THE SACRED CHASE

Also by Cap Daniels

THE SACRED CHASE

CHASE FULTON NOVEL #34

CAP DANIELS

ANCHOR WATCH
PUBLISHING
** USA **

The Sacred Chase
Chase Fulton Novel #34
Cap Daniels

This is a work of fiction. Names, characters, places, historical events, and incidents are the product of the author's imagination or have been used fictitiously. Although many locations used in this work actually exist, they are used fictitiously and may have been relocated, exaggerated, or otherwise modified by creative license for the purpose of this work. Although many characters are based on personalities, physical attributes, skills, or intellect of actual individuals, all the characters in this work are products of the author's imagination.

Published by:

⚓

ANCHOR WATCH
PUBLISHING
** USA **

13 Digit ISBN: 978-1-951021-77-1
Library of Congress Control Number: 2026931062

Cover Design: German Creative

Printed in the United States of America

The Sacred Chase

CAP DANIELS

Chapter 1

To Tell of Demons

2018 – St. Marys, GA

"What do you know about demons?"

The man's question landed in the center of my chest where I had never been precisely punched, stabbed, or shot before that moment. My mind spun itself into a web I would never attempt to put into words for the man wearing his collar backward and sitting only feet in front of me.

I've been in holes so dark and deep that I could swear no sun had ever shone in the sky above. I've been so cold that I begged for the fires of Hell to lap at my feet. I've stared into the eyes of men so haunted and empty that I doubted if they could've ever contained the same life that lived inside me. I've known the man's demons. I've danced with them. I've known the agony of thousands of them clawing at my soul and tearing at my mind with talons of flame.

I've fought beside men of such honor and valor who would die a thousand deaths at the hands of unconscionable evil just to see goodness prevail, if only for one more moment upon this Earth. I've taken lives when there was no other course, and I've preserved life when it would've perished without my hand. I've changed the lives of people who've yet to draw their first breath under God's Heaven, and I've stood in stoic silence as life's breath abandoned the bodies of those who never deserved to taste it.

My body has drunk from the fountain, and my mind has dined from the table of the worst and the best that humanity can be. The best is never pure, and the worst is never absolute. Those who are frail exist in the mist, while we, who are iron tempered by fire, tread at the extremes, away from the weakness of fear, pity, and apathy.

I'm a warrior, less human than many and more beast than most, but a warrior to the end. So, the demon—although not a creature with whom I dine nor drink—is no stranger to my blade, and I am no foreigner to his.

The answer that came from my lips was far less philosophical than the thoughts pouring through my mind. "I know demons are real."

Instead of standing, he crossed his legs, his black pants and shoes matching everything about his attire except the crisp band of white resting just beneath his Adam's apple.

"I would agree with you on that point, Dr. Fulton. Forgive me for not introducing myself. I am Isaiah Lamb."

I laughed and checked over my shoulders in search of my team, who were, no doubt, hiding and recording the ridiculous exchange, amused at my expense.

"Okay," I said, in a weak attempt to gather myself. "I'll play along with a Catholic bearing a Jewish first name and rather sacrificial surname. Tell me, Friar Lamb, what has my ragtag collection of friends put you up to?"

He was either a remarkable actor or truly hurt. I was still leaning toward the good clergyman being of the thespianic order, but I had nothing more pressing to do. So, I turned the twelve-year-old psychologist in my head loose to have a little fun. "Let's hear about this demon of yours, sacrificial Isaiah Lamb."

"Oh, it's not *my* demon, Dr. Fulton. I'm afraid it may be yours. Is there somewhere we can talk more privately?"

The twelve-year-old was gone, and suddenly, I wasn't looking over my shoulder for my laughing teammates anymore. I was looking for Singer, my Southern Baptist sniper and the most devout man of God I'd ever known.

"Let me make a call. Can I get you anything while you wait?"

The priest shook his head and pulled rosary beads from a pocket.

I stepped from the gazebo and froze. "Wait a minute. Why are you here and not at my office?"

He smiled for the first time. "I'm surprised it took you so long to ask. Make your phone call. I'll wait here, and then we can go someplace a little more secure so I can tell you why I'm really here."

"Stand up and put both hands on the cannon," I said.

The gazebo was the one place on Earth I could go to escape almost everything. Its centerpiece was a cannon that sank to the bottom of Cumberland Sound during an early battle of the War of 1812 from the deck of a burning English—or possibly captured French—man-o'-war. Clark Johnson, a dear friend, mentor, and one of the reasons I was still alive, helped me drag it from the mud and filthy muck where it had lain for centuries before tasting the salty air of coastal Georgia again. It would never fire another round in anger, but the man dressed as a priest would get two good handfuls of it while I determined if he planned to put a bullet in my back as I walked away.

He offered no resistance as he stood, spread his feet, and palmed the ancient cannon barrel.

I patted him down and said, "Normally, I'd apologize for this, but I'm having one of the strangest mornings of my life. I was sitting here, minding my own business, and thinking about riding horses with my daughter that I hate . . ."

He jerked his head to meet my gaze. "You hate your daughter?"

"I will break you in half if you move again, Padre. Of course I don't hate my daughter. I love my daughter. She's the closest thing to perfection there is on this Earth, but I hate every drop of blood in those horses' bodies."

With my pat-down complete, I said, "You can have a seat. I'm sure you understand the need for caution."

His answer surprised me far more than I expected. "Oh, I understand completely, Dr. Fulton, but I'm quite certain that you do not."

I stepped away and pulled out my phone. Technology had never been my strong suit, but I was learning, so I held my phone close to my lips and said, "Call Skipper."

What few whispering skills my phone possessed must have been learned inside a sawmill.

She yelled back at me, "Calling Skipper!"

Our intelligence analyst somehow never sounded busy, although she always was. "Hey, Chase. I thought you were supposed to be riding with Pogonya."

"I am, but she's not here yet, and my morning is getting weird. A priest came to visit me."

"Oh, that's creative," she said. "I've heard you come up with a lot of reasons to avoid the horses, but this is a first. Lying about a priest has to be a special category of sin."

"Believe it or not, I'd rather be on the horse. This guy is freaking me out."

"You're freaked out by priests? I'll add that to the ever-expanding list of weird things about Chase Fulton. What freaks you out about him?"

"He's dressed like a priest, but he hasn't actually claimed to be one yet. He hasn't offered to shake my hand. And his name is Isaiah Lamb —or at least he says it is."

"What does he want?"

"This is where it really gets weird. He wants me to tell him what I know about demons."

"Why would a priest come to you to ask about demons?"

I said, "I told you it was weird. Get the team together. I don't know what this is, but 'Father' Lamb let me pat him down as if he expected it, so I doubt he's really a priest."

She said, "I've got good news. The team is already together. Singer's doing some scenario training with them in the shoot house."

"That's perfect, but I haven't heard any shooting yet."

She said, "Hang on a minute. I'll pull up the video."

Skipper spent the bulk of her time locked inside the state-of-the-art op center on the third floor of the house at Bonaventure, my family's ancestral home on the banks of the North River in St. Marys, Georgia. From there, she could keep an eye on almost every inch of the sprawling property that had become the training grounds for Tactical Team Twenty-One, the ragtag bunch of misfit toys I was honored to lead all over the world.

She said, "They're in the briefing room and geared up from head to toe. It looks like the live-fire portion may start any minute. Should I tell them you're coming?"

"Yeah. Tell 'em we're coming, but have them start shooting hard and fast. I like the psychological advantage. The good friar and I will be there in five minutes."

I jogged back to the gazebo. "Are you a runner, Isaiah?"

He hopped to his feet. "Only when something's chasing me. Why?"

"My team is about to begin a live-fire training exercise, and I want to catch them before they get started."

He leapt down the wooden steps and made a point of falling in beside me to my left. Within four strides, he matched my pace, so I picked it up a little. He didn't lag.

I ran every day, and usually with guys younger, stronger, and faster than me, so pushing a dude pretending to be a priest amused me. When we hit the six-minute-mile pace, his breathing picked up, and the gunfire began. He flinched, but it was the instantaneous reaction of being startled rather than afraid. I was learning a kettle full of information about our clergyman on our riverside jog.

"So, where's your parish?"

His breathing was coming harder. "Could we maybe slow down a little?"

Ah, another morsel for my kettle of data on the priest.

I slowed to a fast walk. "Sure. It doesn't matter now. They're already shooting. Do you shoot?"

He shrugged. "I know how to shoot a little, I guess. I mean, it's not like I'm on the Swiss Guard or the Gendarmeria Pontifica."

"But you went to military school," I said.

He stopped by the slow-flowing blackwater river and looked up at me. "How could you possibly know that?"

I laid a hand on his back. "Come on. We're almost there."

We finished our walk in relative silence, with only the sounds of the horses to our left, the river to our right, and the repetition of gunfire inside the shoot house ahead. I thumbed the code, led us through the first door, and waited for it to close before unlocking the second door into the foyer. The dim, slightly red light seemed to catch Isaiah by surprise, so I didn't peg him as a former operator.

My implanted hearing aids acted as both amplifiers and sound suppressors, but I tossed a pair of high-tech hearing protection to our visitor, and we slid on glasses before climbing the stairs to the catwalk above the training rooms. Our hearing protection allowed us to speak softly and hear each other perfectly while still protecting us from the high-decibel sound of the weapons being fired a few feet below us.

I motioned down from the catwalk. "As you can see, our training facility looks like typical rooms inside houses, apartments, or offices, and we can configure it to look like almost any space in any building anywhere in the world."

He stood in apparent awe, shaking his head. "This is astonishing."

"This is where we practice chasing demons . . . just maybe not the same kind you chase." I flipped open a panel and activated a switch that flashed a series of lights in the room below.

Jimmy "Singer" Grossmann, our lead sniper and the team's moral compass, called, "Cease fire! Cease fire! Make all weapons safe and stand down."

The echo of "cease fire" rolled through the room, and as rifles fell tight against body armor on their slings and sidearms locked into holsters, all eyes rose toward me and then to the man in black beside me.

I said, "Sorry to interrupt the training, but we have a guest who needs to speak with us about an issue of some importance. If you'll meet us in the briefing room, this gentleman apparently has a demon he'd like us to hunt down."

Chapter 2
To Tell the Truth

Isaiah and I descended the steps while the team cleared the live-fire training area and began doffing their gear in the cage, but I stuck my head through the door. "Keep it on for now. I like the look."

Having the team appear more like an assault squad than a sweaty bunch of forty-somethings with unkempt beards and dirty boots gave us an advantage I planned to exploit to its fullest extent, with one exception.

As the team filed out of the cage, I caught Anya by the arm. "Pull off your gear from the waist up and sit on the front row."

"This is very sexist thing to say, and I feel like object of—"

"Just do it," I said. "You can file your sexual harassment suit later."

The only female member of our hard-hitting tactical team was Anastasia "Anya" Burinkova, a former Russian assassin trained by the KGB and SVR as a sparrow and edged weapons specialist. Since defecting to the U.S. in her twenties, she'd become an expert in far more than seduction and sharp metal objects. She was one of the deadliest people I'd ever known, regardless of X and Y chromosomes, and undeniably one of the most physically beautiful. In addition to being exactly who I'd want beside me in a fight to the death, she was the mother of Pogonya, my perfect daughter, with whom I should've been riding horses instead of entertaining the musings of a potentially insane man of the cloth.

The team filed into the briefing room and spread the chairs haphazardly to accommodate their increased bulk due to the gear hanging from their bodies. Empty Gatorade bottles bounced across the floor, and the air took on the odor of a post-game locker room. The scene in front of me was living proof that professionalism comes in innumerable shapes and sizes. The cherry on top made her entrance with a pair of fighting knives strapped to her thighs and the tightest black T-shirt she could find tucked into her cargo pants. Shaking out her blonde ponytail was a nice touch I hadn't expected, but one that Isaiah clearly didn't want to miss.

It would appear that our collar-wearing brother isn't immune to the allure most other red-blooded men of the free world—and not-so-free world—feel as well.

I kicked an uncomfortable plastic chair—that was just like everyone else's—toward him and planted myself on mine. "We can make individual introductions if you're interested, but I'd say you've seen enough already for names to be pretty meaningless at this point."

The fact that he didn't appear uncomfortable made me uncomfortable. His opening impressed me, and that wasn't an easy task for anyone to pull off.

He slid a thumb beneath the white square of his collar and pulled it from his black shirt. "Let's get this out of the way. To clear up any misconceptions, I *am* an ordained Jesuit priest, but I do not have a parish. I wore the collarino today for effect. If it makes you uncomfortable, I can dress more like you." He glanced at Anya. "Well, maybe not quite like you, but anyway, my name is Isaiah Lamb."

A priest with a sense of humor.

He said, "Any Catholics in the room?"

No one raised a hand or spoke until Mongo pointed toward our sniper. "That's Singer. He's kind of our de facto chaplain. He's a Baptist minister, and I guess you could say we're mostly Protestant nondenominationals."

Isaiah's eyes fell back on Anya, not unlike most men's eyes tend to do. "I heard you speak earlier. You're Eastern European. Orthodox?"

She said, "You have good ear, but no. I was born inside Soviet Union, but I am now American and Christian, but never Russian Orthodox. Why does this matter to you?"

He said, "All of it matters because I'm going to show you something that you will find impossible to believe. Actually, I'm going to show you two things that you'll likely find impossible to believe. The first is possibly demonically spiritual, and the second is perhaps even more evil than the first, if that's possible. I might be able to explain the first, but despite my education, faith, and even the collar, I'm completely unable to explain the second. That's where all of you come in."

I said, "Let's start with who you really are. You show up here wearing . . . what did you call it?"

"A collarino. It's the traditional black shirt with a standing collar to hold a white insert that everybody recognizes as the badge of a priest."

I continued. "So, you show up wearing the collarino. You didn't freak out when I patted you down for weapons. That means you probably expected it. You fell in on my left side when we started our run from the gazebo to the shoot house. That's a military respect thing. You assumed I outranked you, so you moved to my left out of a habit you learned either at military school or as an enlisted soldier. The shooting didn't frighten you, so you have some familiarity with firearms. You may be ordained, but you're more than just a priest."

He sighed. "You guys are good."

I said, "You knew that before you got here. Otherwise, you would've shown up in somebody else's gazebo. I've got your DNA from your sweat. I've got your fingerprints from your safety glasses. I'll know who and what you are in less than an hour." I paused, more for dramatic effect than anything else. "Take a gander around the room. Do we look like the kind of people who can't keep you here against your will for an hour?"

He said, "I'm not here against my will, and I have nothing to hide from you. Please run my DNA and prints. I'll gladly give you a much better sample than my sweat." He repositioned himself in the chair.

"My name really is Isaiah Lamb. My mother was Jewish by birth and converted when she married my Irish Catholic father. I attended Jesuit high school, and then Notre Dame on an ROTC scholarship, with plans to be a military intelligence officer."

"That explains your answer about being able to shoot a little and running on my left," I said. "But how'd you end up wearing a collar instead of body armor?"

The priest cast a thumb toward the river. "You saw me try to run out there. I've got a pair of malformed bones in my ankles. The Army discovered them during my sophomore year at Notre Dame, and my ROTC scholarship went out the window. That's how I ended up in seminary."

Mongo crossed his ankle over his enormous opposite knee. "So, you figured if you couldn't be an Army intel officer, you'd spy for the Pope?"

Isaiah bounced his foot against the floor. "Have you ever heard of a papal nuncio or apostolic nuncio?"

Mongo huffed. "I was just messing with you, but I was right, wasn't I?"

"Not exactly," Isaiah said. "A nuncio is sort of like—well, no, not sort of—it's exactly like a diplomat of the Vatican to a foreign country."

"The Pope's got political ambassadors?" Kodiak said. "Who knew?"

Isaiah said, "The Vatican is the world's smallest country. The Curia is . . . how do I put this? Think of it like the court."

"Like a criminal or civil court?" Gator asked.

Gator was the youngest of our team, but far from the least capable. He was quickly becoming an expert in every skill the rest of us possessed, especially Singer's sniping gig.

"Not that kind of court," Isaiah said. "Like a king's court. Like King Arthur's court. It's an ancient concept. The Curia was created by Pope Urban the Second sometime between ten eighty-eight and ten ninety-nine, so, to say the least, it's not a new concept."

I tapped my watch. "The history lesson is fascinating, but it'd be nice to get to a point sometime soon, Padre."

Isaiah threw up his hands. "Sorry. As I said, I don't have a parish, so

I don't get to say Mass. Having a real audience is a treat for me, but I get a bit longwinded. Anyway, I'm now part of a division of the Holy See known as the Dicastery for the Doctrine of the Faith. We were once known as the Supreme Sacred Congregation of the Roman and Universal Inquisition, and we're the oldest of the dicasteries of the Roman Curia. Our job, ultimately, is to defend the Catholic faith. That's an extreme oversimplification, but it'll have to do for now."

I said, "We've got your résumé and pedigree, and I assume you're not looking for a job. So, when are you going to show us whatever it is you came here to show us?"

He said, "You need to know a little more information first. Can I have just ten more minutes?"

"You've got eight, and the clock is ticking."

He swallowed hard. "Okay, so the nuncio has an enormous staff—"

I interrupted. "How enormous?"

"Maybe a hundred thousand or more."

Kodiak blurted out, "A hundred thousand people in the diplomatic corps of the world's smallest country?"

The priest screwed up his face. "Is this cutting into my eight minutes?"

I said, "No. Answer the question."

"It's just the world's smallest country in area. There are almost one and a half billion Catholics in the world, but just a tiny portion of them live and work inside Vatican City, which is less than half a square kilometer."

I said, "The clock is ticking again."

He started talking quickly. "Like I said, part of my job is defending the faith. That means checking on people who are doing horrific things and claiming to be doing them in the name of God and His Holiness, the Pope. That's what this is about. The two things I want to show you may have a connection. The first is a possible demonic possession and attempted, supposed exorcism. The second is the possible exploitation of that . . . let's call it a *situation*, for lack of a better term at this point."

I leaned in. "So, you think they're related."

"I didn't say that. I said there *may* be a connection and the second could be an exploitation of the first. There may be no relationship, but just because they aren't related doesn't mean someone with ill intent can't capitalize on the evil of the first to commit equal or greater subsequent evil."

"Like an ambulance-chasing lawyer," Shawn said.

The priest looked up to see our SEAL staring back at him. "Exactly. And may I ask you a question?"

"You just did," Shawn said.

That got a few chuckles, and Isaiah said, "You don't move like the rest of the team inside the rooms. Why is that?"

"Can you speak Italian?" Shawn asked.

Isaiah nodded, and Shawn said, "I'll bet you don't sound like Pope Francis when you speak Italian."

"Well, no, of course not."

"Why not?" the SEAL asked. "It's the same language, and you're both speaking it."

"We learned the language from different people in different parts of the world, and it was his native language. Mine was English."

Shawn grinned. "I learned to kill people at the Naval Special Warfare Training Center in Coronado, California, and most of these guys learned it at Fort Benning, Georgia. Your Italian means the same thing as the Pope's, and a bad guy is just as dead, no matter which one of us puts a double-tap in his face."

I said, "I've heard enough. It's time to see what you came to show us. Gator, will you set up the big monitor?"

Our young warfighter hopped to his feet. "You got it, boss."

The priest turned to me with a coldness in his blue eyes I hadn't seen before that moment. "There's no need for a monitor, Dr. Fulton. I don't have a video for you. We're going to see this man in person. He's in the supermax prison in North Central Florida."

I slapped my hands together and rubbed them maniacally. "Okay, then, Padre. Let's go meet this demon of yours."

Chapter 3
The Warhorse

The team stowed their gear in the cage, and I led the entourage from the shoot house. As I stepped through the second security door and into the midday sun, I came face-to-face with a tall, striking, Eastern European beauty. She wore distinctly British riding clothes, but her accent hinted more toward the British Isles than the Eastern Bloc. "I thought I would find you hiding here, Father. I'm sorry I am late."

Short of starting WWIII, there was little she could do that would require an apology, at least in my mind, and even the WWIII thing might be justified under the right circumstances. I threw my arms around her, and we hugged while the stack behind me simply had to wait.

When we parted, I turned to our guest with the empty collarino. "Isaiah Lamb, meet my daughter, Pogonya Fulton. Pogonya, meet Isaiah. He's a Jesuit priest, my dear."

Isaiah stuck out a hand, but Pogonya curtsied. "Pleasure to meet you, sir, but I'm afraid you've come to a flock without need of a shepherd. Surely, you've met Singer."

The priest chuckled, and I swelled with pride.

He said, "She does say exactly what she's thinking, so there's no question she's your daughter." He spun to see Anya. "And also yours. The resemblance is uncanny."

Anya almost blushed. "I was never so beautiful, but you are kind. Thank you."

Pogonya peered around me at the column of sweaty warfighters. "I hate that I wasn't here to shoot with you. I'm getting better."

"There's plenty of time for that," I said. "And you're right. You're getting much better. It's in your blood."

She giggled. "I wish I could say the same for your riding. You're not going to come up with another lame excuse this time, are you?"

"Is a demon a lame excuse?"

She rolled her eyes. "The lamest. I'll meet you at the stables. Do you ride, Priest, or only say Mass and exorcise demons?"

He cleared his throat and checked his watch, but before he could speak, she said, "You look like you're about Kodiak's size. Kodiak, he can borrow some jeans, right?"

The amused former Green Beret said, "Absolutely, but only if you put him on Pecan."

Pogonya said, "Done."

Isaiah argued. "But I've not ridden in years. We've got some very important things to do, and we don't have time to . . ."

My daughter, who clearly carried half my DNA, patted the man in black on the center of his chest. "I thought you were a Jesuit. You're protesting like a Protestant. Follow Kodiak, and get some jeans, a T-shirt, and boots. You wouldn't want to soil your priestly . . . whatever-you-call-that 'outfit.'"

He turned to me but soon realized he hadn't found an ally.

I said, "You're the one who interrupted my day, remember? I promised my daughter we'd ride. If you want to show me a demon, I doubt the gnarly beast is going to flee because we're two hours late. I'll go with you, but first, you're riding with us."

By the time Isaiah returned dressed like Kodiak, Pogonya and I had the horses saddled and ready. I'd broken more than my share of promises in the four decades I'd spent on the planet, but I was determined to break as few as possible to that girl. If I told her I'd ride, I'd ride, no matter how much I'd rather bathe in African killer bees or visit an incarcerated demon at the North Central Florida supermax prison.

I gave her a leg up onto Praline, the chestnut-colored quarter horse seemingly built to fit beneath Pogonya. My mount was Richter, a majestic, glistening black Arabian warhorse who looked like he belonged on the cover of a romance novel, with some guy who looked like Shawn, our SEAL, shirtless and rescuing a damsel in distress. However, looks can not only be deceiving but also just plain wrong. Richter was barely smarter than a tomato and often forgot his way back to the stables after a long ride. But he was gentle enough to keep me in the saddle, and he was cooperative when I tried to cowboy up and show off in front of my equestrian goddess of a daughter.

To say that I hate and fear horses is far from true, but only because I lack words stronger than those two to describe my real feelings toward the animals in general. Richter, on the other hand, was the exception. The gorgeous beast was a gift from my daughter, and because of that, I treasured him as if he were of royal blood. I feared him a little, and I'd never fully trust him—he was too big and far too powerful. But he obeyed me out of training, lack of intellect, and perhaps a sense of self-amusement. There were moments when I actually liked him. He never tried to bite, kick, or intentionally step on me. His IQ sometimes left him stumbling into me, but I never believed there was malice afoot . . . or ahoof. He could kill me in a breath if he chose to, or he could lumber through life enjoying the treatment, treats, and best accommodations my wonderfully blessed life could provide. I loved the gift, but I never would've bought him for myself.

Richter and I had a few things in common that also kept me from truly hating him. Intellect was on the list. I wasn't the sharpest bulb in the quiver, as Clark Johnson would say, so being able to get away with goofiness together made the relationship with Richter simple. And sometimes, simplicity is the core of quality. He could run without complaining, and I loved that about him. I was grateful to have inherited that quality from my father. No matter how hard I was pushed, I kept running and fighting until it was no longer required. I didn't cry, whine, or moan about it, and when it was over, I went for a swim in the river, rolled around in the grass, and munched on clover, just like Richter did. Birds of a feather. I couldn't swat flies with my tail, but I envied that ability.

We shared another trait that was neither pleasant nor our choice: we were both geldings. Pogonya was conceived prior to my unfortunate accident atop the Khyber Pass, where I was fighting to save the lives of the men who would become my team and family. Richter's was surgical in nature and came at the hand of a veterinarian. To me, that's a shame. If there had to be horses in the world, there should've been more like him. Perhaps his Khyber Pass moment is what made him gentle enough—and dumb enough—to tolerate me.

By breed alone, he was a warhorse. I'd never seen that side of him, but something in his eyes told me it was there. Perhaps one day he'd show me that we shared that one additional element that made us a little more than just two mammals who entertained each other.

Our clergyman was on the verge of redefining a word he thought he'd been taught well in seminary. Pecan wasn't young, but apparently, evil spirits don't age on the same scale as living, breathing creatures we understand. They seem to progress in both strength and fury, through their teens, until they reach a level no man can manage, regardless of how smooth the edges of his rosary beads are rubbed.

Mongo put the priest in the saddle, mainly because he was the only human in the state of Georgia capable of rescuing Padre if Pecan went into a death spiral before Isaiah got both boots in the stirrups. Once that was accomplished, Mongo's responsibility was finished.

Pogonya and I carried lariats as if I possessed some rodeo skill that gave me the ability to stay aboard Richter, lasso any part of Pecan, and control the beast while the only Jesuit I knew leapt to safety.

My goal that day was to stay behind Pecan so I could watch him bounce the priest off the planet, just as the horse had done to me every time I'd been temporarily on his back. Riding the creature wasn't possible for anyone other than Pogonya, and even for her, it was a potential moonshot waiting to happen.

While the team cleaned and locked their weapons inside the armory, Isaiah, Pogonya, and I began our ride along the North River. To my surprise, Pecan behaved as if he'd been a tourist operation's trail horse for a decade. He ambled along, occasionally nipping a mouthful of grass while practically ignoring Isaiah. Praline was the typical, spirited fairy, dancing and prancing her way beneath Pogonya as if performing for a crowd. She often spent more time trotting sideways than moving forward, but her playfulness wasn't misbehavior. It was merely her nature.

Richter held his head high and watched every movement in sight. On two occasions, he almost fell into the river while watching dragonflies flittering around his nose. He was beautiful, but he'd never pass the entrance exam for Mensa.

Pogonya and Praline trotted beside Isaiah. "How are you doing?"

"Great," he said. "I'd forgotten how peaceful this is. I'm sorry I was so resistant earlier. It's easy to get wrapped up in—"

It was at that moment Pecan seemed to remember his ancestral roots as a wild mustang on the western plains—or perhaps some alien planet no one can pronounce—and his hind legs shot skyward above his own head.

Richter turned, obviously no longer amused by the dragonflies, and trotted diagonally away, keeping me centered perfectly in the saddle while never taking his focus from Pecan, who'd obviously lost his mind.

Pogonya yelled, "Isaiah, dig in your heels and hold the saddle horn. Pecan, easy! Easy, boy! Easy!"

I had no idea what to do, and the amusement I expected to feel quickly morphed into fear for Isaiah. I was instantly ashamed for having wanted to see the priest fly through the air from the Pecan catapult.

Pogonya kicked Praline and rode away in an expanding arc as Pecan continued his vertical explosion. Isaiah was doing well at staying in the saddle, but the look on his face said he was on the verge of making his exit.

As Pogonya's arc closed, she rode in beside Pecan from his left hind quarters and reached for the priest with her right arm. "Lean into me, and I'll pull you off."

I'd seen the maneuver at rodeos when cowboys—called pickup men —would ride beside the bucking bronco riders and pull them off after a successful ride. I was impressed that my daughter could do it, but it was apparently Isaiah's first time.

He leaned toward her and laced an arm around her back as Pecan continued lunging and kicking as if under attack from some invisible force.

Isaiah's right foot came across the saddle, and he landed behind Pogonya on his side at the same instant Pecan spun to the right. The violent turn yanked the priest from the safety of Praline's back with his left foot stuck in Pecan's stirrup.

Pecan kept jumping, spinning, and bucking in every direction, thrashing Isaiah like a ragdoll beneath him. The priest fought for several seconds, grabbing for the stirrup with both hands and twisting with all of his might, until exhaustion—or unconsciousness—overtook him and he sagged facedown beneath the wild animal.

"Rope him, Father! You must rope him!"

Pogonya was on another arcing turn with her lariat spinning in the air above her head and closing on Pecan, but I was fifty feet closer. I studied her technique for an instant and lifted my rope. It felt awkward in my grasp, but I soon had it spinning above my head.

The gorgeous creature beneath me, who was barely bright enough to eat and stand up at the same time, made a sound I'd never heard him make, and his front feet simultaneously left the ground a few inches. He turned downriver and lunged as if he'd been fired by a cannon, but his posture didn't allow me to be thrown back. He'd somehow lowered his shoulders and kept me in the saddle, where I had absolutely no business being.

Richter's speed increased as I kept twirling the waxed lariat over my head, and the distance between us and Pecan closed by the second.

Moving with him felt like riding a world-class motorcycle. I leaned with him instead of against every turn, and the balance felt natural, as if we were moving as one. I gave him no direction because I didn't know what to tell him. I had no idea where to be or what to do. I was only slightly less of a victim than the priest, but Richter seemed to know exactly what to do.

He put me abeam Pecan at three feet, a distance from which even a child couldn't miss a lasso throw. I gave the lariat two more circuits and released it just ahead of Pecan's nose. The loop fell across his head as if I'd done it a thousand times, and I was confident the battle was won.

With my right hand, I wrapped the end of the rope around the saddle horn until I'd wrapped so many turns that there was no way the horse could pull away. Richter backed off, applying the brakes to bring Pecan under control. I let out a sigh of relief until I watched and felt the rope tighten around my left leg—the only real leg I had left.

Somehow, in the craziness of the moment, I had allowed the rope to wrap itself around my leg before, during, or maybe after throwing it. Another leap by Pecan, or another stride by Richter, would sever the leg, and I was left with an impossible decision. Hoofbeats pounded behind me, but the sound wasn't sharp enough to determine how far away Pogonya was or if I had time to wait another instant for her to get a rope around Pecan's neck before I lost another appendage.

The rope pulled tighter, and the decision was made. I unwound the wrap as quickly as my hand would move and yelled, "Pull away, Isaiah! Pull away!"

He didn't move, but Pecan did.

As soon as my rope fell slack, Pecan bounded skyward, and the whistle of Pogonya's lasso cut through the air. The powerful horse dodged the lariat and thrust himself toward Praline. The mighty collision sent both rider and smaller horse into the river.

I dismounted before conscious thought entered my mind. My daughter being in the water beneath a thousand-pound animal was enough to send the rest of my world into utter darkness, and I dived into the black water.

Pogonya surfaced at the same moment I disappeared beneath the obsidian ripples, so I arched my back and kicked for the top. As soon as I could brush the water from my face, I watched in disbelief as Richter stood face-to-face with Pecan. Both animals had raised onto their hind legs, their front hooves in the air, and they were pawing at each other like prize fighters. Isaiah dangled from Pecan's left stirrup, and I sent up a silent prayer for the priest.

Richter leapt forward until his face was pressed against his opponent's, and he wrapped his right front leg across Pecan's neck. They snorted and blew as thousands of pounds of muscle and might fought it out with a Jesuit priest hanging in the balance. With his leg still across Pecan's neck, Richter thrust his full weight forward, forcing Pecan back to the earth and pinning him to the ground like the warhorse I'd seen deep in his black eyes—the warhorse he'd been bred to be.

Chapter 4

Is It Not?

"Are you hurt, Pogo?"

She brushed wet hair from her face. "I am okay. Are you?"

I said, "I'm good. How about Praline?"

We watched the horse climb the bank, and Pogonya said, "She appears to be fine."

We crawled up the muddy slope and scampered toward the motionless priest with his left foot still twisted through Pecan's stirrup. Richter knelt, still pinning Pecan to the ground as I slid to a stop beside Isaiah's shoulder. I put one hand beneath his nose and a pair of fingers on his neck. "I've got a good pulse and respirations. How's the leg?"

I'd spent the entirety of my adult life filthy, under enemy fire, and alongside highly trained combatants who knew more about keeping dying victims alive than some ER docs. As near perfect as Pogonya was, she did not fall into that elite category of field medics.

Her voice cracked. "I have no idea."

I drew my knife and thumbed open the blade. "Cut the stirrup from the saddle and get the horse away from him."

She didn't reach for the knife, so I shook it and got louder. "Cut him free!"

"I've already removed the stirrup. He's free."

I ordered, "Get the horses out of here. We can't risk them stepping on him."

With absolute faith she could accomplish that task with zero involvement from me, I went to work on our cowboy clergyman. I started by stabilizing his head and neck with my boots and belt since I didn't make a habit of carrying a C-collar in Richter's saddlebag.

My assessment continued down Isaiah's body while I reached for my phone. Getting him into an ER was on the short list of necessities, regardless of what I found in the coming minutes of my exam, but the next discovery I made was the absence of my phone. A diver with two hours of time and an abundance of patience might find it in the black mud of the North River, but that was of little concern.

Isaiah wasn't cut, and neither of his arms appeared to be broken. His hands and fingers weren't as fortunate, but broken fingers were temporary annoyances more than serious injuries. His ribs felt okay, but it was impossible to diagnose broken ribs or severe internal injuries in the field unless bones were exposed through flesh. Thankfully, all of his parts that were designed to be internal still were.

His upper legs looked and felt okay, but his left ankle had an entirely different story to tell. The rule of combat medicine when packing a wounded warrior for shipping was to move a broken appendage only once and strap it down, but there was no singular direction in which I could move his ankle that would improve its condition.

However, movement was the least of my limitations. Even if I moved it only once, I had no way to strap it down. The priest and I needed help, and quickly.

Richter was standing fifty feet away with his eyes trained on me as if assessing and judging my every move. To his left, a cloud of dust rose with Pogonya and Praline at its prow, sprinting toward me.

They arrived, and she slid from the saddle with a finger pointed skyward. "I called nine one one."

As I followed her pointed finger into the air, the belly of a red-and-black medivac helicopter came into focus. It touched down several feet downwind of Isaiah and me to avoid covering us with dust and debris.

A duo I recognized emerged from the helo, clad in flight suits with medical kits slung diagonally across their bodies. As they approached, I read the titles of "flight nurse" and "paramedic" stitched on their nameplates. From that moment forward, the Padre was in far better hands than mine, so I backed away and briefed what I knew.

"His name is Isaiah Lamb. Mid-thirties, in apparent good health prior to the accident that occurred approximately ten minutes ago. He was thrown from a horse and dragged by his left foot in the stirrup for several seconds, perhaps up to half a minute or more. Lost consciousness after fifteen to twenty seconds. I stabilized his neck with a field-expedient collar. Heart rate was seventy, and respirations were twenty about seven to eight minutes ago. Primary injury appears to be to his left ankle. Secondary injuries to both hands. No compound fractures detected and no serious bleeding. Unconscious with no apparent head wounds, but pupils are reactive to light bilaterally."

The paramedic took notes while the flight nurse did her assessment. Seconds later, Isaiah was strapped to a gurney and headed for his next, far more comfortable ride.

"Do you want your 'field-expedient C-collar' back?" the nurse quipped.

"Yes, that'd be nice. Thanks."

She tossed the boots and belt toward me. "Nice work, Dr. Fulton. You should've been a real doctor. We'll take good care of him. Is there anything else we should know?"

"He's a Catholic priest, if that matters . . ."

She grinned. "We could take him to Baptist just for fun."

"You could."

"We'll take him to St. Vincent's. I'm a little concerned about internals. Is the horse okay?"

I waved her off. "Get out of here."

Seconds later, the chopper was airborne, and Richter was at my side watching the helo grow smaller to the southwest.

I threw an arm across his back. "You did a good thing, boy. I guess you're a lot smarter than I gave you credit for. I'm sorry for doubting you."

He bowed his head as if humbly accepting my apology, and then he freaked out, dancing and squirming wildly as he stared at the ground at my feet.

I watched in disbelief at his behavior and turned to my daughter. "What's he doing, Pogo? He's losing his mind."

She laughed hysterically. "I think you spoke too soon, Father. Pick up your belt. He thinks it's a snake."

I pulled on my soaking-wet boots and laced my scary belt around my waist. "You bought me the dumbest horse on Earth."

She giggled. "Maybe, but he saved the priest's life."

"Yeah, that, he did."

She said, "I don't think anyone should ride Pecan again except maybe me. What do you think?"

"I don't like the idea of you riding him, either."

She shrugged. "Maybe you're right. We're definitely going to work on your roping skills. What was that?"

"It's a long story. We can talk about it later, but I think we should get cleaned up and go check on Isaiah."

* * *

After showers and a snack, I made the benevolent decision that no one had to make the trip to the hospital if they truly didn't want to go. No sane person ever really wants to visit a hospital, so it became a family affair. Singer—because he considered Isaiah to be a brother, even though he wore his collar backward—volunteered, and the three remaining members who shared DNA climbed into the Suburban. Pogonya felt bad about being part of the horse incident, I wanted to learn more about the priest and his demon, and Anya couldn't stand the idea of not spending every available second with our daughter. The foursome made sense on some bizarre level, but even I, as the team psychologist, wouldn't dare try to decipher the weirdness of it all.

The drive to Jacksonville took a little over an hour, but parking took an eternity until Singer remembered a secret weapon that wasn't a single-use tool for the day. He hooked his clergy permit to the mirror and parked fifty feet from the hospital entrance.

Between his clergy pass and my hospital credentials to the psych department, we were given unlimited access to the interior of the hospital while more deserving families and friends waited for hours, stacked like firewood in overcrowded waiting rooms across the massive facility.

Nuns don't freak me out, but I didn't expect to see them flittering about inside a hospital, so their presence took me by surprise when we rounded a corner and discovered a gaggle of them sharing a can of Pringles and harmonizing. I was certain that Singer was tempted to join in.

Gaggle can't be the right word for a group of nuns, but it'll come to me.

At the nurses' station, I flashed my creds. "I'm Dr. Fulton. We're looking for Isaiah Lamb, a patient who came by med-flight a couple of hours ago."

The young man typed and then pointed over his head. "He should be out of surgery on six west. I'm sure you know how to get there, Doctor."

I shoved my ID back into my pocket. "Of course. Thanks."

I knew what the number six meant, and I fully understood that west was the opposite of east, but that was the limit of my comprehension of the information we obtained from the nurse. We were, however, slightly smarter than Richter, so I had faith we could figure it out.

We did, and the nurse was correct. I learned something else about Catholic hospitals that day. Rank apparently has its privileges. Father Isaiah Lamb wasn't recovering in the typical tiny room in which most parishioners would convalesce. Being a priest apparently comes with an upgraded post-surgical package.

"Nice digs, Padre. How's the foot?"

Isaiah peered up at me through his narcotic-induced euphoria. "Chase. You came. I'd get up, but you know, I have that rude habit."

I said, "Rude habit. There's a nun joke in there somewhere. I just know it."

"Don't make nun jokes in a Catholic hospital, Chase. One of them will jump out of the closet and slap you on the wrist with a ruler. They do that, you know."

"So I've heard," I said. "We saw a gaggle of them downstairs eating chips and singing. They're really good."

He grinned. "Yeah, I love chips, too."

I wrote it off to the narcotics, but he snapped his fingers and said, "Got you! It's a better idea to just call them a group and not a gaggle. I think that's reserved for geese, and the sisters wouldn't like that."

"Okay, so group it is. Back to the foot. How is it?"

"Broken," he said. "But it's not bad. Remember when I told you the Army found a malformation and kicked me out of ROTC?"

"I remember."

He said, "It turns out that was a good thing, in this case. The bones grew together in a strange way that actually made them stronger. Where the bone broke is just above that malformation. It made it easy to repair, and it should heal more quickly. They said I'll be on crutches for up to a couple of weeks and then a walking cast. Is the horse okay?"

"You're worried about the horse?" I asked.

"Well, yes, of course. There was a nest of yellowjackets."

Pogonya gasped. "So, he didn't just spook on his own?"

"No, of course not," Isaiah said. "He stepped on the nest, and they swarmed out."

"I'm glad to hear he didn't just lose his mind," I said. "What did the doctors say about additional injuries?"

He held up his hands. "A couple of broken fingers, but I've had worse from playing basketball. No big deal. I have a few bruised ribs, but I spend enough time in the gym to keep my core tough enough to take a beating without falling apart."

"How long are they going to keep you?" Singer asked.

"If everything looks good in the morning, they told me I can go home tomorrow afternoon. That means we can go see Fitzsimon day after tomorrow."

"Fitzsimon?" Singer asked.

Isaiah nodded. "Yes, Garland Fitzsimon at North Central Florida supermax. He's what all of this is about."

Singer pulled a chair from beside the window and sat on its arm beside Isaiah's bed. "What makes him so important?"

Isaiah sat in silence for a moment as if considering his answer. "This man in prison . . . they tell me he murdered two NSA agents, a former Mossad officer, and a Russian FSB officer on a boat in Key West. I'm a simple priest. I don't even know what any of that means, but the important thing to me is that the church believes Fitzsimon is possessed by a demon."

Singer didn't flinch. "But you don't agree."

The priest stared directly back at our Southern Baptist sniper. "Why would you say that?"

Singer focused. "Because you said the church *believes*. If you agreed, you would've made the statement that Garland Fitzsimon *is* possessed by a demon because you're a priest of the Dicastery for the Doctrine of the Faith. That's your calling from God and the Holy See. Is it not?"

Chapter 5
Jay-Dub

There have been great researchers down through history, but when the books are opened one day and the true greats are named, the best of them won't make the list. Her name and face will remain in the shadows, and she wouldn't have it any other way. She was one of the many reasons my team and I were some of the most successful tactical operators on the planet.

Elizabeth "Skipper" Woodley ran the operation center like a perfectly oiled machine, and that's exactly how the door felt as it pivoted open on silent hinges when I walked inside to find her buried between an array of monitors and beneath stacks of paperwork.

"Why do you still print things?"

She silenced me with a raised finger, and I settled onto the chair that had been mine since we built the third-floor op center after an arsonist destroyed the original house that had been in my family since before Georgia became a state. The rest of my team sat around what I enjoyed calling our "round table," although I'd never think of myself as King Arthur. We were equals in every imaginable way except one. In my mind, I bore full responsibility for every failure we suffered, and nothing anyone in that room could ever say or do would change that. They looked to me for direction, and I looked to them for reassurance that I could be the man they deserved at the tip of the spear we had become.

Mine would always be the first boot onto the battlefield, and I prayed I'd always taste the sting of incoming fire so they wouldn't have to. Each of them could step into my boots and fill my role in an instant, but none of them believed that ultimate truth. That's one of the things that made them some of the greatest warriors in any fight against any foe. The most capable warriors are those who continually forge themselves into harder, sharper weapons because they see and feel their flaws within rather than admiring their own strength. We didn't hang mirrors in our gym to watch ourselves flex—we did it to see ourselves tremble and shake and fail under the burden of the demands we placed on ourselves.

"This guy is some piece of work," Skipper said.

She had our attention the instant the primary overhead monitor filled with a photograph of a tattooed man. He had a shaved head and eyes like those of someone who'd stolen at least one of them.

"Whoa! Check out those eyes," Gator said.

I studied the picture on the screen. "It's called heterochromia. It's a genetic condition giving a person two different-colored eyes, but I've never seen such a dramatic case."

Kodiak said, "I've seen some scary-looking dudes, but that guy's in a whole other category. Is he our demon carrier?"

Skipper said, "His name is Garland Fitzsimon. His last known non-incarcerated address was Ponce de Leon, Florida, a small, rural town in the panhandle of about five hundred people—ninety-two percent white, two percent black, three percent Hispanic, median income around twenty-five thousand per year."

"Why would Fitzsimon live there?" I asked.

Skipper said, "That's why you're the boss, because you ask the right questions. That's where the woman he believed to be his maternal grandmother lived."

I held up my hand. "We're getting ahead of ourselves. What did he do to get himself into the supermax?"

Skipper said, "His rap sheet reads like a self-help manual for good boys looking to go bad. It started out with petty stuff like vandalism and shoplifting and progressed to some drug trafficking and assault and battery. Apparently, he made sure his grandmother got the lion's share of everything he scored, whether it was legal or not."

"So he loved his grandma. Who doesn't?" Kodiak said.

Skipper continued. "A couple of small-time B and E convictions led to his first serious felony. It was an armed robbery that went badly wrong. A store clerk ended up facedown in a pool of his own blood, but fortunately for everyone involved, he survived. The lucky-to-be-alive clerk fingered Fitzsimon as the shooter at trial, but store video told a different story. Our boy was there and armed, but he clearly wasn't the shooter. A court-appointed attorney, who was apparently better than most, got our boy a pretty good deal of seven to ten without an attempted murder rap tagged on. And he worked it out so Garland could do his time close to home."

I said, "Let's back up even further to something you said earlier. When I asked why Fitzsimon lived in . . . where was it?"

"Ponce de Leon."

"Right. You said he lived there because that's where the woman he *believed* to be his maternal grandmother lived."

"That's right," Skipper said. "We don't know who his real parents were. After he was born, he was sort of adopted by a volunteer fireman and his live-in girlfriend."

"*Sort of* adopted?" I asked. "What does that mean?"

She sighed. "You've heard of dropping babies off at the fire department, right?"

"Sure."

"Well, apparently, Fitzsimon's birth mother didn't know the difference between a fire department, where actual firemen stay twenty-four-seven, and volunteer fire stations. She picked the wrong one, the week before Thanksgiving."

"How long was he out there in the cold?" Singer asked.

Skipper shrugged. "Nobody knows. If someone had been there, they probably would've picked him up instead of just starting the clock, don't you think?"

"Good point," Singer confessed.

Skipper said, "I guess somebody left a turkey in the oven too long and it caught a trailer on fire. That was lucky for little Garland. Otherwise, the fire alarm wouldn't have gone off, and nobody would've been at the volunteer fire station for God knows how long." She shuffled through some papers. "So, this young fireman, who could barely afford to feed himself and his crackhead girlfriend, scooped him up and took him home. Holmes County—that's the county where Ponce de Leon is—messed around and couldn't find a foster home for Garland, so he fell through the cracks."

Singer said, "Let me guess, the crackhead girlfriend's mother caught him when he fell through."

Skipper pretended to ring a bell. "Ding! We have a winner. Pat Fitzsimon was her name. She tried, but life isn't easy for a woman like her in a place like that."

We all leaned toward our analyst, and I asked, "What do you mean by a woman like her?"

Skipper motioned toward a second overhead monitor. "Remember the demographics of the booming metropolis of Ponce de Leon? Our girl Pat doesn't exactly fit in."

The image on the screen showed a disfigured woman whose heritage was impossible to determine. Her skin bore the darkened shade of someone who'd either spent a lifetime in the sun or who'd been born to immigrants from somewhere Caucasians didn't consider home. Her hair could've been that of Caribbean islanders who descended from African slaves or even the native islanders before the Europeans ever stepped foot on the Antilles or Indies.

"Did she have people in Ponce, or how'd she get there?" Singer asked.

Skipper said, "I don't know yet. She could be Creole and migrated from the bayous of Louisiana, or it's possible she could be the descendant of slaves in the area."

Singer said, "Fitzsimon is about as white as a name gets, so I'm not buying the Creole angle. Other than Garland, does she have any family left? What about her daughter, the one living with the fireman?"

"Other than the daughter, she didn't have any family, and the daughter overdosed in Panama City seven years ago."

"So, where's Pat now? Is she still alive?" Singer asked.

Skipper took a long breath. "I don't know."

"You don't know?" Singer said. "The woman is either alive or dead. How can you not know?"

"Just like I said—I don't know. She was alive and well when Garland was doing seven to ten at Walton Correctional Institution. That's a Florida state prison about half an hour from where Pat lived in Ponce. That was part of the deal the public defender got for Garland."

I tapped my pen on the table. "You're being way too cryptic with this one. Tell us what you know, and stop holding back."

Skipper spun in her chair. "That's the problem. I don't know enough, and it's frustrating the crap out of me. It doesn't make sense."

I said, "Pour it out for us, and maybe we can piece it together . . . together."

It wasn't meant to make her chuckle, but I was pleased that it did.

She said, "Okay, here it is. Pat Fitzsimon went to see Garland every Wednesday, without fail. She never missed a visit, not one. She spent exactly one hour with him and rode back home. It was the same schedule every Wednesday. It never changed."

I interrupted. "You said she rode. Did she not drive?"

"No. She didn't have a car or a license. A friend of Garland's drove her every week. It wasn't always the same friend, but she always found somebody. I'm working on names and contact information, but as you might imagine, ex-cons don't exactly keep a Rolodex."

"I'm sorry to have interrupted. Please continue."

She said, "One day, five and a half years into Garland's seven-to-ten-year sentence, they turned him loose."

"Who turned him loose?" Singer asked.

"I'm still working on that, too. The court filings are sealed."

"Sealed?" Singer blurted out. "An adult felony conviction resulting in an early release is sealed? It wasn't federal, was it?"

"No, the crime was local, and he was doing time in a state prison."

Singer shook his head. "And some judge just cut him loose?"

I continued my efforts to focus and bring everything together. "Did he go back to Ponce de Leon?"

It was Skipper's turn to wave us off. "Slow down, guys. I can only answer one question at a time. Yes, obviously, some judge cut him loose, and I'm working on finding the order, but if it exists, it's sealed."

Singer groaned. "That's insane. Somebody has to know."

"Yes, somebody knows, and I'll find it. It's just going to take some time. Now, to Chase's question. I actually have that answer."

"I can't wait," I said.

"Garland did run home, but not to his dear old grandma. He stole a car from a school parking lot."

I dropped my pen. "What? On his first day out of prison, he stole a car?"

"Not only on his first day, but in his first hour."

"Was he picked up?"

She laughed. "Oh, yeah, but not by the cops. Well, sort of not by the cops. The guy who picked him up was a fed of some sort. I just haven't figured all of it out yet. So, here's the story. Garland stole a Toyota from an elementary school parking lot in Ponce de Leon, and this guy who only seems to be identified as Jay-Dub chased him down in a mud-covered pickup truck, ran him off the road, punched out the window, and dragged him from the stolen car by his neck."

Mongo said, "I like this guy. Maybe we should give him an interview."

Skipper huffed. "Stop interrupting me. This story is long enough without stopping every thirty seconds. So, a pair of real feds showed up on the scene, and this Jay-Dub guy had Garland by the ankle, and he's swinging him around like an axe or something and beating him against the stolen car."

Mongo slapped the table. "I don't care if the story takes another hour. Get this Jay-Dub guy on the phone. He's my new drinking buddy since Chase has gone dry. I love this dude already."

Skipper said. "Anyway . . . The feds—we still don't know their official affiliation, by the way—Tased your new drinking buddy and spent way longer than expected getting Garland away from him. Apparently, Jay-Dub gave them quite a whipping, even with the Taser barbs in him."

I was still trying to cut through the insanity. "Did you say this Jay-Dub guy was also a fed of some kind?"

"Yeah, but apparently not law enforcement. He's got something to do with Army or Air Force aviation search and rescue, or something like that. It's not important to the story."

Mongo said, "It's important to me. I want to know if the guy wants to wrestle."

I said, "Let's focus here. So, two feds of undetermined affiliation are tailing Garland when he steals a car, and they just let him get away with it. A third coincidental government employee intervenes, and the feds rescue Garland instead of arresting him. Is that what I'm hearing?"

"Exactly," Skipper said.

"And he didn't go back to jail?"

"Nope."

"How about Jay-Dub?" I asked. "What happened to him?"

Skipper said, "The coincidences get weirder. It turns out that the stolen car belonged to Jay-Dub's wife, who was a teacher at the school, and he just happened to be there dropping off something for an event when he saw Garland steal the car."

Singer said, "So, nobody went to jail. Is that right?"

"That's right."

I asked, "So, what happened to Garland? Did he see his grandmother?"

Skipper sighed. "You're forcing me to say the phrase I hate the most again. I don't know. Pat Fitzsimon has never been seen or heard

from again, and the next time Garland surfaced, he was in police custody in Monroe County, Florida. I can't find any record of the official charges, but if the priest is right, it has to be connected to the
murders of the NSA agents, the Mossad officer, and the FSB officer
in Key West, right?"

Chapter 6
One Final Demand

I lay on my back, staring at the bedroom ceiling that had been Penny's and mine, and I tried to come up with a reasonable explanation why a small-town criminal would murder four intel operatives after somehow walking away from half of a seven-to-ten-year stint for armed robbery. Answers weren't coming, and nothing on that ceiling gave me any reason to believe they would. What came through my door unannounced and uninvited gave even less promise of any answers . . . or so I thought.

"I do not believe person is real priest."

"Hello, Anya. You could've knocked."

"Yes, but it would be rude to wake you by knocking."

I wanted to believe there was some logic in there somewhere, but I was too afraid to dig for it. "Then I guess I should thank you for not being rude."

She sat on the edge of my bed. "You are welcome. Did you hear me tell to you that I do not believe he is priest?"

I pressed the remote control and rose in the adjustable bed that I'd argued against but had grown to love. "Surely there's some sort of priest registry or something, isn't there? Skipper can check him out in the morning."

She spun and lay her head on the pillow beside me. "What do you think is happening?"

"The first thing that's going to happen is you're going to get out of my bed."

"I am not *in* your bed. I am *on* your bed. You are *in* bed."

"Oh, you're teaching me English prepositions now?"

She stood and nestled onto a bedside dressing chair. "This is less tempting for you, yes?"

"We're not playing this game tonight, Anya. What are you doing here?"

She sighed. "I came to talk about priest and because I knew you would not be able to sleep. We can go for walk if you want. I promise to maybe not flirt with you."

"Where's our daughter?"

She smiled. "She is so much like her father. She cannot sleep either. Her head is inside book in library."

"Fiction or non-fiction?"

"Biology. She is going to be physician, I think."

"She's going to be everything."

Anya tapped the floor with the toe of her shoe. "She has already more education than me."

"What are you talking about? She's in her first year of college."

"Yes, I know this. I do not have graduation from even high school."

"What?" I threw back the cover. "But you went through all the schools with—"

She said, "I have been to many schools, and I performed always well, but these are not kind of schools that give to students degrees and diplomas."

"Hand me my leg. I think I'll take you up on that walk."

She laughed. "This sounds funny when you say to me, 'Hand me my leg.'"

I hopped from the bed on my one remaining foot. "Laugh it up, beauty school dropout. I'll get it myself."

She leapt to her feet. "Finally, I know one. That is song from *Grease*. I have not seen Broadway musical play, but I watched movie with friend Gwynn on television."

"You're becoming more American every day."

She reached into her pocket, but I held up a hand. "You don't have to pull out the flag. I know you have it."

It didn't stop her.

Over time, I'd become very good at donning my prosthetic, even while standing. Dr. Ham, the orthopedic genius at UAB who designed the remarkable device and fitted me with several iterations of the hardware, made sure I could operate every aspect of it, especially getting into and out of it with unmatched efficiency. In my line of work, the eighteen inches beneath my knee was pretty important.

"Come on, intruder. Let's take our daughter for a walk."

Anya furrowed her brow. "I did not say I wanted her to come with us for walk."

"And I didn't say I wanted you to come barging into my bedroom at ten o'clock at night."

She brushed a strand of hair behind her ear. "You are only man in all of world who would not want me to do this."

It wasn't arrogance on her part. She was right. She was a classic beauty, and I was endlessly grateful our daughter looked far more like her than me. It wasn't a lack of physical attraction that made me kick her out of—or off of—my bed. It was the fact that half of that bed still belonged to the even more beautiful woman I still loved more than I could ever love anyone else as long as I lived.

We descended the slightly arching main staircase at Bonaventure and crossed the foyer to the library, a room I loved more than any other in the rebuilt colonial. It remained the most original of any room in the house, with its wavy window glass and ornate fireplace. Built-in bookcases towered far higher than even Mongo could reach, but a beautifully ornate ladder with rollers on brass rails doubled the capacity of the magnificent storehouse of wisdom and fantasy. The desk was smaller than the room deserved, but also grander in style and history since it had belonged to a sea captain and sailed the world before the days of steam and iron. The wood bore scars I imagined to be those of sword fights and splinters that I dreamed were left by flying cannonballs. In truth, the captain and his ships had likely been merchantmen, and the wounds had probably been those of drunken nights upon stormy seas left by broken glass and falling cargo.

The frosted double doors leading into the room stood barely ajar, and I leaned in to find Pogonya reclining in one of the wingbacks in front of the fireplace with an open book lying across her lap. Most people look like drooling, melting wax figures when they fall asleep, but even in her slumber, our daughter was perfect.

I gently pulled the doors closed, pressed a finger to my lips, and Anya smiled. We slipped through the kitchen door and down the gallery stairs.

I said, "What makes you think he's not a priest?"

"I cannot put on finger, but is something. I will question him and catch him inside lie if he is not really priest."

I stopped by the gazebo. "You'll do no such thing. We're playing this out to its natural end. I want to know what this whole thing's about, even if the priest is an impostor."

She scowled. "Why do you care so much?"

"The Fitzsimon guy killed four intelligence operatives. Why *don't* you care?"

She shrugged. "Two were *former* operatives, maybe. Skipper said NSA. They could have been clerks or analysts. Third is Mossad, maybe. It will be impossible to verify this. And fourth is FSB. He deserved to die."

I chuckled. "You're biased."

"You know what Soviet Union did to me, Chasechka. You would be also biased."

"You're right. I can't argue with that one except to say that it wasn't entirely the Soviet Union. The wall did come down, and it became the Russian Federation."

She grabbed my hand and jerked it to her side. "Come with me."

We crossed the lawn to an enormous tree that had stood on the property for hundreds of years.

She pressed my face against the rough bark. "If someone drove stakes into ground and tied you to them, and then cut down this tree to make it fall on you, would it matter if they call it oak tree or pecan tree?"

Our walk became friendlier after my Eastern Bloc botany lesson, and it was actually nice. For several minutes at a time, I found myself believing Penny was walking beside me, and in those moments, I wanted to reach for her hand. I'm glad I didn't, but it would've been easy to let it happen.

"You go every day to her grave, yes?"

I nodded.

"Maybe one day I can come with you."

Instead of answering, I asked, "How did Penny react when you told her about Pogonya in Switzerland?"

We stopped by a fallen log and took a seat.

"She was very angry at first and did not believe me. She thought I was only trying to be cruel."

"That makes sense."

She nodded. "Yes, it does. Inside mind of woman is strange place. Is impossible for man to know."

I laughed. "Trust me. I know exactly what you mean. Every man on Earth knows what you mean."

"Some women might do this. They might say things like, 'I have child of man you love' to be cruel and hurtful, but I am not kind of person who would do this."

"No, you're not," I said.

"Is true, Pogonya does not look like you so much, but she has very much eyes of your mother, and I know for certain she is your child, Chasechka."

"I know. I don't have any doubts about that. Besides, Dr. Mankiller ran the DNA test Skipper demanded."

Anya gently took my hand in hers. "There was no DNA test. Skipper changed her mind, but there is something you must know. There could be no other father because since first time you and I were together on sailboat, you have been only man I have been with."

"That can't be true. Anya, that was twenty years ago, and you lived with Mongo, and there was—"

She cupped my face in her hands. "Mongo and I were only friends. He wanted more, but I could not. There was one man named Pyotr Evanhoff. I cared very much for him, but he was killed on mission with Department of Justice. We did not have romance, but if he was not killed, maybe."

"I'm sorry. I didn't know."

"Do not be sorry. You could not know. Is much better this way. I would rather live life forever with you and me as Pogonya's parents, even if we are not, you know, together."

I was left speechless, but she said, "I did not finish answering all of question. Penny was first angry with me for saying to her Pogonya was your child because she thought I was being cruel, but this was for only short time. After this, she was angry—very angry—with me for not telling you. She said it was not fair to you and to Pogonya. She said both of you deserved to know, and it was terrible of me to keep both of you from each other."

"She was right."

"Yes, of course she was right. She was always right, and she had perfect taste in men, but this is not all of story."

"What's the rest of the story?"

"Is important for you to know that Penny and Pogonya liked each other very much. They spent many hours together and talked much about you. Penny told silly stories of you and made Pogonya laugh. It made me happy inside heart, but I was angry with myself for keeping silent for so long. I believed I was doing thing that was right, but I know it was not, and I am sorry."

I tossed a leg across the log and pulled Anya against me. "It doesn't do any good to be sorry. We can't erase anything. We can only move forward and make the most of the time we have with our daughter, and that's exactly what I'm going to do."

She hugged me tightly. "We must do this together."

"We will, but for now, it has to be a different kind of together."

"I know, and I understand, but maybe there will come time when . . ."

"Like I told Pogo, if that time comes, it'll be you, Anya, and no one else."

I don't know how long we held each other, but it was exactly the right amount of time.

When she pulled away, she said, "There is one more thing you must know, and it proves again that Penny was always right." She wiped a tear from her eye. "I insisted we bring Pogonya with us to meet you together, but she said that wasn't right way to do it. She said she wanted to talk with you so you understood she would not be angry before you met Pogonya."

It felt as if I'd been punched in the chest, and I couldn't catch my breath. "Are you saying . . ."

Anya nodded. "Yes, Chasechka. If I made decision, our daughter would have been on airplane when we were shot down and your wife was killed, but Penny demanded that Pogonya stay behind in Switzerland."

Chapter 7

A Vow by Any Other Name

My phone chirped on the drive to Jacksonville the following morning. I pressed the speaker button, but before I could answer, Skipper said, "By the way, he's really a priest. I checked with the diocese."

"Did Anya put you up to that?"

"No, I was just trying to cover all the bases. There's a lot wrong with this whole case, and I don't want to miss anything. I spoke with a Monsignor Mastronardi—which is fun to say, by the way—and he confirmed that Father Isaiah Lamb is, indeed, a Jesuit priest in good standing with the church but officially on sabbatical from his duties with the Holy See."

"Sabbatical?" I asked.

Anya jumped. "I told you he was not real priest."

"He's obviously a real priest," I said. "The church confirmed that. Being on sabbatical doesn't mean he isn't real. It just means he's not on official church business."

Skipper said, "Yeah, he's freelancing."

Singer said, "I've never heard of a priest with a side gig."

I said, "I agree. Do you think we should bring the Triad in yet?"

The Triad was a group of three men who loosely directed our operation. It was made up of two retired special operations command generals and one career covert operator who just happened to be my original handler and the father of my current handler.

"Not yet," Skipper said. "I'm not sure we're fully committed yet. We haven't voted."

That got a hearty round of laughter and a chorus of "This ain't a democracy."

I shook my head. "All right, that's enough. You're right. We're not fully committed yet, but I do want to meet this Garland Fitzsimon guy, who's supposedly possessed by a demon. But we have to spring our priest from the hospital first."

Skipper said, "Oh, yeah. They just called and said he can leave as soon as someone can pick him up."

"That was quick," I said. "I thought it would be this afternoon before they'd turn him loose."

"Don't forget. He's got that whole white-collar thing working for him," Singer said. "Maybe I need to get me one of those."

Kodiak did something with his hands that looked more like a gang sign than anything holy. "Do we need to start calling you Reverend, Dr., Father, Pastor, Preacher, Minister, Friar James Singer Grossmann?"

"I'm just Singer, and my name's Jimmy. You know my folks were too poor to name their boy James."

* * *

Isaiah refused the wheelchair—perhaps yet another priestly privilege—and made his way to our short bus on simple wooden crutches with a small canvas bag hung diagonally across his chest. He refused our assistance with the bag and mounting the vehicle. His independence, if genuine, was enough to earn at least a modicum of respect from me, and I suspected the same was true of the rest of the team.

"This is an interesting vehicle," Isaiah said as he tried to make himself comfortable with his new footwear.

"It's our short bus," I said. "It used to belong to the Camden County school system until it was neglected and fell into disrepair behind the county maintenance garage. We rescued it, and our favorite mechanic—you'll meet her later—turned it into this."

"It looks like a limousine inside," he said.

Shawn, our SEAL, said, "It was originally a school bus, but now we use it exclusively for transporting exorcists."

The priest's eyes turned to saucers. "I'm no exorcist, and please understand this is no joking matter."

Shawn threw up his hands. "Sorry. Sometimes I tend to . . . never mind. I could play the guitar or something if you want. I know a bunch of gospel, but I don't know what Catholics sing."

Isaiah asked, "Do you happen to know 'I'm a One-Legged Priest on a Bus Full of Mercenaries'?"

Shawn opened up his guitar case. "I think so. The original is in G, but I like to sing it in E if that's all right with you."

That broke the tension, but only until Anya relocated Isaiah's crutches and nestled beside our clergyman. Every part of me wanted to intercede except for the curious, mischievous psych student who still hung out somewhere behind my left eye.

Anya said, "Do you have official paper to prove you are really priest?"

Ah, that's the boulevard she chose. Disappointing.

Isaiah struck back. "Are you asking to see my papers? That's a very Soviet thing to do."

Anya seemed unfazed and tugged Isaiah's sleeve. "I could go to place where this is sold and buy clothes of priest. It would be easy to pretend."

He laughed, and she scowled. "What is funny about this?"

He said, "I was thinking about you dressed as a priest. There are no female Roman Catholic priests. You could purchase a habit and convince someone you're a nun, or you could wear the collar and pretend to be clergy of another faith, but not a Catholic priest."

"This is technicality only."

He said, "You're correct. I carry an official card from the Vatican identifying me as an ordained priest and servant of the Dicastery for the Doctrine of the Faith. I could show you the card, but if you doubt my word, you will, of course, doubt a credential that could so easily be counterfeited. I have an idea. I could tell you about my vows. If you are who and what you claim to be, and if I'm an impostor, you'll identify me as a liar within seconds."

I expected her to say "I'm listening," but she fooled me.

"I made no claims. You made assumptions because of accent that could be also counterfeit, but tell to me vows, *Priest*."

I doubted he was taking the pain medication the doctors prescribed, but his smile said otherwise. If Anya had induced the smile, I was certain that, alone, was a violation of at least one of his vows.

He began. "As a Jesuit, I took three vows that appear on their surface to be quite simple, but, in fact, they are remarkably deep."

He turned to face his inquisitor, and I liked the move. It gave her an unobstructed view of both of his eyes and demonstrated his willingness to openly face his accuser—if that's what he perceived her to be.

"The first and most well-known of the priestly vows is, of course, Chastity. This is the full reservation of all of one's love, affection, desire, and passion, wholly and solely for God alone."

Anya shifted in her seat, and the psych student in my skull and I detected a touch of discomfort in her body language. After all, the core of her early training as an operative had been based wholly and solely on the exact opposite of the priest's vow of chastity.

Isaiah also seemed to notice. "I know. This is in defiance to one of the most basic natures of humanity. We are physically attracted to others for the purpose of procreation. That attraction, however, is often perverted into an obsession rather than its original purpose."

He glanced away, and I couldn't wait for the next sentence to leap from his mouth. He didn't disappoint.

"Just because I took the vow and meant it—I retake it constantly and mean it constantly, by the way—doesn't mean I'm not physically attracted to women."

Anya smiled. "Thank you."

Isaiah cleared his throat. "Yes, well . . . back to the vow. Please don't mistake it to mean that I withhold all love of any kind from everyone except God. We are commanded throughout Scripture to love without end. That is not the kind of love the vow forbids. Of course I love people. I've devoted my life to sharing the Gospel with them out of love. The vow of chastity is a devotion of purity of mind, body, and spirit for God alone. It isn't always easy, and that's part of the point. Devotion to anything meaningful and good requires sacrifice and never comes easily for sinful humans, priests included."

Anya spoke just above a whisper. "I believe you."

"Shall I continue?" he asked.

She said, "You are going to tell me of Obedience and Poverty, no?"

He stuttered. "Well . . . um . . . yes, I was going to."

"Tell to me, instead, of fourth vow."

His eyes widened, and a smile replaced the look he'd worn seconds before. "I'd like that."

He paused, but only for a moment, as if carefully considering the wording for his attentive audience—an audience for whom his first vow was specifically designed. "The fourth vow of the Jesuit is known as a special promise to the sovereign pontiff and not so much as an actual vow, which is made to God. We promise to make ourselves totally available and obedient to our superiors, accepting orders to go anywhere in the world, even if we're required to live in extreme conditions, no matter what the mission requires."

"That sounds familiar," Mongo said. "Almost everybody on this bus made a similar promise. We called it the Oath of Enlistment. We raised our right hands in front of an officer in uniform and said, 'I do solemnly swear that I will support and defend the Constitution of the United States against all enemies, foreign and domestic; that I will bear true faith and allegiance to the same; and that I will obey the orders of the president of the United States and the orders of the officers appointed over me, according to regulations and the Uniform Code of Military Justice. So help me God.'"

By the time he was finished, nearly everyone aboard joined in, repeating the oath they'd taken more than once. Anya, Gator, and I were the exceptions since the three of us had never served in uniform.

Isaiah nodded. "It's more similar than you know. The leading founder of the Jesuits, St. Ignatius, was a nobleman and a man of military service. In fact, the opening lines of the founding documents of Jesuits declare that we were founded specifically for 'whoever desires to serve as a soldier of God.' In some parts of the world, we're even called God's soldiers or the Company. Perhaps we aren't so different as we might appear on the surface."

* * *

Gator looked up into the massive mirror still hanging in the front of the bus. "We're here, guys."

I stood and drew my credentials. "I guess that's my cue."

Isaiah lifted a crutch and stuck the toe in my sternum. "No, I believe it's mine."

We rolled to a stop, and a uniformed officer stepped aboard the bus. "Good morning, and welcome to the North Central Florida supermax. I'm Corporal Leonard. Oh, hey, Father Lamb. I didn't see you there. What happened to the foot?"

"Horseback riding accident."

The officer said, "I guess you weren't cut out to be one of those Knights Templar, huh?"

"I guess not. I brought a few friends to see—"

"You don't have to say it. I know who you're here to see." The corporal laid a hand on Gator's shoulder. "Pull into the sallyport, and we'll search the vehicle. Any weapons or contraband on board?"

Everyone except the priest drew a pistol, and Shawn unlocked the floor-mounted rifle vault.

Corporal Leonard stood with his mouth agape. "Uh, who are you guys?"

I turned to Isaiah. "May I?"

He nodded, and I produced my Secret Service credentials.

The officer examined them closely. "You guys don't usually come through the main gate. What's up with that?"

"What do you mean?" I asked.

He said, "When you feds come, you always come through the warden's office, and it's always the same guy."

I made a pile of mental notes a mile high and did my best acting job by waving a hand. "That's a different branch. We're just observers from Treasury with Father Lamb. We're not here on any kind of official federal capacity . . . Just doing a favor for the Pope. You know how it is. You've gotta score all the points you can, am I right?"

He tossed my cred-pack back. "You're right about that. I'll log the weapons and lock them up unless you want to secure them in your floor vault and take our bus to the main building."

I said, "That sounds a lot simpler for us and less paperwork for you."

He chuckled. "That's what I'm saying. Lock 'em up, and we'll secure your vehicle. I'm sorry for this, but we have to pat you down. It *is* a supermax, you know."

Corporal Leonard and two of his fellow officers took our ink pens, belts, pocketknives, watches, and sunglasses, and they almost took the priest's crutches. They x-rayed his cast and sent us through half a dozen metal detectors, where we set off more buzzers and red lights than a carnival ride. Warfighters with as much downrange experience as my team tend to collect a lot of metal on their bodies, and we were no exception.

After scrutiny that made the TSA look like Girl Scouts, we were finally allowed inside the reception station. It took over an hour to finally progress into unit G-7, where we were met by a gentleman who looked as if he hadn't shaved in a week and probably hadn't slept in far longer than that.

He didn't offer a hand or so much as a nod, but Isaiah made an effort at introductions. "Dr. Brian Plum, meet Dr. Chase Fulton. Dr.

Plum is the chief neurological officer for the North Central District of the Department of Corrections. He oversees all of the—"

Dr. Plum said, "Are you here to see your pet project, Lamb?"

"I am."

"He's strapped down in Delta Eight. You can take yourself and two more back there. That's it. If he breaks anything, you're paying for it."

Plum stormed off without looking up, and I said, "Seems like a nice guy."

"He's overworked, underpaid, and you're minutes away from understanding why he looks sixty-five when he just turned forty."

"You said he's the chief neuro officer. Is he a psychiatrist or neurologist?"

Lamb shrugged. "He's responsible for the mental health of a thousand inmates who, by definition, are the opposite of mentally healthy, so if you're looking for a job, I'm sure he'd love to give you his."

"No, thank you."

Our escort, a twenty-something correctional officer with no neck, led us down the Delta corridor and to a heavy steel door marked with a white eight. "You know the protocol, right, Father?"

Isaiah said, "I do, but brief it for my associates, please."

The officer sighed. "The glass is three inches thick, so there's no danger of the inmate harming you. He's restrained but extremely volatile. That can be a little alarming at first. He may overpower the restraints. He's done it before. If it happens, just let me know, and we'll take care of it. The large black plungers close the blinds. Use that if anything happens that you don't want to see. The yellow plungers stop the audio from the prisoner's side. Use that if anything happens that you don't want to hear. The orange plunger opens audio instead of stopping it from your side. Use that if you want the prisoner to hear what you're saying. The red ones mean get me out of here. There are three of those. I'll be right here, so I can pull you out of there in less than two seconds. Got it?"

Singer and I locked eyes and nodded in unison as if the priest and the correctional officer weren't there, but when the door opened, there was nothing I could've done to prepare myself for what I saw on the other side of the thickest pane of glass I'd ever seen.

Chapter 8

Facie ad Faciem

The space was the size of an apartment kitchen, with three seats, a countertop, and a wall of glass four feet tall. Beyond the glass sat a form that had once been a human being, reduced to a form wrapped in a Department of Corrections jumpsuit and strapped partially upright to a fixture for which there could be no name. The only sound was Fitzsimon's deep, resonant breathing that seemed to ooze like mud from the walls within the chamber.

Isaiah turned sideways and moved through the opening on his crutches. Singer followed, and I stepped through last, unable to force my eyes from Fitzsimon's. I had anticipated and even prepared myself for his heterochromia, but there was more to the eyes than their difference in color. Although his left was the blue of an Alaskan husky's, and his right could've been Richter's, black as obsidian glass, there was a helplessness behind them, a child's yearning for his mother's—or his grandmother's—embrace. Everything else about him spoke of terrifying hatred and perpetual evil, but the man behind those eyes wasn't the man who wore them.

The priest whispered a prayer I'd heard hundreds of times and crossed himself while Singer sat in stoic silence, watching every move Garland Fitzsimon didn't make.

"Can he hear us?" I whispered.

Isaiah slowly shook his head. "No. As the officer said, he can only hear us when we press the orange plunger. Be very careful what you tell him, though. You do not want that man inside your head, Chase."

No matter where I moved in the room, Fitzsimon's eyes never left mine. Type-A personalities tend to force eye contact until someone breaks, but his wasn't a challenge. It was the awareness of both predator and prey. He needed to know into which category I fell, and regardless of the answer, knowing *where* I was in the room remained crucial for survival inside the mind of the predator he believed himself to be and the prey he feared he could become.

Singer spoke softly. "It's interesting how his eyes never leave mine."

"What?" I asked.

He looked up at me. "Fitzsimon. He never takes his eyes from mine, no matter where I move."

"That can't be," the priest said. "He's doing the same to me."

I took a long breath, more to reassure myself than anything else. "It's an optical illusion with the thick glass. I'm seeing it, too. Don't let it bother you. What do you make of his breathing?"

Isaiah said, "It's been just like that every time I've seen him calm. It sounds like he's breathing through a respirator, like Darth Vader or something."

"Have you ever heard him breathe naturally?" I asked.

"Do you mean, like in the same room with him?"

"Yes."

"No, I've never . . ."

"Are you afraid of him?" I asked.

The priest said, "I'm not afraid of dying, if that's what you're asking."

"That's not what I'm asking. He can't hurt you. He's obviously restrained. I'm asking if you're afraid to be in the same room with him."

Isaiah didn't answer, so Singer said, "I'd like to talk with him."

The priest straightened his collar. "Okay, but don't tell him your name or anything personal. Try not to provoke him. Keeping him calm is the best way to keep him lucid."

Singer eyed the Jesuit. "Lucid, you say. We're looking through three inches of glass at a man strapped to a steel chair, and you're talking to me about keeping him lucid."

As Isaiah backed away, Singer slowly approached the glass and laid a gentle hand against the orange plunger. "Hello, Garland. I'm Singer. I'd like—"

The prisoner hissed. "I wanna talk to the one back there that ain't no priest."

I pointed a finger toward my chest, and he said, "Yeah, you."

Singer said, "I'm not a priest, Garland."

The man roared like an enraged beast as spittle and blood exploded from his mouth. "*Numquam mentiari ultimo!*"

Singer released the plunger, and I covered my mouth with a cupped hand. "Relax. He's just playing games with us."

Singer turned to Isaiah. "Was that Latin?"

I didn't give him a chance to answer. With my mouth still covered so Garland couldn't see, I said, "It was elementary Latin any tenth grader could pick up. He just said, 'Don't lie to a liar.' He's just trying to scare us."

Singer said, "He identified me as a priest."

"Look down at your hand," I said.

Singer glanced down to see the silver cross he wore as a ring on his right hand any time we weren't deployed downrange.

I said, "He's clever, but he's done a lot of prison time. Cons are very good with details. Just stay calm, and let's see what he has to say to me."

Isaiah turned his back to Fitzsimon. "But that's not what he said."

"What are you talking about?" I asked.

"You told us Garland said, 'Don't lie to a liar.' Maybe in tenth grade Latin, you're right, but what he actually said was, 'Never lie to the ultimate liar.'"

I lowered my hand and stepped toward the glass. Before I could put my hand on the plunger to speak, Fitzsimon spoke in his original Southern tone. "You're one of 'em."

"One of who?" I asked.

"You know the truth, and you ain't doing nothin' about it. That's who."

"What truth, Garland?"

He tightened his previously relaxed hands into fists of iron as the veins in his neck bulged and his face turned from the pale pallor of a man who never saw the sun to bright red.

Singer asked, "Should we call the guard?"

I laid a hand on his arm. "No. I'm sure they're monitoring. Give me a minute."

Pressing the plunger, I said, "Garland, who do you think I am? I'm here because my friend, Father—"

Isaiah slapped my hand from the plunger. "I told you not to give him any of our names."

I pressed the button again. "I'm sorry about that. I'm here because someone I trust believes we may be able to help you."

"*Fides est fundamentum mendaciorum.*"

I ignored his outburst. "I need you to relax, Garland. I just want to talk with you. Let's talk about your grandmother, Pat."

What happened next came so quickly, it would be impossible to describe in real time. Garland ripped his left hand from the restraint, tearing flesh from bone as if he had no regard for pain. In the next instant, he tore at the remaining restraints until his fingernails peeled from his skin and blood poured from beneath. His head twisted at such an angle that it was impossible to believe the vertebrae of his neck could remain connected until his head slipped from the bands holding his forehead to the top of the chair. Bent at the waist, he chewed through the restraints at his ankles and then threw himself against the glass with such force that I felt myself tremble to my very core as I retreated toward the back wall. Although mine rocketed beyond a measurable rate, Fitzsimon's pace of breathing never changed throughout the entire affair.

The priest closed his eyes, laid a hand on the black plunger, and made the sign of the cross over his chest.

* * *

Back aboard our bus and outside the supermax sallyport, Singer prayed in silence, the priest did the same, and I stared out the window until Anya laid a hand against my knee and whispered, "You are okay, my Chasechka?"

"I don't know. I've seen a lot of terrible things in my life, but I've never come face-to-face with anything like that."

"*Facie ad faciem*," Isaiah whispered. "It means face-to-face in Latin."

"Have you ever seen him do that before?" I asked.

"Several times . . ."

"And you still don't believe he possessed?"

Kodiak said, "Okay, somebody's gotta be the one, so I'll do it. Tell us what happened in there."

I relayed the story poorly, but I can't imagine anyone telling it well. No one spoke until we made it back to the interstate, and I should've predicted it would be Singer who finally broke the silence.

"You're the psychologist. What did you see?"

"I saw a madman who speaks Latin."

Singer huffed. "A career criminal from a tiny little place smaller than the rathole I crawled out of, who never finished high school, who speaks Latin?"

"Not just Latin," Isaiah said. "But good Latin. Proper Latin."

Kodiak asked, "The kind of Latin a demon would know?"

Isaiah shrugged. "How should I know? I've never met a demon."

Singer pointed behind us. "Are you sure?"

The priest ignored him. "Fitzsimon said, '*Fides est fundamentum mendaciorum.*'"

Gator checked the mirror. "What's that mean?"

I said, "It means trust is the foundation of lies."

The priest held up a finger. "Again, you're close, but not quite. It actually means faith is the foundation of lies."

"What's the difference to an inmate doing life in the supermax?" Gator asked.

"The difference to you and me is that we *trust* the truck driver beside us not to change lanes and kill us. We have *faith* that if he does, we'll wake up in Heaven. I have no idea what the difference is to an inmate at the supermax."

"He identified me as a fed," I said. "I don't know how. I don't think I have *the look*. He said I was one of them who knows the truth. I have no idea what he's talking about."

Shawn said, "How much weight have you gained since you bought those pants?"

"What kind of question is that?"

"Just tell me."

I said, "I don't know. Maybe ten pounds. I lost a lot of weight after Penny died, okay?"

The SEAL said, "I'm not beating you up. I'm just telling you how Fitzsimon knew you were a fed. Stand up and turn around so everybody can get a good look at your cute little butt . . . or what used to be a little butt."

When I stood and checked Gator's giant mirror, the outline of my Secret Service credentials pack shone like a beacon in my hip pocket.

Singer said, "Now I don't feel so bad about my ring."

I reclaimed my seat. "Okay, so that answers the mystery of how he knew I was a fed, even though I'm not a real one. But it doesn't answer the question of how or why he knows Latin so well."

Singer asked, "How many times have you seen him, Isaiah?"

"Today made . . . nine?"

"Have you ever had what could be considered a normal conversation with him?"

"Not really. Maybe for a few minutes at a time, but it always ends up out of control."

"Have you ever tried speaking Latin with him?"

"It's a dead language," Isaiah said. "Nobody speaks Latin, so nobody really knows how it was spoken or how it's supposed to sound."

"Yeah, but you know the rules of the grammar, and you can get the pronunciation close, right?"

He said, "I've tried answering him in short passages."

Singer leaned in. "And?"

The priest sighed. "He can do it."

"Do what?"

"Fitzsimon can communicate in Latin."

I said, "So, it's not just a few phrases he's memorized from exorcism movies."

"No," Isaiah said. "Definitely not."

Singer laid his head back against the seat. "I'm not ready to concede that he's possessed, but I want you to make me understand why *you* don't believe he's possessed."

The Jesuit pulled out his rosary beads, wound them around his hand, and spoke with quiet confidence. "What I am about to say is controversial, even within the church, but I believe it to be true. Evil is not an entity. Lucifer, Satan, whatever you choose to call him, is not a force that is equal and opposite to God. Evil is the same as darkness. It doesn't truly exist. Darkness is simply the absence of light. Evil is simply the absence of good, the absence of God. Darkness cannot exist in the presence of light, just as evil cannot exist in the presence of God. In the nine times I have seen Garland Fitzsimon, I have never experienced the absence of God."

Chapter 9

Broken Vows

"How far are we from Ponce de Leon?" I asked no one in particular.

No one answered, so I yanked my phone from my pocket and dialed the op center.

Skipper answered immediately. "So, is he possessed? Tell me everything."

"I don't have time to tell you everything, but the short answer is maybe. Singer thinks so, but the priest still says no."

"Well, there's a plot twist for you."

"I know," I said. "But that's not why I'm calling. We just got back on the interstate a few miles from the supermax, and I want to find this Jay-Dub character who beat up Fitzsimon after he stole his wife's car. Can you do it?"

She blew a raspberry. "Does the pope wear a funny hat? Oh, my gosh. I'm not on speaker, am I?"

"You are, and Isaiah is trying hard not to laugh."

I could almost see her blushing through the phone.

She said, "I really wish I could take that back, but yes, of course I can find him. Do you want to talk to him on the phone or face-to-face?"

I said, "*Facie ad faciem.*"

"Learn that from the demon, did you?"

"Actually, the priest taught me that one."

"Well, turn around. Believe it or not, you're closer to Ponce de Leon than to St. Marys. If you really want to talk to this guy, make a

U-turn and head west. I'll start digging, and I'll have an address for you by the time you make the exit."

Isaiah reached for the phone, and I hesitantly surrendered the device.

He said, "He doesn't always wear the hats, but he has several funny ones. I'll get some pictures for you if you'd like."

Skipper said, "Have you really met him?"

"Only once, but very briefly, and we didn't chat."

"Seriously, I hope I didn't offend you with the hat thing."

Isaiah said, "Skipper, we just watched a man rip his fingernails off, almost break his own neck, and chew himself out of leather restraints. A joke about pontifical headwear isn't going to offend me."

"You're pretty cool for a priest, you know that?"

"So I've been told."

He gave back the phone, and I tucked it away. "I assume you don't have any place to be since you're on sabbatical, huh?"

He bowed his head. "So, I guess that means you know about that. I'm sorry. I should've told you."

A chorus echoed through the bus. "Don't be sorry. Be better!"

He recoiled. "Wow. It's almost like you practiced that one just for me."

"It's not unique to you," I said. "It's kind of our team motto. You've got nothing to apologize for. You didn't lie to us, as far as I know. We didn't ask if you were on an official mission, and you didn't claim to be."

"Still, I should've told you."

"So, tell us now," Anya said. "You are really priest, yes?"

"Yes, I really am. I've taken final vows."

"I do not know what this means, but it does not matter. I believe you. Tell to us what you should have in place of first."

He cocked his head. "Place of first?"

I chuckled. "She's only been in America for a couple dozen years, so she's still learning the language. She meant, tell us what you should've told us in the first place."

Although the moment called for anything except laughter, he chuckled. "Oh, yes. Well, what I should've told you is that the archbishop appears to hold the unofficial position that Fitzsimon is the victim of demonic possession."

I said, "You didn't specifically name the official who held that opinion before, but you didn't hide that fact from us."

He continued. "Yes, but what I left out was the fact that when I questioned the archbishop's position, I was overstepping my vow. It was not then, nor is it now, my place to question the spiritual wisdom of the leadership within the church. As a Jesuit, I am bound only to serve and obey."

I groaned. "So, your sabbatical . . . Are you being punished for disagreeing with the archbishop?"

He bowed his head again, and I stuck a finger beneath his chin. "Look at me. *Facie ad faciem*, remember? Are you on a priestly suspension or something like that?"

He closed his eyes for a moment and mouthed "God forgive me" before saying, "I'm supposed to be at a Jesuit center called Ignatius House, spending all my time in prayer, contemplation, and service. Have you heard of it?"

Singer said, "I have. It's a Catholic retreat in Sandy Springs, near Atlanta, right?"

"That's right," Isaiah said. "I was there for almost three months and became close friends with a priest who suggested that my time would be better spent in silence at a Trappist monastery in Moncks Corner, South Carolina."

Singer gripped the seat as if he were going to tear it from its foundation.

The priest nodded at our sniper. "Yes, I know that's where your brother died. In an extremely rare and precious moment, one of the monks broke his silence to pray and talk with me. That's how I came to be in the gazebo at Bonaventure the morning Chase found me there."

Singer released his grip on the seat and wrapped the priest in a hug that only true men of God understand. "We may disagree about doctrine, but whatever this thing is, brother, we'll figure it out."

* * *

Gator took the exit to Ponce de Leon at the same time my phone chirped. "This is Chase."

"Hey, it's Skipper. I know it's hard to believe, but I'm striking out. Jay-Dub is obviously some kind of nickname. I'm still digging, but whoever he is, the guy doesn't have an online footprint."

"No worries," I said. "We're almost there. We need diesel and chow, so we have to make a couple of stops anyway. We'll do some good old-fashioned detective work and see what we can come up with. This place is even smaller than St. Marys. How many Jay-Dubs can there be in a town of five hundred people, right?"

"Good luck, and please be careful. Take a look around. You guys aren't exactly going to fit in down there."

"What are you talking about? We've got a giant, a priest, and an African American sniper. We precisely mirror the demographics of this place."

She groaned. "Yeah, right. What could possibly go wrong? Keep me posted."

Gator rolled to a stop beside the diesel pump at a Tom Thumb station at the corner of Highway 90 and SR 81. While he pumped, I took a walk inside the store. The young man behind the counter with a Colt 1911 on his hip gave me a friendly nod, and I returned the gesture.

He rang up fifty-four dollars' worth of snacks and drinks, and I asked, "You don't happen to know a guy named Jay-Dub who lives around here, do you?"

Without looking up, he said, "Never heard of him."

I paid with three twenties. "Keep the change. Oh, and is there a good place to eat close by? We've been on the road a while."

He motioned across his shoulder. "If you like barbeque, Four C's is the best around. It's just right there."

"Thanks."

I climbed back aboard the bus to an audience of faces full of anticipation. "I planted the seed but got nothing. We'll see if it sprouts. Is anybody opposed to barbecue?"

The store clerk was right. The barbecue was amazing, and the atmosphere was exactly as expected. Picnic tables beneath a tin roof was the perfect spot to enjoy more smoked pork than anybody needed to shove in their mouths.

I asked four more people if they knew Jay-Dub, and I got identical answers. "Never heard of him."

Any other answer would've concerned me, but that one was exactly what I was hoping to hear. We cleaned our table, left a courteous but unmemorable tip, and headed north on the county road.

"Please tell me you've got a plan," Gator said as he accelerated to the posted blazing speed limit of thirty-five miles per hour.

"With a little patience, I've got a feeling our plan will come directly to us. Just keep an eye out for that elementary school where Garland stole the Toyota."

We continued north, and the speed limit increased.

"There it is," Isaiah said, pointing through the window.

I watched the small, one-story school pass. "Keep driving, Gator. Just be patient."

A white pickup truck that hadn't been washed, maybe ever, pulled behind us from a driveway and matched our speed. That was my cue to move to the front seat.

Gator said, "I'd really like to know what's going on."

I motioned through the windshield. "See that big sign that says 'Vortex Springs'? Turn down that dirt road, and go nice and slow."

"Uh, that looks like a great way to get ambushed."

I said, "With any luck, we can certainly hope so."

He followed my instructions, and the pickup made the turn with us. Somebody jumped from the bed of the truck while it was still moving and pulled the gate closed across the dirt road leading to the springs, but the driver didn't wait for the gateman to catch up. Instead, he accelerated and passed us in a cloud of dust.

He made an aggressive move that ended in a power slide across the red dirt road in front of us. It was a good maneuver—not Navy SEAL quality—but it was good. The driver threw open his door, leapt from the cab, and leveled an AR across the toolbox of the truck, directly through the windshield of our bus. A second gunman followed him through the driver's side door and joined him behind the cover of the toolbox.

I was impressed. So far, they'd pinned us in with a closed steel gate to the rear, blocked our forward progress with a three-quarter-ton pickup, covered us with two pretty good rifles, and taken decent cover behind enough steel to stop any small-caliber fire we sent their way. They were doing all right, but they weren't finished impressing me.

The gateman apparently had some friends with four-wheelers. Three of them flanked us from our four and seven o'clock positions from the tree lines and took relatively good cover behind their ATVs. We weren't facing battle-hardened warriors, but in many ways, we were up against far more dangerous opponents. Untrained, trigger-happy, good-ol' boys are some of my favorite people on the planet, but they aren't always the most predictable lot.

I stood, but Mongo forced me back into my seat with his giant hand on my shoulder. In his other hand, he held a jug of Jack Daniel's Black Label. "I've got this one, boss."

Our giant ambled down the steps of our short bus, and Gator opened the split doors. Mongo stepped to the red dirt road and raised his island-sized paws well above his head. A grizzly bear would've been intimidated, but the two men behind the truck's toolbox showed no signs of fear.

Mongo said, "I figure one of you two is Jay-Dub. My name's

Mongo, and I'd really like to sit on the tailgate of that truck and have a drink with you."

The barrel-chested brawler behind the truck flipped the selector switch of his AR from semi to safe, and half a dozen sighs of relief sounded from inside our bus.

"Who are you, and why've you been asking about me all over town?"

Mongo said, "I'm trying to get to the truth about Garland Fitzsimon, the guy who tried to steal your wife's car."

"You a cop?" Jay-Dub asked.

Mongo shook his head. "Nope."

"You willing to take the first drink out of that bottle to prove it ain't spiked?"

"Yep."

Jay-Dub said, "Let's open this road back up, and you guys can follow me back down to the barn. I can't take you to my house 'cause my wife would lose her ever-lovin' mind."

* * *

Jay-Dub's barn wasn't exactly a barn by most people's definition. It was a lot more like the ultimate man cave with two pool tables, several televisions, trophy bucks mounted around the perimeter, an extremely well-stocked kitchen, and even a pair of bathrooms.

"We have church in here sometimes," he said. "My dad's a preacher, and his church leaks when it rains heavy. Find yourselves a seat, and we'll talk about Fitzsimon."

Introductions were made, and there was absolutely none of the awkwardness Skipper feared might be an issue.

Jay-Dub said, "Sorry 'bout bearing down on you, but we're a pretty tight community around here, and when folks start asking around, well, you know."

"I get it," I said. "We'd do the same thing in our town."

He said, "Tell the truth. You let us pin you down, didn't you?"

I shrugged. "You boys did all right."

He spat a long stream of tobacco juice into a Dr. Pepper bottle and shoved it back into his pocket. "I saw your arsenal in that fancy bus of yours while you were eating at Four C. It's good barbecue, ain't it? Whoever you boys are, you're the real deal."

"We're just some volunteers looking into the situation with Fitzsimon. Did you know him before he stole your wife's car?"

"Yeah, I knew him. I know everybody around here. He's been a good-for-nothin' piece of crap his whole life. We went to school together 'til he quit."

"He loved his grandmother," I said.

Jay-Dub took a drink. "Yeah, that's for sure, but she wasn't really his grandma. Somebody dropped him off at the fire station when he was a baby, and she adopted him. She loved him, too. That sorry daughter of hers . . . you probably know about her, too, right?"

I nodded. "We know she overdosed."

"Yeah, it was bound to happen. She wasn't nothin' but trouble. What do you think happened to Ms. Pat?"

I glanced at the priest, and he said, "We were hoping you could tell us."

"I ain't got no idea. Nobody around here knows. She just up and disappeared the same time Garland killed that fed down in the Keys. She was here one day—and bam!—gone the next. Nobody ever heard nothin' from her again."

"What about her house?" Isaiah asked.

"It was a trailer. It just rotted to the ground, and nobody cared. A bunch of kids played in it for a while, and some crackheads dealt dope out of it, I guess, but it's just a pile of junk now. I can take you to it if you want me to."

I said, "There's no need. I'd like to know more about Garland, though. You said you went to school with him. Did he learn Latin in school?"

Jay-Dub shot whiskey through his nose. "Latin? That's a good one!

He couldn't speak English, let alone Latin. Nobody at our school could teach him Latin. We had Spanish if you wanted to learn a foreign language, but that boy never went to school long enough to learn nothin'."

"He dropped out early?"

"He never really went. He was the smartest dumb guy I ever met, though. He'd work harder to avoid work than anybody you know. Stole everything he touched. Lied every time he opened his mouth. Whooped everybody he fought, except me. And them crazy eyes of his . . . that's some crazy stuff. Have you seen his eyes? I heard he's in the supermax over in Greenville now. Is that right?"

"That's right. Why do you think they didn't arrest him for stealing your wife's car?"

Jay-Dub held out his glass toward Mongo. "It's pretty simple to me. Ain't it to you? He was working with them feds on some kind of deal. If he wasn't, they wouldn't have paid for the car, and at least one of us would've gone to jail."

"Wait a minute," I said. "The feds who picked him up paid you for the car?"

"Yeah, they paid me for it, and they paid in cash. That sorry SOB broke the window out and jimmied the ignition. It was gonna cost a couple thousand dollars to get that fixed, but I ran him off the road, and that probably totaled it."

I leaned toward him. "So, you're telling me they paid for the car in cash."

"Ain't you listening? Yeah, they paid me cash. Fifty thousand bucks in cash for a thirty-thousand-dollar car. I may not be the smartest person in the room, but I ain't the dumbest. I'll take that deal all day every day. I bought her a new, nicer car and me a new rifle."

I leaned back and crossed my legs. "I want to hear your theory."

"On what?" Jay-Dub asked.

"On all of it."

He thanked Mongo for the refill and said, "It's pretty simple if you ask me. The feds put him up to killing that boy in the Keys to cover something up."

"What about the grandmother?" I asked.

Jay-Dub said, "I already told you, nobody knows what happened to her, including me."

"Yeah, I know that's what you said, but you also said you ain't the dumbest guy in the room, so I want to hear your theory . . . just for fun."

He made another deposit into the Dr. Pepper bottle. "All right, then. If you ask me, I'd say in return for him killing them boys down in the Keys, them feds put his Mamaw in witness protection or whatever you call it."

I nodded. "Don't you think they'd make the same promise to put Fitzsimon in WITSEC?"

"Well, yeah, of course they would, but I've worked for the government my whole adult life. They lie every day. Breaking promises is what they do. Ask the priest. He looks like he's broken a vow or two in his day."

Isaiah looked away, and I asked. "Is there anything else you can think of that might help us out?"

Jay-Dub eyed Mongo up and down. "I don't reckon it'd help you out, but I'd kinda like to wrestle with that big fella, just to see if I could pin him."

Our giant threw up his hands. "Oh, no, not me. I'm a pacifist, totally against fighting in every form. Gator, on the other hand—he's the tall, skinny one—he loves to wrestle."

Chapter 10

That Fed

I spent the long drive back to St. Marys silently studying the complexity of what little we knew about Garland Fitzsimon and why any of us should be involved at any level.

There's a long list of terrible side effects of being a sheepdog. Mine began where my right foot used to be, and a high-tech prosthetic now rested in its place. The scars continued over nearly every inch of my body and reached their apex inside my ears, where my body no longer had the natural ability to hear and process sound in the range most people spoke. Much like the electronics and mechanics that replaced my leg below the knee, my hearing worked only because brilliant biomechanical engineers developed devices that converted the world's vibrations into electronic ones and zeros that my brain interpreted as sound.

The greatest advantage of that device was my ability to turn it and the world around me off. Doing so gave me the freedom to hear with my eyes, and that changed everything. I watched, and by doing so, heard Singer and Isaiah sitting side by side, discussing everything that mattered in eternity. I heard Shawn snoring away and dreaming of the Nashville recording contract he turned down to join the Navy a lifetime ago. I heard Gator behind the wheel with his heart still breaking at the loss of his family and a promising NFL career. I heard Kodiak growing older beneath the red mop of hair and beard that should've turned grey, but somehow all those years beneath a Green Beret must've been a fountain of youth for him. I heard Anya wishing that our little girl, on the brink of becoming a woman, could remain a little girl forever. Finally, I heard Mongo, my second-in-command, listening to my silence, and I called to him without a word.

A flip of a switch brought the noise of the world back inside my head, and the giant beside me said, "This is none of our business."

I pointed toward our Southern Baptist sniper and the Jesuit priest who'd dumped this whole thing in our laps, sitting together on the wide front seat. "Try telling that to those two."

The big man shook his head. "Not everything is a mission from God just because some priest brought it to us, especially when that priest has been sent to the principal's office."

"I know, and I'm not saying this one is, but something about it sure doesn't smell good."

He sighed. "Everything about it stinks to high heaven. That corn-fed plowboy back there in Ponce nailed it. This whole thing is a rotten conspiracy, but if we jumped in the middle of every government conspiracy, we'd never stop jumping, boss."

"Are you saying we should walk away from this one?"

He huffed. "I don't know."

"You didn't see what they're doing to that guy."

"What guy?"

"Fitzsimon," I said.

Mongo furrowed his brow. "You're worried about him?"

"The priest is right. He's not possessed. He's doped out of his mind. He's scary as hell, but he's scared, too. I saw it in his eyes before he went crazy."

Mongo had always been rock-solid when it came to keeping me in my place, and it was time for another replanting. He said, "You're a psychologist—not a psychiatrist—who saw a recidivist for a few minutes at most. You've got no idea what drugs he's on, and you've never examined him. You just made a psychiatric clinical assessment without the credentials, tools, or time to do so. Take a step back before you fall off the cliff."

I took a long breath. "You're right, but did you catch what Jay-Dub said exactly?"

"What are you talking about?"

"He said *that* fed, not *those* feds."

"Huh?"

I said, "When he was talking about who Fitzsimon killed in the Keys, he only said one guy. He doesn't know about the other three guys. That means when the story broke in the news down here, they only mentioned Fitzsimon killing one guy."

"I missed that," he said, "but I can't see how that matters."

"It matters because Skipper knows about all four guys, but the locals where Fitzsimon lived don't. We need to know exactly who and what he was convicted of killing. If it was a federal agent, what's Fitzsimon doing in a *state* prison?"

Mongo shook his head. "Remember that step back we talked about? You're not taking it."

"This *is* me taking a step back. Normally, I would've already been over the edge."

"All right, but at least give me this one. Let's not freelance it. Let's bring in the Triad and get some approval and funding. If you're right about this being a government cover-up, have you considered the possibility that what it's covering up might be worth keeping under cover?"

* * *

After a longer drive than any of us wanted to experience, we pulled into the pecan tree–lined drive at Bonaventure and poured ourselves from the bus. We stretched and squirmed and swore we'd never take another road trip . . . until next time.

After bathroom breaks and sandwiches, Mongo and I pulled Isaiah into the library.

I said, "Have a seat. We've got a lot to talk about."

The priest settled into a wingback and propped his crutches against the arm of the chair. "This is the part where you tell me you can't do anything about any of this, isn't it?"

"You're supposed to be a man of faith. Don't jump to conclusions. We're not here to tell you anything like that."

"I'm relieved."

I said, "Let's get some logistics out of the way first. You've got that whole vow of poverty thing going on, so I assume that means you don't have a car, a place to sleep, food to eat, or money for any of these things. Am I right?"

"I have some clothes and a few dollars to give to the needy and feed the hungry."

"Right now, I'd say you fall into both of those categories."

He shook his head. "I can return to the monastery."

"If that's what you want to do, we'll get you there, but you're welcome to stay here with us while we figure this out. We'll feed you and give you a bedroom. There's even a Catholic church in town if you want to, I don't know . . . do something with them."

"Does this mean you'll do something about Garland?"

Mongo and I leaned back as if in practiced unison, and the big man asked, "Exactly what is it you want us to do about Garland?"

"Have I not made that clear?" the priest asked.

Mongo and I shook our heads, and Isaiah said, "I want you to find out why the Catholic church is involved at all. Fitzsimon never went to church a day in his life, as far as I can tell, and neither did the woman he believed to be his grandmother."

"That's all you want?" I asked.

"Of course I want humane treatment for Garland, but yes, essentially, I want to know why I was so harshly dealt with for my role in what I believed was a simple prison ministry."

Mongo palmed his forehead. "Oh, boy. We're in it for sure now. Listen, Isaiah. None of us is going to call you Father, by the way. I'm not sure what you think we are, but we're not private investigators or the A-Team—although Singer would look cool with a mohawk and gold chains. We're sort of . . ."

He paused, and I tagged in. "We don't take private cases. We work for an organization that directs our operations, and what we do has to be funneled through that organization. I'm willing to talk with them about this situation, but I can't promise they'll bless it." I hesitated. "Sorry, that may not have been the best choice of words. What I meant was, I'm not sure they'll approve our involvement. If they do, we'll have our analyst dive into the research phase."

Mongo locked eyes with me, and I nodded, granting the permission he wanted.

He said, "The truth is, she's already doing the research. Even if our governing body doesn't approve our involvement, we'll give you what we find, as long as it's not classified, of course."

Mongo shot another look, and I gave another nod before I continued the talk. "Some things will happen over the next two or three days that you can't see, hear, or be involved in. It's a matter of security and your safety. There's plenty to do around here, and like I said, the church is in town if you want to hang out with the priest over there."

He bit his lip, and Mongo said, "Spit it out, Priest. What's on your mind?"

"It's just that I'm still not technically within my vow. I'm not at the Jesuit center or the monastery. If I were to serve in the church here, word would get back to the archbishop, and—"

"I get it," I said. "You need a quiet, private place to pray and contemplate your vows. You're a Jesuit priest, so you can bless a place and make it a . . . I don't know . . . retreat or something, right?"

He muffled a laugh. "It's not necessary that a place be blessed by me or any other priest, but a quiet, serene place where I could pray, study, and meditate would be very nice. Of course, I don't expect anything without labor in return from me. I can work, and I will gladly do so."

"We may take you up on that, but for now, I've got just the spot in mind where you won't have to worry about the local priest ratting you out to the archbishop while we figure out what our next move is on this thing."

Isaiah nodded, and Mongo pointed across his shoulder toward Cumberland Sound. I gave him a wink and picked up the phone.

The pleasant young lady said, "Good afternoon. Cumberland Island Ferry. This is Cynthia."

"Hey, Cynthia. It's Chase Fulton. I need to borrow the Alberty House area for a few days if you don't have anything scheduled up there."

"Oh, hey, Chase. I'm sure it'll be fine, but let me check with the ranger. You're not going to be shooting this time, are you?"

"We certainly hope not."

"Hang on. I'll be right back."

She kept her word and returned in seconds. "You still there, Chase?"

"Yes, ma'am."

"Good. The chief ranger said it's all yours as long as you're not going to kill anybody or blow anything up."

"I promise to do none of the above . . . this time."

She giggled. "Is Gator still happily married?"

"I'm afraid so, but I'll tell him you asked."

"Don't you dare. Skipper would kill me. I'm scared of her."

"So am I, Cynthia. Tell Ranger Rick I said thanks."

She said, "He hates it when you call him that, you know."

"Yeah, I know. That's why I do it. Have a great evening."

I hung up and said to Mongo, "Have Singer pack a bag for Isaiah and meet me on the back lawn in half an hour."

"You got it, boss. And I like what you're thinking."

* * *

I drove to the airport and into our rebuilt hangar that felt like a cavernous wasteland, but it wouldn't feel that way for much longer. It took only a few minutes to tow out the Bell 412 and take off. The look on the priest's face was well worth the cost of the jet fuel when I touched down a hundred yards from the gazebo. Singer helped him aboard and climbed in behind him.

They donned headsets, and I asked, "Have you been in a helicopter before, Isaiah?"

"First time."

"If you can get that cast between the seats, climb up here with me."

He finagled the cast through the opening and settled in beside me.

I helped him with the shoulder harness and said, "Wrap your hand around the cyclic between your knees. I'll manage the collective and the pedals. Once we're clear of the trees and the mast of the sailboat, you can do the flying."

I raised the collective and pressed enough left pedal to keep the nose pointed into the wind. We climbed easily from the lawn and over the towering pecan trees as Cumberland Sound spread out in front of us.

I said, "She's all yours. Just move the cyclic the direction you want to go, and I'll do the rest."

"Seriously?"

"Yep, just do it gently. She's very responsive."

He eased the cyclic forward, and we accelerated over the water. The look on his face was priceless.

We made a few turns, and his smile grew with every maneuver until he said, "Thank you for this, but I must ask you to do it. This is beyond the simple life I have vowed to live."

I didn't believe God would be angry with the priest for enjoying the experience, but I wasn't going to argue with him.

"I have the controls," I said, and turned the chopper to the northeast.

We touched down at the extreme north end of Cumberland Island in a clearing in the trees barely big enough for us to fit beside a small, simple structure. I shut down, and the rotor spun to a stop over our heads as Singer helped Isaiah from the cockpit. I shouldered the priest's pack and followed the two men of God as the feet of Isaiah's crutches sank into the sandy soil of the island.

Singer led him up four steps of the small wooden building and pushed open the doors. They walked through together and settled onto the first of four worn pews.

"What is this place?" the priest asked.

Singer sighed as if breathing in the history around him. "This is the First African Baptist Church of Cumberland Island. It was built by former slaves in eighteen ninety-three. I could be descended from some of the people who built it. I kinda hope so."

He paused and ran a hand across the pew in front of him. "It was rebuilt in the thirties, but we don't know why. It might've been a fire, or maybe it caved in on the soft sand. John Kennedy Jr. and Carolyn Bessette got married here in ninety-six, but that was a publicity stunt. The real history of this place is meaningful. What some actress and politician's son do can't change the world. Believers with hammers and nails do that."

Although the priest obviously didn't share Singer's Protestant faith, he clearly understood his love and passion for the old church and for the value of what truly matters in life and beyond.

Singer said, "There's no crucifix or bowl of holy water, but it's quiet, and nobody will bother you. There's a satellite phone, food, water, and a sleeping bag in your gear. You take care of you right now. We'll take care of things on our end and be back for you in a couple of days."

Singer stood, and I asked, "Will this place do?"

Isaiah said, "The Vatican itself wouldn't be any better."

Chapter 11
Old Birds

Although everybody in my life could be perfectly described as "a unique character," Clark Johnson fit the bill more solidly than most. When I left training and survived Anya's attempt to seduce, flip, or kill me, Clark stepped into my life to pick up where the Russian left off. Well, not the seduction part. She did just fine in that department. It was the flipping or killing area in which she let down her countrymen. She neither flipped nor killed me, and although Clark never actually admitted he'd been dispatched to end me if he believed I'd been recruited as a Russian asset, I had no doubt he would've slit my throat without hesitation. Twenty years later, I believed he would fight an army of chainsaws naked with nothing but a toothpick and a plastic spoon to keep me alive. He became my greatest teacher, mentor, partner, and friend. When the day finally came when his country asked for one too many fights from his war-torn body, he stepped from the battlefield and became my handler. I respected and loved him more than words or even actions could ever express, and until I draw my dying breath, I'll believe he feels the same about me.

"It's about time you got here, College Boy. We've been wondering if you'd ever show up."

I yanked Clark from *my* chair in the op center and threw my arms around him. "It's good to see you, old man."

"You too, but we've got a lot to talk about."

I took my seat, and he settled for another. "I guess that means you know, huh?"

He inspected the toothpick that rarely left his mouth. "We don't miss much, but why don't you start by telling me about the priest?"

Clark and I weren't alone in the room. The whole team was on deck, including Skipper, our analyst, and I asked, "Should we bring in the Triad?"

Clark motioned toward the overhead monitors. "They're standing by, but I wanna hear about the priest before we get My Three Dads involved."

One of the three members of the Triad was, quite literally, Clark's biological father, Dominic Fontana. But that relationship had been far from familial for well over thirty years.

"There's not much to tell," I said.

Clark's last drink of water exited his nose at high speed. "A Catholic priest shows up unannounced, and you start letting him lead you around by the nose, and you call that 'not much to tell'? That's cute, College Boy. Start again, and try a little harder to be honest this time."

"Fine," I said. "He got his wrist slapped for sticking his nose into a situation with an inmate named Garland Fitzsimon at the supermax over in Greenville, Florida."

Clark waved a hand. "Yeah, we know about Fitzsimon. Forget about him. Tell me how you got involved with the priest."

"Never mind the priest," I said. "Why and how do you know about Fitzsimon?"

"We'll get to that, I promise. Just tell me how that crazy priest wound up in your lap."

I gave him the same crooked grin he'd worn all over the world for most of his life. "I kinda like knowing something you don't. I think I'll hold onto it for a little while longer and savor the moment."

He leaned back in his chair, crossed his legs, and shrugged. "Fine with me. I think I'll hold onto your disbursement and savor it in my bank account for a moment. We'll see who likes it more."

"Okay, you win."

"I always do."

I said, "The priest stuck his nose where it didn't belong and got it slapped. Some archbishop—whatever that is—sent him to dust erasers after class at a Jesuit retreat in Georgia, where he was supposed to think about what he did wrong and never do it again. I'm sure there's a name for that, but I don't know what it is."

Clark raised his eyebrows. "Are we getting to the part where he became your ward at some point?"

"I'm getting there. Some priest at this retreat told him it might be good to spend some time at a monastery. Guess which one he picked."

Clark turned to Singer, and our sniper nodded.

Singer's brother committed suicide in the Trappist monastery at Moncks Corner after spending his teenage years there following their horrific childhood that culminated in Singer being forced to take their father's life in a failed attempt to save their mother's.

Singer picked up the story. "I don't know how he did it, but somehow, the priest got one of the monks to break his silence, and apparently, he told the priest about us. That's how he ended up here."

Clark huffed. "That monk needs to shut his big mouth."

Singer smirked. "You're right. He's probably said fewer than three dozen words in fifty years. That guy's a real blabbermouth. I'll creep in there under the cover of darkness and take him out with a two-thousand-yard fifty-cal shot. You wanna crawl in with me and spot for me?"

Clark thew up his hands. "So, now it's a mission from God?"

"Nothing like that," I said. "But there's a lot more going on than CNN and Fox News know about. All right, I showed you mine. Now, let's see yours."

Clark curled a pair of fingers in the air. "Bring 'em up, Skipper."

Three somber faces who'd seen more than their share of the world's dark side filled the screens, and retired Major General Bradford Michaels, the ranking member of the Triad, spoke first.

"Gentlemen . . . and ladies. Good evening. You've had quite a day."

I said, "Indeed we have, General, and it would appear you know more about it than we do."

"You can call me Brad, Chase. You've been through enough to earn that privilege. If you and I are ever fortunate enough to testify before Congress together, maybe you should refer to me as General, but in this setting, Brad is fine."

I was unsure if I was being set up or if the general was sincere, so I simply nodded, parlaying my bet to see what came next.

Retired Brigadier General Clinton McFarland was what came next. He scoffed. "I guess if the guy I have to salute says you can call him Brad, that means you can call me Clint, but trust me, I'll never testify before Congress. I've got lifetime immunity."

"How did you get that deal?" I asked.

He said, "I haven't decided yet, but it'll come to me."

The third member of the Triad waved a hand at the camera. "You've been calling me Dominic for twenty years. I think I'd like it if you called me General for a change."

I said, "I might be able to manage Commodore, but General just doesn't feel right."

Dominic grinned. "I'll take it. Listen, Chase. You've fallen into a pile of stuff you're going to have trouble getting off your boots . . . if you know what I'm saying."

"I've been interpreting what comes out of your son's mouth for a long time, so I think I'm smart enough to piece that one together. Are you going to tell us what really happened with Fitzsimon and the four guys he killed in the Keys?"

Dominic surrendered the floor back to the boss, and Brad Michaels said, "No, we're not."

That chilled the air in the room, and I sat up in my seat. "In that case, I request that you authorize us to investigate the situation to determine what happened, who was involved, and if American National Security was compromised."

"There are official agencies in place for that," General Michaels said.

"Have those agencies conducted such an investigation?" I asked.

The general shrugged. "If they have, I've not seen the reports."

I stared into the camera. "Are you going to consider my request?"

The general said, "Please tell me you're not finished asking questions, Chase."

Where's he leading me? What does he want me to ask?

I let my eyes meet every other pair in the room, hoping somebody knew which of the narrow paths at the bevy of forks in the plethora of roads I needed to take. I feared my only course was through the looking glass, where sanity was a liability. Perhaps I was running low enough on that commodity to cease worrying about it being a problem for me.

"Why is the Catholic church involved?"

All three men on the screens shook their heads.

I slammed my palm onto the table. "Conviction! What did they actually convict the man of doing?"

The generals—and Commodore—smiled in unison.

Skipper's fingers turned to blurs of speed and accuracy as they raced across the keys and then froze. The small screens built into the conference table in front of us filled with the official criminal filing and conviction from *State of Florida v. Garland Fitzsimon*:

Aircraft piracy — 1 count

Aggravated stalking — 1 count

Felony murder — 1 count

My mind felt like Skipper's fingers looked, and I had thousands more questions. The Triad no longer mattered. The conversation was mine and Skipper's, and no one else existed.

"Who was he convicted of murdering?"

She said, "An unnamed former officer of the United States Government."

"Former? Meaning he was a former officer at the time he was murdered, right?"

"That's how it reads," she said. "But it's a court document, so who knows what it really means?"

"That explains why Fitzsimon is in state prison and not a federal facility. This mysterious *former* officer wasn't a government employee at the time of the murder. If he had been, it would've been a federal crime."

Mongo tapped the table. "What does aircraft piracy and aggravated stalking have to do with any of this? I thought he killed those guys on a boat. And why is there only one count of murder?"

I said, "I can't answer the piracy thing, but I think sometimes they try only one case when there are multiple victims in case they don't get a conviction. That way, they can always come back and try again with another victim without the problem of double jeopardy."

Mongo chewed his lip. "Okay, maybe I'll buy that, but even the court documents don't name the victim. There's a pretty big shroud around this thing. From the official record to the public information, there's only one victim."

Singer said, "Isaiah knows there were four men killed, though, and none of you corrected Chase when he said Fitzsimon killed four guys in the Keys. That means the church knows and you guys know."

Gator had been silent for the entirety of the meeting until that moment, but he looked up and softly asked, "Who are they protecting? And who are they?"

Major General Bradford Michaels clicked his pen. "I think it may be time for a new team leader down there at Team Twenty-One. Someone is *finally* asking the right question." He pointed directly into the camera. "That's the mission we'll authorize, fund, and fully support. Answer those two questions, and all of the other answers will fall into place. Just be careful whose feathers you ruffle. A lot of those old birds are packing heat under those dusty old plumes."

Chapter 12
Dead Drop

The monitors went dark, and the team and I were left sitting in silence in the op center. My gut told me everyone felt some variation of the same thing that was eating at me. What on earth were we supposed to do next?

Gator looked mortified when I met his gaze. "Hey, look. I was just asking a question. I wasn't trying to jump to the front of the line."

I laughed. "You can have this chair any time you want it, Hotshot. In fact, I'd be more than happy to write a pretty big check to anybody who wants it right now. We may have a mission, but I'll be the first to admit that I've got no idea where to start."

Shawn said, "I get it, man. Point me at something and tell me to kill it, but this kind of stuff is way beyond trigger-pulling."

Every eye at the table drifted toward the two big brains in the room.

Mongo redirected. "Don't look at me. Skipper's the only one who's got a shot at getting us started down the right road on this one."

I looked in a different direction. "Unless . . ."

Skipper seemed to appreciate the break, but Clark didn't like the fresh attention on him. "Whoa, what do you think I know?"

I said, "I think you know more than we do, otherwise, you wouldn't be here. So, tell me about the four guys in the Keys."

Clark could be goofy and carefree, but when the moment demanded, he was a bad-guy-killing, freedom-defending, steely-eyed warfighter, and that moment had come. He swallowed what remained of the water in his bottle. "We need to start by putting the screws to the priest."

I grabbed the edge of the table. "What?"

"You told me he knew about the four guys. You said he's the one who told you. We need to know how he knows."

I said, "I agree, but I'm not going to waterboard a priest before I know everything you know."

"That's the problem," Clark said. "We don't even know if they're dead. We know an NSA contractor's body washed up on Boca Chica with part of Garland Fitzsimon's ear in his stomach."

Skipper said, "Okay, that's nasty."

"That's how he got busted," Clark said. "It's my theory that he would've gotten off scot-free if the NSA guy hadn't bitten off his ear and swallowed it. That's the only way anybody even knew Fitzsimon was involved. They had his DNA in the system since he'd already been in prison."

Mongo said, "So, you agree that the whole thing was a setup by the feds."

Clark grabbed another bottle of water from his cargo pocket. "There's no question about it. Just like your buddy over in Podunk, Florida, said, the feds made a deal to get Fitzsimon out of prison and tuck his granny away somewhere nice and comfy in return for Garland doing them the favor of knocking off these four guys they needed to disappear."

Kodiak shook his head. "Nope. There's too many holes in it. The feds have plenty of guys to knock off four intel operators if they wanted them dead. They don't need a small-time con from the panhandle with no experience in big-time hits."

Clark said, "Look, *why* they did it doesn't matter. We just know they did. We know one body washed up, for sure, but we've never found the other three, dead *or* alive. That likely means they're dead."

"So, Garland probably pulled it off," Shawn said. "Maybe he's more of a hard hitter than we thought, but why let the county pick him up and the state try him and convict him?"

"What do you mean?" Clark asked.

"You said the feds were going to let him get off scot-free. Why would they let him get convicted?"

My handler sighed. "Maybe once the wheels were rolling, it was out of their hands."

I said, "I've got a better question. Why didn't he mention any of this to his attorney during the trial?"

"That's easy," Clark said. "He was looking out for his grandmother. He knew if he said a word, the feds would put a bullet in her head."

"I want to talk to him," I said.

Clark laughed. "He won't talk to you. Even though his boy got convicted, he's still protected under attorney-client confidentiality."

"I don't mean the lawyer," I said. "I want to talk to Garland Fitzsimon."

Singer scoffed. "You saw him. He's out of his mind, or maybe worse. You can't have a conversation with a guy like that."

"I can if I can get to the real Garland Fitzsimon. If I can get through the meds . . ." I froze, replaying every detail of the visit to the super-max. "What was that corporal's name? The one who came on the bus when we first got to the prison."

Gator said, "Leonard."

"That's it. Corporal Leonard. When he saw my Secret Service credentials, he assumed we were all feds, and he made the comment that the only fed who ever comes always comes alone and always comes through the warden's office. We need to know who that fed is, why he's there, and who he sees."

The familiar sound of Skipper's fingers on her keyboard filled my ears, and I turned to watch her work. Two minutes later, she said, "According to the official visitors' logs, the only federal officials who've visited that prison in the past six months have been three different FBI agents and one federal prosecutor."

"It sounds like the corporal's story is falling apart," I said. "I wonder how many other stories we heard in that place have holes in them."

The looks on the faces around the table said interest was piqued, so I said, "Let's take a vote. Option one is to waterboard the priest, and option number two is to rattle the cage of one Florida State Prison System Corporal Leonard until he tells us why he lied about one single fed coming through one single door."

Gator frowned. "I thought this wasn't a democracy."

"You're right," I said. "It's not. Go get the priest and a bucket."

He froze, and I couldn't hold back the laughter.

Anya had been too quiet, and that always made me nervous, so I slid a pen across the table toward the Russian. "Don't you have anything to add?"

"Is not FSB," she said.

"What?"

"This person on boat with others. If they were NSA and Mossad, fourth person was not from FSB. He was maybe SVR, but definitely not FSB. There would be only one reason two Americans, one Israeli, and one Russian intelligence operative were together."

She paused and said, "No, this is not true. There could be two reasons. Maybe all of them did not know who and what all of others were. This is other possibility, but if they knew, they were having conspiracy. Think inside mind what is only thing all four of these people could want in common."

I let my chair recline to its limit. "No way. This whole thing *cannot* be about Iran."

Clark pulled off his cap and tossed it onto the table. "Why not?"

I stared at the ceiling. "Because you don't pull a guy like Garland Fitzsimon out of prison to break up an international intelligence gathering conglomerate against the country of Iran."

Clark repeated, "Why not?"

"Because it's not the kind of thing we do."

He said, "And that's exactly why we'd do it—because nobody would ever believe we would."

Anya said, "There is one more very big mystery. Why not kill Garland Fitzsimon? Is easy inside prison. He is only dangerous piece in all of puzzle. He is maybe only person who knows what happened on boat and with other three people. It does not make sense they would let him be still alive."

I kicked a heel against the carpet and spun toward Skipper, but she beat me to the punch. "I'm already on it. Corporal Peter Leonard has breakfast at Lucy's Diner in Monticello on Highway ninety, twelve miles west of Greenville every morning at six thirty before his shift at the supermax."

I asked her, "Do you have a navy-blue pantsuit and some sunglasses that'll make you pass as a fed?"

"Of course, but I'll need a badge and a gun," she said.

Anya spoke up. "I have badge from Department of Justice, and there are maybe one million guns downstairs inside armory. This is maybe exaggeration, but only small one."

"Now we just need somebody who looks like a lawyer," I said.

Clark threw out his arms. "Uh, I'm right here."

"Do you even own a necktie . . . or a razor?"

Skipper said, "I've still got a couple of Tony's suits. He was the same size as Clark. And there are plenty of razors lying around."

I said, "We'll need a subpoena and a couple of business cards."

Skipper asked, "How closely will they be scrutinized?"

"Not at all if I play it right."

She gave me a wink. "Then you'd better make sure you play it right."

* * *

At 4:00 a.m. the next morning, Clark, Skipper, and I were westbound on I-10 toward Monticello, Florida, and Lucy's Diner. Skipper looked the part, and Clark was passable as a federal prosecutor from thirty feet away, but up close, he still looked and smelled like a door-kicker.

We parked across the street from the diner and waited for Corporal

Leonard to make his appearance. Something told me that punctuality wasn't an area in which the corporal was lacking, and I would soon be proved correct.

At precisely 6:28 a.m., he pulled open the door and took a seat by himself in a booth that appeared to be reserved just for him. A waitress at least twice his age smiled and slid a cup of coffee onto the table in front of the uniformed officer, no doubt exactly as she'd done hundreds of times before. Leonard didn't look at the menu or pick up the morning paper. He simply sat alone, staring out the window onto a world he likely wished was as good and pure as it looked through the dingy glass of the decades-old diner in the small Southern town.

I pulled the Suburban from our hidden position and directly in front of the restaurant. The three of us stepped from the blacked-out, very government-looking vehicle, and I made a show of stopping Skipper and Clark on the sidewalk. Each of them produced a business card Skipper had printed the night before, and our newly-minted Treasury officer made certain her badge and gun were on broad display for the corporal. Clark straightened his tie in the reflection of the glass and then handed me the folded subpoena that came off the same printer as the business cards tucked neatly in my palm.

"Wish me luck," I said.

Instead of responding, both of my co-conspirators simply stared through the glass at our target. If Leonard called my bluff, our charade would crumble, but with a little luck and a good cup of roadside diner coffee, that wouldn't happen.

Without an invitation, I slid onto the vinyl seat opposite the corporal and pulled off my sunglasses, letting the business cards spill from my palm and onto the table. The Seal of the United States behind the titles of "Assistant U.S. District Attorney" and "Special Agent" is hard to ignore.

"Good morning, Pete. Remember me?"

He licked his lips and narrowed his gaze. "Yep, you're the one who claimed he wasn't on an official visit."

"That's right. But you're the one who officially lied to me about the other feds who've visited the prison recently."

I bounced the worthless, folded subpoena on the table. "I thought I'd give you a chance to get that story straight before I dropped off this little document cordially inviting you to join my friends out there in federal court to answer our questions under oath."

"Can I get anything for you, sugar?"

I glanced up at the waitress who'd delivered Leonard's coffee, and I pointed at his steaming mug. She nodded and disappeared.

"You'd rather talk to me here than to them on camera, wouldn't you?"

"Do I need a lawyer?"

I leaned back and played with the subpoena. "That's up to you, but you're not under arrest. We're just two guys having breakfast and a chat . . . for now. I think both of us would prefer to keep it that way."

My coffee arrived, and I took the first sip as Peter Leonard grew more nervous by the second.

Finally, he said, "I wasn't lying. I was just trying to show off a little, I guess. I've got a pretty boring life. A prison guard is what I am, but they call us correctional officers now because it sounds better. You know, like sanitary engineer instead of janitor. I don't even remember exactly what I told you, but I didn't mean anything by it, whatever it was."

"You told me there was only one other fed who came to the prison, and that he was always alone, and he always came through the warden's office."

"Oh, that. No, that's true, a hundred percent."

"No, it isn't, Corporal Leonard. We checked the records. Three FBI agents and a federal prosecutor have been there in the past six months."

He furrowed his brow. "But you know they come through the attorney's processing center. They come to talk with inmates about cases they're investigating—like when the inmates are witnesses or something like that. All of that is done through the Access-Alpha System.

That's why you could pull it up on the official record. I wasn't talking about that."

"Then what were you talking about?"

His breakfast arrived, and it looked amazing.

The waitress said, "Are you sure I can't get you anything to eat, baby?"

I motioned through the window. "Could you take a couple of cups of coffee out to those two, please?"

"Sure, darlin'. No problem."

"So, what were you talking about, Leonard?"

"I don't know. All of this is starting to feel a little weird to me."

He reached for the business cards, and I upped my bluff. "Okay, if that's how you want to play it, Peter Leonard, you are hereby ordered to appear before—"

He held up his fork. "Hold on a minute. I don't need this kind of stuff in my life. I'm just a—"

"I know. You think that you're just a simple prison guard, but that's not true, Peter. You're an important man. You control who and what goes in and out of one of the highest-security facilities in the state of Florida. You're far more than a guard. You're the eyes and ears of the people of this state, and even this country, when it comes to the supermax. What goes in and out of that facility affects the security of all of us. We rely on men like you to protect us when systems like that break down. You witnessed a breakdown, Peter, and you have an opportunity to make it right without anybody knowing it was you who reported it."

He laid down his fork and stared out the window again. His eyes didn't fall on Clark and Skipper, though. They seemed to fall on the flag flying above the post office as the wind sent it waving in the morning sun.

My sales pitch wasn't quite complete, but I needed him to keep staring at that flag, so I spoke barely loud enough for him to hear. "Nobody will ever know it was you, Pete. Nobody except you and me.

Whatever's going on inside that prison shouldn't involve the federal government, and you know it. That's a state prison—your state prison —and you're responsible for it."

He didn't look back at me. "I don't know who the guy is, but I can get you the video footage of him coming and going. I can't leave a trail, though. I'd lose my job, and my job is all I've got."

"No, it's not, Pete. You've got your integrity, and that's worth more than any job in the world. I swear to you, though, I won't do anything to risk your career. Have you ever heard of a dead drop?"

"Like in the spy movies?"

"Exactly like that," I said. "How long will it take you to get the video footage?"

"I can probably get it today."

I checked over my shoulder to heighten the intrigue. "I'll call you on Friday night from a number you won't recognize. Answer the call, Pete. It may not be my voice that you hear, but it'll be instructions for the dead drop. Follow those instructions to the letter, and"—I held up the subpoena and made a show of tearing it in half—"you can forget all about this."

I replaced the business cards on the table with two twenty-dollar bills and left Monticello, Florida, having recruited a spy while enjoying the best forty-dollar cup of coffee I'd had in years.

Chapter 13

Kiss the Girl

Clark leaned forward and checked the mirror outside the passenger's side window. "You had us scared for a minute there, College Boy. I thought it was falling apart."

"Me, too. I saved it, though. He just needed somebody to believe in him."

Skipper said, "If he comes through with video we can use to identify the fed he's talking about, he may turn out to be the most important person in this whole puzzle."

I accelerated onto the interstate. "Maybe not the most important piece, but it'll make him a corner piece of our puzzle, for sure."

"What if he gets nervous and chickens out?" Skipper asked.

I drummed my fingers against the steering wheel. "Then I'll have to be more convincing next time."

She said, "As cheesy as it is, I think what you're doing is the right play. He's obviously a loner who enjoys the attention. I've got an idea about how we can dangle a little more bait and set the hook even deeper if you think Anya's up for it."

* * *

"Uh, hello?" Peter Leonard said as if he'd never answered a tele-phone before.

Doing my best to play out the cloak-and-dagger routine, I asked, "Are you alone?"

"Yes."

"Good. Do you have it? Don't say what it is."

"Uh, yeah, I've got it. But it wasn't easy."

I took my first breath of the call. "I knew you could do it. Change of plans, though. The dead drop is too risky. How do you feel about a brush pass?"

He stammered. "I, um . . . I mean, I know what that is, but I don't really know how—"

"It's okay," I said. "We'll play it modified with an experienced oper-ator and make it easy for you. You'll like it, I promise. Are you off for the weekend?"

"Yeah, but I've got my niece's soccer match in the morning in Talla-hassee. We can't do it there, though. No way. My sister—"

"Relax," I said. "We're not going to involve your family in any of this. I wouldn't do that, Pete."

"It's Peter, okay? My stepdad called me Pete, and I hated it."

"Sorry. It won't happen again. What time will the soccer match be over?"

"It'll be over by noon, but I always take them to lunch. Can we do it at maybe two?"

I covered the phone so my spy couldn't hear me laughing at the ab-surdity of him negotiating the drop time of his stolen intel. "Sure, Pe-ter. Two is fine. Are you familiar with the Florida State University Museum of Fine Arts?"

"Yeah, I think so. It's behind the theater. The uh . . . Fallon The-atre, right?"

Skipper typed furiously before nodding at me.

I said, "Yep, that's the place. There's an exhibit on loan from St. Pe-tersburg, Russia, to the museum. You can't miss it. Be there at two with 'the item' in your left hand. It is small enough to palm, right?"

He said, "Oh, yeah. It's on a—"

"Hey! I told you not to say it. This is serious."

"Sorry. I'm not, you know . . . This is all new to me."

"It's okay," I said. "I was a rookie, too, and I made mistakes. The difference is that you're not going to bleed out in a gutter in Budapest if this goes south."

"That happened to you?"

"One mission at a time, Peter. Keep your eye on the egg."

Before he could ask another ridiculous question or force me to tell another outlandish lie about my experience in the realm of international espionage, I pressed the end button and powered down the throwaway cell from which we'd made the call.

"Too over the top?" I asked.

Skipper grinned. "Perfect! He's online right now trying to figure out the 'keep your eye on the egg' comment. It won't take him long. I looked up his academic records. He did okay in school, so he'll figure it out."

Gator leaned back in his chair and propped his feet on the table. "If I were a prison guard and not in this crazy world of ours, I'd think it was cool, too. This guy probably thinks he's in the middle of some James Bond stuff."

"He very well may be," I said. "I've got a theory, and if I'm right, this thing runs deep and ugly."

"Let's hear it," he said.

I glanced over my shoulder. "Toss me an envelope."

Skipper pulled one from a drawer and held it toward me.

I slipped it from her fingers. "Thanks. I'll write what I'm thinking and lock it up. When all of this is over, we'll crack it open and see how close I was."

He pulled out his wallet and slid a one-hundred-dollar bill across the table. "I've got a hundred bucks that says your theory is wrong. You pick the judge."

I wrote a brief synopsis of my theory and slipped it into the envelope, along with Gator's cash and mine. We sealed it, signed the flap, and slid it into the safe. "I pick Shawn to be the judge."

Gator nodded. "Fair enough."

* * *

Saturday came, and we positioned ourselves inside the Florida State University Museum of Fine Arts with only one of our teammates in plain sight—the only one who fit in with the Russian exhibit on display.

A lady with horn-rimmed glasses dangling from a chain around her neck stepped behind the locked-and-guarded display and then pulled on a pair of bright white gloves. From my vantage point, I found it difficult to believe she was actually going to handle the delicate, multi-million-dollar contents of the case.

"Ladies and gentlemen, I'd like to thank you for joining us this afternoon. We're honored to have a sampling on loan from the incomparable Fabergé Museum in Saint Petersburg, Russia. As you may know, the museum is located inside the Naryshkin-Shuvalov Palace and is privately owned. It was established by Viktor Vekselberg to repatriate as much of the priceless art of Russia and the Soviet Union as possible that was lost through centuries of war, conflict, and unrest."

She paused long enough to adjust her gloves. "The crown jewel, if you will, of the museum's impressive collection is its nine Imperial Easter eggs created by Fabergé for the last two Russian Tsars. You can see before you one of the most famous of these eggs, the breathtaking Cockerel egg."

The small crowd, including Corporal Leonard, who obviously knew little if anything of Peter Carl Fabergé, clapped softly.

The lady continued her obnoxiously self-indulgent spiel. "The Cockerel, or as it is sometimes called, the Cuckoo Clock egg, was given by Tsar Nicholas II to Empress Maria Feodorovna in nineteen hundred. Although we, of course, do not wind the clock, it is believed to still function as it did over a hundred years ago."

She motioned for the armed guard to unlock the case, and he did as she instructed. If she lifted the egg from the case, I would throat-punch the rent-a-cop and snatch Princess Feodorovna's egg from the woman's gloved claws. If anyone deserved to handle the astonishing work of art, it certainly wasn't the self-important art professor, Dr. Hootie-Hoo from FSU.

She reached inside the case and traced the back of her hand over the outline of the gorgeous egg, but she dared not come within three inches of its gold and porcelain surface. "As you can see, the egg has a mechanism on the top that allows this dainty bird to come out and move about at the top of every hour. There is one missing pearl, but aside from that detail, the egg is complete based on early photographs and drawings."

The crowd clapped softly again, and the lady drank it in as she instructed her underling to resecure the case.

He obeyed again, and she said, "I am, as you know, intimately familiar with the entire Fabergé collection, and I will make myself available for"—she paused and checked her watch—"oh, I could spare perhaps twenty minutes for questions."

Anya, obviously unable to tolerate another second of the woman's performance, stepped around her, leaned toward the case, and said in her strongest native accent, "Is, of course, extremely good quality replica for display only. Viktor Vekselberg would never allow original to leave Russia under any circumstances."

My favorite Russian took two steps away from the case, turned, and handed the guard the pistol she lifted from his holster as she passed. "Is also, of course, replica of real police officer."

She continued her walk as the crowd collapsed around the display and the supposed academic expert.

While the egg and professor had everyone's attention, Anya slipped her right hand into Peter Leonard's left, sliding the thumb drive from his palm. In the next instant, she laced her left hand beneath his ear and pulled his lips to hers, delivering a kiss precisely as she was trained to do so many years before on the banks of the Volga River at State School 4, where she became a Russian Sparrow.

"Oh, my darling. I have missed you so. Thank you for coming. We will now go, yes?"

Peter stood frozen, likely having the best day of his life, and the former Russian assassin led him from the museum like the obedient puppy he'd become.

With the passing of the thumb drive complete and the exfil underway, the team dispersed ahead of Anya and Peter. When she led our grown-up spy through the front door of the museum, she released his hand and whispered, "You were perfect. Walk now to your car and drive away like nothing happened."

He hesitated but stepped away. Anya should've slipped into the Suburban, but she paused as well. "Oh, and Peter. Next time you kiss girl, kiss her exactly like that. It will make her want to kiss you many more times."

With that, she climbed inside and pulled the door closed behind her. I didn't like how it made me feel to see her kiss another man, even if it was an act entirely for the benefit of an operation.

She bounced the thumb drive in her palm. "Got it."

I caught it on the third hop. "Let's just hope there's something on it we can use."

She cocked her head. "What is wrong, Chasechka? You think I should not have taken gun from guard, no?"

"No, that was fine. He deserved it. Nothing's wrong. Just get this to Skipper."

She took back the drive and plugged it into her tablet while I dialed the op center.

Skipper answered almost instantly. "Did you get it?"

Anya said, "We did. Is very large file, but is coming now."

My phone clicked, and I checked the screen. "Hey, Skipper, I need to take this call. We'll call you back."

"No problem. I'll process the video as soon—"

I clicked over. "Gordo! How's it going?"

Gordo was an interesting story—one I knew well and almost nothing about. He was the kind of man whose veins ran full of ice water when the world around him caught on fire, and I envied everything about that quality. He was also one of the most highly qualified airplane drivers I knew. Gordo and his crew were the newest members of our team, and I'd been waiting for his call for weeks.

He said, "You'll never believe it, but we're test-flying the Herk this afternoon."

Gordo and his copilot, Tubs, had slid a civilianized C-130 onto the Celtic Sea with my team strapped into the back after a saboteur poured enough gelatin into the fuel tanks to put the turbines to sleep over the North Atlantic. After months in the hands of some of Lockheed's finest mechanics, the highly modified C-130J was on the verge of claiming her rightful spot back in the air and inside our vacant hangar.

"That's great news," I said. "Do you have any concerns?"

"A few. I wrecked it in the ocean the last time I flew it, so there's that."

"You didn't wreck it. You ditched it and saved it and us."

He chuckled. "Yeah, well, it felt like a wreck from the front seat."

I joined him in laughter. "Now that you mention it, it kinda felt that way from the back seats, too. If everything goes well, how long will it be before she'll be mission-ready?"

He said, "I'm not sure. It all depends on what we find. The first flight will be short. We'll never pull the gear up, and we'll stay right over the airport. We'll run it long enough to get everything up to temperature and pressure and stick her back on the ground."

"Here's hoping it's perfect. Keep me posted. We've got a mission, and we could use you and the airplane."

He said, "You can have us, but the plane is questionable."

"That's what I figured. Call me tonight and let me know how it went."

"You got it. Oh, and Chase. We really appreciate you paying us, even though we're not doing much of anything."

"You're earning every penny. Managing the refit of the airplane is a huge job that I can't do, and nobody knows that bird like her crew. I'm happy to write that check every month."

My phone clicked again, and the screen reported it as the op center. My initial reaction was frustration that Skipper would interrupt when I told her I'd call back, but I said, "Thanks for the good news, Gordo. We'll talk soon."

I clicked over. "Go ahead, Skipper."

"Your boy really came through. The video is solid. The guy's not a fed, though."

"Who is he?" I asked.

She scoffed. "I'm not telling you over the phone. Not even on *this* phone. I assure you that you're not going to like it, though."

Chapter 14
Don't Be Afraid

The Suburban's massive engine wasn't capable of producing the horse-power required to get us back to Bonaventure quickly enough for me, but I pushed the workhorse to its absolute limit. The blacked-out vehicle looked official enough to avoid pursuit by the Florida Highway Patrol, and the moment we left I-95 headed into St. Marys, every officer on the road knew exactly who and what we were, so there was no risk of being wrangled by the locals.

We may have closed the doors after sliding to a stop and dismounting, but no one cared. Every boot on the team sprinted up the stairs as if we were running from the devil himself, but I feared we may have been running directly into his waiting arms.

To my surprise, Skipper left the op center door open an inch to avoid the extra seconds it would've taken to buzz us through the high-security hatch.

"Sit down, and find something to hold onto," Skipper said. "You're not going to like what I'm about to show you."

I skipped both the sitting and holding and demanded, "Just tell us."

"Fine. His name is Gregory McDonald, but that isn't the part that's going to kick you in the gut. He's the special assistant to the deputy chief of staff to the vice president."

I grabbed the back of my chair. "Of the United States?"

"Oh, yeah."

It was time to take that seat Skipper suggested. "Take me through it."

She pulled up video on three monitors. "Here he is on three separate occasions, entering the prison just like your little spy said."

Mongo grunted. "Those are some good cameras."

Skipper nodded. "Yes, they are, but not quite good enough for perfect facial recognition at that distance. When I created a mosaic from the three videos, I got a hit on Gregory McDonald with just over eighty-nine percent certainty."

"That's not great," I said.

Mongo cocked his head and closed one eye. "If I'm doing the math correctly, that leaves a little over four hundred million possibilities."

"You're right," Skipper said, "but I wasn't finished. You have to throw out everyone who isn't Caucasian and between thirty-five and fifty years old."

Mongo said, "I'll admit that narrows the field, but that's still a lot of possibilities, including most of the people in this room."

Skipper held up a finger. "You're still correct until . . ." She overlaid a collection of stick figures on top of the man as he approached the prison entrance, and the whole team leaned in.

"What's that?" I asked.

"It's called gait modeling. It's like fingerprints for people's strides. We all have a unique gait, but we don't have the database to use it for ID yet. We have most of the fingerprints in the U.S. and a lot of DNA, but we don't have video of everybody walking yet."

"So, what good does any of this do us?" I asked.

"Keep your shirt on, Dr. Impatient. I'm getting there. Since we— well, I—know a lot, and I mean a *lot*, about Gregory McDonald, I dug up a ton of video footage of him over the years, and thanks to the supercomputer you paid for, when I combined the gait-modeling data with facial recognition, I got a ninety-nine point two percent certainty that the man in those three videos is none other than Gregory Rod-Man McDonald."

"Rod-Man?" Gator said. "Where'd that come from?"

Skipper grinned. "Oh, you're going to love this. It came from his days as a Marine. Apparently, he stabbed an Iraqi with an iron rod after the guy climbed on top of his tank. His platoon started calling him Rod-Man, and the name stuck."

Gator said, "Okay, cool story, but how'd a guy like that get to be on the vice president's staff?"

"Simple," Skipper said. "McDonald became a Florida State Trooper after he got out of the Marines and ended up on a temporary security detail for the congressman from Florida's second congressional district. Some whack job drew a pistol at a campaign event, and McDonald took him down like a linebacker."

I said, "Ah, so the congressman found himself some inside, dependable muscle, and brought him on full time."

"You got it. And that very congressman just happened to get himself elected as our vice president in the last election. So, guess who moved to D.C.? That's right, boys and girls—good ol' Gregory Rod-Man McDonald."

Silence overtook the room, but thunder roared inside my skull. Skipper had just tied the vice president of the United States of America to the murder of four intelligence operatives with a long and winding string of players no one in their right mind would ever connect, and it was up to me to somehow stack all of those parts, pieces, and players into a neat little bundle, tie a ribbon around them, and present them to the Triad. I had somewhere around a billion questions running amok in my head, but the one that kept bouncing the loudest fell out of my mouth first. "But why and how is the priest involved in any of this?"

Mongo said, "From the looks of things, the priest is the last thing we need to worry about. Before we take this one step further, I say we brief the Triad. It may be time for us to wash our hands and walk away like Pontius Pilate."

I turned to Clark. "I'm not a big fan of walking away. How about you?"

He sighed. "Oh, College Boy. What tangled webs we paint ourselves into. Can I have the room for ten minutes?"

Anya took my arm as we stepped through the door. "We must warn Peter."

It was my turn to sigh. "You're right. This thing is a big game of cops and robbers to him, and people are going to get hurt before it's over."

She said, "It should come from you. He knows you are serious. It would not be good idea for me to tell him. Is wrong message from me to see him again."

"Yeah, about that . . ."

She squeezed my arm and smiled. "I like when you are jealous, Chasechka, but this is not why I made with him kiss."

"I know why you did it, and it was the right move. I shouldn't have mentioned it. It's not my place to—"

She took my hand and laid it over her heart. "Your place is here, Chasechka. Is only for you to make decision when is right time."

"Ahem. Having fun feeling up my mom?"

I jerked my hand away and turned to see Pogonya stepping onto the landing behind me. "We were just talking."

She giggled. "Yeah, that's how I got here, by you two 'just talking.' Is everything okay? You guys came in like the world was on fire or something."

I wrapped an arm around our daughter and pulled her between us. "I think the world may be on fire, sweetheart, and it might be up to us to put it out."

"Will I ever get to do that with you?" she asked.

I squeezed her against me. "I hope not. This isn't a side of the world I ever want you to see. You're too beautiful for anything this filthy."

"But who will do it when you cannot?"

It was her mother's turn to share the wisdom she'd earned in ways I'm certain she couldn't fathom Pogonya experiencing. "My perfect child, this life is not what it appears to be from outside. Is terrible place filled with unthinkable people. For you, world is waiting with arms open. What your father and I do is not for people like you. You are so much more than we could ever be. You are best of both of us and even more."

"You can't protect me forever, you know. If I don't go to the world, it will come to me, and what have you done for me if you let it come and I'm not prepared?"

Perhaps the wisdom of her youth ran deeper than either Anya or I could fathom.

"Preparation is one thing," I said, "but charging onto a battlefield to wage a war that's not yours is a fool's suicide. We'll teach you to fight and to protect yourself and others, but we won't stand you in harm's way as long as either of us can stand there instead."

"This scares me," she said.

Anya asked, "What scares you, my child?"

Pogonya said, "Seeing the two of you like this. You're both scared, but you're too proud to admit it. Father, you're afraid you'll lose Mama, just like you lost Penny, but you're even more afraid of what you really feel every time Mama touches you or smiles only for you."

Anya scowled. "Pogonya, it is not your place to tell your father—"

Our headstrong daughter cut her off. "And Mama, you're afraid that you'll never be able to fill the empty hole inside Father's heart."

Anya glared at her. "You should not speak of things you do not yet understand."

"It's just love, Mama. When the two of you look at me, that's what I see and what I feel."

Our daughter placed my hand back over her mother's heart. "You two are fearless in every other aspect of your lives, so don't be afraid of what you both feel."

She left us standing there like fools as she bounded down the stairs, but she stopped a few strides away. "Oh, I almost forgot. You can go save the world now. Apparently, it needs you."

I glanced up to see Clark curling a finger through a narrow opening between the door and jamb of the op center. "Get in here, you two."

Anya and I followed him back into the op center, and he wasted no time issuing orders. "Get that priest back over here on the mainland, and do something to keep your little prison guard from running his mouth and getting himself killed. I talked to the Triad. It doesn't matter if this thing goes all the way to the Oval Office. We're working it, and we've got whatever assets we need—practically a blank check."

I laid a hand on Skipper's shoulder. "Have Gator and Singer go pick up Isaiah. I think the best place for him is back at the monkery."

Clark let out a sharp burst of laughter. "I'm rubbing off on you, College Boy. Even I know it's called a monastery. I don't think *monkery* is a word."

"Whatever," I said. "Let's just get him back here. We'll deal with getting him someplace safe tomorrow. And give me a throwaway. I need to call Peter."

Skipper tossed a cheap plastic cell phone toward me, and I made the catch. She had Gator on the line before I could get Peter to pick up, and she said, "Take Singer and the chopper. Chase wants you to bring the priest back here ASAP."

Finally, Peter's voicemail picked up, and I waited for the tone. "Peter, listen. Things are heating up, and it is crucial that you keep silent about everything . . . absolutely everything. If you've got any vacation time coming, now would be a very good time to burn it. I need you to call the number I'm about to give you. I'll see that you have the money for a nice vacation somewhere unforgettable so you can forget all about the supermax for a couple of weeks."

I gave him a temporary number that would ring in the op center and said, "A woman will answer, and she'll make all the arrangements. Listen to me, Peter. Not a word to anybody. People are going to get hurt, and I couldn't stand it if you were one of those people. You're a good guy with a great heart. The world needs a billion more just like you. Call the number, Peter."

Chapter 15
Hoofbeats of Snakes

Although Gator wasn't ready to command the space shuttle, his flying skills and collection of licenses were accumulating nicely. With every passing day, he stepped a little deeper into my boots. The love and respect he and Skipper shared and showed each other gave me even greater confidence in him, but he still had a lot to learn and scars to collect.

With the precision of a surgeon, our young pilot kissed the ground beside the gazebo with the skids of the Bell 412, and our priest hobbled from the sliding door. I gave the slicing signal across my throat, and Gator shut down the turbines, allowing the rotor to spin to a stop while Isaiah and I settled onto a pair of Adirondacks.

I asked, "How was the island?"

He slid his hands across the arms of his chair, apparently ignoring my question. "Here we are, back where all of this began, and based on the look on your face, I'd guess you're about to tell me this is where it ends."

I crossed my legs and watched a lizard climb the carriage of the cannon in pursuit of an elusive insect just beyond his reach.

I feel your pain, little buddy.

"I'll be honest with you, Isaiah. I wish I could tell you that's what's happening, but lying to a priest doesn't feel like a great move on my part."

He brightened. "Does that mean you're going to help?"

"No. Helping isn't what we do. We're door-kickers, not personal assistants. When we take on a project, it becomes ours, and we turn it inside out until we shake the bad guys and every ounce of truth out of it, no matter who and what they are. That's what this conversation is about."

He licked his lips and swallowed hard.

I glanced at the house and then back at the priest. "Yep, we figured out that you haven't exactly been forthcoming with everything you know about this case."

"Is that what it is now? A case?"

"The games are over, Isaiah. The guys want me to waterboard you, and I'm not convinced they aren't serious."

He reached for his rosary beads. "Is waterboarding a real thing?"

"It's one of the worst but most effective things I do. Clark calls it tactical baptism, but trust me, it's not a sacrament you want to experience."

He pressed himself against his chair. "You're not serious."

"Relax. I'm not going to torture you, but you *are* going to come clean about what you know. Let's start with Gregory McDonald."

The priest flinched. "What about him?"

"You could've mentioned him."

He furrowed his brow as if I'd accused him of failing to introduce himself. "What are you talking about? I told you he's the reason I was sent away from my duties with the dicastery."

It was my turn to furrow. "No, you didn't. You never mentioned him."

Isaiah leaned forward in what I hoped was an attempt to close the mighty chasm of misunderstanding between us. "Chase, Gregory Mc-Donald is the archbishop who had me sent to Ignatius House, the Jesuit Center in Georgia, where I was to spend my time in prayer, contemplation, and service. I told you all of this."

I shook my head in disbelief and disappointment. "Isaiah, I'm so very sorry. There's been a huge misunderstanding, and I came down on the wrong side. I should've assumed you weren't hiding anything.

Instead, though, I stuck you in the same category as most of the rest of the world and assumed you had something to hide. I apologize."

"I still don't get it," he said. "What is the misunderstanding?"

I leaned back and said, "Relax. I've got a lot to tell you. While you were on the island, we were given the authorization to pursue the operation, and we've begun. Do you remember Corporal Leonard, the correctional officer at the supermax?"

He nestled back into his chair. "Of course. He's a very pleasant guy. A little socially awkward, I'd say, but he's always been extremely kind to me."

"You hit the nail on the head there," I said. "He's a little different but seems to have a good heart. He did us a huge favor and helped us identify the man he referred to as 'a fed who makes regular visits to the prison directly through the warden's office.'"

"Sure, I remember him mentioning that, but that doesn't have anything to do with the archbishop."

I said, "Well, you'd think that would be the case, but just wait until I tell you that guy's name. It's Gregory McDonald."

The priest shuddered. "Wait. What? Are you saying the archbishop is visiting the prison and representing himself as a federal agent?"

I laughed. "I wish it were that simple."

Isaiah recoiled. "Simple? That would be the exact opposite of simple. That would be unimaginable."

"Trust me. In my world, that would be the simplest explanation for all of this, but when I hear hoofbeats, I don't look for horses . . . or zebras. I look for snakes, and in this case, we already found one."

He smiled. "You know, Chase, if this gazebo were a confessional, I'd make a priestly absolution, but since you're not a Catholic, nor is that cannon a confessional screen, I'll just say that I forgive you for accusing me of hiding things from you. Even if I'm the only person for whom this is true, I have nothing to hide."

"No holy water or Hail Mary requirements?"

He said, "We should be constantly in prayer, but no holy water required. Are you allowed to tell me what you've learned so far and who this other Gregory McDonald guy is?"

I said, "*Allowed* is an interesting word. No one is going to throw me in jail or send me to a Jesuit Center in Georgia for telling you what I know, but this operation is already extremely sensitive."

"I'll take that as a no, meaning you're not going to tell me."

I kicked a boot onto the carriage of the cannon, accidentally exposing a section of my prosthetic. "I'll tell you who Gregory McDonald is, but I'm afraid that's all we really know so far."

He tapped my inhuman leg with a crutch, and a smile crossed his lips. "Let me guess. You were defending someone or something with enormous valor when you lost the leg."

"I don't know about the valor part, but I was in a fight that left my right leg a foot and a half shorter than my left."

The priest continued the smile, and I motioned toward his face. "What's that look about?"

He said, "Ignatius de Loyola was struck in the leg by a cannonball during the battle for Pamplona in fifteen twenty-one before his conversion to Christianity. He was still a womanizing, hard-drinking, rabble-rouser back then. Maybe you have even more in common with the patron saint of us Jesuits than I first suspected."

"I don't drink anymore. I'm definitely not a womanizer these days. And I'm not certain what a rabble-rouser is, but I doubt I'm one of those either."

"Neither was Ignatius after his conversion, but I was talking about your leg."

"I'm no saint, and I never will be, but if your boy Ignatius wasn't afraid of a fight, maybe he and I would've gotten along pretty well. I probably could've even used him in a few fights along the way."

The priest crossed himself and looked through the roof of the gazebo as if staring directly into Heaven. "I still do . . ."

Unsure if I was being recruited or redirected, I said, "Do you still want to hear about the op?"

"I do. I apologize for the distraction."

"Okay, I'll be brief. Gregory McDonald—*my* Gregory McDonald—is a special assistant to the deputy chief of staff to the vice president of the United States. He's got a storied history with the VP, and it looks like he and the politician have a mutual back-scratching agreement. McDonald just happens to scratch a little harder than most."

Isaiah frowned. "Special assistant to a deputy chief of staff doesn't sound like a very prestigious position."

"It's not," I said. "McDonald is apparently muscle, not political finesse. He'll never get close to the VP on paper or in the public eye, but I get the impression that he's the guy the VP calls when he needs to keep a dirty little secret a secret."

"Is Garland Fitzsimon one of those dirty little secrets?"

I laughed. "You may be better at this ops game than the typical priest."

"I'm a Jesuit, one of God's soldiers, Chase. I don't stand in pulpits, deliver sermons, and baptize babies. I go to battle for the faith, wherever that battle and that faith demands."

"I appreciate that, and I have a lot of respect for it, I do. But this isn't a spiritual battle. This is espionage and politics, and in those worlds, good people get hurt. Even worse, *very* good people get hurt *very* badly. I don't want to see that happen to you. I recommend you go back to the monastery and serve out the rest of your penance. You'll be safe there while my team and I get to the bottom of this thing."

He traced the outline of his cast with a crutch. "Under normal circumstances, I would argue with you, but in my current state, you may be right. I would be little more than dead weight, so I'll do as you ask and stay out of the way, even though it's outside my nature and my commitment."

I said, "I do have one more question, though. When you originally told me about the murders in the Keys, you said something like, 'They told me he murdered two NSA officers, a Mossad officer, and an FSB officer.' Do you remember telling me that?"

"I do."

"Who is *they*? Who told you that?"

He bit his lip. "When I made my plea before the archbishop to minister directly to Fitzsimon in prison, he pulled me aside and privately told me what Garland had done. So, that makes the archbishop the *they* who told me."

I let that percolate in my head for a moment. "Okay. That's one more mystery we'll have to solve before we get to the bottom of this whole ordeal. Can I ask you for another favor that's outside your nature?"

"Sure, go ahead."

"Can you stay quiet and out of this until we solve it? The more you talk to anybody, even the silent monks, the more dangerous it becomes for you, and the more difficult it becomes for us. If you could just pretend to be a humble, submissive priest who is silently taking his licks, that would be best for everyone involved."

"I am humble," he said. "And I am submissive before God and the Pope. It's the silent part that's tough for me. I'm eternally thankful I was called to the priesthood and not to the life of a monk."

"Is that a yes?"

He nodded. "Yes, I'll be a good boy and keep quiet."

"Thank you. In return, I'll keep you posted on our progress. The reports won't come regularly or as often as you'd want, but they'll come. Are you permitted to have a cell phone at the monastery?"

"Yes. Of course, I can't use it on the grounds, so I'll have to leave the monastery to make or receive calls."

"That's what I thought. We'll give you a phone, and Skipper will teach you how to use it. She'll come up with a solar charger in case they don't want you charging it in your room. Anyway, check your voicemail every other day or so, and we'll leave instructions for you to call for updates. The phone isn't the typical off-the-shelf model. It's extremely specialized, so please use it only to communicate with us and only for this operation. When this is over, we'll need it back."

"I understand. Now I have a favor to ask of you."

"Let's hear it."

He raised his cast and crutches. "It's a long walk back to the monastery from here."

I stood. "It sure is. That should give you plenty of time to think, reflect, and pray. Good night, Priest."

I left him sitting alone in the gazebo as I jogged up the path toward the house. On the third step to the gallery, I spun and called across the lawn. "I'm just messing with you. Your room is still yours inside, and the shower works. You could use one."

He hobbled from the gazebo. "You're a cruel man, Chase Fulton."

I said, "Just wait 'til you see me cut the head off of a hoofed snake or two."

Chapter 16
Coconut Telegraph

There was only one reason for me to be in the water, breathing from a regulator, and sliding gloved hands along the keel of the 80-foot Mark V patrol boat resting peacefully on the dark surface of the North River. The hull was fine. The inspection was completely unnecessary, but the mission was crucial.

Even though the sun shone brightly in the morning sky over coastal Georgia, from my vantage point, I could've been on the dark side of the moon. What little light penetrated the inky water failed to find its way into the shadow beneath the massive vessel overhead. The only way to know my partner was still with me was the brush of an arm or the gentle tug against the short tether that bound us together. Both came in routine intervals that gave me reassurance that the diver beside me was not only comfortable in the environment that would terrify most people, but also capable of maintaining focus on a mundane task under such stressful conditions. Training works, but it has its limitations. I can simulate enemy fire, but how a shooter will perform when bad guys' bullets start flying can only be determined when the incoming fire is real, and the black water of the North River was as real as it gets.

When we surfaced at the stern of the vessel, my partner pulled her backup mask from her face and let it dangle around her neck. "Father, that was cruel. Why did you tear away my mask?"

The full facemasks we'd worn when we descended into the shallow water provided light, communication, and continuous airflow, making the dive far more comfortable than it would've been in conventional scuba gear.

"Because gear fails, sweetheart. How we react to those failures is often the difference between staying alive and becoming a statistic. I'm pretty fond of you being alive, so I want to make sure you have the skill to stay that way."

Pogonya splashed me with a massive wave from both hands. "It's still cruel, but how'd I do?"

"Perfectly. Were you afraid?"

"A little," she admitted. "But I had a good teacher. I just remembered the steps, remained calm, and worked the problem, just like you taught me."

"Don't you dare tell her I said this, but you're already a better diver than your mother. She's nervous in the water."

"No, she is not. Don't say that."

"It's true," I said. "She's better than ninety-nine percent of divers, but water work is one of her few weaknesses."

She thumbed the back of her regulator, spraying water and air into my face. "I'm telling her you said that."

"Go ahead, but she already knows. Seriously, though, you did very well under there. Most people—most men—would freak out, but you were as cool as any operator on the team. I'm proud of you."

She finned close and wrapped her arms around me. "Thank you for this. I know you have work to do, but spending time together like this is really special to me."

I wouldn't let her see the tear, but I felt it. "Yeah, I kinda like it, too. Almost as much as riding the horses."

She planted both hands on top of my head and shoved me beneath the surface. We splashed our way out of the water and onto the dock.

"You don't really hate the horses, do you?"

"Hate is a strong word," I said. "I love Richter, mostly because he was a gift from you, but Pecan and I aren't ever going to be pals."

The whop of the Bell 412's rotor blades echoed through the trees, and we shaded our eyes against the sun.

She said, "I guess that means it's time for you to go to work, huh?"

"That's what it means."

"And I still can't come."

"No, you still can't come, but the good news is that we're not going far. This operation is practically in our backyard."

"That's good, I guess. But I have to get back to school anyway, so it doesn't really matter."

We pulled off our gear and gave it a thorough wash before hanging it to dry. Between the salt in the brackish water and the muck from the bottom of the river, the thousands of dollars' worth of gear would turn to worthless trash in a matter of days if we didn't keep it spotless.

Pogonya showered and changed in the boathouse and pranced through the door. "I'm going to see the horses. Please don't leave without saying goodbye."

"I wouldn't dare."

* * *

Gator and Singer walked into the op center, and I asked, "Did you get our holy man tucked in?"

Skipper hopped from her seat and kissed her husband on the cheek. "We've been waiting. What took you so long?"

Gator checked his watch and eyed me. "You get me into some weird situations. The dock at the monastery broke from its mooring and floated downstream about a mile. Singer spotted it and somehow negotiated for us to drag it back upstream for them. Have you ever seen a negotiation when only one person does the talking? It's weird. Monks are weird. Not talking is weird."

I laughed. "Nothing surprises me anymore. Have a seat. We've got a plan."

Skipper cocked her head, "Oh, *we* do, do we? And when were you going to brief your analyst on this plan of *ours*?"

"Right now," I said. "Here's the working theory. Gregory McDonald, the special assistant guy, not the archbishop, is making regular visits to the prison. We don't know why, but we can assume it has something to do with Garland Fitzsimon. We need to know who he sees while he's there. Skipper, can you do anything with that?"

"I can try, but there's probably no official record of him being there, so, most likely, there won't be an electronic trail for me to sniff."

"Give it a shot, but don't chase your tail. If you don't pick up a scent quickly, move on."

"Got it."

I said, "Next is the psychiatrist, Dr. Brian Plum. What do we have on him?"

Skipper said, "Board-certified psychiatrist. Been with the Department of Corrections for just over eight years on some program where the state pays back his student loan debt if he gives them ten years of service."

"So, he's two-thirds of the way through his sentence," Mongo said. "We may be able to use that."

"Maybe so," I said. "If they're doping Fitzsimon, Dr. Plum has to be in on it. There's no way around it."

"I've been thinking about that," Kodiak said. "And I still can't figure out why they don't just kill the guy or let him kill himself. It doesn't make any sense that they're keeping him alive."

"For me, that's the biggest mystery of all," I said. "But there's no way to figure it out from the surface. We'll have to dive in, and I say we start in Cayo Hueso. We need to know what really happened down there."

Shawn closed one eye as if aiming at me. "So, you're going to ride into Key West and start asking strangers if they know anything about four intel operators getting killed offshore. That's your plan?"

"Yeah, pretty much. Have you got a better one?"

He showed me his palms. "I got nothing, but I'll pack a bikini and some Coppertone. Let's go."

* * *

One of the air assets that wasn't destroyed in the attack on our airport was an amphibious de Havilland Twin Otter we acquired during an operation a long way from home a long time ago. It was time to pull the old girl out of the hangar and toss her into the ring.

I dialed Gordo's cell. "Mornin', Chase. How's it going?"

"Not bad, except for one thing. I told my chief pilot to call me after the test flight, and he didn't."

Gordo said, "That's because we haven't made the flight yet. We did some high-speed taxi runs and discovered a vibration that threatened to shake the wings off the thing. So, that put her back in the shop."

"You still should've called."

"Sorry. It won't happen again."

"I'm just bustin' your chops. You're the chief pilot. Just keep doing that pilot stuff. Speaking of which, are you current in the Twin Otter?"

He said, "I'll need a few landings to be legal, but otherwise, sure. Why?"

"I want to put her to work, and nobody here is current. We need you to sign us off."

"All right. I can be there this afternoon, but any seaplane instructor—"

I cut him off. "I want you."

"We'll be there in three hours, boss."

* * *

We towed the Twin Otter out, fueled her, did a thorough preflight inspection, and ran the engines long enough to get the temperatures up, just to make sure she was up to the task.

Gordo, Tubs, and Slider landed just after lunch in a beautiful King Air and taxied to the main hangar.

I met the loadmaster as soon as his foot hit the tarmac. "Nice ride. Where'd you steal it?"

He shook my hand. "If I tell you, that'll make you an accomplice."

Slider was not only a brilliant loadmaster, but he was also a flight engineer and A&P mechanic with exceptional wrench skills. He was a force multiplier for the team, giving us the ability to repair most anything we could break anywhere in the world. Our assets were stacking up, but on our current operation, the pile of liabilities was nothing to scoff at.

Tubbs, the copilot, was next through the door, and I stuck out a hand. He shook it and whispered, "Don't let Gordo blame me for that bounce. He was on the controls."

"I have no doubt," I said.

Finally, Gordo strolled down the steps, and I made a double-take. "I thought it was Tom Cruise for a minute, there."

He ran a hand through his hair. "He only wishes he could look this good."

"Nice bounce, by the way."

He shot a look at Tubbs, and I said, "It wasn't him. I saw who was doing the flying. The windows work both ways."

He waggled a finger at his copilot. "You'll pay for that one."

After bathroom calls and snacks, Gordo made his landings both on the water and the runway before having Tubbs, Gator, and me join him in the Twin Otter. We ran through a refresher on normal ops, as well as emergency procedures, before spending several hours getting all of us up to standard and honing some rusty skills.

Gator did well, even though he had the fewest flight hours of anyone and just enough seaplane time to call himself an amphib pilot. I'd yet to see him under fire in the cockpit, but everything pointed toward him being just as cool at the controls as Pogo was underwater.

We had dinner family-style and caught up on the progress with the C-130.

Gordo said, "They found the problem with the vibration, so she'll be ready to fly day after tomorrow. You don't need us for the mission, do you?"

I said, "No, that's why I had you get us current, but you're welcome to come along if you need a break. It'll be work for us, but you guys are welcome to hang out on the beach and drink Cuba Libres."

"Thanks, but we need to get back. I don't want those Lockheed test pilots anywhere near my cockpit."

The whole team crashed for the night, and we were wheels up just after the sun showed her face over Cumberland Island the next morning. Gordo and the King Air headed northwest, and Gator pointed the Twin Otter south for our two-and-a-half-hour trip to the southernmost point of the continental U.S.

When we touched down, Shawn bumped my shoulder. "You're not really going to ask random people about the murders, are you?"

"No, they're not random," I said. "The boat captains down here know everything that happens between here and Havana. There's no such thing as a secret on this or any other island. It's called the coconut telegraph, and I plan to tap into it and do a lot of listening."

Chapter 17
Moments of Weakness

Key West thrives on tourism, but the heart of the island is its people, the residents who call it home. Some of them live on the street while others squander their wealth on magnificent homes destined to become bull's-eyes for the relentless hurricanes that always win. The bulk of the residents are hardworking people living their lives in what the tourists call 'paradise' and the nightly freaks on Duval Street call 'the mother ship.' The island began as a haven for wreckers who thrived on the cargo of ships whose unfortunate captains got a little too close to the reef just offshore. Not much has changed since those days. Shopkeepers leer from their windows, just waiting for drunken tourists with pockets full of cash to stumble into their stores. And the fishermen, who spend their lives at the end of a line, fill the marinas, waiting for their next charters and the next big catch. And that's exactly what I was doing when fortune smiled on me and opportunity fell in my lap.

As we walked from the airplane across the scalding tarmac, a disheveled guy, who could've been thirty or seventy, wiped his brow with a filthy Boston Red Sox hat. "Is that your Twin Otter, mister?"

I glanced back at our airplane as if uncertain exactly what the man was asking. "That's right. It's ours."

"You wouldn't be interested in chartering it for a few hours, would you? I've got a bunch of boat captains chomping at the bit to get airborne and go spottin', but my old Caravan laid down on me . . . again."

I said, "I'm sorry. What?"

"Your airplane. Can I rent it from you for maybe four hours?"

When the gift of his question finally hit me, I couldn't believe my luck. "No, I'm sorry. I can't rent it to you. My insurance company would lose its mind, but I'll fly the charter for you, and you can ride in the right seat."

He squinted up at me. "How much?"

"How much do you charge?"

He seemed to consider the question and decide whether to lie. "I charge twenty-five hundred for four hours, and the captains split it between them. As long as I stay under max gross, I don't care how many they shove in there."

"I'll make a deal with you," I said. "I know how it feels to have a broken-down airplane. I've been there. If you'll pay for the fuel, you can keep the rest of the cash. Do you have a multi-engine ticket?"

"Yeah, of course I do."

I said, "In that case, you can do the flying, and I'll have my pilot in the right seat to make the insurance man happy. There's just one catch, though."

"Yeah, what's that?"

"I get a seat in the back. I want to talk to some of the charter captains."

He said, "Fine by me, but they're usually pretty focused on spottin' fish. I can't make you any promises about how talkative they'll be."

"You let me worry about that. You just find the fish for them. What time are we leaving?"

He checked the spot on his arm where a watch used to be. "Wouldn't you know it?"

I said, "It's ten fifteen."

"They like to be out over the strait when the sun's high, so what do you say about eleven thirty?"

"Sounds great to me. We'll get checked in and meet you back here a little after eleven."

"I really appreciate this. You're a lifesaver. I'm Bobby Gibson, by the way."

I slapped him on the back. "Nice to meet you, Bobby. I'm Chase. I know a good traveling mechanic up in New Smyrna if you want him to come down and take a look at your Caravan. He knows them well. He took care of mine for years."

"I just might take you up on that. Thanks again."

We parted ways, and Anya took my arm. She pointed across the highway to Smathers Beach. "Do you remember many years ago we sat on sand right over there and you were frightened that I might be pregnant?"

"Ha! Yeah, I'd forgotten all about that. It seems like a lifetime ago."

"It was," she said. "I was not pregnant that day, but look at us now. We have beautiful girl who will soon be woman."

"She's a better diver than you."

She laughed. "I know. She told me. I will give back to you arm now so people will not think we are lovers. This is what you want, yes?"

I squeezed my arm against my side, trapping her hand beneath my elbow. "Let 'em talk. They're just jealous."

We checked into the house Skipper rented for us, and I explained what was about to happen. "Gator and I are going to fly the charter. I want the rest of you to hit the marinas and see what you can dig up. We're going to get some crazy stories, but we're looking for common threads. Fishermen are storytellers, but if there's a tiny piece of truth that jumps out of every story, or at least most of the stories, that's what we need."

* * *

Six charter captains showed up, and two of them brought their first mates. That made eleven souls on board, including Gator, the other pilot, and me.

I took the opportunity as a teaching moment and pulled Gator aside. "Count the bodies and guess the average weight. Add ten percent. We need at least five hours of fuel for a four-hour trip. Run the weight and balance calculations, and let me know what you come up with."

He pulled out his phone and opened the app, but I covered the screen. "Nope. You can use the calculator, but not the app."

Two minutes later, he said, "Somebody has to stay behind."

"I thought that might be the case. Do you want to break the news, or shall I do it?"

He said, "I'm the pilot in command. I'll do it."

Twenty minutes after culling the herd, we took off without the two first mates and climbed out to the south over the Straits of Florida. Everyone wore a headset, so conversation was easy, and Bobby did a nice job of handling the airplane. Gator was careful to stay close behind him on the controls during takeoff, but once in cruise flight, he relaxed a little and watched for other aircraft.

Bobby pointed out a few schools of fish running the straits, and we even spotted a pod of whales I hadn't expected to see.

"That's a good sign," one of the fishing captains said. "Whales and big fish eat the same things. If the whales are eating, so are the blue marlin."

Somebody said, "Jimmy Griggs had a charter last week that landed a four-hundred-pound swordfish."

"It was three eighty-eight. I saw it," another of the captains said. "The thing was a monster. I heard they tipped him three grand. It was some big real estate guy from Texas, from what I heard. Took 'em five hours to land the thing."

The stories continued and grew as the afternoon played out. At the peak of story time, I popped the question I'd been sitting on for days. "While we're telling fishing stories, I've got a question about something that happened down here a couple of years ago. Maybe you guys heard about it."

I suddenly had everyone's attention, so I said, "I heard about four guys getting killed on a boat between Key West and Havana. Did any of you hear about that?"

I was surprised when my answer came in the form of laughter. Finally, one of the captains said, "You'll have to be a little more specific. Dead guys on boats aren't big stories down here."

"One of these guys washed up on the Naval Air Station with part of the killer's ear in his stomach."

The laughter ceased, and I was suddenly uncomfortable in my own airplane.

"Are you some kind of cop or something?" one of the captains asked.

I threw up my hands. "Not a chance. How many cops do you know who own airplanes like this? I write books for a living. I'm just working on some research for a story."

"Like a documentary story kind of thing?"

"No, nothing like that. I write fiction, but it's always interesting to hear about real-life events that are too wild to believe."

One of the captains slapped another on the shoulder. "Go ahead, Iggy. Tell him."

When the man they called Iggy turned around, the look on his face was not amusement. "I seen it happen."

My heart nearly leapt from my chest, but I didn't say a word. Iggy clearly wasn't a big talker, but I had no interest in interrupting him.

He said, "It was about two o'clock in the morning. I was doing something I didn't have no business doing in a place I didn't have no business being, if you get what I'm saying."

I nodded, and he continued. "I was running dark, 'cause, well, you know. Anyhow, I was dodging three or four boats that was out there on radar. I didn't know who none of 'em was, but I didn't want nobody to see me."

At that moment, I wanted more than anything on earth to be alone with Captain Iggy, a pair of good Cubans, and a bottle of whatever he liked to drink, so I said, "Maybe you and I could sit down and talk about it tonight when we're not bouncing around over the ocean in an airplane."

"I've got a charter tonight, but if you really want to hear about it, I guess I could tell you the story for my normal charter rate tomorrow night. I can't exactly afford to be givin' up a night's pay for storytelling."

I said, "How 'bout I buy you dinner and pay your normal charter fee when we get back? It shouldn't take you more than an hour to tell me the story."

"Suits me," he said. "It's your money."

"How many people can your boat carry for a charter?" I asked.

"She can carry twelve or fifteen pretty easy, but I generally run her like a six-pack. Keeps the Coast Guard off my back, you know?"

"I get it," I said. "Where do you like to eat?"

He said, "Let's go to Schooner Wharf Bar. Michael McCloud's picking and singing this evening. I like him, and they do a good hogfish in there."

Gator nailed the landing, and Iggy was exactly right about the hogfish. It was the best I'd ever had. We sat in a pair of white plastic chairs on the edge of the gravel-lined area designated as the Schooner Wharf Bar's dining room, and Michael McCloud played "Moments of Weakness" on stage.

My team was stationed strategically around the perimeter of the bar, and I caught Anya's eye during the first chorus. She smiled as the man who wrote it sang the song I'd sung for years in the shower and on sailboats all over the world.

Iggy broke my trance. "So, you wanna hear about them killings, and you're sure you ain't no cop or nothing like that?"

"I'm sure."

"All right, then. Let's go for a walk. I ain't talkin' about it in here."

I paid our bill and tipped Michael. The old island troubadour watched the hundred fall into his jar and said, "Thank you. If there's anything you want to hear, just let me know."

"I'll be back in a while, and I'd love to hear "Chasing the Wind" if you can remember the words."

He said, "Keep puttin' those hundreds in that jar, and I'll write one especially for you."

"You already did," I said. "You just played it."

Our walk took us away from the bar's lights and noise. I was well armed and completely sober, but Iggy would've been a handful if he decided he wanted to put me in the ocean. Thankfully, he did not.

We stopped by what was left of a rusted-out bench, and he took a seat. I calculated the unlikeliness of the bench supporting both of us, so I planted myself on the pier.

He lit a cigarette and blew a stream of smoke into the air. "Want one?"

"No, thanks. I'm more of a cigar man myself."

"Yeah, me too, but good ones are expensive, and cheap ones taste like the inside of a garbage can."

I pulled a pair of Cuban Cohibas from my shirt pocket. "I don't smoke garbage, my friend."

He flicked the cigarette into the water and lifted the cigar from my hand. "No, sir, you sure don't."

Instead of punching the end, he bit the tip and stuck it in his mouth. Not wanting to appear pretentious, I did the same, and we lit up.

He studied the cigar for a long moment. "It sure is a shame these things are embargoed."

I kicked a shell from the edge of the dock, into the placid water, and watched the ripples expand. "Yes, it is, but I'm sure you have a source."

"Yeah, but they're still expensive."

I didn't push. I just let the evening play out and pretended to be patient.

After a few minutes of silent enjoyment, he said, "So, I guess you figured out I was running dope."

"That's none of my business. What a man does to feed his family is his. I just want to hear the story. That's all."

"I appreciate that. So, like I told you, I was runnin' dark and dodgin' boats when I come up on three or four in a bunch out there. When I first seen 'em, I thought it had to be the Coast Guard or Border Patrol, but it weren't."

I didn't move or make a sound.

"It was some kinda deal going on. I figured at the time it was dope, but the longer I watched, the more I knew I was wrong about that. It was real curious looking, so I cut the motors and just listened in the dark."

I pretended to relight my cigar, even though it was still burning just fine, and he kept talking.

"They weren't speaking English or Spanish. 'Course, you know I speak English, but my Spanish ain't bad neither. I ain't sure what language they were speaking, but they got louder and louder. You know, trying to talk over each other. All of 'em had something to say, I guess."

"Could it have been Russian?" I asked.

"Don't know. I don't guess I've ever heard nobody speak Russian."

"*Eto zvuchalo kak-to tak?*"

"Is that Russian?"

"It is."

"Do some more. Say something longer, like you're mad at somebody."

I gave him a few more sentences, and he said, "It could've been Russian, I guess. It's been a couple years, so I can't be sure, but it sounded something like that."

I asked, "Were you close enough to see anybody?"

"I laid off about a quarter of a mile or maybe a little more, but I've got some good binoculars on the boat. I'll be glad to show you my boat if you want to see it. I've still got the binoculars. They're some foreign name—Swarovski or something like that."

"Those are good binos," I said. "Some of the best in the world."

He shrugged. "They work pretty good. Anyway, I wasn't close enough to see them without the glasses, but I was watching and listening. Say, you're not going to put this in your book, are you? I mean, I don't want to get mixed up in nothing."

"I don't even know your name," I said. "And we'll keep it that way. We're just two guys smoking Cubans and telling lies."

He took a long draw and exhaled a cloud of smoke. "That's when the shooting started, but it didn't last long. It was maybe three or four shots—maybe a few more than that—but it turned into a brawl. I guess somebody got the gun away from the guy."

"How many people were fighting?"

"There was five of 'em. One of 'em went down during the shooting. Three turned on the guy who done the shooting, and they were giving it to him pretty good, but he was a fighter. The other guys weren't slouches, either. They fought for a while, but apparently, the guy had another gun. It sounded like a twenty-two. You know, something small. The first one was a nine-millimeter, at least."

I took a chance. "If I showed you a picture of a guy, do you think you could tell me if he was one of the men in the fight?"

Iggy said, "I don't know. Maybe."

I pulled out my phone and brought up a picture of Garland Fitzsimon in street clothes.

"Hey, that could be the guy with the gun, but that's a picture somebody took before that night, isn't it?"

I nodded, and he said, "Yeah, I knew it, 'cause one of them guys bit off his ear while they were fighting, and that guy in the picture's still got both of his."

I almost swallowed my cigar. "What happened next?"

"That was it," he said. "It was over when that guy in the picture went in the water. Everybody was shot, but that little gun wasn't enough to kill 'em. I figure that guy bled to death or the sharks got him. You know how your ear bleeds when you cut it. Just imagine how much he was pumping into the water with it bit clean off like that."

"What about the other boats?" I asked. "What did they do when it was all over?"

"I don't know. I cranked up and got out of there. I was already in over my head, and the last thing I needed was to get in the middle of something like that with a boat full of square grouper."

"How much is your charter, Iggy?"

"I get eight hundred for half a day or twelve for a full day."

I dropped five grand in banded hundreds on the bench beside him and laid my last two Cohibas on top of the stack. "Thanks, Captain. I hope you catch a swordfish that could swallow that three-hundred-eighty-eight pounder."

"From your lips to God's ears. Thanks for the smokes." He scooped up the stack and weighed the cash. "Are you serious? This is way too much."

"I'm a sucker for a good story. As Michael McCloud says, just call it a moment of weakness."

Chapter 18

It's Key West, Baby

Sunsets on Mallory Square at the north end of Duval Street have brought tourists to the island for decades, and the show that night was just one more example of why there's no better spot on Earth to watch Sol make her way beyond the horizon. We didn't see the elusive green flash, but the spectacle was still breathtaking. As important as our mission was, something about seeing the sunset on that particular day called to me. Something inside me needed to see it, to experience it, to feel it, and as the crowd dispersed, an old man beside me dropped what looked like Tylenol into the gentle waves lapping at the seawall.

He caught me watching and grinned up through his white beard. "Strange thing to see somebody do, huh?"

"A little bit," I said. "May I ask?"

He held up a velvet bag and pulled open the top. "Take a look in there, son."

I leaned down and peered into the pouch that greatly resembled a Crown Royal bag. "It looks like a bunch of pills."

"Capsules," he said. "My youngest son is a pharmacist. This whole thing was his idea. His mother and I were married for almost seventy-one years. This was her favorite place to watch the sunset. We've seen them all over the world, believe me, but this place was always her favorite."

I glanced back up at the darkening sky, streaked with orange and purple bands no artist could ever truly capture, as my family stood a few feet away watching and listening to my exchange with the old man. "I've seen a few myself, and I have to agree with your wife. This one's pretty special."

"Alzheimer's took her from me back in the spring. I always thought I'd go first, but now, I'm glad she got to go ahead. The thought of her heart breaking the way mine does every day when I wake up and she's not there would be too much for me to bear. I'd rather carry that pain myself."

"I get it," I said. "I lost my wife last year, and I never knew it was possible to hurt so badly."

He shook the bag. "That's what these capsules are for. Every one of them has a little bit of her ashes in them. I told you our son was a pharmacist, didn't I?"

"Yes, sir. You did."

"I'm taking her with me around the world again and leaving a little piece of her everywhere she loved. I didn't count them, but I hope I've got enough of these things to drop the last one on the day I die, and I'll get to wake up the next morning beside Marilynn again."

"That's a beautiful story. I'm sure you'll see her again, and she'll be just as beautiful as she was on your wedding day."

His mind seemed to take him somewhere far away. "Sounds like a long time, doesn't it? Seventy-one years. It's not. It's just the blink of a young man's eye. Before he knows it, his eyes are old and alone. Don't turn into me, son. Don't spend what time you've got left throwing tiny pieces of what used to be your life into the wind all over the world."

Without another word, he turned and walked away, his cane pressing into the ground with every step, and the velvet bag clenched in his fist.

"Who was that?" Shawn asked when I turned to join the team.

"I don't know. It might've been me."

* * *

Although my belly was full, the rest of the team insisted on dinner at Blue Heaven. I drank tea and nibbled off everyone else's plates as the old man and his bag of capsuled ashes consumed my thoughts. I watched my team—my family—eat, drink, and laugh together as if Penny never existed. She was gone, and with every passing day, the reality of her grew a little fainter, replaced by priceless memories I'd carry with me throughout eternity. They wouldn't fit inside any capsule or velvet bag, but I'd cling to them just as the old man did. I couldn't leave pieces of her behind, but slowly, the pieces of me she left behind seemed to fall back together, and it was the people around the table in front of me who made that happen.

"I wish Pogonya could be here. She would love this place." I smiled back at Anya. "We'll bring her down here when we're not working and we have time to relax and enjoy the island."

She bit her bottom lip. "*We* is a very nice word."

* * *

Back at the house, we settled into loungers on the deck overlooking the tranquil ocean. The stars danced on the water, and an occasional boat passed by on its way to another night of God knows what off the Florida Keys.

Mongo said, "We all heard your man's story. Do you want to hear ours?"

"I do," I said.

He pulled out his pad and skimmed through some notes he'd made throughout the day. "The stories we pieced together all happened after what your guy said. Apparently, a couple on their honeymoon, taking a seaplane sightseeing excursion, spotted a guy in the water. According to what we heard, the pilot landed in the water and picked up a man who was missing most of his left ear. He brought him back to Key West so the ambulance could take him to the hospital."

"Sounds like our guy," I said.

Mongo frowned. "Like all so-called eye-witness stories, it gets a little shaky on details, but apparently, the guy was out of his mind and mumbling stuff about spies and working for the government. Some people even said they heard he tried to take over the airplane."

I said, "That may explain the piracy of an airplane charge they hung on him. He was probably delirious from blood loss and dehydration. How long was he in the water?"

Mongo said, "From what we could pick up, it was early to midafternoon when they found him, so he would've been in the water over twelve hours."

"That's a long time after losing a fight against four guys."

Gator jumped in. "I talked to Skipper, and she said the story checks out with hospital records, but she wouldn't say how she got access to the records."

Kodiak said, "All of this is fascinating, but how does it get us any closer to finding out what it's all about?"

I said, "I don't know yet, but the more information we have, the better chance we've got of discovering something meaningful. I really want to know what those four guys were talking about on that boat that night."

Anya said, "I do not think they were speaking Russian. If is true only one of them was Russian, then why would other three speak also Russian?"

"Maybe it was their only common language," I said.

"This cannot be true," Anya said. "If two were American, and one was Mossad, all three would speak English. If fourth was Russian, and he was officer of SVR, he would also speak at least some English."

I sighed. "Yeah, you've got a good point. And if Fitzsimon was part of the conversation, I doubt he spoke Russian."

Singer coughed as if he were choking on something. "He speaks Latin. Why not Russian?"

"How, when, and where did Fitzsimon get arrested?" I asked.

"That's another one for Skipper," Gator said as he pulled out his phone.

It took only seconds for our analyst to turn sassy. "It must be nice hanging out in the Keys while some of us actually have to work."

"It is," I said. "We've just been lounging and doing nothing all day."

"Yeah, right. What do you want, and when are you bringing my husband home?"

I said, "We want to know when and where Fitzsimon was arrested."

"That's an easy one. Monroe County deputies arrested him in a bar in Islamorada two days after he left the hospital, against medical advice in Key West, and three days after the coroner found part of his ear in the dead NSA contractor's stomach on Boca Chica."

"What was the original charge?"

"The police report is a little vague, but apparently, there was a fight in the bar, and Fitzsimon got a drunk and disorderly charge and a night in the county lockup on Marathon."

Shawn laughed. "Imagine going to jail for a bar fight and ending up in the supermax."

Anya asked, "Why would this story not be on every newspaper and television station when it happened?"

I said, "It's Key West, baby. Down here, the only thing that's considered weird is when everything is normal. Nobody freaks out about dead bodies in the water or missing ears. It's a different world."

Mongo raised a finger. "You have to keep in mind, too, that none of this would've seemed connected at the time. We're looking at it in hindsight, but back then, Fitzsimon was just another drunk fisherman who fell overboard and left the hospital without telling anybody. That's not out of the ordinary for the Keys. When he got picked up an hour away in a bar fight, nobody would've cared."

Our Russian scowled. "This is very strange place."

I laughed. "Truer words . . ."

We spent some family time together on the deck before turning in for the night. Having gathered all the intel I thought we could glean from the island, an early flight back to St. Marys seemed like the next reasonable step in whatever lay ahead.

The early part didn't work out as well as I'd hoped. The gang insisted on Blue Heaven one last time for breakfast before mounting our trusty steed . . . or otter.

By the time we made it to the airport, the sun was high in the sky, and dark clouds threatened from the west.

Before I could ask, Gator said, "I already checked the weather. As long as we're out of here within the next hour and we stay east of Orlando, we'll miss the storms."

"In that case, let's load up."

On my way out of the FBO after paying for fuel and overnight ramp space, Bobby Gibson whistled from beneath a palm tree. I turned to see him motioning for me to join him, so I obeyed and strolled into the shade.

"Good morning, Bobby. Any luck with your Caravan?"

"It's an electrical gremlin," he said. "I've been chasing it for weeks, and I think it finally won. I'd like to get that mechanic's name from up in New Smyrna if you wouldn't mind."

I gave him Cotton Jackson's contact information and said, "Make sure you tell him I sent you. He's a busy guy, but he'll move you to the front of the line if you let him know."

He glanced across the tarmac, and the look on his face said he wanted more than just Cotton's number. "What is it?"

He kicked a palm frond and said, "I wanted to thank you again for yesterday. You know, for letting me use your plane and all."

"No problem. Like I said, I know how it feels to be broken down. I've got an airplane in the shop now that's been down for almost a year. It's not so bad for me, but since you use yours to make a living, it's a different story. Cotton will get you fixed up."

He dragged the frond through the sand with his toe. "There's one other thing, and I really don't know if I should say anything."

I took a half step closer. "What is it?"

He checked the ramp again and even leaned to peer around me. "That guy yesterday. Iggy. You know, the one who was telling you about what he saw out there."

"Yeah, what about him?"

He wiped his nose with the back of his hand. "It's just that he's got a reputation."

"What kind of reputation?"

Bobby let out a long sigh. "It's like this. He got in trouble a while back—the kind of trouble that should've put him away for a while—but he didn't do any time. He came back like nothing happened and went back to work running charters. It's just that he got a lot friendlier when he came back . . . talking to everybody and talking a lot, if you get my drift."

I took the half step back to ease the stress I had intentionally imposed on my new friend. "This trouble he got into, was it the local kind or bigger?"

"Bigger," he said. "A *lot* bigger. Did he tell you he used to run dope out of Cuba?"

"He did. And that struck me as odd. I wondered why he'd tell a complete stranger something like that. I figured he was just bragging to add credibility to his story about what he saw."

Bobby said, "You seem like the kind of guy who's been around enough to know what goes on down here, and I'm a guy with an airplane in the Keys. You can imagine the kind of offers I get. There's no shortage of guys who make a little extra money on square grouper or whatever needs to be moved, but it's weird for somebody to talk about it like Iggy does."

My stomach turned, and I stuck out my hand. "Thanks, Bobby. I appreciate the information, and I'll let Cotton know you'll be calling. Could I ask you for one more thing?"

He said, "Sure, whatever you need."

"Could you give me a call if you hear anybody asking questions about me or any of the guys with me? I don't want to get mixed up in anything, and it's nice to have a heads-up if trouble's on the horizon."

He pointed into the western sky. "You mean like those storm clouds?"

"Exactly like that."

I left Bobby under his tree and kicked myself all the way across the ramp for not picking up on the flashing neon signs over Captain Iggy's head.

Gator climbed us out to the northeast, being careful to avoid the airspace over the Naval Air Station. The sun-kissed sky was a little more turbulent than I liked, but something told me that was just the foreshadowing of things to come.

Mongo shot a thumb back toward the airport. "What was that little meeting about?"

I choked on the words I didn't want to say out loud, but I had no choice. The team had to know. "I got played, and I really stepped in it this time. Our job just got a lot harder than it already was. It would seem that good ol' Captain Iggy is a federal narc."

Chapter 19

I'm Your Girl

Back at Bonaventure, I slammed myself into my chair at the op center table. "I should've seen that coming. It was too easy. Everything fell right into place, and that never happens."

Mongo picked a pebble from the tread of his boot. "Stop beating yourself up. All of us should've caught it, but we took the bait, just the same as you."

Clark played with his toothpick. "I told you that you should've taken me with you, College Boy."

"You did not."

"Well, I may not have said it out loud, but you should've known it was implied."

"Yeah, that's you, the king of implication. How bad is it?"

He swirled the contents of his cup. "We don't know yet. We'll have to wait and see. If this Iggy character reports the contact to his handler, it may die there. If he's working for the DEA, they probably don't know anything about the Fitzsimon case, and they probably don't care. That's the best we can hope for."

Anya said, "This is not truth. We can hope Iggy tells no one, especially not his handler. That is best case."

Clark conceded. "I'll give you that one, but the chances of him not mentioning it are slim at best."

"How often do we deal in best-case scenarios?" I asked. "What if he reports it and his handler is a young, overly ambitious agent who can't wait to send it up the chain?"

"That would put a shoe of a different color on a horse in the bush."

I shook my head. "I'm pretty sure part of my brain just melted."

"You know what I mean," Clark said.

"This time, believe it or not, I do know what you mean, and I don't like it. I wanted to keep this thing covert as long as possible, but that's out the window. We have to tell the Triad."

"They already know," Clark said. "And they've got feelers out to see how far upstream the story floats."

Kodiak said, "Surely, they have some contacts at the DEA. Can't they quash the story there?"

"I don't think *quash* is a word," Clark said. "But sometimes, trying to shut down a story gives it even bigger wings. Some sharp-eyed analyst, like ours, might want to know why we're trying to kill the story and start digging. We don't need that."

I said, "What we need is to talk to Garland Fitzsimon again."

Singer adjusted in his seat. "What's that going to accomplish?"

"You still think he's possessed, don't you?"

"Demonic possession is real, and it's way outside my wheelhouse. I'll be honest. I think it's possible, and that's not something I'm willing to play with."

"Maybe you're right," I said, "but there's only one way to know for sure. We need to look him in the eye and talk to him like a human being instead of a caged animal."

"Are you talking about meeting with him face-to-face?"

"Not yet. We can still learn a lot through the glass. What are the chances of us getting permission to see him again?"

Singer said, "A hundred percent. I'm on the registry as clergy, and you've got Secret Service credentials. We can walk into that prison any time we want, but what are you hoping to see?"

I said, "It's not hope. It's a hunch. Skipper, have you had any luck getting access to the medication list?"

"Not yet, but I'm still on it. I've got a bot crawling the system."

I drummed my fingertips against the table. "I don't know what that means, but I trust you. If we're blown anyway, though, why don't we grab Dr. Plum and shake it out of him?"

Clark threw up a hand. "Easy. We're not blown yet, but we will be if you start manhandling the doctor."

"How about the warden?" I said. "I could have a little off-the-record chat with him and see what I can get him to spill."

"I don't hate it," Clark said, "but you can't go scorched earth. You have to be subtle."

I laughed. "A bulldozer just told a fox to be subtle."

"Oh, so you think you're a fox, huh?"

I said, "Compared to you, I am. I remember you describing yourself as a freight train on Main Street once."

He waved me off. "That was another lifetime. I'm just a little lamb these days."

Gator gazed at the ceiling, and his look caught my attention. "What's going on in that head of yours?"

He sighed. "I was just making a list of people who might be on our side in this thing."

"And?"

"Since we're concerned about our cover being blown, it might be a good idea to talk to some people who aren't likely to call the vice president when we start asking questions."

"Okay," I said. "Let's have your list of friendlies."

Gator pulled out his notepad. "I don't really have a list yet, but we could start with Fitzsimon's attorney. He's obligated by law to work in his client's best interest."

"Who else?" I asked.

He dropped his pad. "I guess it's a pretty short list."

Anya said, "There is one more person."

Everyone turned to the Russian, and she said, "Pat Fitzsimon."

"The grandmother?" I asked.

"Yes. She may not know all of truth, but she knows more than we do."

I let that potential interview play out in my mind. "You're right, but she's in WITSEC, if she's still alive. The chances of finding her—"

Skipper said, "Oh, ye of little faith."

I spun in my chair. "No way."

"*Maybe* way. I've been working on it. Patricia Marie Fitzsimon, born May first, nineteen forty-five. That would make her seventy-three now and, statistically, still alive. Like her grandson, she has a criminal record. She was arrested twice on minor drug charges—once for prostitution, and one drunk driving bust."

Gator said, "That's good info, but none of it gets us closer to finding her."

"What happens when you get arrested?" Skipper asked. "That's right. You get fingerprinted. What happens to those fingerprint records when a person goes into the Witness Security Program?"

The team sat in silence as Skipper continued. "Great question. Thanks for asking. The answer is, they go away. The old-school fingerprint cards on file with small-town agencies get confiscated by the Marshals Service. The same is true for DNA samples and records, if they exist. Those prints and DNA records get reassigned to the person's new identity in WITSEC. I just need a sample of the grandmother's DNA or her fingerprints."

I said, "Surely, it can't be that simple."

"Oh, it's not," Skipper said. "It's a ton of work, and it means committing a few dozen felonies, but if anybody can do it, I'm your girl."

Anya yanked her pad from the cubby, wrote a note in Cyrillic, and slid it across the table.

Нет. Я твоя девушка.

It took longer than it should have for me to translate the script, but I had to chuckle when the characters finally fell into place.

No, I'm your girl.

Some force I can't explain made me fold the paper in half and tuck it into my shirt pocket. A roomful of operators doesn't ignore details like that, so perhaps it was self-imposed guilt that prompted me to change the subject. "How about the lawyer? Have you found him yet?"

It felt as if Skipper's eyes wouldn't leave my shirt pocket. "Dylan Duncan. It looks like Dylan is a partner with Duncan and Miller in St. Augustine. It's a small firm doing *some* criminal defense, but mostly family law, from what I can dig up."

"I'm intrigued," I said. "Why would Fitzsimon end up with a part-time criminal defense attorney in a capital murder case?"

Skipper said, "Not sure, but you've got an appointment with Dylan Duncan, *Esquire*, at three thirty this afternoon to discuss a criminal matter."

"Thanks, I think. I guess that means I'd better come up with a plan on my way to St. Augustine. In the meantime, I want a DNA or fingerprint sample from Patricia Fitzsimon, and I don't care how you get it."

Skipper recoiled. "Are you talking to me?"

I motioned around the table. "No. I'm talking to them, on your behalf. If you're going to find Grandma Pat, we have to start somewhere."

Everyone stood, and I pointed at the only other person in the room who could read and write Cyrillic. "You're coming with me."

* * *

"This is not what I thought office of attorney would look like," Anya whispered.

We sat side by side in a pair of torturous chairs, in what barely qualified as a waiting area, inside suite six-A in the Ponce de Leon retail center, a strip mall a few blocks from the Old City of St. Augustine.

A lady in her mid-thirties stepped around what had clearly once been a retail clothing rack. "Mr. and Mrs. Fulton? Come on back."

Anya glanced at me with a smirk and whispered, "Is not lie. I can show to you driving license with name Ana Fulton."

"Just go," I said, "or this'll turn into a divorce case before we're even married."

We followed the woman into a small office, and she pointed to a pair of slightly more comfortable chairs. "I'm Dylan Duncan. Sorry to have kept you waiting."

I made a mental note to find a way to punish Skipper for failing to mention that Dylan wasn't a dude.

"No problem," I said. "I'm sure you're busy, so we won't take up much of your time. I'm Chase, and this is Anya."

"It's nice to meet you both." She slid a finger down a page of notes beside her keyboard. "You're on the schedule for a criminal consultation, so what can I do for you?"

I squirmed in my seat. "I'm afraid my secretary may have been a little misleading when she made the appointment. It's hard to find good help. I'm a writer, and I'm researching a case involving a client of yours named Garland Fitzsimon."

The muscles of Ms. Duncan's neck and jaws tightened, and she gripped her pen a little too aggressively. "I'm sure you know I can't discuss the details of any of my cases. Attorney-client confidentiality prohibits it."

"I understand, and I would never ask you to violate your ethics. I just have a couple of questions about the case in general."

She tugged at the shoulders of her jacket. "I'm afraid I'm extremely busy with clients who—"

"I understand," I said. "We're not asking for pro bono time, Ms. Duncan. We'll gladly pay your hourly rate. In fact, we may need your input as a legal consultant for the details of the book I'm working on."

The meager office gave the impression that Duncan and Miller were in no position to turn down a paying client, even if it meant skirting the edges of attorney-client confidentiality.

Dylan laid her pen on the legal pad resting beneath her hand. "In that case, we'll need to draft a client agreement and collect a retainer. Our consultation rate is two hundred—"

I interrupted. "Will ten thousand dollars be a sufficient retainer?"

She swallowed the hook and reclaimed her pen. "Yes, I think that will be sufficient. You may consider yourselves clients of Duncan and Miller."

Anya and I exchanged smiles as if we'd just won the drawing for the day's door prize. "Thank you, Ms. Duncan."

"Please call me Dylan. We don't get hung up on formality around here. Now, what exactly is it you want to discuss?"

I pulled my pad from my attaché. "As I mentioned, we're doing some research for a potential project, and Mr. Garland Fitzsimon is one of the possible topics of the story. May I ask how you came to be involved in his case?"

Down went her pen again. "I can't discuss specifics, of course, but I'll tell you what I can. I was an associate at a firm in Jacksonville, not long out of law school at the time. I happened to be in court on a completely unrelated criminal matter the morning Mr. Fitzsimon was arraigned, and the judge assigned me to be his court-appointed attorney."

"Is that common?" I asked.

"Unfortunately, it is. The public defender's office is swamped up there, and private-practice lawyers are often assigned indigent defendants and paid minimal fees to provide the defense all of us are entitled to. It's not much money, but for a small firm, it can be enough to keep the lights on, barely."

Anya frowned. "You are forced to do this?"

Dylan grimaced. "Not exactly forced. If we can prove we have other caseloads that would prevent us from providing adequate representation, we can be excused, but it's all part of practicing trial law in Florida."

I said, "So, you ended up being Fitzsimon's attorney. Had you ever tried a capital murder case prior to that one?"

"Heavens, no, and I've not tried one since. I spend most of my time on DUI cases and divorces. The most serious criminal case I've tried since Mr. Fitzsimon was a vehicular manslaughter case. In case you care, I won that one."

"Congratulations. So, are you representing Mr. Fitzsimon for his appeals?"

"Appeals? There are no appeals when a defendant takes a plea deal."

"A plea deal?" I asked. "I thought he was convicted of aircraft piracy, aggravated stalking, and felony murder."

"That's right. In the state of Florida, a plea is entered as a summary judgment of guilty. It's the same as a conviction without a trial."

I asked, "Did you encourage him to take the plea deal?"

Dylan stood, stuck her head into the hallway, and closed the door before returning to her seat. "We're off the record here, and this is absolutely off the table for your book, but that was the stupidest plea deal in the history of criminal proceedings. Any sober, second-year law student could've gotten him off if that case had gone to trial. He didn't have any memory of committing the crime, and he wasn't faking it. He had no idea what he'd done."

I stiffened to hide my surprise, but the look on the lawyer's face said I'd failed.

She said, "You don't know the truth of what happened in that case, do you, Mr. Fulton?"

Chapter 20

A Dangerous Man

Anya squeezed my hand, and I got the message loud and clear. We'd just taken an enormous stride forward, and I had to solidify our footing on the new ground. I pulled a checkbook from my case, wrote the retainer, and slid it across Dylan's desk. "Now, we're your clients."

The attorney slid the check into her drawer. "Welcome to the family. Where would you like to start?"

"I want you to tell me everything you can legally and morally share about Garland Fitzsimon."

She lifted the phone from her desk. "Do I have any more appointments this afternoon?" She waited for an answer and said, "Good. That can wait. I'll be with the Fultons for the rest of the day. Please don't interrupt us unless the building is on fire again."

I said, "As much as I'd love to hear the fire story, let's talk about Garland Fitzsimon."

She pulled three bottles of water from a tiny refrigerator behind her and passed them out. "Okay, writer. Get your pen ready. You're not going to believe this one."

I took a sip and situated myself to take copious notes. Little did I know I'd learn more than I could've hoped for before my pen even touched the paper.

Dylan said, "As I told you already, I was assigned the case as Fitzsimon's court-appointed attorney. I was in over my head, and even though I was nervous, part of me was excited about the case." She seemed to consider the limits of what she could say before continuing. "Every defendant claims to be innocent, and Garland was no different in that respect, but his way of denying responsibility was different."

"How so?" I asked.

She grimaced. "It was as if he had no idea what I was talking about. He seemed to have absolutely no memory of committing the crimes he was accused of, and I believed him. No one is a good enough actor to pull that off as well as he did."

I studied her face carefully for any signs of deception, but there were none. She seemed bewildered as she replayed the events in her mind before sharing them out loud.

"Of course, we scheduled a psychological evaluation to determine if he was mentally competent to stand trial. I know, most people believe all violent criminals are mentally ill, but that's not what I mean. The man I interviewed didn't deny any of his previous criminal activity. He was open and blunt about it. He even admitted to starting the fight in the bar that got him arrested in Islamorada."

"So, what did you think was going on with him?" Anya asked.

"Honestly," she said, "I thought it might be some kind of trauma-induced amnesia. There's a name for it, but I can't remember what it's called."

I said, "You may be thinking about lacunar amnesia."

She snapped her fingers. "That's it. I remember now. It's often caused by a stroke or severe injury and eliminates the victim's ability to remember a specific event or series of events, right?"

"That's right. Such a condition could prove to be quite convenient for a defendant."

She laughed. "Wouldn't it, though? But as I remember, it's almost impossible to prove, and even harder to get an expert witness to testify to such a diagnosis. None of that mattered in this case, though. We never got that far."

"You never had him examined?" I asked.

"Oh, no. We had a psychiatrist examine him, and he had some mental deficiencies, but nothing that would prevent him from standing trial. In talking with the doctor, I learned that he also believed Garland's absence of memory of the event. Unfortunately, just because you can't remember doing something doesn't mean you're not guilty."

"Did the psychiatrist have any thoughts on the possibility of lacunar amnesia?"

"He's the one who brought it up, but he wasn't willing to stick his neck out far enough to make a formal diagnosis."

"I understand," I said. "What did you mean when you said you never got that far?"

She held up a finger. "Before we go there, let me tell you one more strange element. Garland kept asking me about his grandmother. He wanted to know if she was all right. So, of course, I tried to find her, but she vanished into thin air. I know that sounds impossible, but—"

I said, "We know about the grandmother, and what you're saying makes sense."

"Then maybe you could explain it to me."

"You'll have to read the book."

"Anyway, when I told Garland about his grandmother being impossible to find, he was relieved. Of all things, he was happy about his own grandmother disappearing." She took a sip of her water and said, "Completely off the record, I have to admit that the thought crossed my mind that maybe he'd done something with his grandmother."

Anya frowned. "You thought your client killed his own grandmother?"

Dylan waved both hands. "No, nothing like that. I thought maybe he'd gotten somebody to move her away from Florida so she wouldn't have to hear about his trial."

I sighed. "You may not be as far off base as you think with that theory, but please continue."

She said, "A capital murder case is a complex undertaking. I had a couple dozen pre-trial motions that I planned to bring before the judge, and I was preparing those motions and briefs when I got a call from the jail about a visitor who came to see Garland."

"Is that routine?" I asked. "Does the jail usually tell the defense attorney about visitors?"

"No, but I made some friends down there, and one of them gave me a call because, as she put it, something didn't seem right about the whole thing."

I was hanging on every word, but she pushed away from her desk. "Hang on a second. Let me pull the file."

"You've got the case file?" I asked.

"Sure. Even though I was with another firm at the time, Garland was still my client, so I retained a copy of his file."

She left the room, and Anya leaned toward me. "Do you have guess?"

"Yep, and I bet it's the same as yours."

When Dylan returned, she opened the file and thumbed through the contents. "Okay, here it is."

She slid a printout of a grainy photograph across the desk. "This is a picture my friend at the jail took with her cell phone of the guy who came to visit Garland. It's not great, but you can see his face. He signed in as William Scott and had a driver's license in the same name, but when I ran the license, there was no record of it."

I swallowed the lump in my throat as I stared down at the photograph of Gregory McDonald, special assistant to the deputy chief of staff to the vice president of the United States.

"You know who he is, don't you?"

I looked up at the lawyer. "Maybe."

"What do you mean, maybe? You either know who he is, or you don't."

I said, "We'll come back to that, but tell me what happened next."

"The prosecutor proffered a plea agreement—twenty to life for a guilty plea to the three counts you already know."

"And Garland took it," Anya said.

Dylan slumped in her seat. "He took it, but I begged him not to. Like I said, a second-year law student could've gotten him off or pleaded it down to five years as a worst-case scenario. It was ludicrous for him to take the deal the prosecution offered, but nothing I said or did could convince him to go to trial or even negotiate a better plea deal." She drank the last of her water and checked her watch. "Well, that didn't take as long as I expected."

I lifted my attaché from the floor beside me. "We're not finished."

I produced three printed photographs of Gregory McDonald walking into the supermax. "Your client's mysterious visitor is still visiting."

She stared at the photos as if someone had just pulled the rug from beneath her feet. "Who is this guy?"

"Trust me, you don't want to know."

"Oh, that's where you're wrong. I've wanted to know who he is since the second my friend called from the jail." She pulled my check from her drawer and slid it back across the desk. "If you tell me who he is, you can keep this."

I held up a hand. "You'd better hold onto that. I have a feeling we're going to burn through it pretty quickly if you're willing."

"Who is he?" she demanded.

"His name is McDonald, and he works for the federal government. That's all I can say right now, but I'll tell you everything as soon as I can . . . on one condition."

"What condition is that?"

"You're still technically his lawyer, right?"

She nodded, and I said, "Then I want you to get a judge to order the release of your client's medication list from the supermax. We need to know what they're shoving down his throat."

Dylan leaned back in her chair. "You're not writing any book, are you? This is something else."

"You're my lawyer, too, right?"

She slid the check back into the drawer. "Yes."

"Good. How long will it take to get the medication list?"

She waved a finger. "No, no. You're not getting off that easy. What's really going on here? I'm not going to be a pawn in a game I don't understand."

I said, "The truth is that I'm researching a criminal case that may be ongoing, and your client just might be the victim in that case. Whether or not that research results in a book is irrelevant."

She said, "It's two-fifty an hour. I can file the writ this week and probably get in front of a judge within ten days. What are they doing to my client, Mr. Fulton?"

"That's exactly what I want to know as well."

She bit her lip and stared back at me. "How is he?"

"Garland?"

She nodded, and I said, "Not good. That's why we need you to get the med list. Is it possible to get a blood sample to compare against the list of meds?"

The hesitance in her eyes turned to intrigue. "It depends on which judge I get, but maybe."

"I need you to try, and I'm perfectly fine with you doubling your hourly rate for anything you do on this case. If it turns out the way I expect, you're working for two clients on this one."

She said, "I'm starting to get the impression that the client in my office is far more dangerous than the one locked up at the supermax."

I tapped a finger against the pictures of Gregory McDonald. "If I'm right about this, I'm only dangerous to this guy and the people he works for."

Chapter 21
Not Cool, Chase

I fell in love with the Columbia Restaurant during my first visit to St. Augustine and never missed an opportunity to revisit my old favorite.

Anya took in every inch of the courtyard and brilliant interior. "This is beautiful place."

I held up two fingers to the hostess. "Just wait 'til you taste what comes out of the kitchen."

"Chase? Is that you?"

I looked up to see an old familiar smile. "Elizabeth? You're still here."

The woman wrapped her arms around me and leaned back as if conducting an inspection. She said, "You look amazing. How have you been? *Where* have you been?"

A glance at Anya made it clear what my next words should be. "Elizabeth, meet Anya. Anya, this is Elizabeth. She makes the best tableside mojitos you've ever had."

They shook hands. "Is nice to meet you, Elizabeth. You know my Chasechka."

"Well, I don't really know what that means, but I knew this guy a long time ago."

I said, "I met Elizabeth the first time I came here almost twenty years ago. She's an amazing waitress."

She blushed. "Thank you, but not anymore. I'm the front-of-the-house manager now."

"Congratulations. I hope you passed your cocktail skills along to the next generation."

She laughed. "Nobody will ever do it like me, but they're learning. Come on, I'll find you a great table."

Anya slid her hand into mine in an age-old ceremony I called 'peeing on your tree.' The territorial marking ritual never failed to amuse me.

Elizabeth led us to a table overlooking the courtyard. "Last time you were here, you beat up that pervert in the parking lot, and if I remember correctly, there was some drama with a nun."

"Wow, that was a long time ago," I said.

Anya cocked her head. "I must hear this story. But first, where is restroom?"

Elizabeth directed Anya toward the ladies' room and slid onto the seat next to me. After a glance across her shoulder, she said, "Oh, my gosh. It's amazing to see you. What's with the hot foreign chick, and what happened to Penny? What did you do?"

I took a long breath. "Penny passed away two years ago. It's a long story, and Anya, well, she's an even longer story." I pulled out my phone and brought up several pictures of Pogonya. "After Penny died, I learned Anya and I have a daughter together—from before I was married, of course."

Elizabeth yanked the phone from my hand. "What? She is gorgeous. How did you not know?"

Anya returned and glanced at the screen. "This is Pogonya. She is *our* daughter."

"Chase was just telling me about her. She looks so much like you. She's beautiful."

Anya took her seat and smiled. "Yes, she is. Thank you."

Elizabeth stood. "I'm really sorry to hear about Penny. I always loved her."

"Thanks. It was tough, but we have to move on."

"You're right about that. What can I get you guys to drink? Mojitos?"

"Not for me, thanks. I don't drink anymore, but—"

Anya said, "I would love to try mojito."

Elizabeth hurried toward the kitchen, and Anya asked, "She is old girlfriend, no?"

I laughed. "Not hardly. She's just a friend I met here a long time ago. I've actually never seen her outside this restaurant."

"Oh, good. She is too young for you, and she did not give to us menus."

"We don't need menus here."

"This is very strange place."

Elizabeth reappeared with a glass of water for me and her mojito cart. "You'll have to bear with me. It's been a while since I've done this, but I think I still remember how." As if she'd never missed a day, she put on the same brilliant show of creating the pitcher of mojitos and poured one for my date.

Anya lifted the cocktail. "I think I have never had mojito."

I slid a stick of sugar cane into my mouth and watched the Russian try her first sip.

"Oh, is very good. Thank you."

Elizabeth took a little bow. "You're quite welcome. It's nice to know I've still got it. You don't want menus, right?"

I shook my head. "No, of course not. You've never let me down."

Anya continued sipping her drink, and I refilled her glass from the bright blue pitcher.

I said, "Cool place, huh?"

She inspected a stick of sugar cane before carefully tasting it. "Yes, is very cool, but I still do not understand about having no menu. Other people have them."

"Trust me. We're not *other people*, and I promise you'll love it."

She said, "Lawyer was interesting, yes?"

"Very. I just hope she can get a judge to order that blood test for Fitzsimon."

Dinner began with the famous 1905 Salad tossed tableside, followed by Shrimp Al Ajillo. Every bite was as unforgettable as the first time I discovered the Columbia.

A server cleared our salad and appetizer plates, refilled my water, and said, "The main course will be out soon."

I watched him walk away, and my attention fell on a woman sitting three tables away behind Anya. She was eating what appeared to be chicken on the bone, but she was eating it with her fingers instead of a knife and fork. The woman seemed enraptured by every bite, as if no one else were in the room. Although not glamorous by any measure, she was beautiful with delicate features and a blonde ponytail draped over her shoulder.

"Chase. Chasechka. Are you okay?"

I flinched. "Yeah. I'm good. Sorry. I was just—"

"You were someplace else with very strange look on face. Are you sure you are okay?"

I traced a fingertip between the knuckles of Anya's left hand. "I'm fine. This is nice."

"You are thinking of Penny, no?"

I closed my eyes. "No, I was thinking about the case."

"This is new thing for you to say. We have always only *mission*, never *case* until this one."

I said, "I guess I haven't really thought about that. This one just feels like a case to me. We're not working our way toward a gunfight."

"Are you certain of this?"

I was drawn back to the woman eating chicken from the bone. Something about her left me wanting to know more about her. She was alone, but the white button-down she wore was clearly made for a man. The look was confident and unconcerned.

Anya squeezed my hand. "You are doing it again. Tell to me what you are thinking."

"Sorry. I . . . it's just . . ."

Elizabeth's arrival with a massive tray saved me. "Here you go, guys. You're going to love this. Pompano en Papillot for Ms. Anya. It's fillet of pompano stuffed with shrimp, crabmeat, artichoke, butter, and white wine. The rice alone is to die for." She slid the plate onto the table and turned back to her tray. "And for you, Chase-catch-ka, or whatever she called you, Lechón Asado. It's a garlic-and-citrus-marinated pork shoulder, slow-roasted and served with black beans and rice, yuca, and extra plátanos, because I know how much you love them."

I pulled my plate close. "Everything looks amazing. Thank you."

"My pleasure. Let me know if there's anything else you need. My little brother, Michael, will take care of you if I'm busy."

Anya took Elizabeth's wrist. "Before you go, may I see menu, please?"

"Uh, sure. Do you not like pompano? Oh, my gosh. You don't have a fish allergy, do you?"

"No, is nothing like that. I love fish. I made for Chase fish stew on sailing boat first time we were . . . together."

More tree pee, and it made me laugh.

"Oh, okay, sure. Just a second."

Elizabeth retrieved a menu and slid it onto the corner of the table. "Let me know if you'd prefer something else. I'm usually really good at . . ."

Anya smiled up at her. "No, this is perfect. I want to make plan for next visit."

Before opening the menu, she took her first bite and let out a sensual sigh that left me wishing I had the pompano.

"It certainly sounds like you're enjoying it."

"Is wonderful," she said as she flipped open the menu.

I tried my first two bites while Anya perused the list of delicacies. "Mine is delicious, too. Want a bite?"

She leaned forward. "I do."

I slid a bite of pork into her mouth, and she closed her eyes as she savored the taste. "Oh, that is wonderful. Why have you never brought me to this place?"

"I guess we've just never had the opportunity. If I remember correctly, the last time you were in St. Augustine, you got arrested by the feds."

Her shoulders sagged. "Yes, that was very bad night."

"So, what's with the menu?"

She said, "I wanted to make test inside mind. If I had menu, I would have probably ordered this dish. How is it possible Elizabeth could know this?"

"It's her superpower. I've probably been here a dozen times, and I've never seen the menu. She always gets it right, and it's always something new."

Anya frowned. "She does this also with other people?"

"I guess so. It's part of why I love this place. It's like a psychic dinner."

She giggled and dived back into her pompano and mojitos as white-shirt-and-ponytail caught my attention again. This time, the woman caught me looking, but I didn't turn away. She smiled, licked the tips of her fingers, and turned back to her dinner.

Anya startled me with a forkful of fish an inch from my lips. "You must try."

I did, and she was right. "That's fantastic."

"We must come here again soon. Is my new favorite restaurant."

A well-dressed man with his tie pulled loose appeared at the woman's table and took a seat across from my new "friend." The look on her face and the glance at her watch told the whole story, and I watched the man try to explain his tardiness. At some point during the conversation, the woman seemed to surrender. She slid her hand into his, and I felt a stab of jealousy pierce my gut.

What am I doing? I'm sitting across the table from one of the most beautiful women on Earth and checking out somebody else. Not cool, Chase. Not cool at all.

Since the moment Penny died, I hadn't looked at another woman —not even Anya—with the slightest hint of desire or interest, and I couldn't understand why the woman in the white shirt had been the one to flip the switch inside my head.

"They have also dessert?"

My attention was suddenly back where it belonged, and I discovered Anya's plate to be completely empty.

"Yes, they have dessert," I said. "And it's just as good—or better—than the main course."

"Does Elizabeth do also psychic trick for dessert, or do I get to choose?"

"Let's play a game," I said. "Take a look at the menu and make a selection, but don't tell her. Let's see if she can guess."

Anya snatched the menu. "I like this game. She will not guess correctly. I am sure of this."

She helped me finish my pork shoulder, and a young man showed up to clear our plates.

"You must be Michael," I said.

"Yes, sir. Elizabeth wanted me to tell you that your dessert will be right out. Would you like coffee?"

Anya set her jaw, and I said, "Yes, please."

When Michael left, Anya whispered, "She will be wrong."

"What did you pick?"

She spun the menu toward me, and her finger landed on one of my favorites.

Michael arrived with coffee, and Elizabeth was hot on his heels. "I took a flyer, but I think I might be on the money."

She slid a plate onto the table in front of Anya. "Guava Turnover Carmita. It's guava and melted sweet cream cheese baked in this perfect flaky pastry with crystallized sugar and vanilla bean sauce."

Anya slammed the menu closed. "How do you do that?"

Elizabeth shrugged. "It's sort of my thing. And, of course, white chocolate bread pudding for Chase."

We left plenty of cash on the table, hugged Elizabeth, and walked our way through the Old City back to our Suburban still parked in front of the attorney's office in the shopping center.

I opened the door for Anya, but she glanced around the hood of the SUV. "I must go inside store for one moment. You will be fine here waiting for me, yes?"

Spontaneous shopping wasn't one of the Russian's habits, so I was intrigued. "Sure. Take your time. I'll be right here."

I climbed behind the wheel and started the engine at the same instant my phone chirped.

"Hello, this is Chase."

"Hey, it's Shawn. How'd it go with the lawyer?"

"Good, I think. Any luck on Grandma Pat's DNA?"

"Probably not, but we've got some fingerprints."

"How'd you pull that off?"

He said, "Our old buddy in Ponce came through. Gator flew us over here, and Jay-Dub took us to what was left of Pat's trailer. It was a disaster area, so we didn't find anything we could use. But remember the volunteer fireman who found Garland at the fire station?"

"I remember the story," I said.

"It turns out that Jay-Dub knows the guy. I'm pretty sure he knows everybody, but that's beside the point. He took us to the guy's house, and he had an old photo album in a box from when he used to date Pat's daughter. There must be a hundred pages of pictures, and the fireman said that, as far as he knew, Pat was the only person who ever put a picture in the book."

I said, "That means it's full of her fingerprints. Did you lift any?"

"Not yet," Shawn said, "but we've got the book. I figured it would be best if we let Dr. Mankiller do the forensic work."

"Great thinking. We'll be on our way home from St. Augustine in a few minutes."

Shawn said, "We just landed, so I'll get the book over to the doc's lab. It'll be late by the time you get here, but we'll see you in the morning. Breakfast?"

"Sure. Tell the rest of the guys to meet us at the diner at eight."

"We'll be there," he said. "Oh, and Chase."

"Yeah?"

"Jay-Dub told me to tell you 'duh-huh.' He said you'd know what he meant. Do you?"

"No idea," I said, "but I think it's funny."

"See you in the morning."

I hung up, and my favorite Russian came through the door of the boutique with her hair in a loose ponytail and wearing a man's white button-down. She had the bottom of the shirt tied in a knot just above her jeans, and I immediately felt like the jerk I was.

Chapter 22
A Solid Ruling

Anya climbed onto the passenger's seat and turned to face me. "You like?"

I've spent very little time in my life being speechless, but that was one of those rare moments when I could think of nothing to say that would improve my position. Anything that came out of my mouth would only serve to dig my hole deeper than I'd already dug.

She leaned across the console, stroked my arm, and kissed my cheek. "There was mirror behind you inside restaurant. You are terrible spy."

"I'm sorr—"

She pressed a finger to my lips. "Do not be sorry. Be better."

The quip gave me the break I needed to let myself off the hook. "I know. Still, I'm sorry. I shouldn't have—"

She pressed her finger against my lips for a second time. "You are not only terrible spy, but also apparently bad psychologist, too. You have no reason to be sorry. You should know what happened tonight, and you should know why I am dressed like this. Is permission."

"Permission?"

"Yes, of course, silly boy. Is permission from yourself to feel what you felt when pretty woman smiled at you. You will always love Penny, but she is gone. Do you believe she would want you to forever be alone without her?"

I had to smile. "Maybe."

Anya joined me. "Okay, maybe is true. She was little bit possessive, but you are wonderful man. Is perfectly understandable she would be this way."

"I do like the white button-down," I admitted.

She glanced down at herself. "I am maybe prettier than woman inside restaurant?"

"You're maybe prettier than everybody else on the planet."

She giggled. "This is not true. Our daughter has this award."

"Okay, I'll give you that one, but you're a close second."

She squeezed my hand. "I am not pushing, but I think you know I am here waiting for you, just like I have been for many years."

* * *

Time, they say, passes at a measurable, constant rate, but *they* never spent time as a covert operator. Dr. Celeste Mankiller lifted over a hundred prints from Pat Fitzsimon's scrapbook, and Skipper's computer churned away, prowling the electronic world for matches.

"How long is this going to take?" I asked.

Skipper huffed. "Would you please go find something to do? It could take an hour or two hundred hours. It's not like we're the FBI searching the federal database. I could do that in twenty minutes, but this isn't the same. We're looking for somebody the feds are trying hard to hide. It's going to take a while."

I abandoned the op center with no destination in mind other than finding someone else to prod. I chose the library as my destination and Dylan Duncan, attorney at law, as my target.

"Duncan and Miller," the cheerful receptionist said after two rings.

"Good morning. This is Chase Fulton. Is—"

"Oh, good. I'm glad you called, Mr. Fulton. This is Melanie. I'm Ms. Duncan's paralegal."

"Hello, Melanie."

"Hey. So, I was planning to call you this morning. Ms. Duncan filed the petition for Mr. Fitzsimon's medical records and a blood and urine sample with the court, and Judge Mays has her on the docket for an in-chambers hearing tomorrow afternoon."

"What does that mean?"

"It basically means the judge will listen to our argument and make a ruling privately from her chambers instead of in open court."

"Will the judge issue a ruling during the hearing?"

Melanie said, "It's impossible to know, but maybe. Judge Mays is pretty efficient, and she's not a political animal. She makes solid rulings that actually make sense."

"We could use a few thousand more just like her. Should I be there for the hearing?"

"Oh, definitely not. You aren't a party to the petition. Ms. Duncan is representing the continued interest of Mr. Fitzsimon."

"I see. Will you let me know as soon as the judge makes a ruling?"

"Definitely. You'll be the first person we call. That's actually one of the reasons I was planning to call you today. Ms. Duncan wants to know what we should do with the blood and urine samples if the judge rules in our favor."

"We'll test them against Garland's medical records to verify the medication they claim to be giving him."

She said, "Yes, of course, but do you have a lab in mind to conduct the testing?"

"Oh, sorry. I thought you were asking what to do with the samples in general. Yes, we have our own lab, and we'll do the testing. If it's possible to acquire two sets of samples, that would be great. We'll conduct the tests in our lab, and we can have the results independently verified by a second lab if it becomes necessary."

"I'll pass the information along to Ms. Duncan, and I'll be in touch as soon as we hear from the judge."

"Thanks, Melanie."

Singer stepped through the door of the library when I hung up the phone.

He said, "Got a minute?"

I motioned to a wingback. "Sure, come on in."

He parked himself in the chair and wasted no time getting to the point. "So, how are you? And don't give me the casual 'I'm fine' business."

"Honestly," I said, "I'm consumed by this case. I can't stop thinking about it, and I don't know why."

"We can all see that, and it's out of character for you. You seem to be eating this incoming fire all by yourself, and that's not what good teams let their leaders do."

I leaned back and let his accusation wash over me. "You know what? You're right, and we'll fix that. There's something else I want to talk with you about first, though."

"Send it."

I spent ten minutes describing what happened in the Columbia Restaurant with the woman three tables away and with Anya afterwards. I expected a spiritual consultation and some deep, thought-provoking insight, but instead, he said, "I think Anya's right. Mourning Penny is important. You have to go through that process, but two years is long enough. It's time to be Chase again instead of Chase the widower."

"That's it?"

He said, "I can make it more complicated if you want, but that's what it boils down to. We need our leader back, and you need yourself back. All of us deserve that Chase instead of the Chase we've had for two years."

I held up a finger. "Hold that thought."

With the press of a button, I had Skipper on the line two floors above our heads.

She said, "I thought I told you to go bother somebody else."

"I am, I promise. It's Singer at the moment, but I'm about to spread the love. I need you to find Dr. Plum, the psychiatrist from the supermax."

"Too easy. I just sent his dossier to the whole team's phones and tablets. I'm running an active track on his cell phone, as well as the GPS in his car. I can tell you where he is at any moment."

"What would I do without you?"

She laughed. "Drink too much and accomplish nothing meaningful."

"The question was rhetorical."

"Not for me, it wasn't. See ya!"

Singer and I assembled the team at the shoot house, and I briefed my plan.

"With any luck, we'll have medical records along with blood and urine samples from Fitzsimon within a couple of days. I expect the files and samples to disagree with each other. When that happens, this becomes a tactical operation, and we need to be ready for it."

We spent the rest of the day burning ammunition, pouring sweat, and becoming brothers again. Anya, of course, wasn't left out of the brotherhood. When the fight begins, she'll always be one of the boys, but Singer wanted to make sure.

When the training broke up, he stayed behind and tossed me a bottle of water. "Let's finish our conversation from earlier."

"I thought we already finished it," I said.

"If it's all right with you, let's do each other a favor and consider our conversations never truly finished."

I swallowed the contents of the bottle. "I'm good with that. What's on your mind?"

He tossed a pebble into the river. "It's about Anya."

"What about her? She did well today."

"She always does well. I'd go to war with her by my side any day. The team and I just need to know that you feel the same way."

"What do you mean? Of course I feel the same. She's one of the best operators alive."

He said, "Nobody's questioning that, and nobody's going to be surprised when the two of you end up, you know . . . together."

"Slow down," I said. "We're a long way from anything like that."

He tossed another stone. "I think you're not seeing the forest for the trees. We all see it. You're the one who's not looking. A relationship between the two of you is inevitable, but we need to know that your head is going to stay in the game if she goes down in a fight."

It was my turn to toss a pebble. "Of course my answer is yes, and I want it to be the truth, but until it happens, I can't swear I won't look at her differently."

He laid a hand on my back. "That's exactly the right answer, my friend. Anything else would've been a lie. Chivalry ain't sexism."

"You're just *full* of wisdom today."

He hopped to his feet. "Full of wisdom and all sorts of other stuff. Thanks for playing with the boys today. We needed that."

"We're not finished," I said. "Let's continue in the morning."

* * *

It took thirty-six more hours and a few thousand dollars' worth of ammunition, but my phone finally rang.

"Hello, this is Chase."

"Mr. Fulton, it's Dylan Duncan. I hope I'm not interrupting anything."

"Not at all. I've been waiting for your call. Has the judge made a ruling?"

"She has, and we won . . . for now."

"What does that mean?"

"It means somebody doesn't like us messing around with the Fitzsimon case."

"Can you break that down for me?"

She said, "Judge Mays ordered the release of the records, as well as blood and urine samples. She actually ordered four sets of samples, but somebody immediately filed for a temporary injunction in federal court to halt the collection of samples and release of records."

"Who is this somebody?"

"We don't know yet, but we will soon. The request for injunction was filed in the U.S. District Court for the Northern District of Florida, which has jurisdiction in Madison County, where Fitzsimon is being held. The Florida Department of Corrections has five days to comply with Judge Mays' order."

"I'm not a lawyer, Ms. Duncan, so I need you to make it simple for me."

She sighed. "Quite simply, it means that if the prison has something to hide, they're going to drag their feet and not provide the records and samples until the very last minute. Depending on which federal judge they get, it's possible the injunction hearing could take place tomorrow and halt the release altogether."

"What can we do to force the prison to comply with the judge's order quickly before the injunction hearing?"

She said, "I can go back to court and ask for an acceleration order, but with pending federal litigation, it's a waste of time."

"So, you're saying there's nothing we can do, right?"

"There's nothing we can legally do other than wait for the federal judge to hear the case. With any luck, he or she will dismiss the claim and allow Judge Mays' order to stand."

"I'm not a fan of relying on luck, Ms. Duncan. My checkbook is open. Do something."

"As much as I appreciate that, this isn't a matter of writing checks. It's a matter of waiting and watching."

I hung up and immediately dialed the op center. "You're still tracking Dr. Plum, right?"

Skipper said, "Of course."

"Outstanding. We're going to have a little chat with the good doctor and convince him to comply in a timely manner."

"Comply with what?" she asked.

"A solid ruling that actually makes sense."

Chapter 23

Just Pretend

My team and I had been in position for almost two hours by the time the sun rose over Dr. Brian Plum's rented property a few miles north of Madison, Florida. The rural setting made the perfect stage for our performance, and I was determined to make an impression the overworked doctor would not soon forget.

One of the few luxuries the doctor allowed himself while he was working, primarily to have the state of Florida pay off his crushing student loan debt, was his Mercedes-Benz C-Class sedan. He backed the gleaming car from the garage and turned in the widened driveway, just as he did every morning on his way to the prison and into the world that seemed to weigh on him like a torturous press he couldn't overcome.

The twin reports of the sniper rifles echoed through the air as Singer and Gator surgically placed rounds on each front tire of the doctor's posh ride. The warning lights on the dash held Plum's attention as I opened the rear door and slipped onto the seat behind him. A loop of 550-cord across his head and around his neck was enough to send his attention away from the dash and into the rearview mirror.

"Sorry to disappoint you, Doc," I said through my balaclava, "but you really don't want to see my face. If that happens, I'm afraid I'll have to cut off your head."

"What do you want?" Plum demanded.

"I just want you to do what the court ordered you to do."

He jerked and bucked against the cord. "What are you talking about?"

"Let's not play dumb, Brian. It's beneath you. You know exactly what I'm talking about. You'll release the records and blood and urine samples this morning before doing anything else."

"Who are you?"

I pulled the loop tighter. "I'll be happy to tell you, but they'll be the last words you ever hear. Is that what you really want?"

As his face turned red, he pawed at the cord. "Okay, okay, but I can't give you what you want."

I wrapped a second loop over his head and pulled again. "You're the only person who *can* do it."

He choked against the pressure. "You don't understand. The warden—."

I pulled hard enough to silence his protest. "I don't care about the warden. I care about what you're pumping into Garland Fitzsimon. You have two options. You can tell me now, or you can provide the samples. Pick one."

His face bloomed bright red, and panic filled his eyes, so I eased my pull enough to give him one breath.

In a move I anticipated long before he mustered the courage to attempt it, he threw both hands over his head in a desperate grab at my face. I released the 550-cord only long enough to cuff both of his wrists behind the headrest with my favorite pair of black Smith & Wesson handcuffs.

"Nice try, Doc, but I'm a lot better at this than you. So, let's hear it. What are you giving him?"

He struggled against the restraints and the cord I was again pulling hard enough to keep him uncomfortable. "I've got two thousand patients. You can't expect me to remember the meds of every one of them."

"I don't care about the others. Just Fitzsimon."

"I'm telling you. I don't know."

With a handful of his hair in my left hand, I directed his attention through the windshield. "Focus on that shiny Mercedes emblem out there. See it?"

He tried to nod, and the crack of Singer's rifle echoed an instant after the emblem vanished from the tip of the supersonic rifle round.

I shook his head. "My sniper is over a thousand yards away, and with one word from me, he can put the next round through your right eye without splashing a single drop of blood on me. Does that help your memory?"

He broke. "Why are you doing this?"

"You know exactly why we're doing it. Now, talk."

"He's likely on the same cocktail as most of the psychotic inmates in the country. I'm sure he gets quetiapine and probably clozapine."

"Why the combination?"

"I don't know about the meds for sure. I'm just guessing. But Fitzsimon is an extreme case. He has to be controlled."

"Controlled," I said. "We don't use drugs to control inmates in this country. We use drugs to treat their conditions."

He let out a guttural groan. "Grow up. How much time have you spent around murderous psychopaths?"

"How do you know there's not one in the back seat of your car, Doctor?"

"Kill me if you want," he choked out, "but it won't change anything. If you think I make the decisions about what goes into inmates like Fitzsimon, you're delusional. I'm just the guy with the FDA number."

I eased the pressure and unlocked one of the handcuffs. "If you were feeding Fitzsimon quetiapine and clozapine, he'd be a zombie, not an animal."

"Just tell me what it is you want," he said with a submissive tone.

"I want a blood sample from Fitzsimon."

"How am I supposed to do that?"

"That's not my problem. When you leave the prison today, you'll have the blood sample with you, or you'll never see another sunrise."

He groaned. "I don't have that kind of access."

I removed the other cuff and slipped the 550-cord from his neck. "Okay, leave the prison this afternoon without my sample, and tonight we'll feed what's left of you to the sharks off Jacksonville. And tomorrow, we'll find someone who does have that kind of access. Have a good day, Doctor."

As quickly as I'd appeared, I was gone, and Dr. Brian Plum was left likely questioning every decision he'd ever made and making the most important one of his life.

Eight minutes later, my team was huddled inside a Suburban, watching video of the doctor pacing back and forth with his phone pressed to his ear.

"Don't worry," Skipper said through the sat-com. "He's calling the auto club to come change the tires."

He made a second call to the prison to notify the warden that he'd be late, and Skipper's tap on his cell let us hear every word. His tone was solid enough to avoid suspicion.

Mongo said, "Sounds like he's still going to work."

"He better go," I said. "Otherwise, we're out of options at this point."

The service truck arrived, and a mechanic had both front tires changed in minutes. That gave the team and me eight hours to kill while we waited, and Skipper continued tracking the doctor.

* * *

The trapping maneuver would've been easier with three Suburbans, but we weren't dealing with a trained tactical target. Kodiak accelerated around the Mercedes a half mile north of Highway 90. Barely clear of the front bumper, he jerked the wheel to the right and hit the brakes. Gator moved in on the rear bumper of the car and angled to prevent Dr. Plum from backing out of the trap.

Singer and Shawn dismounted ahead of me and trained their rifles on the doctor, through the glass, as I pulled my balaclava across my face for the second time in one day. I pulled the rear door handle with my gloved fingertips, but it didn't budge, so Shawn tapped his muzzle against the windshield.

Plum got the message and pressed the button to unlock all four doors. I slipped inside and pressed my pistol to his skull. "No cord this time, Doctor. Just a bullet if you don't hand me a test tube full of Fitzsimon's blood in the next three seconds."

He pointed toward his case lying on the passenger's seat. "It's in there."

I switched my pistol into my left hand and reached across the seat with my right. "By the way, we have Fitzsimon's DNA profile, so if the blood doesn't match, there's going to be a school of very happy sharks off Jacksonville Beach."

I retreated from the car and pulled open the case. Two glass vials of what appeared to be blood rested inside, so I pocketed them and tossed the case back into the car. "Relax, Doc. You did good. If you didn't screw us, you'll never see or hear from us again, but if you're trying to pull a fast one, this is your last chance to come clean. Trust me, you don't want us to show up again."

Dr. Plum squeezed the steering wheel. "It's his blood. I drew it myself."

"Good. You can go live your life now and forget any of this ever happened."

We backed away and disappeared before the doctor could react, and I said, "We've got it, Skipper. Jam the phone."

She said, "It's already done, but he's not trying to make any calls."

"How about his dashcam?"

"I shut it down before he backed out of his garage this morning. You guys are in the clear. Now, get back here so we can put that blood in Celeste's hands right away."

Gator and I leapt from the Suburban and into the waiting helicopter, with the blood samples tucked away in my bag. I played the role of passenger while Gator built more time at the controls. He grew more confident in the chopper with every passing minute.

We beat the Suburbans home by almost an hour, and Gator touched down on the ramp in front of the hangar that Celeste converted into her state-of-the-art laboratory. I climbed out and trotted inside.

Just inside the door, our mad scientist waited with outstretched hands, and I surrendered the goods.

"How confident are you that it's really his blood?" she asked.

"I told Dr. Plum we had Fitzsimon's DNA profile, and he didn't flinch, so I'm pretty sure it's authentic."

"We'll know soon."

"How soon?"

She said, "I'll have the chems run in a couple of hours, but the DNA will take quite a bit longer. That process isn't as simple."

"Let me know as soon as you have the chem panel. I've got some calls to make."

She disappeared into her lair, and I headed for Bonaventure.

The phone rang five times before a hurried voice said, "Duncan and Miller."

"Melanie?" I asked.

"Yes, who's calling?"

"It's Chase Fulton."

"Oh, hey, Mr. Fulton. You barely caught me. I was headed out the door."

I said, "I won't keep you. I just wanted to check on the status of the case."

"Nothing new. The Department of Corrections still hasn't released the file or the samples, but we didn't expect them to. The injunction hearing is set for tomorrow morning at ten. Dylan—I mean, Ms. Duncan—will be there, but federal court is different. She probably won't get a chance to make a full argument."

"I don't know what that means, but would it make any difference if we had an unofficial blood sample and complete chemical analysis?"

"What? How could that happen?"

"Just pretend it happened. Would the results make any difference in the hearing?"

"I'm just a paralegal, but I'd have to say no. There's no way the results would be admissible. You don't really have a sample, do you?"

"Have Dylan call me in the morning before she leaves for federal court, will you?"

Melanie said, "I'll tell her, but . . . how did you get a blood sample?"

"I don't know what you're talking about. I didn't say I had a sample. I just said pretend."

Chapter 24

Our Demon Hunter

"Chase, wake up! I found her!"

I opened only one eye, just in case it was a dream, but Skipper standing at my bedroom door and waving a sheet of paper forced my other eye open.

"Found who?"

"Pat Fitzsimon. Well, her name is Marge Baker now, but I found her."

I sat up. "Unless you want to see a naked one-legged man, you may want to turn around."

"Ooh, thanks for the warning. I'll be in the op center. I could send Anya up. I'm sure she'd—"

"Get out!"

After a quick shower, installation of my prosthetic, and a couple of layers of clothes, I stepped into Skipper's lair. "Are you sure it's her?"

She spun in her seat. "Do you want me to shoot you in the face? How dare you ask such a question? Of course I'm sure. She's in Sedona, Arizona."

I poured a cup of coffee and rolled a chair beside the analyst. "Am I allowed to ask *how* you found her?"

She waggled both hands above her keyboard. "Magic fingers, baby. Well, that plus the supercomputer you paid for."

"It's worth every penny."

"You have no idea," she said. "It was the fingerprints. She screwed up and let herself get arrested and booked before the U.S. Marshals could intervene. I would've found her anyway, but that little mistake made it a lot easier."

"Nice work. What is she doing in Sedona?"

"Living out her days in a retirement village called Western Wind. Original, huh?"

"Quite. So, I guess I'm headed to Arizona."

She said, "I wouldn't recommend that yet unless you've got a plan I don't know about."

"My plan is to ask her how she wound up in Sedona."

Skipper said, "The Marshals will cut you off at the knees—well, the knee—before you get through the door."

"That's hurtful."

She rolled her eyes. "Deal with it. Oh, hang on. That's Celeste calling."

She punched a button. "Good morning, Dr. Do-Little."

Our technical services officer laughed. "That's me. I'm just resting on my laurels over here, whatever laurels are. Do you know if Chase is out of bed yet? I tried calling him, but he didn't pick up."

"I'm here, Celeste. *Someone* yanked me out of bed, so I forgot my phone downstairs."

"That sounds interesting, but not as interesting as what I found in Garland Fitzsimon's blood. It is *his* blood, by the way."

"What did you find?"

"In addition to the barbiturates we expected, I found massive—and I do mean massive—amounts of a synthetic amphetamine of sorts."

I leaned back in my chair. "It looks like you just found our demon."

Dr. Mankiller said, "I've had a lot of titles in my career, but I've never been a demon hunter."

"You can add that one to your résumé," I said. "Can you narrow down the chemistry to a specific manufacturer?"

"Funny you should ask. I'm working on that right now, and I'm coming up empty. Teva Pharmaceuticals manufactures the most common prescription amphetamine salt combination under the name Adderall. I'm sure you're familiar, but that's definitely not what this is. The compound doesn't match any of the generic manufacturers' formulas either. This is something special."

"Special how?" I asked.

"If you really want to geek out on the chemistry, come down to the lab and I'll show you."

I said, "I wouldn't understand it even if you drew me a map, but stay on it. I want to know exactly what it is and who created it. I'm pretty sure I know who's delivering it."

She said, "Your delivery boy isn't getting it on the commercial market. I assure you of that. The FDA would never approve whatever this stuff is."

"If the source is who and what I suspect, they don't need a commercial source."

She said, "That might explain a couple more things that don't make sense."

"Don't leave anything out. I need to know everything you know about what's in that blood."

She groaned. "I hesitate to mention it because it could be a false positive, but I picked up extremely trace amounts of two substances that resemble trimethoxy phenethylamine and lysergic acid diethylamide."

"I don't know what either of those things are."

"Yes, you do. On the street, they're called mescaline and LSD."

"Wait a minute! LSD? You can't be serious."

"That's why I didn't mention it at first. The chemistry isn't identical to either of those drugs, and it's definitely synthetic. I'll need several more hours to isolate the compounds and analyze them completely."

"You said they're similar in composition, right?"

"That's right, but as I said, without closer analysis, I can't say with certainty what either compound is."

"Nice work. Stay on it, and let me know as soon as you figure out what else is in his system."

"You got it," she said, and the line went dead.

Skipper laced her fingers together on top of her head. "Well, that's interesting. Why would they dose him with uppers, mescaline, and LSD, on *top* of the sedatives? What were they called? Quetiapine and clozapine?"

I tapped out a rhythm on my thigh. "I don't know yet, but I intend to find out. What time is it?"

Skipper glanced at her monitor. "Almost eight, why?"

I stood. "I'm expecting a call from the lawyer, so I need to grab my phone. Do you want or need anything?"

"Some sleep."

"How long have you been awake?"

She shrugged. "What day is it?"

I pulled her chair away from the console. "Go to bed. There's nothing about this case that's important enough for you to be awake around the clock. I need you sharp."

"Chase, stop it. I've got too much work to do."

"Take the next twenty-four hours off. I mean it. This thing is going to get nasty, and when it does, you can camp out right here, but for now, take care of you so you can take care of us later."

She huffed. "Fine, but call me if anything happens."

"No. I absolutely will not, and *you* will turn off your phone. If the world stops turning without you, I'll have Gator wake you up. Otherwise, you're off duty."

After securing the op center, I collected my phone and opted out of waiting for the attorney's call. Melanie, the paralegal, was right. Nothing we found in Fitzsimon's blood could be used in court, and our chances of coming away from a federal courtroom with a victory were minuscule at best. But I still wanted the bug in Dylan Duncan's ear, just in case she was given the opportunity to make even a partial argument.

"Duncan and Miller."

"Good morning, Melanie. It's Chase Fulton."

"Great timing, Mr. Fulton. Ms. Duncan just walked in. Hold on a sec."

Dylan picked up. "Good morning, Chase. How's it going?"

"Not bad. Have you had a chance to talk with Melanie about our conversation from last night?"

The lawyer said, "Briefly. She said something about pretending to have a blood sample. What's that about?"

"It's all hypothetical, of course, but let's say I acquired a sample of Fitzsimon's blood and had it analyzed by an extremely reliable laboratory. And let's say that lab came back saying that in addition to the sedatives Fitzsimon is supposed to be on, he's also being given synthetic amphetamines and possibly mescaline and LSD."

"Did such a lab produce such findings? Hypothetically, of course."

"It did."

"Do I want to know how you hypothetically acquired the supposed blood sample?"

"You do not," I said. "But hypothetically, the sample matches Fitzsimon's DNA profile exactly."

"Who are you, Chase Fulton?"

"Just a bloodhound of a writer sniffing out an interesting story for a manuscript."

"Right, and I'm Ruth Bader Ginsburg."

I said, "Good luck in federal court this morning, Your Honor."

"There's no such thing as luck in federal court, and I can't use anything you've told me."

"I still thought you should know. Call me when you get out of court, will you?"

"Of course, but don't expect good news."

"I never do," I said.

With the call complete, I headed for my thinking place. I actually had three such places: the gazebo, the library, and my absolute favorite of all . . .

Penny's Secret was a 1944 North American P-51D Mustang that I inherited from my mentor—and Anya's father—Dr. Robert Richter, the greatest psych professor who ever lived. Although not that particular airframe, he'd flown Mustangs over Europe during WWII, including a close air support mission for the D-Day invasion, during which he was shot down and rescued from the waters of the English Channel.

My Mustang had worn the nose art of a stunning Russian brunette—who happened to be Anya's mother—above the moniker *Katerina's Heart*, but after I slid the old warhorse down the runway in a cloud of smoke, dust, and airplane parts, she was reborn under the skilled hands of Cotton Jackson and christened *Penny's Secret*.

The twelve-cylinder Rolls-Royce supercharged engine belched to life and loped its signature tune as I taxied away from the hangar. It had been far too long since the Mustang and I had shared any quality time together, but that was about to change. We thundered down the runway and into the calling sky. I cranked in trim as my right leg trembled from the pressure I applied to the right rudder pedal to overcome the incredible torque of the massive engine and propeller.

Eleven thousand five hundred feet over the Atlantic, with airspeed approaching three hundred fifty knots, I put the airplane and myself through our paces. *Penny's Secret* barely noticed the stress I put on her, but my body felt every tug, twist, and turn. Flying a machine like the Mustang to the limits of her ability requires concentration and absolute attention to every detail; however, in cruise flight with the wings and nose level, the warbird was as docile as a kitten. And that's when I let my brain go wherever it goes when I need it to answer questions I'm not smart enough to understand.

It has to be Gregory Rod-Man McDonald, right? He has to be the one delivering the drugs, but why? Why do that to an inmate they could easily kill and no one would care? Why is Garland Fitzsimon, a small-time criminal, so important to the vice president of the United States that he'd have an underling keep him drugged out of his mind? What could Fitzsimon possibly know that would drive the Washington elite to such lengths? What are they hiding? No! Not, what . . . who! Who are they protecting?

I banked hard and shoved the throttle forward. With the nose pointed directly at St. Marys, I thumbed the Bluetooth switch on my headset, connecting my phone to the Mustang's intercom.

Clark answered before I heard the first ring. "What's up, College Boy?"

"Do you know how to set up a video conference call with the Triad from the op center?"

"Yeah, sure. Just tell Skipper to do it."

"I ordered her to take the day off. She's been killing herself on this mission, but I need a secure line to the bosses. I think I've got it figured out."

"Got what figured out?" Clark asked.

"The Fitzsimon situation. Not all of it, but it's a cover-up, and I think I know who they're shielding."

He said, "I'll meet you in the op center, and we'll figure it out. Where are you, anyway? It sounds like you're in a hurricane."

"It's no hurricane," I said. "I'm riding a wild Mustang, and I'll be there in half an hour."

Chapter 25

Smokin' in the Boys' Room

There's nothing easy about landing a Mustang. They were built to fly and fight, not roll down the runway, but I got lucky and greased the landing. A great landing in the Mustang is always a gift from above, and I took it as a good omen of things to come. Even in my haste to get to the op center, I wouldn't neglect my prized possession, so I wiped down the fuselage of oil and grime from the engine and exhaust. The old girl was beautiful, but she was messy. When her bath was finally finished, I tucked her in, right where she belonged, and draped the cover over everything except the engine, which still had an hour or more before it would be cool enough to wrap up.

I expected to find Clark alone in the op center when I made my way through the door, but to my surprise, the table was full. The whole team, including Skipper, was waiting for me.

"I thought I ordered you to take the next twenty-four hours off," I said when Skipper's eyes met mine.

"Gator woke me up because the world was about to stop turning. Now, do you want to argue or brief the Triad?"

"Both," I said. "But we'll temporarily postpone the fight you're going to lose."

"That's what I thought," she said. "The Triad is standing by. Are you ready?"

Clark jumped in. "Maybe it'd be a good idea to let the rest of us in on what you think you figured out before you start spitballing with our bosses."

"Just let me do the talking," I said. "You boys in the band can watch me for the chord changes and try to keep up. Fire it up, Skipper."

The three faces of our directors filled the monitors, and I said, "Sorry to call you unannounced, but I need you to know what's happening in the Fitzsimon mission."

Anya rustled in her seat, and I noticed but didn't respond.

General Michaels said, "Don't apologize. That's why we're here, Chase. What's going on?"

I briefed the acquisition and testing of Fitzsimon's blood, as well as the legal battle and injunction hearing.

General McFarland said, "Do we know for certain that such a combination of drugs in the prison system is unusual?"

I said, "I don't have a baseline other than my knowledge of pharmacology and Dr. Mankiller's opinion."

"Is it possible that some of the drugs that appear in Fitzsimon's system are contraband? We all know prisons are full of things that aren't supposed to be there. I think it's a little early to accuse the Florida Department of Corrections of dosing an inmate when it's possible, and maybe even probable, that Fitzsimon acquired the drugs inside the prison, either from crooked correctional officers or other inmates."

I slumped in my seat. "I hadn't considered that."

My phone chirped, and I glanced at the screen. "This is the attorney."

"Well, answer it," McFarland said. "I'm sure we'd all love to hear what she has to say."

I thumbed the button. "Hello, Ms. Duncan. You're on speaker."

"Speaker with whom?"

I stumbled. "Uh . . . my agent and publisher. You know, the bosses."

"Okay, well, I'm sorry to say that it went exactly as I expected. The judge ordered the injunction, so we're not getting blood, urine, or medical records anytime soon."

"So, where does that leave us?" I asked.

"It leaves us exactly where we were yesterday. With nothing."

"Can we appeal?"

"Sure, but you'll have to write a much bigger check. As much as I'd love to spend your money, I'm afraid we'd just be hitting our heads against the wall. There's no way we'd ever get this case in front of the Supreme Court, and short of that, we're dead in the water."

I glanced up at the monitor to gauge the Triad's reactions. All three of them were huddled together, apparently whispering to each other.

I said, "Okay. Thanks, Dylan. I'll give you a call this afternoon to discuss what to do next."

She said, "I just told you there is no next."

"There's always a next," I said. "It just may not be in the same direction we started. We'll talk soon."

General McFarland said, "I get the impression you haven't told us what this call is really about yet, so could you get to the point?"

"Certainly, General. When all of this began, Isaiah Lamb, the priest, mentioned the nuncio. Are you familiar?"

Dominic Fontana took the floor. "Chase, it would be wise to be very careful about what you say and do next. If you're about to accuse the Diplomatic Corps of the Vatican of being involved in the murder of intelligence operatives, you're going to call down lightning and thunder from on high."

"I'm not accusing anyone of anything yet. I'm just asking questions. I think there was a deal going on that somebody on a high throne didn't like, and that somebody used a nobody named Garland Fitzsimon to break it up."

"But why?" General Michaels asked. "Why wouldn't that person or people use operators like you to kill the deal, so to speak?"

I said, "I don't have an answer for that yet, but we'll figure it out by the time all of this is over. In the meantime, I plan to question the priest again and get him to elaborate on his theory of how any or all of this ties to the nuncio."

The general waved a hand. "Then do it. You don't need our permission to conduct your mission, Chase. We're not hall monitors. We're facilitators."

"Thank you. I also want to talk with Fitzsimon's grandmother."

General McFarland said, "I'm afraid there's not much we can do to help you in that regard. If she's in WITSEC, even we can't pierce that veil."

"We've already torn the veil to shreds, General. We know exactly who and where she is."

Dominic smiled and leaned toward the camera. "Like the General said, we're not hall monitors, Chase. You don't need to raise your hand and ask permission to go to the bathroom. Just don't get caught smokin' in the boys' room."

"How about the nuncio?" I asked. "When I make a connection there, do I need permission shake the Pope's diplomatic tree? That's who I think is being protected in all of this."

"The Pope?" General Michaels asked.

"Well, ultimately, I'd say yes, but I was thinking more specifically about the Pope's ambassador or nuncio."

"Tread lightly, and be prepared for some serious fallout if you shake that tree too hard," McFarland said. "The things that fall out of that particular tree hurt when they hit you in the head."

"Fallout doesn't scare me."

McFarland narrowed his gaze. "It probably didn't scare those four intel officers on that boat in the Florida Straits, either, but look what happened to them."

"I'm glad you brought that up," I said. "Can you pull any strings to get me the names of three guys who didn't wash up with part of Fitzsimon's ear in their bellies?"

"We can try," General Michaels said, "but we can't make any promises."

I said, "I understand. In the meantime, I think I'll make some inquiries about what drugs are floating around on the black market inside the supermax."

"Call us if you need us," Dominic said, and the monitors went black.

Clark huffed. "Yeah, you definitely should've briefed me on that before the call. You can't just start accusing the Vatican of being involved with four murders."

"I didn't make that accusation. As far as we know for sure, there was only one murder. The other three guys may not have walked back into the real world, but that doesn't mean they're not still out there doing whatever they were discussing on the boat that night."

"Okay, run with that if you think it's a bone you can carry."

"I like that one," I said. "It actually makes sense for once. Let's have a little get-together. Gator, I want you and Singer to fetch the priest."

Gator said, "You got it. When?"

"Have him here tonight. Shawn and I need the chopper, though, so you'll have to pick him up in one of the Suburbans."

Singer said, "We could take the Otter. There's an airport not far from the monastery."

"That's fine. I don't care how you get him here, but the SEAL and I are headed back to Madison for another visit with our favorite prison psychiatrist."

I turned to Anya. "And what was that little thing you did in your seat when I told the Triad my theory?"

She said, "You are very observant, but so am I, Chasechka. You stopped calling this a *case* and is now *mission*."

"I guess you're right. The gloves are coming off. It's time to do some bareknuckle boxing."

* * *

I walked through the high-security door into Dr. Mankiller's lab and found the scientist dipping a banana into a jar of peanut butter. "That looks disgusting."

She scooped a dollop onto the banana and held it toward me. "It's great. Have a bite."

"No thanks. How's the blood analysis coming along?"

She devoured the snack and screwed the lid back onto the jar. "I was right about the trace compounds. They're definitely *almost* mescaline and LSD."

"Almost?"

"The compounds are nearly identical to what you could buy on the street, but they're cleaner. Nobody cooked them up in a high school chemistry lab. Somebody knew exactly what they were doing."

"Is there any way to trace them back to a manufacturer?"

"I'm working on that now," she said. "And if my hunch is right, you're not going to like the answer."

"Let's hear this hunch of yours."

She licked a tiny smear of peanut butter from the tip of her finger. "Have you ever heard of a government program called MKUltra?"

"It rings a bell, but I don't know the specifics."

She motioned toward a stool. "Have a seat. You're about to hear a science teacher give an American history lesson."

I settled onto the stool, and Shawn propped against the corner of a table as Celeste began.

"MKUltra was a program the CIA began in the nineteen fifties. It was highly illegal and even more unethical. At the foundation of the program was the belief that certain drug combinations could be administered in adequate doses to make a person do unthinkable things —the kinds of things that person would never be capable or willing to do otherwise. Think of it like an ultimate soldier scenario. Take a normal person and turn him into a killing machine with absolutely no conscience. They were trying to create temporary psychopaths out of normal, healthy people."

I said, "Yeah, I remember now. They conducted those tests on a bunch of people who didn't know they were being used as guinea pigs, right?"

"That's right," she said. "Tens of thousands of them. They used inmates as one of their primary sets of test subjects. They used CIA officers, students at several universities across the country, and even soldiers. It's one of the worst things our government has ever done."

"What happened to the program?"

"President Ford finally shut it down in the seventies, when some senator whose name I can't remember discovered it and started peeling back the layers."

I said, "You're not suggesting that MKUltra is still going on behind the scenes, are you?"

"I'm just telling you about my hunch. Mescaline and LSD were two of the primary drugs they used in the experiments, and the CIA created the drugs in their own lab. That work was done by some of my predecessors in the technical services branch way back then."

Shawn unperched himself and pointed toward Celeste's workbench. "Are you telling us the drugs you found in Fitzsimon's blood came from a CIA lab?"

She bit her lip and hesitated before saying, "Again, it's just a hunch. I'm still running analysis, but I have access to the baseline formula the CIA lab used during MKUltra. Don't ask me how I got it, but if I'm right, I'll tell you within twelve hours if the same formula was used to create the drugs in Fitzsimon's blood."

I ran my fingers through my beard. "This thing just keeps getting messier by the minute. Can you give us a printed report on what you found in the blood?"

She stepped to her computer, and after a few clicks of the mouse, the printer produced a single-page report.

I read through it and folded it in half. "It's all Greek to me, but we're headed out on a little field trip to see just the guy who'll understand every word."

Chapter 26
Lawyers, Guns, and Money

When Dr. Brian Plum pulled his gleaming Mercedes with four brand-new tires into his garage and then stepped from the car, Shawn slipped from the shadows and slammed the car's door behind him. The doctor turned to see the SEAL, his face hidden behind a balaclava identical to mine, and he sighed. "Not again."

I lifted the briefcase from Plum's hand and said, "Remember me?"

"What do you want this time?"

I said, "Let's go inside and have a little chat. No handcuffs, no garrotes, just three grown-ups—two of whom are capable of unimaginable violence—having a nice, cordial conversation."

The doctor motioned toward the door, and we followed him into the kitchen. From my limited vantage point, the house was clean, neat, and almost empty.

"It must get lonely out here all by yourself, huh, Brian?"

He pulled out a barstool and took a seat. "Thanks to you guys, it's not as lonely as it used to be."

I unfolded the lab report from Dr. Mankiller and slid it in front of him. "Give that a read and let me know what you think."

Dr. Plum pulled a pair of reading glasses from his pocket and lifted the report. Half a minute later, he removed the glasses and dropped the paper. "May I have my briefcase, please?"

I lifted the case from the floor and laid it on the counter. "Sure, but I think I'll open it. We wouldn't want you pulling a pistol on us. That would ruin the rest of your night and leave us with a terrible mess to clean up."

"Come on. I work in a supermax prison. Do you really think I carry a pistol in my briefcase?"

I popped open the latches. "I like your attitude, Doctor. You seem to have accepted that we're part of your life now."

He said, "If you had any idea of the hell that is my life, you'd understand why you guys are a breath of fresh air. There's a file in the top section marked 'Case Study.'"

I slid the folder from the partition and laid it in front of the doctor.

He flipped it open. "This is Fitzsimon's medical record since he's been at the supermax. His current prescription list is on page three."

I pulled the file in front of me and flipped to the third page. "I see quetiapine and clozapine, as well as olmesartan for blood pressure, but there's nothing here about the other substances we found. Care to take a stab at how the amphetamines, mescaline, and LSD got into his system?"

"Look, I've got a year and a half left with the state, and I'll be debt-free. If you get me fired, or worse, I will have wasted over eight years of my miserable life for nothing. I've given you everything you asked for. Can you please just leave me out of this . . . whatever it is?"

"The drugs, Brian. Where is Fitzsimon getting the drugs that showed up in his blood?"

He ran a hand through his hair and pointed to a cabinet. "At least let me have a drink."

Shawn opened the cabinet and pulled out a glass and a bottle of Jim Beam. He poured the doctor a double and slid it across the countertop.

Dr. Plum killed the drink and slid the glass back for a refill.

Shawn capped the bottle. "Answer the boss's question first."

Plum said, "The Adderall makes sense. That's easy to get inside. It's everywhere, but not the others. Who did the lab work?"

I smiled behind my balaclava. "Nice try, Doc. Are you saying the mescaline and LSD aren't floating around in your prison?"

"First, it's not *my* prison. And second, no, I've never seen either of those drugs show up, but . . ." He planted his face in his hands, and I motioned for Shawn to pour another.

The SEAL played bartender again and slid the glass toward the doctor.

"But what?" I asked.

He swallowed the bourbon and slammed the glass back onto the counter. "Those damned priests!"

"What about the priests?"

"They came in there and did their little Broadway production, calling it an exorcism."

"Wait a minute," I said. "Are you telling me the Catholic church sent a priest to exorcise a demon inside the supermax?"

"Yeah, yeah," he said. "It was the most ridiculous thing I've ever seen."

He grabbed the lab report from Dr. Mankiller. "Here's your demon right here."

I said, "Hold on. The priest who did the exorcism—was it Father Lamb?"

"No, it wasn't Lamb. He's the only one of them with any sense. It's easy to get cold and cynical when you live your professional life inside a prison like I do. I expect everybody to have an agenda, but Lamb is different. I'm not a religious guy, but he's the real deal—a true believer, for whatever that's worth."

"Let's get back to this exorcism. How many times have you seen that happen while you've been at the supermax?"

"That's the only one," he said. "Technically, it's a religious ceremony, and the inmates have a right to what the state calls Sacred Observance."

"So, you don't believe in demons?"

"Of course I believe in them. I live with eighteen hundred of them every day of my life, and I'm supposed to see to their mental health. If exorcisms worked, I'd become a priest instead of a psychiatrist, for God's sake."

I slipped Dr. Mankiller's lab report into Fitzsimon's medical file and tucked it beneath my arm. "You won't see us or hear from us again, Dr. Plum. I hope you survive the rest of your sentence. I have a feeling you would've been better off paying your student loans yourself."

He reached across the counter for the bottle in front of Shawn. "You're right about that. I don't know who you are or who you're working for, but for what it's worth, I don't think Fitzsimon murdered anybody."

I froze in place. "Why's that?"

He poured his own third drink. "Think about it. I look murderers in the face every single day. I've been Fitzsimon's psychiatrist since the time he showed up at the supermax, and I'm telling you, he's not a killer."

I stepped toward the door, and Plum pointed at the file beneath my arm. "None of that's admissible, you know. And I can't testify."

Shawn stepped back. "We're not building a court case, Dr. Plum. You've heard the old phrase, 'Send lawyers, guns, and money'? We're the guns."

* * *

When Shawn and I made it back to Bonaventure, I was happy to see Father Isaiah Lamb sitting in the gazebo where we'd first met.

"Welcome back," I said as I settled into my preferred Adirondack.

"Thank you. It's nice to be back. The monastery is a beautiful place, but I was called to serve, and I can't do that behind those walls. Everybody there is already a believer. I belong out here in the real world where sinners and saints collide."

I said, "It's not always easy to tell the difference in today's world."

He laughed. "You're right about that. I assume that since you called me back, you've made some progress and maybe you need my help."

"I don't know if it's technically considered progress, but we're now certain Garland Fitzsimon isn't possessed. Did you know about the exorcism?"

He screwed up his face. "What exorcism?"

"Dr. Plum, the prison psychiatrist, said the church sent a priest to perform an exorcism on Fitzsimon."

He slid forward in his seat. "I don't think that happened, but if it did, it wasn't sanctioned by the Vatican. Priests don't just run around performing exorcisms without the blessing of the Holy See."

"I'm just telling you what the doctor told us."

"When did you see him?"

I checked my watch. "Two hours ago. And he gave us this." I handed the medical file across the cannon. "The first page is the lab results from Fitzsimon's bloodwork. We ran it ourselves. The rest is his medical record from the prison."

The priest thumbed through the pages. "This doesn't make sense. How did those drugs end up in Fitzsimon's blood if they're not in his medical record?"

"Beats me," I said, "but I'm going to find out. That's not why you're here, though. I need to know about the connection with the nuncio. You mentioned him the first day we met, but you never elaborated."

Isaiah said, "A nuncio, as I'm sure you know, is an ambassador to a country from the Vatican. Father Leonardo Vincetti is the nuncio to the United States. Have you heard of him?"

I shook my head, and he continued.

"Most people haven't. He's not a Jesuit, so he has great ambition for advancement within the papal hierarchy. We Jesuits don't seek recognition or advancement. Father Vincetti is of an entirely different mindset."

"Keep talking," I said.

"He and Archbishop McDonald are contemporaries and friends. You may remember the archbishop is the one who had me sanctioned, and if he has his way, I'll likely be excommunicated."

I said, "That feud is between you and McDonald. I need to know how the nuncio ties to Fitzsimon's case."

"It's supposition on my part, but it's based in personal observation and a little ungodly snooping on my part. The lifestyles of Archbishop McDonald and Father Vincetti changed dramatically when Fitzsimon went to prison."

"How do you know?" I asked.

"As I said, personal observation and amateur detective work. The archbishop's salary is one hundred ninety thousand dollars per year, plus a stipend for housing, transportation, and meals."

"That's nothing to sneeze at."

"No, it's a very comfortable living, but if you'll do a little digging, you'll find that the archbishop owns well over two million dollars' worth of oceanfront real estate. It's in the name of a corporation, of course, but it's his."

"And the church isn't paying for the real estate, I assume."

Isaiah said, "No, the church doesn't do that—not even for archbishops."

"So, what about Vincetti?"

"His salary is slightly less than Archbishop McDonald's, but I suggest snooping into his financials as well. I don't have the resources you do, but I was able to find bank accounts and real estate well in excess of ten million dollars, also in corporations under Father Vincetti's control."

"Where's the money coming from?"

"I don't know, but if it were legitimate, they wouldn't make an effort to hide it in corporations."

"There are tax advantages to holding assets under a corporate structure."

Isaiah smiled. "Perhaps in your world, but these men are clergy and a foreign diplomat."

"Ah, I see. That *is* a different story."

He said, "I can't prove anything sinister, but it certainly doesn't look good. It may be a total coincidence, but both McDonald and

Vincetti had almost no financial net worth prior to Fitzsimon going to prison."

"We'll look into it. By the way, we found the grandmother."

"You can't be serious."

"She's in Arizona. Wanna come?"

He stared back at me with total disbelief. "How did you find her? I thought she was in the Witness Protection Program."

"It's actually called Witness Security, and she is, but we're very good at what we do."

"And you plan to just walk up and introduce yourself? What are you going to tell her?"

"I don't know yet, but I'll think of something. I was actually thinking an introduction from a Jesuit priest might be a good place to start."

He closed his eyes and whispered softly for a moment before crossing himself. "Of course I want to come. When are we leaving?"

"Tomorrow, if we can find a ride."

Chapter 27
You Wouldn't Understand

Isaiah and I climbed the gallery stairs and made our way into the kitchen just as Anya pulled a pan from the oven. "I made for you chocolate chip cookies. Is your favorite, yes?"

"How did you know?" Isaiah asked.

The Russian giggled. "I was talking to Chasechka, but I am also happy that you like cookies. These are chewy and do not make crunch."

"Perfect," Isaiah said. "Just how they should be."

I reached for one, but she slapped my hand away. "You will burn fingers on pan, silly boy. I will bring for you on plate. You would like also milk, yes?"

Domestic Anya was a new creature in my life, and she made me nervous. "Sure, milk sounds good. Is everything okay?"

I don't know if Eastern Europeans are taught to look stern as children or if it's somehow interwoven into their genes, but a sincere smile from a Russian woman is a rare treat, and Anya's was my favorite.

"Yes, of course, everything is fine. I just wanted to make for you cookies. You have had long day."

Still uneasy, I continued through the kitchen. "We'll be in the library. I have to find us a ride to Arizona tomorrow."

With the Russian Betty Crocker behind us, I led Isaiah to the library.

"I like this room," he said as he slid a hand along the shelf of an ornate bookcase. "It's beautiful. I love books, and you have quite the collection."

I took a seat. "You should see Singer's collection of Bibles. He has an original King James Version printed in sixteen twenty-nine on the same press that printed the very first KJV."

"I'd love to see it. Do you think he'd let me?"

"Of course he would," I said. "He has it locked away in a dark, airtight case, but I've seen him pull on the white gloves and take it out several times."

The priest said, "There's an original Gutenberg Bible at the Vatican, but I've never seen it. Someday, I'd like to."

"Singer would tell you it's just a book."

Isaiah raised both eyebrows. "Singer would be terribly wrong about that."

"Hear me out. He says the Bible is the greatest love story ever written, but the true value is the love itself, not the ink and paper. And that having Christ alive in us is the treasure, not the leatherbound earthly volumes."

Isaiah took a seat. "In that case, I'd have to agree with him. You're lucky to have him in your life, Chase."

"It's not luck, Padre. I'll always believe God sent that man to me. I would've fallen away from everything that matters a long time ago without him."

Anya came through the door with a plate of still-steaming cookies and two glasses of milk. "I hope you like."

We took the goodies, and I said, "I'm sure they're delicious. Thank you for doing this. I've known you for twenty years, but I never knew you could bake."

"Is new thing for me. Perhaps someday maybe I will be housewife with apron and recipe books."

I chuckled. "I'd like to see you in an apron."

She gave me a wink that said more than I would be comfortable hearing her say in front of a priest. "I have airplane you bought for me. You do not have to search for other ride to Arizona."

"This is a business trip. We shouldn't put the hours on your plane when we can use company assets."

She said, "Everything that is mine is also yours, Chasechka. Take airplane. I will even fly for you if you would like."

Isaiah looked back and forth between Anya and me. "You two have an interesting dynamic."

"Is something maybe you would not understand since you are celibate priest."

He blushed. "Well, I didn't mean to . . ."

I tried to save him. "Thank you for the cookies and for the offer of your airplane, Anya. It's very kind of you, and I'll take you up on both."

Another rare Russian smile appeared. "Good. What time shall we leave?"

"How about eight?" I asked, glancing between the priest and the pilot.

In perfect unison, they both said, "Great."

When Anya closed the door on her way back to wherever she was going, Isaiah asked, "Are the two of you . . ."

I said, "Not yet, but probably."

"I see. Okay, so, about Garland's grandmother. How did you find her?"

"Skipper did it, thanks to a little help from Jay-Dub in Ponce de Leon. You remember him, don't you?"

"Oh, yeah. Who could forget Jay-Dub? I have to tell you, if I weren't a priest, I think I'd like to work with you."

I waved him off. "Trust me, you don't want this job. People rarely shoot at priests, but I've got more bullet holes in me than most folks could survive."

"You forget that I'm a Jesuit, a soldier for Christ. Bullets don't frighten me."

"That's because you've never had one tear through your flesh like a lightning bolt. Bullets scare everyone, especially soldiers like us."

He held up a cookie. "These are amazing. You should probably keep her around."

I took my first bite. "You're right, I'm definitely keeping her, but her skills in the kitchen aren't the reason she's here."

He blushed again. "I got that impression."

"No, that's not what I meant. She's an incredible operator. I've never seen anyone more dangerous with a knife than she is. She's as much a part of this team as any man will ever be."

He took another bite. "And she makes great cookies."

"Yes, she does."

* * *

Eight o'clock arrived as Gator and Anya retracted the landing gear on the climb-out from St. Marys.

"I've never flown in a private jet before," Isaiah said, gliding his palm over the leather armrest.

"It's nice work if you can get it," I said. "I've got a plan, by the way. Wanna hear it?"

"Absolutely."

I crossed my legs. "I think I'll go with honesty. I'll tell her who we are and what we're doing."

"Novel approach," he said, "but I respect it. What do you expect from her?"

"I don't know, but depending on her reaction, we may have an extra passenger on the eastbound leg this afternoon."

* * *

Western Wind Retirement Village was a collection of duplexes in the desert on the outskirts of Sedona. I was pleased to see that it wasn't a nursing home. Getting the woman out of a full-time care facility would be almost as challenging as breaking her out of prison.

The lines on Pat Fitzsimon's—aka Marge Baker's—face told the story of a life that had been anything but easy as she peered through the blinds on the front door of her taxpayer-provided duplex.

"Who are you, and what do you want?"

I reached for my Secret Service credentials but remembered my plan to stick with the truth. "My name is Chase, and I'm trying to help a man named Garland Fitzsimon. May we please come inside?"

The blinds fell closed at the sound of Garland's name, and I stood there wondering how long it would be before a deputy U.S. Marshal arrived to cuff me and haul me away.

An eternity later, the woman pulled the door open an inch. "What did you say your name was?"

"I'm Chase Fulton, and these are my friends. We're trying to help . . ."

She pulled the door fully open and leaned out to look in both directions. "Why did you bring a priest? Oh, my God. Garland's dead, isn't he?"

"No, ma'am, he's not dead, but we need to talk with you. May we please come inside?"

She eyed Isaiah. "Why's he here? I ain't no Catholic."

I said, "He's the reason we're trying to help your grandson."

Her eyes widened as she continued scanning the road behind us. "Is anybody out there in a dark-blue four-door?"

"No, ma'am, they aren't here. If they were, they'd do their best to stop us from helping your grandson."

She stepped back. "Get inside quick, and don't track no sand in here. That stuff gets everywhere, and there ain't nothin' you can do about it out here."

We stepped inside and followed her down a short hallway to the living room.

"It ain't much, but it's what I've got. You want some coffee or something?"

I said, "No, ma'am. Thank you. We just want to talk."

"How'd you find me?"

"We're very resourceful, but I assure you that we're no threat. We believe your grandson was framed, and we're trying to find the people who set him up, Ms. Fitzsimon."

She flinched. "Don't call me that name. I'm Marge Baker now. They told me I could never say my real name ever again."

"I understand. Can you tell me a little about what happened before Garland went to prison?"

"Which time?"

"The most recent."

"Oh, that." She seemed to drift off into a world only she could see. When she finally came back, she said, "The whole thing was just weird all the way around. He come home from prison—they let him out early, you know, and he told me everything was gonna be all right. He said he was working with the government, and some people were going to come and take me away somewhere safe and make sure I had plenty of money and a good place to live. He said he set it all up for me and everything was going to be fine."

We listened intently as she kept talking.

"I didn't understand nothing about it, and I just figured it was another one of his schemes. You've got to understand, he was a troubled boy. He had a tough life, even though I did everything I could for him."

"We know his background and yours," I said. "We're not here to judge anybody. We just want to make sure your grandson isn't serving time for somebody else's crime."

"I'll tell you one thing. My boy ain't no killer, if that's what you're asking. He ain't got it in him. He's a thief, and he's been known to mess around with drugs, just like my daughter did. Do you know about her, too?"

"We do," I said. "And I'm sorry you lost her."

The old woman wiped a tear away before it could escape. "I wish I could've done better for them kids. If I could've just caught a break, maybe I could've done better."

"It's okay. It's not your fault. Could you tell us what happened after Garland told you everything was going to be all right?"

She said, "Are you sure you don't want no coffee? It's Maxwell House, the good kind, and I've got a Mr. Coffee."

I gave in. "Thank you. That would be nice."

She scooped coffee grounds into a filter. "What'll happen to me if you get Garland out of prison?"

"I didn't say we were going to get him out."

She spun. "You said you were trying to help him. What other way can you help him other than getting him out of that prison?"

Isaiah finally joined the conversation. "I've met Garland several times, Ms. Baker. He never struck me as a murderer. I'm the one who asked Chase and his team for help. I believe we've uncovered a conspiracy that put your grandson in prison for a crime he didn't commit. We might not be able to get him out of prison, but it is possible we can successfully get him into a better facility where he can receive the help he needs."

She poured a pot of water into the machine. "What about them other people, the ones who done this to him? Are they going to prison?"

"I don't know," Isaiah said. "That's not up to me. But it would help us a great deal if you'd tell us every detail you can remember about what happened after you last saw Garland."

The Mr. Coffee sputtered and dripped black liquid into the pot. "The Marshals come and got me one day and brung me out here. They told me it was a new life where I'd be safe and taken care of. They told me it's what Garland wanted for me. That boy loves me, and I love him."

"I'm sure you do," Isaiah said. "Can you tell us more?"

"That's it, really. I get a little money in my account every month from the government, I guess. I'm supposed to tell people I'm a widow and my late husband left me enough money to live out here. I ain't no widow woman. I had a couple of husbands, but weren't neither of 'em the kind of man who'd leave me nothing—especially not the sort of money it would take to live in a place like this."

I asked, "Have you spoken with Garland since he's been in prison this time?"

The pot gurgled, and she turned off the machine. "No, that's part of the deal. I ain't allowed no contact with him at all. Probably never again. I'll die 'fore they let him out. I'm an old woman, as you can see. How do you like your coffee?"

"Just black all around. Thank you."

She poured five cups, and Gator joined her in the small kitchen to help carry the load.

After everyone had a cup, I said, "Thank you. If I could make it happen, would you be interested in seeing Garland again?"

She froze. "How's that possible?"

I blew across the surface of the steaming coffee. "It'll require a little lie, but if you're willing to play along, I think we can pull it off."

Chapter 28
The Hornet's Nest

After a second cup of Maxwell House—the good stuff—Marge Baker said, "Do you really think you can get me in to see my boy without ruining my setup with the Marshals?"

I took a long breath. "I promised myself I'd be completely honest with you, so here's the harsh reality of the situation. It is possible that the Marshals Service may find out what we're doing. I don't know what the fallout would be for you if that happened. I can, however, promise that we'll do everything in our power to slip you out of here, get you some face time with Garland, and bring you back home without anyone knowing you were ever gone."

"But what will they do to Garland if they find out it's me?"

"I don't know, but he's already serving a life sentence for something I'm not sure he did, so anything they do to him can't be much worse than—"

She cut me off. "I already told you he didn't do it. That boy ain't no killer. I'm telling you."

"I tend to agree," I said. "That's part of why we're doing this. I'm not trying to force your hand, but we have to go. If you want to come with us, you're welcome. If not, I understand, but that won't stop us from working to figure out what really happened and seeing that the real criminals are punished for what they did."

She didn't hesitate any further. "Let me wash these dishes, and I'll be ready to go."

Anya stood. "I will clean dishes. You should pack bag for three or maybe five days."

Marge recoiled. "Whoa! I didn't expect that. Where you from, girly?"

Anya collected our empty cups. "I am American girl from Georgia now, but I was born inside Soviet Union."

"I don't guess I've ever met nobody from Russia before. Is it as bad as they say it is over there? I mean, with the bread lines and communism and all?"

Anya said, "I will answer this way. I am very happy to be American now."

I pulled Isaiah aside and briefed him while Marge packed. He didn't love my plan, but he reluctantly agreed and said, "There's a diocese here and a fairly large church, so I'll see what I can do."

On our drive back to the airport in our rented SUV, Gator pulled into the parking lot of a gorgeous Catholic church. Its spire soared into the sky above an architectural masterpiece that fit into the desert landscape as if God Himself had carved the building with His own hands.

Isaiah straightened his collar and slid from the seat. "Wish me luck."

"What's he doing?" Marge asked.

I said, "Shopping."

She frowned. "Maybe instead of shopping, he should light a candle and say a prayer while he's in there."

"I don't know about the candle, but I think he prays almost constantly. He's a good man, Marge. He's one of the primary reasons we're doing this."

"I reckon that makes you folks pretty good people, too."

Isaiah returned with a paper bag and climbed back inside the truck.

"Well?" I asked. "Did you get it?"

He turned to Marge. "Are you about a size ten?"

She groaned. "I'm an eight, thank you very much."

The priest handed her the bag. "Good, then this should fit just fine."

As Gator pulled out of the parking lot, Marge dumped the contents of the bag onto her lap. "Oh, no! I ain't wearing this. This is one of them nun's outfits, ain't it?"

"Yes, ma'am," Isaiah said. "It's called a habit, and if you want to get into the prison to see Garland, you have no choice but to wear it."

She shoved it back into the bag. "Okay, fine. I wear a ten in some things. Will it still fit?"

"They make the habits a little big, so I think it'll be perfect."

Gator had us at the airport in no time, and we climbed the stairs into Anya's Citation.

Marge eyed the interior with disbelief. "You're gonna let that Russian girl fly this thing?"

"It's her jet," I said, "and she's a fantastic pilot. Gator's the copilot, and he's excellent in the cockpit as well. You've got nothing to worry about."

She strapped in as I closed the door and the engines whistled to life. "This sure is fancy. I've never been in anything like this. Other than regular airliners, I flew in a little airplane one time. It had a propeller, though. It weren't no jet like this."

"It's a nice ride, and the westerly wind will make our trip a little faster. If you'd like a snack or something to drink, just let me know."

We taxied away from the FBO, and my phone chirped.

"Hello, this is Chase."

"Father?" Pogonya said.

"Yes. Is everything all right?"

"No, I don't think so."

"What's going on? Are you hurt?"

"No, it's nothing like that. I came out of my condo to go to class, but I had a flat tire."

I relaxed. "Oh, that's not a big deal. Just call the number on the insurance card, and they'll send someone out to change it for you."

She said, "No, that's not necessary. A man already changed it for me. He was coincidentally walking through the parking lot when I discovered the flat."

"Okay. So, what's the problem?"

"When the man finished changing the tire, he told me to call my dad and tell him that little girls get hurt when their fathers make bad decisions."

My blood ran ice cold. "Where are you now?"

"Inside my room with all of the doors locked. Should I call the police?"

I said, "No, baby. Get in your car immediately and drive to the campus police station. Drive as fast as you can, and don't even slow down for traffic lights or stop signs. Call me from inside the station, then give the phone to the desk sergeant. Do you understand?"

"Yes, I understand, but will you stay on the phone with me?"

"Of course I will. You have your pepper spray, right?"

"I always have it with me."

I tapped Isaiah's foot with mine and mouthed, "Give me your phone."

He pulled out the phone I'd given him and laid it in my hand.

I dialed the number, and Skipper said, "Op center."

"Pogo's in trouble. She's on her way to the campus police station. Get everyone you can up to Athens right now."

I expected a dozen questions, but instead, Skipper had the rest of the team on the phone in seconds.

She said, "Pogonya's in trouble. Chase wants you guys at the main police station at UGA right now."

She came back on the line. "They're on their way. Is she okay?"

From my phone, Pogonya asked, "Who are you talking to?"

"I'm talking to Skipper on another phone. She's got the team en route. I want you to stay inside the station until they get there. It'll be Mongo, Singer, Shawn, and Clark."

"Why aren't you coming?"

"I'm on my way home from Arizona, but I'll be there as soon as I can."

"Okay," she said. "I'm heading to the car now. Stay with me."

"I'm here, baby. Keep your eyes open, and don't talk to anybody."

The door slammed, and the sound of the engine starting eased my mind, if only slightly.

"Okay, I'm on the road. Please don't make me hang up. I need you on the phone with me."

"I'm right here," I said. "I'm not going anywhere."

Thumbing my seat belt free, I stuck my head through the cockpit opening and pressed the mute button. "Change of plans. We're going to Athens. I think Gregory McDonald just threatened our little girl."

Anya scowled. "I will tear his—"

"Relax," I said. "It's under control. I've got Pogo on the line, and she's headed to the police station. The team's on their way from Bonaventure."

Gator was on the controls and taxiing the airplane from the ramp to the runway, but Anya grabbed the yoke and shoved the throttles to their forward stops. We accelerated down the taxiway and leapt into the air, climbing directly over a pair of smaller planes waiting to take the runway.

I gave her a nudge. "Nice work."

"Father, are you there?"

I tapped the mute button again. "Yes, I'm here. We're airborne now, and your mother is at the controls. We'll be there as soon as possible. We can make Athens nonstop, but the team will be there before us."

She said, "I don't think anybody is following me."

"That's good, but don't worry about what's behind you. Did you lock the condo?"

"Yes, but Father, I'm scared."

"It's okay. We're coming, and the campus police will keep you safe until we get there."

She said, "I can see the police station. I'm almost there."

"Take the closest parking spot to the door, even if it's marked handicapped or police cars only, and get inside."

Anya said, "Gator, you have controls. Give to me phone!"

"Wait a minute," I said. "I'm about to talk with the desk sergeant."

Pogonya said, "Okay, I'm inside."

A confident, firm voice came on the line. "This is Sergeant Williams, UGA Police Department."

I said, "Sergeant Williams. I'm Chase Fulton. My daughter is the one who just gave you the phone."

"I know who you are, Dr. Fulton, and we know Pogonya. What can I do for you?"

"A man approached her in the parking lot of her condo and had her relay a threatening message to me. I need you to sit on her until some of my men get there."

"I'll put out an APB, and we'll catch him if he's still on campus."

I said, "That's a waste of time. He's long gone by now, I'm sure of it. But I still want you to keep my daughter in the station with you until we arrive. Can you do that?"

"Of course we can, but what's the harm in looking for the guy?"

I considered his question. "You know what? You're right. Get a description from Pogonya, and go after the guy. If you get lucky, I'll take him off your hands when I get there."

"That's not exactly how it works, Dr. Fulton, but I understand. I'll see that Pogonya is safe, and we'll put out the APB."

He apparently handed the phone back to Pogo, and I said to Anya, "She's safe in the police station."

Anya snatched the phone from my hand and pushed her way past me.

I took her seat and turned to Gator. "I guess that means I need a cockpit briefing."

He said, "We're through thirty-two for flight level four-one-oh with a one-hundred-fifteen-knot tailwind. That'll put us in Athens in less than three hours, as long as the wind holds. All systems are operational, and we're on frequency with Albuquerque Center. I have the controls, and you have the radios."

"I have the radios," I said.

Two hours into the longest flight of my life, Anya slithered back into the cockpit opening. She said, "Mongo has Pogonya, and they are taking her home. Change destination."

I called Memphis Center and amended our flight plan for St. Marys.

The controller said, "Citation Eight-Alpha-Foxtrot is now cleared direct Bonaventure Field. Descend and maintain flight level three-seven-oh, and expect that as a final altitude."

I keyed the mic. "Eight-Alpha-Fox is cleared direct Bonaventure and leaving four-one-oh for three-seven-oh."

I reprogrammed the GPS, and Gator gave me the nod to initiate the new course. At the touch of a button, the Citation rolled ten degrees to the right, her nose pointed directly at coastal Georgia, where the team and I would deal with the swarm of hornets from the nest we'd just kicked.

Chapter 29
Dragon Slayer

We touched down and taxied to the ramp ten minutes ahead of Pogonya and the rest of the team. When they finally arrived, the door came open, and Pogo sprinted from the Twin Otter, across the tarmac, and into my arms. The look on Anya's face said she didn't fully approve of her running to me first, but as long as our little girl felt safe, I didn't care which of us she reached for.

"I wanted to kill him, Father. I was so scared."

I squeezed her against me. "Don't worry, baby. I'll make sure you never have to see him again."

She pulled away. "Oh, no. Don't do that. I *want* to see him again. I want to see the fear in his eyes when you find him."

The proper parenting technique in that moment probably involved a discussion about revenge being wrong, but something in my gut made me proud to know my daughter believed I would slay her dragon and that she would get to witness my sword piercing his scales.

Mongo stepped beside me. "I just got off the phone with campus police, and they haven't found the guy yet."

"I didn't expect them to, but we'll find him."

Our giant glanced down at Pogonya. "She drew a sketch, and I think it's good enough for Skipper to do our hunting for us."

I redirected my attention to my daughter. "You can draw?"

She shrugged. "A little. I drew a picture of him for the police."

"Did they keep it?"

She pulled a folded sheet of paper from her pocket. "They made a copy, but I kept the original."

I unfolded the paper and couldn't believe what I saw. "Pogo, this looks like a photograph. I had no idea you could do this."

Anya joined us. "She is very talented, like her mother."

Pogo hugged Anya, and they held each other. The girl was so mature for sixteen, but there were moments when the child in her rose to the surface, and it made me angry that I hadn't been there during those early years.

Mongo took the sketch from my hands. "I'll get this up to Skipper."

Don Maynard, our airport manager, rolled up in the fuel truck. "Is everything all right, boss?"

"It will be, Don. Thanks for coming out. Can you get the planes topped off and put them away? We've got a lot to do."

"No problem. Is there anything else you need?"

"I'm sure there is," I said. "We're neck-deep, and the water's still rising, but I can't think of anything else I need at the moment."

He straightened his cap. "Well, I'll see to the planes, and I'll keep everything ready to go. Just let me know if you need me. Your girl's a real sweetheart, by the way. You should be proud."

"You'll have to credit her mother with that one. I didn't have the privilege of being her daddy when I should've been."

He eyed Anya and Pogonya, still locked in their beautiful embrace. "Looks to me like you're making up for it pretty good. I'll be around if you need me."

When we made it to the op center, Skipper motioned to an overhead monitor. "Meet Gregory McDonald. Pogonya's sketch was good enough to ID him."

"How long will it take you to find him?" I asked.

"Oh, that's already done. He's not as covert as he thinks he is. Are you going to kill him, or does Anya get the pleasure?"

I said, "We may flip for it, but something tells me it'll be a case of heads she wins, tails I lose."

"That's what I figured," Skipper said. "He's in Pensacola and traveling aboard a King Air owned by the taxpayers."

"Can you track him, or just the airplane?"

She huffed. "How long have we been doing this, Chase?"

"Sorry, I didn't mean to question your skills. I'm just trying to prioritize our next steps."

She said, "Did you talk Grandma Pat into coming home with you?"

"She's downstairs with Isaiah. He scored a nun's habit for her, and I plan on taking her into the prison looking like Mother Teresa. Can you work up an ID for her?"

"You bet. I'll get her picture and put one together, but you probably want to know how I'm tracking McDonald, right?"

"I do."

She said, "Three phone calls were made from inside the King Air from two different numbers. One of the numbers dialed the flight service station, so it probably belongs to one of the pilots. The other phone called a number in Washington, D.C. I haven't identified it . . . yet. And then it called a cell phone in Pensacola that belongs to the Catholic diocese."

"That has to be McDonald," I said. "Can you keep tracking the phone?"

"Of course. I'm tracking both of them, and I'm still working on the D.C. number. It's a landline, but it's locked down tight. I thought about calling it just to see who picks up."

"Let's save that as a last resort. But I'm curious, too."

Skipper said, "I'd bet dollars to donuts it rings in the Naval Observatory."

"The vice president's house? No way. McDonald wouldn't be that sloppy."

She rolled her eyes. "He threatened the daughter of the two deadliest people I know. Let's not give the man any credit for good decision-making skills. Can I make a suggestion?"

"When have you ever needed permission?"

She said, "Send Gator and Singer to watch him in Pensacola. They can stay on him without anyone knowing they're there while you get Granny in to see her boy."

I said, "GMTA."

She swooned. "I love it when you call me a great mind."

"I love that you let me lump my brain in with yours. Get on that ID for Pat, and we'll plan to hit the prison first thing tomorrow morning."

I dispatched our two snipers to the western end of the Florida Panhandle to keep an eye on Gregory McDonald. "If he moves, you move with him. Got it?"

Gator said, "If he's got a King Air, we can't keep up with him in the Otter."

"You will take Citation," Anya said.

I turned. "I didn't know you were here."

"I can be very sneaky when is necessary, but is Pogonya's fault this time. She likes when you and I are inside same room."

Pogo groaned. "Mama, your English is getting worse. Please . . . And don't lie—you like being in the same room with Father, too."

* * *

Singer and Gator blasted off, and I pulled Isaiah and Pat Fitzsimon into the library.

"Have a seat. We need to talk about what's going to happen tomorrow at the prison."

The priest and future temporary nun settled onto the wingbacks, and I asked, "How's the foot?"

Isaiah lifted his boot into the air. "It's getting better every day. I'm glad to be off the crutches."

"Are you doing okay, Ms. Fitzsimon?"

"If you don't mind, call me Marge or Ms. Baker. It took me a long time to learn to be somebody I'm not, and I don't want to slip out of that character if I don't have to."

"Of course," I said. "Tomorrow will be tough for you. You're going to see Garland in a condition you've never seen before, and it won't be pleasant."

She sighed. "I've seen that boy strung out like you can't imagine. I don't think I'll see anything that surprises me, but I can't wait to lay eyes on him. He's had a tough road."

"Yes, he has," I said. "But I'm not sure the most recent bumps have been entirely his fault, and I'm working on a plan to resolve as much of that as possible."

"Are you saying you can get my boy out of prison?"

"No, ma'am, I'm not saying that at all. But if things go our way, maybe, just maybe, we can get him somewhere a little more comfortable where they'll take better care of him."

"Forgive me," she said, "but exactly who are you people?"

I glanced at the priest. "In this case, Ms. Baker, we're the good guys."

Clearly unsatisfied with my answer, she said, "And what was all that business with your daughter?"

The priest's vow and celibacy suddenly seemed easier than my vow of honesty to Pat Fitzsimon, aka Marge Baker.

"A man who we believe is a major player in your grandson's situation threatened my daughter, so I put a couple of men on him, and we'll have a talk with him before this is over."

"I don't understand. Why would that have anything to do with Garland?"

I said, "When a den of snakes is uncovered, they strike, and in this case, they struck at my daughter. Serpents are supposed to be cunning, but trying to bite my daughter was a terrible decision on their part . . . and the surest way to get their heads cut off."

"So, what'll happen if people at the prison figure out I'm not really a nun?"

"I don't know," I admitted. "But your agreement with the federal government restricts you from having any contact with Garland. I need you to keep that in mind tomorrow. If you blow your cover and reveal who you really are, your life will change dramatically, and most likely, it won't be a change for the better."

A knock came at the door, and Skipper stepped into the library. "Sorry to interrupt, but I need to get a picture of Ms. . . . ."

"Baker," I said.

Skipper nodded. "Yeah, Baker. Got it. But that won't be your name tomorrow. I've decided you'll be Sister Mary Katherine Morgan."

Marge smiled. "That sounds like a good nun's name. All of this has to be a sin, though, right? I mean, impersonating a nun can't be legal."

Isaiah laid a hand on Marge's arm. "There are certain situations in which God understands the necessity of secrecy. Christ Himself didn't reveal His true identity for the first thirty years of his life on Earth. Are you a believer, Ms. Baker?"

"I ain't never gone to church as a regular thing, if that's what you mean, but I believe in God. I pray for Garland, but I can't say it's ever done much good."

The priest said, "Look around. These people may not look like angels sent from on high, but God answers prayers using all sorts of people and situations. Nobody was fighting for Garland until Chase and his people agreed to step in. Don't discount the value of prayer just because you don't understand God's answer."

Although he hadn't directed the comment at me, the priest's wisdom hit me like a falling hammer.

How many times had I questioned God's timing? How many hours had I wasted in raging anger at Him for allowing Penny to be murdered? How could I look into Pogonya's beautiful eyes and see my mother's face without thanking God for giving her to me, regardless of the circumstances . . . and the schedule?

Isaiah helped Marge into her habit and arranged the garment as a nun would wear it so Skipper could take the pictures she needed.

"It just don't feel right," Marge said. "But if it gets me in to see my boy, even for a little while, I guess it'll be worth it. What if he calls out my name, though? You can give me all this talk about how I'm supposed to behave, but who's gonna tell Garland not to call me Mamaw?"

Isaiah said, "Don't worry about that. I'll be there with you, and I'll do my best to make sure Garland doesn't do anything to threaten this operation."

"Operation?" Marge asked. "How about telling me the truth about why you're doing all of this. Why risk sneaking me in there? What good can come of it?"

I took the floor and held fast to my vow of honesty. "The truth is, Marge, I believe having Garland see you is our best chance of cutting through the medication-induced state they keep him in. I believe that what he reveals when he sees you will change everything about this case."

Chapter 30

An Unlikely Ally

Sister Mary Katherine Morgan looked the part in her tunic and veil.

Isaiah pressed a long strand of beads with a wooden cross at the end into her palm. "This is my rosary. Holding it in your hand will not only give you something to do with your nervous energy, but it will also lend an air of authenticity. Just don't let it dangle like an accessory, okay?"

She squirmed beneath the habit as we approached the gate. "Thank you."

A young, uniformed guard approached, and I handed him Father Isaiah Lamb's ID. I said, "Where's Corporal Leonard?"

The guard examined the ID and leaned into the Suburban. "I need everyone's ID, and I need all of you to step out of the vehicle."

I pressed an Alabama driver's license bearing the name Mary Katherine Morgan into his palm and held up my Secret Service credentials. "Where did you say Corporal Leonard is?"

The guard ignored the driver's license and stared at my cred-pack. "Oh, I didn't realize you were—"

"Yes, I am."

He stepped back. "You can pull forward and wait for the gate to close behind you."

I didn't move. "I asked you about Peter Leonard."

"Oh, yeah, sorry. He got promoted. He's over in Tallahassee now as a sergeant in admin."

"Is that right? Good for him."

The guard said, "It was kind of a surprise for everybody, but he's a good guy. He deserves it."

I pulled forward into the sallyport, and the twelve-foot-tall gate slowly closed behind me. The second gate in front of us slid open even more slowly than the first had closed.

With the IDs back in their appropriate hands, I said, "Okay, that's one. Only a couple hundred more checkpoints to go."

"I'm sweating already," Marge said.

"Just try to act like a nun," I said.

She coughed. "I ain't never even met a nun. I seen *Sister Act* on TV, but I can't sing, so how am I supposed to act like something I don't know nothing about?"

It was far too late, and we were in way too deep to change the game, so I said, "You're doing fine. Just keep your head bowed as much as possible, and try not to make eye contact with anybody other than Isaiah and me."

"I'll try," she said.

Once inside, we moved through a pair of metal detectors, and my body turned the machines into light shows. Raising my pant leg, I exposed my prosthetic, and the guard nodded. He still patted me down, but thankfully, he didn't make me leave my leg at the checkpoint.

A guard frisked Isaiah, too, but no one laid a hand on our nun. The lines on her face and the strands of grey hair falling from her veil made her look much older than she was, and that somehow added to the disguise.

A pair of guards led us toward unit G-7, down a corridor in which every footstep echoed like thunder, and one of the guards said, "You know the protocol, right?"

Isaiah nodded. "We do. We've been here many times."

Before we reached the visitation rooms, a pair of footsteps approached from the opposite direction, and I looked into the face of Dr. Brian Plum. His eyes met mine, and he froze momentarily. It took every ounce of strength I possessed to merely nod and continue walking.

Did he recognize me? Is everything blown? Am I about to leave this prison in handcuffs?

A large round mirror at the end of the corridor showed Dr. Plum turning to watch us walk by, and my heart pounded like stampeding hoofbeats.

"Fitzsimon is in D-Six. We'll be right outside the door if you need us. You've got twenty minutes."

The room was identical to the first one where I'd met Garland Fitzsimon, but the feeling in my chest was quite different than it had been on that day, which seemed both distant and still raw.

We took seats at the wall of glass as the stench of the prison washed over us.

"Hello, Garland. It's Father Lamb. Good to see you again. How are you feeling?"

The inmate looked up. "I'm tired. I don't think I can do this much . . ."

Pat Fitzsimon looked up into her grandson's face for the first time in years and pulled the veil from her head.

I panicked. She was on the verge of destroying every hope we had of helping the man on the other side of the glass, but to my surprise, she pressed a finger to her lips and spoke barely loud enough to be heard. "Don't be afraid, my child. Angels are looking over you."

A shiver ran down my spine, and Garland Fitzsimon stared back at the woman who'd loved him since the day he was found outside the volunteer fire department in Ponce de Leon.

He mouthed, "You."

The look of utter disbelief in his glassy eyes gave me the first glimpse of humanity in the man who'd spent most of his adult life behind prison bars.

I sat in silence as Garland and Pat stared at each other without a word. Each of them shed tears neither could explain, and the same look of fear Pogonya wore when she ran from the airplane and into my arms consumed Fitzsimon's face. I suddenly wanted to tear through the glass and carry the troubled young man out of the North Central Florida supermax, but slaying his dragon would require a sword far mightier than mine.

"Times up!" came a call through the door.

I couldn't believe how quickly twenty minutes had passed. So few words had been spoken, yet so much had been said.

Garland drew in a long breath. "They're killing me. You should give it to the priest."

The door opened behind us with a thundering report. "I said time's up. Let's go."

Isaiah stood and took a few steps toward the guard. "We're praying with Mr. Fitzsimon. May we please have just a moment more?"

"Sorry," the guard growled. "It's not up to me."

The priest helped replace Pat's veil and helped her to her feet. Her knees trembled beneath the black tunic, and she squeezed the worn wooden cross at the end of the beads.

Afraid the guards were on the verge of physically removing us from the visitation room, I took Pat's elbow in my hand and gave one last look through the glass.

Garland Fitzsimon mouthed, "I love you, Mamaw."

As we stepped through the door and back into the corridor, Pat collapsed to the tile floor, and the guard yelled, "Get the doctor!"

"No," I said. "She'll be okay."

"I'm not losing a nun on my watch. We're getting the doctor."

Seconds later, Dr. Plum took a knee in front of the woman he believed to be Sister Mary Katherine Morgan. "Sister, look at me."

She tried, but tears, rage, and boundless agony flowed from behind frozen lids. "He is such a troubled boy. Why can't you help him?"

I squeezed her hand as Dr. Plum felt the pulse in her wrist beneath the rosary.

He looked up at the guard. "Bring some oxygen."

The uniformed officer returned in an instant with an oxygen cylinder in a padded black bag, and the doctor slipped a mask over Pat's mouth and nose. "Just breathe normally. This can be a trying experience."

I kept my eyes on our nun and fought hard to avoid looking at Plum, but he leaned toward me and gripped my arm.

In a voice filled with desperation, he whispered, "You have to help him. Come back to my house tonight. I have the information you need."

I pulled my arm from his grip. "Make sure she's okay."

"She'll be fine," the doctor said. "Just get her out of here, and do what I said."

When our nun caught her breath, we lifted her to her feet, and she took a few trembling steps.

"We can get her a wheelchair if you want," the guard said.

She waved him off. "No. I'll be all right. It was all just so much."

In a move I never expected, she crossed herself, and Isaiah fought back a smile.

It took almost as long to get out of the prison grounds as it took to get inside.

With the supermax getting smaller in the rearview mirror, Pat tore off the tunic and veil. "I can't believe that was my boy. What are they doing to him? You've gotta do something. You've gotta help him."

"I will," I said. "I'll do everything in my power to get him out of there. I'm sorry I did that to you today."

"No! Don't you ever be sorry for that. I got to see my boy, and I didn't think I'd ever see him again. I got to tell him I love him, and he told me. You don't know how much that means to me."

I checked my watch. "I have to get you two back to Bonaventure. My day is far from over, and I have a feeling that what we've seen so far is just the tip of the iceberg."

* * *

The op center was empty, and nothing could've surprised me more —or so I thought. When Skipper didn't answer her phone, my surprise morphed into concern. My next two calls to Anya and Pogo went unanswered, and my anxiety exploded.

I found Isaiah and Pat in the kitchen and said, "Come with me."

We rode the elevator to the third floor, and I locked them inside the op center. "Stay here. Something's going on, and I want to keep you two safe while I figure it out."

The stairs were far faster than the elevator, so I sprinted down, hitting every third or fourth tread on the way. When I burst through the kitchen door onto the back gallery, Kodiak and Mongo were climbing from the water onto the dock in dive gear.

"Hey! Have you guys seen the girls?"

Kodiak pulled off his mask and cupped a hand around his ear. "What's that?"

"Anya, Pogo, and Skipper . . . I can't find them."

He pointed toward the shoot house. "They were out there."

I crossed the distance to the training facility in seconds and threw open the door to find Pogonya pounding away at Skipper with a metal baton. Skipper's pads protected her, but the ferocity of Pogonya's blows surprised me. Anya stood behind our daughter, directing the angle of every strike.

They stopped when I stepped in and said, "What's going on in here?"

"I'm learning to fight, Father."

"It looks like you're doing well."

"I have very good teachers and a willing victim."

"I see that. You guys had me scared. I couldn't find you."

Skipper pulled off her headgear. "We've been out here for a couple of hours. Thanks for the interruption. I needed a break. How did it go at the prison?"

I relayed every detail and said, "The psychiatrist recognized me and told me to come back to his house tonight. He said he had information I needed."

"He recognized you?" Anya asked. "Did you not wear mask last time?"

"Yes, of course we wore balaclavas, but I'm six-four, so I tend to stand out a little."

Skipper said, "You're going tonight, right?"

"Oh, yeah, and I'm taking some help in case it's a setup. My days of walking into other people's traps with my guard down are over. If it goes the way I expect, we may have to extract the doctor and keep him safe until we get this mess cleaned up."

Chapter 31

The Man

I gave up trying to predict Skipper's next move a great many years ago, so her response of taking off her shirt didn't surprise me at all. "Cool. I'll grab a shower and get to work. We need to check on Gator and Singer, too."

Competition between women is far fiercer than it will ever be among men, and Anya proved my point. She lifted the front of her T-shirt, exposing her midriff—which I enjoyed—and said, "You should maybe spend more time inside gym with me and less time in front of computer screen, Skipper."

The analyst scowled. "Gator likes it just fine, and on behalf of all real women everywhere, I'd like to say that we hate you. Would you please start aging at some point? You're really making the rest of us look bad."

Pogo jumped into the ring. "Hey, stop that. I've got those genes, so don't curse me. I pray every day that I'll look as good as Mama when I'm her age."

I cleared my throat. "Uh, we've got work to do, ladies."

Skipper threw her sweaty shirt at me. "I'm on it."

Anya said, "If you can do mission with doctor tonight without me, I would like to stay with Pogonya. I do not like her being alone while all of this is happening."

"Of course," I said. "I think I can handle it with two Green Berets and a SEAL, but I can call in security for Pogo if it would make you feel better."

"I do not think this is necessary as long as one of us can stay with her."

Pogo said, "Hello . . . I'm right here. Don't I get a say in this?"

I laughed. "Sure, let's hear your thoughts. But I can't promise we won't override them."

"Okay, it's like this," she began. "I thought I was pretty tough before this thing happened. Now, I'm learning that I'm pretty easy to scare, and I don't like it. That's why I'm out here learning to take care of myself."

"And you are doing very well," Anya said. "Is okay to be afraid sometimes, though."

"Thank you, but let me finish, Mama. I'd really feel best if I were with either or both of you until this is over. I'm sorry to be so clingy, but that guy really freaked me out. He was so nice while he was changing my tire, but everything changed as soon as he finished."

I grabbed her and pulled her against me. "Come here, Stinky Butt. You need a shower, too. We're not going to override that one. At least one of us will stay with you every minute, and if that becomes impossible, we'll take you with us."

She squeezed me. "That would be amazing. Seeing you guys actually work would be like, I don't know. It would be great."

I shoved her away. "I'll give you a thousand bucks if you can land one solid shot on me with your baton in sixty seconds. Go!"

Before Pogonya could move, Anya stepped between us and pressed her lips to mine in a kiss that left my head spinning, just like she'd done in the shallow water off St. Thomas almost twenty years before.

The second unbelievable and unexpected blow came in the form of Pogo's baton against my prosthetic, hard enough to throw me from my feet and onto my back.

Pogonya threw her hand into the air, slapping her mother's in a powerful high-five. "Nice teamwork, Mama. Let's split the thousand and go shopping."

"Great idea, Pogonyechka!"

The door to the training room opened and closed with me still lying on my back, wondering what just hit me. My girls left, and booted footsteps approached.

"You all right, boss?" Shawn asked. "What are you doing on the floor?"

I hopped to my feet and brushed off my pants. "I'm fine. I just got hit by two forces of nature that nobody can control."

"Been there," he said. "Kodiak and Mongo are washing up their dive gear. They've been working on some cross-bracing under the dock. Skipper said you needed us."

"I do need you. We're going back to Dr. Plum's house tonight."

"Can I waterboard him this time?"

I chuckled. "I'm afraid we'll have to pick another victim for that. Plum recognized me at the prison today and whispered that he had information we could use. He told me to come by his place tonight, so we're going."

Shawn took a step back. "That's a trap."

"I know, but if we can snatch the bait without getting caught in the jaws, it might be worth it."

He said, "I'll brief the others. What time do you want to leave?"

My watch reported ten minutes past three, so I said, "Let's hit the road at four. That'll put us there before sunset, with plenty of time to get into position to keep an eye on the house in case the good doctor isn't alone."

"I like it," he said. "We'll be ready, but . . ."

"But what?"

He contorted his mouth. "I could be wrong."

"About what?"

"About it being a trap. Maybe the doctor came to his senses. We might need to pull him out of there if he's being real."

I said, "My thoughts exactly. We'll be prepared for this to turn into an extraction and protection mission if he's sincere."

Shawn said, "You know, we can't make him come with us if he doesn't want to."

"He may not realize how much danger he's in, so it'll be up to us to make him understand."

"Balaclavas and sidearms?"

"No masks," I said. "We're out in the open now, but don't you dare leave your sidearm behind."

"Yes, sir. We'll be ready when you are."

The drive from Bonaventure to Madison, Florida, took just under two hours, and we nestled into the perfect hiding hole about a thousand yards from Dr. Plum's rented house. Our wait was shorter than I expected. Plum pulled into the driveway a few minutes after seven, just as the sun was sinking behind the trees to the west, but he didn't put his prized Mercedes inside the garage.

"It looks like he's alone," Mongo said.

I watched Plum step from the car with his briefcase as the garage door rose. "Yeah, but he didn't park inside. The car's been inside every time I've been here."

Shawn said, "Agreed. Maybe he's dropping something off and heading back out."

"Maybe, but it's still out of routine for him. That's a red flag."

The garage door descended after Plum was inside, and a few lights came on in the house.

An hour passed, and darkness consumed the rural setting.

I said, "It looks like he's alone and in for the night. Let's move in."

Kodiak laid a hand on my shoulder. "Wait. He's on the move."

Plum's silhouette passed through what I assumed was the living room and toward the kitchen. Lights went out, one by one, as he moved through the house.

"What's he doing?" I asked.

Kodiak said, "Maybe he's trying to tell us he's ready for company."

I stood from my covered position. "I hope you're right. Let's do this."

We press-checked our pistols and ran toward the house with ten yards of space between each of us. If it was a trap, snaring all four of us would be quite an accomplishment for somebody.

With fifty yards remaining between me and the house, a bright flash of light filled the row of windows in the garage door, and a gunshot rang out.

The four of us froze in place and took a knee.

I asked, "Does everyone agree that was a pistol shot from the garage?"

Mongo and Shawn closed on Kodiak and me, and all three heads nodded.

The SEAL groaned. "I didn't see that coming. I guess this isn't an extraction after all, but we'll need to glove up."

I said, "Find some concealment. I'm going in. There's no need to risk putting any more forensic evidence in there than necessary."

Mongo pulled a pair of boot covers from his kit and held them toward me. "Footprints are almost like fingerprints."

I pulled on my gloves and slipped the elastic covers over my boots before inching toward the house. The rest of the team moved to a small grove of trees thirty yards away.

After ten strides, I stopped and reversed course until I was back with my team in the trees. The touch of one button had me in comms with the op center. "Skipper, we think Plum just shot himself in his garage. Can you check for a security system and exterior cameras?"

"I'm on it," she said.

A minute later, she said, "There is a security system in the house, but it's not connected to a monitoring service. I can't find any evidence of cameras. You should be good to approach, but make sure you're wearing gloves and booties."

I said, "Thanks for the tip. We never would've thought of that."

I moved to the house and peered through one of the glass panes on the garage door before jerking away. Our open-mic sat-coms put my voice in the team's ears at the speed of light. "He's down with one to the head. I'm going in."

Squatting in front of the walk-through door into the garage, I picked the lock and stepped inside with my pistol at the ready. "I'm in, and he's definitely missing his soul and most of his skull. It's a revolver . . . looks like a three-fifty-seven Magnum."

"That'll do it," Kodiak said. "Do you want us to search the house?"

I sighed. "No. He left us a care package at his feet."

I lifted the doctor's briefcase, said a silent prayer over his body, and stepped back through the door.

Back in the Suburban, Shawn said, "I guess I was wrong on both points, huh?"

"Which points would those be?" I asked.

"That this was a trap and that Plum didn't know how much danger he was in."

I let out a long breath. "I guess we were both wrong about that. If we had moved in as soon as he came home, he'd still be alive."

Mongo slugged my arm. "Cut that out. None of this is our fault. We're the ones trying to clean it up. The only ones. This is not on you."

"I still wish we had moved in earlier."

Kodiak tapped the briefcase. "Are you gonna open it and see what he left us?"

I pushed his hand away. "Not until Dr. Mankiller scans it for explosives."

"Good thinking," he said, "but I'm not sure I can wait. The anticipation is killing me. Let Shawn sniff it. Aren't SEALs kind of like drug- and explosive-sniffing dogs?"

Shawn barked, and I said, "Down, boy. Anticipation is far more survivable than a pound of C-Four going off in our faces. We'll work on our patience 'til we get home."

Kodiak stroked Shawn's head. "Who's a good boy, huh?"

Skipper's voice filled my ear. "It sounds like you're on the road and having some sort of guy thing that I'm glad I don't understand."

I said, "Sorry, I didn't realize we still had the active comms on. Yeah, we're gone, and we have the case. Plum pulled his own trigger. There was nothing we could do by the time we got in."

She said, "Mongo's right. This one isn't on you. We've got enough to think about without you dragging that anchor around. Get your head straight, and I'll have Celeste stand by to scan the case when you get here."

"Thanks. Have you talked with Gator and Singer?"

She said, "Affirmative. They've got eyes on McDonald. He's at the beach house owned by his namesake, the bishop. He's been on the phone a lot, and I have most of the conversations transcribed."

"Anything we should know from those conversations?" I asked.

"Just that he keeps referring to somebody as 'the man.' It's weird. I haven't figured out who he's talking about yet, but whoever he is, he's obviously important. I've got my theory, but I'm not ready to stick my neck out."

"Stick it out. I won't let anybody cut it off."

"If I had to wager a guess," she said, "I'd put money on the man being the vice president."

Chapter 32

Crocodiles in the Mist

"Let's sniff it first," Dr. Celeste Mankiller said when I laid the briefcase on her stainless-steel table.

Kodiak threw up both hands. "See! I told you. Shawn, you're up. Sniff away, boy, and try not to pee on the floor this time."

Celeste shook her head. "Boys . . . please."

She lifted the case and slid it inside a chamber that hissed and purred beneath her touch. "I'm drawing a vacuum in the chamber. The case isn't airtight, so that'll draw out any air inside, and then we can test the air for traces of potentially explosive or toxic material."

"I hadn't considered toxins," I said.

Celeste shrugged. "If a guy's willing to kill himself, what's stopping him from throwing around a little anthrax on his way out?"

"How long will this take?"

"It's usually less than three minutes, but that's a really nice case and a little tighter than most. It may take five."

"Oh," I said. "I expected hours."

"Not in this lab, Sugar Britches. Isn't that what Earl calls you?"

"Don't *you* start. I've got enough clowns in my circus without adding another."

The machine hummed to a stop, and Celeste turned to the monitor. "Well, would you look at that? It seems our doctor likes to smoke a little weed. That's a pretty healthy dose of THC. It's a good thing

Shawn didn't stick his nose in there. He would've been too chill to fight for a few hours."

I leaned in. "Anything else interesting?"

She said, "Nope. It looks like aftershave and deodorant, which are both flammable, but nothing that's going to kill us or go boom. You want me to nuke it just in case?"

"I do."

Celeste unlocked the cabinet, removed the briefcase, and slid it onto her X-ray table. "Stand back, boys, or your baby-making days end today."

All four of us stepped closer to the table.

She rolled her eyes again. "Cute, boys. Back up."

We followed orders, and she took the shot.

"Oh, that's interesting," she said as the screen filled with the negative image of the case's contents.

"What are those?" I asked.

"If they are what I think they are, it's going to be a very long night in the lab." She pulled the case from the X-ray table and slid it back onto the counter. "Do you want to do the honors?"

"Sure. Why not?"

I thumbed the latch releases, the spring-loaded tabs flew open, and I lifted the top. Just as Celeste predicted, a half-empty bottle of aftershave and a tube of deodorant lay inside with four neatly rolled joints tucked into slots where ink pens should've been.

Kodiak snatched the hand-rolled joints. "I'll take those, thank you."

The rest of us gazed at him as he pocketed the pot.

"Don't look at me like that. I'm just making sure they don't fall into the wrong hands. We can't have Pogonya finding them and . . . experimenting."

Shawn slapped him on the back. "You're always thinking of the children, aren't you, Mr. Humanitarian?"

Kodiak raised an eyebrow. "Just say no to drugs. It's a motto, or credo, or whatever."

Celeste broke up the show. "I'm not interested in the weed. These are what I want to get my hands on."

She opened a pair of pouches with at least a dozen vials of blood in each.

"Is that what you expected to find?" I asked.

"Yep. I'll need some help in the lab tonight. Any volunteers?"

I said, "I'm sure Pogo would love to help. She's really into what you're doing out here."

Celeste looked up. "Really? Well, all right, send her out. I love a young, curious mind that's eager to learn."

"She qualifies," I said, "but she won't be alone. We're keeping security on her around the clock, so Anya will likely never leave her side."

Celeste continued searching the case. "Good. She can help, too." She held up a manila envelope. "And . . . this is probably for you."

I took it and pulled out two sheets of paper stapled together. The front page had a handwritten note.

I have been discovered helping you, and I cannot live with the threats I'm now under. You will find 26 blood samples drawn by me. All were taken from inmates adjacent to Fitzsimon's cell. All are prescribed similar medications. You will find photocopies of each inmate's med list in the file folder, but I did not have time to copy their entire medical files. I've not run the samples. That part is up to you. On page two, you will find a photograph of a man I can't identify, but I suspect he's delivering illegal substances into the prison on a regular basis and providing them to certain correctional officers who administer them when they deliver the inmates' daily prescriptions. I cannot prove any of this, of course, but the blood samples will likely support my suspicions. If I am correct about what I fear is happening, my life is not the only one in danger. Yours is also at great risk.

Godspeed,
Brian D. Plum, M.D. (deceased)

When I flipped the page, I stared into the face of Gregory "Rod-Man" McDonald, special assistant to the deputy chief of staff to the vice president of the United States.

I tossed the papers onto the table. "Oh, boy."

After the rest of the team in the lab devoured the contents of the note, everyone was frozen except our mad scientist. She scooped up both bags of blood samples and darted for the clean room, where she'd spend the next several hours of her life.

I said, "Go get some rest, guys. We'll have to pull security in shifts until I can get us some extra bodies out here. Mongo, as always, you're in command while I'm gone."

"Where are you going?" the big man asked.

"To pick up a guest. We're going to get pretty busy in the next couple of days, so power-load calories and sleep while you can. You'll need plenty of both."

"A guest?" Mongo said. "You're going after McDonald, aren't you?"

I nodded, and my three teammates turned on a dime.

Kodiak said, "Screw the sleep, and we'll eat in the air. We're going with you. When have you ever known any of us to skip a snatch-and-grab?"

Arguing with operators like mine was only slightly less effective than arguing with a crocodile, so I made no protest.

We assembled in the op center, and Anya brought Pogo. "She is coming also inside. This is okay with you, yes? I thought so."

Oh, look. Another crocodile in my life.

Skipper spun in her chair. "So, what's this about?"

I briefed them on Dr. Plum and the care package he left us, fighting off questions as I went. "We don't have any information other than what I just gave you, so stop asking questions. Anya and Pogo, you're on lab duty until Dr. Mankiller releases you. You're okay with that, yes? I thought so."

Skipper said, "I've got something."

I held up a finger. "I'm not finished. Mongo, Kodiak, Shawn, and I are going after McDonald. We can't have him running free while we wrap this up. He's too dangerous out there."

"What are you going to do to him, Father?"

For some reason, I was okay with Pogo's interruption. "I'm going to give him a few things to think about and some quality time alone. Very alone."

She said, "My new baton and I would love a little quality time with him."

I gave Anya a look. "See what you're turning her into?"

The Russian grinned. "You are proud, no?"

Skipper said, "My turn now?"

I sighed. "Sure, go ahead."

"I've been working myself to death trying to find out who else was on that boat, and I'm hitting brick walls in every direction I turn, but I did a thing."

I said, "What kind of thing?"

She squirmed like a kindergartener telling a story. "Okay, so stay with me. Somebody gave the priest . . . where is he, by the way?"

"He's downstairs with Pat."

"Are we taking her back to Arizona?"

I said, "I haven't decided yet. Will you please focus?"

"Sorry. I've got a lot going on in my head. So, anyway, somebody made Isaiah believe there were two American CIA officers—or at least intelligence officers of some kind—which we know isn't true since the guy who washed up was former NSA and just a contractor, but close enough. The other two were supposed to be a Russian and who else?"

I slapped the table. "Mossad!"

She said, "Ding! We have a winner. And who do we know at Mossad?"

"Mr. Rabin," I said.

The analyst threw a stress ball at me, and for the first time in my life, I missed the catch, and the rubber ball bounced off my forehead. Everyone froze in apparent disbelief until Skipper finally said, "It's fine. I distracted you, but that is weird. Like, really weird. Are you okay?"

I threw the ball back. "Focus! Rabin."

"Oh, yeah. Guess who was just selected as the incoming director of Mossad? That's right. Our buddy, Mr. Rabin. And guess who has an audience with him in forty-eight hours?"

I shot a thumb at myself, and she nodded. "Ding! Another winner! Even if you can't catch anymore."

"So, I'm supposed to kidnap a government official from Pensacola *and* be in Jerusalem in the next two days?"

She glanced up at the clock. "Technically, it's forty-two-and-a-half hours, but yes."

I leaned back in my chair to let the reality of my life wash over me. *Why did I miss that ball?*

"Why can't I have my meeting on a secure line with Rabin and save all that dead travel time?"

Skipper eyed Mongo as if to say, "Explain it to him, please."

The big man said, "If a mid-level Mossad officer wanted to talk to you about a classified mission that never happened, would you take him seriously if he wouldn't make the time to put his butt in one of your beloved wingbacks?"

"Are you calling me a mid-level guy?"

Mongo shrugged. "To Rabin, yeah, you probably are."

"I guess that means I'd better find my passport."

Pogonya, whom I'd forgotten was at the table, said, "Ooh, me too? I've never been to Israel."

I held up a hand. "Give me the ball."

Skipper tossed it as if throwing it to a two-year-old, and I snatched it from the air before bouncing it off Pogo's noggin. "Pick one. Baton play with McDonald, or a quick-turnaround trip to Jerusalem. You can't have both."

She turned to her mother for help, but to my surprise, Anya didn't flinch. "Talk with your father, not me. He is in command . . . of this decision."

Pogo squeezed the ball. "I'll sleep on it and let you know when you get back with that terrible man who changed my tire. Come to think of it, I really want new tires, please."

I said, "I think we can manage new tires, and I'll wake you up when we get back from Pensacola."

"On second thought," Pogo said, "I won't sleep on it because I'll be in the lab with Dr. Celeste, so you can just tell me there."

Even though I knew the exact time, something made me eyeball my watch. "Let's suit up, boys. We've got a bad guy to bag, and the clock is ticking."

Chapter 33
The Price

"Get Singer on the line," I said.

Skipper gave me a mock salute. "Aye, Captain."

In an instant, the sniper's calm tone filled the room through the speakers. "Good evening."

I said, "Sitrep."

Singer cleared his throat. "Our subject has a girlfriend."

"Oh, that's very good news. Does the wife know?"

"Apparently not. I'm on McDonald and the lady friend, and Gator's on the wife back at the beach house."

"Did you score a second vehicle?" I asked.

"We did. With them spending time apart, it only made sense to keep both of us mobile."

"Has either of you had any sleep?"

"Here and there, but we're okay. What's on your mind?"

I said, "We finally have a plan, and we're on our way to pick up Mc-Donald. Can you snatch the girlfriend after we grab him?"

"No problem. She's a soft target."

"Have you been inside the house yet?"

"Only once," he said. "I'll send you a sketch."

"Great. Skipper pulled the plans from the building permit, but it's always nice to know exactly what we're walking into. With any luck, though, we'll be able to snatch him off the street without penetrating the house. We'll be there in less than two hours with the full team, minus Anya."

Singer hesitated. "Is everything okay with Anya?"

"It is, but she's keeping Pogo in sight after the incident in Athens."

"I get it, but she'd come in handy managing the women."

"I'll see what I can do, and I'll call you when we're twenty minutes out. If you're confident the wife is in for the night, pull Gator off her. I'd like to have his speed if things get out of hand and this turns into a footrace."

"Done," he said. "One of us will pick you up at the airport. I assume you'll be in the Citation."

"That's right. We'll see you soon."

Skipper ended the call, and I slapped my hands together. "All right, folks. Let's mainline some caffeine and go bag ourselves some unfaithful government muscle."

Anya asked, "What about me?"

"That's up to you," I said. "We'll have McDonald wrapped up, so he won't be a threat if we leave Pogo with Celeste. Singer's right, though. If we're going to snatch the girlfriend, it would be nice to have you out front."

"I could come," Pogonya said.

My immediate reaction was resistance, but she'd been thrust into a world she didn't understand the instant McDonald confronted her with the flat tire, and sheltering her from the reality of what we did wasn't realistic.

Anya's gaze met mine, and I raised an eyebrow in question. Her silent response came in the form of a tiny nod, and I said, "Okay, but you're staying inside the vehicle at all times, and you are to say absolutely nothing. Got it?"

Pogonya smiled, and Anya scowled. "Do not celebrate this. Is very serious thing we are doing, and is not something anyone will enjoy. Is very dangerous, and you must stay out of way and follow instructions exactly at every moment. You understand this, yes?"

"Yes, Mama, I've got it. What about Dr. Celeste?"

Skipper held up one finger as she spoke on the phone. When she hung up, she said, "It's taken care of. A friend from the hospital is coming to help in the lab. She can use the extra cash, and she loves the work."

"Nice job," I said. "Pay her well, and keep her number handy."

Pogonya said, "But don't let her take my place all the time. I love working in the lab, too."

"Don't worry," I said. "There's never a shortage of work to do out there, and you're always welcome to jump in."

I scanned the table. "Anything else?"

Heads shook, so I said, "Let's gear up. Wheels up in fifteen minutes. Anya, are you good to fly?"

"I am. Are you?"

"Yep. Let's move."

* * *

We made the fifteen-minute window and climbed away from Bonaventure with a stone-faced team of commandos who were ready for anything the night could dish out, and one overly excited girl who had no idea what she was about to witness.

I called as planned, and Gator pulled beneath the FBO's portico in his Suburban.

"Where's Singer?" I asked as we climbed inside.

Gator looked at Pogonya and paused. "He's . . . still on McDonald, so instead of swapping places with him, I came to get you. Is *she* on this with us?"

"Good call," I said. "Is the wife in for the night?"

He couldn't look away from Pogonya. "She's already in bed and appears to be sound asleep. Uh . . . what are we going to do with *her*?"

"The wife?" I asked.

He shook his head and pointed at my daughter. "No. Her."

"Tell him, Pogo."

She said, "I'm going to stay in the vehicle with my mouth shut and watch you guys scare this guy even more than he scared me. It's going to be great."

Gator shrugged. "Cool with me, but they told you it's not going to be pretty, right?"

"The uglier, the better."

He shook his head. "You're going to be just as terrifying as your mother."

We pulled away from the airport, and Gator said, "I can borrow a van if you want it for the snatch-and-grab."

I asked, "How can you *borrow* a van in the middle of the night?"

"It's parked at the bishop's beach house with the keys in the ignition. I think it might belong to the diocese or whatever. Anyway, it's there if you want it."

"Side door?"

He gave me a nod and a knowing grin. "Absolutely. Just like you like."

"Is our target still with the girlfriend?"

He tapped his ear. "Do you have your sat-coms on?"

We turned on our radios and ran through checks. "We do now."

Gator said, "Singer, sitrep."

The sniper answered. "It looks like the evening is winding down. What's your ETA?"

"Sixteen minutes," Gator said. "We're picking up the van."

"Perfect. The target vehicle is a block and a half east on the north side of the street. It's the same grey Audi as before. I'll report movement."

We parked on the street a few hundred feet from the bishop's house, and Shawn followed Gator into the backyard on foot. They returned in a dark blue van that wasn't exactly what I would've chosen for a snatch vehicle, but it was a better option than the Suburbans and their narrow doors.

Gator led us to McDonald's grey Audi, and we staged half a block away in the van with Anya and Pogo in the Suburban just in front of us.

"He's coming out," Singer said.

I checked the sidewalks, narrow yard, and porches in every direction. "It's nice and quiet, so let's keep it that way. Are you in your SUV?"

Singer said, "Affirmative."

"Good. Move into position behind the van. You'll be the caboose. Anya will lead and block with SUV number one. Mongo and I will make the grab from the van, and Gator will be ready if McDonald darts."

Shawn said, "Do you want Kodiak and me on the wings?"

"Absolutely. I want you between the houses. If he squirts, I think he'll take the sidewalk, but I don't want to give him an easy out if he shoots for the houses."

The SEAL and former Green Beret stepped from the van and melted into the darkness.

Singer killed his lights and rolled in behind us just as McDonald rounded the corner on foot. He surveyed the street as I expected him to, but our position behind a collection of palms gave us just enough cover and concealment to avoid grabbing his attention.

"Stay on your toes," I said on the open-channel comms. "Target is approaching his vehicle. Be ready to move in five . . . four . . . three . . . two . . . execute!"

We kept our lights off as all three vehicles rolled at the same instant McDonald closed his door. Anya's positioning was textbook-perfect, pinning the Audi in its place against the curb. Gator stopped the van adjacent to the car door, with our front bumper almost touching Anya's. I threw open the van's side door and followed Mongo onto the street.

McDonald was pinned with no avenue of escape, but he obviously thought differently. By the time I pulled open his driver's side door, he had scrambled across the seat and out the passenger-side rear door.

Gator slipped from behind the steering wheel and whispered, "Run, rabbit. Please run."

McDonald could run, but that would only delay the inevitable and leave him breathless and exhausted when we finally threw him headfirst into the van.

I should've anticipated his reaction based on what little I knew of his background and character, but it caught me by surprise. Running obviously wasn't in his plan. McDonald was a fighter, and in my book, throwing him in the van with a bloody nose was even better than Gator's footrace.

McDonald's experience and training clearly made it obvious to him what was happening, and he drew his pistol the second he was clear of the car. The last thing I needed was a gunfight on a beachfront neighborhood at one in the morning.

Shawn and Kodiak burst from between houses and closed on our target as soon as his gun was out. Singer rounded the van's rear with his pistol raised and trained on our target. Anya moved in absolute silence around the front of the next parked car and closed the distance on McDonald.

The man tightened his grip on the pistol, and his knuckles whitened as the muzzle bore directly at my head. The curve of the suppressor was in perfect focus, and I was thankful there would be little noise when he pulled the trigger.

Relaxing my knees, I allowed gravity to clear my head from McDonald's line of fire just as his pistol hissed twice and glass shattered behind and in front of me. Taking temporary cover outside the driver's door, I had no field of vision in front of me, and I couldn't imagine why glass would've broken between me and McDonald. His pistol rounds piercing the van windows behind me made sense, but there was no glass between his muzzle and my head.

The painful huff of exhalation answered my question as I peered over the door. McDonald lay half inside the back seat and half out, his belly resting in the opening where the window had been the moment before Shawn collided with him from behind.

I yanked open the door and dived inside, capturing McDonald's pistol with my right hand and grabbing a handful of hair with my left. Wrenching the silenced pistol from his grip, I sent a thundering blow to his temple with the butt of his weapon before pulling him fully inside the vehicle.

The blow dazed him, but he wasn't out. The fighter in him still had the wherewithal to draw a knife with his left hand and swing it wildly over his head, slashing like a maniac at my arms and face. I withdrew, narrowly avoiding the attack, and heard the unmistakable crack and hiss of Anya's Taser.

Somehow, she had slithered through the passenger-side door and set the probes of her weapon into the flesh of McDonald's back. He spasmed and bellowed until the knife tumbled from his hand and his body fell limp on the back seat.

Gator moved into position beside me, opened the rear door, and pulled the man from the car. He wasted no energy being gentle as he deposited him onto the floor of the van with a thud. "I told you that you should've run. It would've been better for you and a lot more fun for me. But no, you wouldn't listen, would you? You just had to make a stand."

Kodiak stepped into the van, flex-cuffed the man's wrists, and tied his ankles. Yanking the remaining rope from McDonald's ankles, Kodiak looped it around his neck from behind. "There. That should be nice and comfy for you. Maybe it'll help you understand why shooting at the boss isn't such a great idea."

"Let's roll!" I ordered.

We drove several blocks to a darkened gravel parking lot behind what had once been a dive shop.

I said, "That went well, huh?"

"Could've been better," Mongo said. "Are you okay?"

"I'm good. He missed me, but the van is going to need some glass work. Let's make sure those rounds didn't penetrate the house across the street before we go."

Shawn said, "Already checked. One got a tree, and the other is lodged in the seatback of the van."

"Well done," I said. "Anya, you're up. Grab the girlfriend, and introduce her to Mrs. McDonald. Keep Gator and Singer with you. The rest of us are headed home. We'll see you back at Bonaventure. Is Pogo good?"

Anya nodded toward the passenger seat of the Suburban, and I stepped to the window. "You okay, baby girl?"

For the first time, I saw my daughter speechless. She sat with her mouth agape and her head and eyes darting back and forth between the van and the team standing in the gravel lot.

I gave her a moment and asked again. "Hey, are you good?"

She swallowed hard. "He shot at you."

I squeezed her arm. "Yeah, people do that. I'm getting used to it."

"Is he dead?"

"Oh, no, baby. He's very much alive, but he'll soon wish he was dead. He *is* the guy who changed your tire and threatened you, right?"

She wiped a bead of sweat from her upper lip. "I think so. He's the same size, but I didn't get a good look at his face."

I opened the door. "Come take a look. We need to be sure."

She recoiled. "I don't know. Is that really a good idea? I'm not sure I want to."

"You don't have to. I'm sure it's him, but he's hogtied pretty good in there. He's not going to hurt you."

She slowly slid from the seat and took a few timid steps toward the van.

I said, "Let's see his face."

Mongo grabbed McDonald by the shoulders and pulled his head across the threshold of the van's sliding side door until we were staring at his bloody, upside-down face.

Pogonya stepped closer to me until her body was pressed against my side. "That's him. Are you sure he's alive?"

"Look at his chest," I said. "It's rising and falling. He's alive. He's just having a little nap. Do you want to stay with your mother to pick up the girlfriend, or would you rather fly home with us?"

Her body quivered beside me. "Is this what they're going to do to the girl?"

"No. It'll be nothing like this."

"I don't know. I wish I hadn't come. I wasn't expecting anything like this. I thought it would be cool, but this is . . . I don't know what to call it."

I took a knee beside her. "It's called paying the price for scaring my little girl. Nobody gets to do that."

Chapter 34

Worlds Collide

Pogonya opted to fly back to Bonaventure with me instead of witnessing two kidnappings in one night, so I put her in the right seat of the Citation, and we took to the sky. She was silent for the first half of the flight, although she glanced across her shoulder into the cabin at regular intervals along the way.

"You don't have to keep checking. There are three hardcore good guys between you and the bad guy. They won't let him get past them. I promise. Even if they weren't there, McDonald is sound asleep and well bound. His days of threatening you are long gone."

She finally spoke. "It's not that. I just can't believe I'm on an airplane with a guy who scared the crap out of me and tried to shoot you."

"Welcome to my world."

"If somebody tried to kill me, I'd never be the same. You just blew it off like it's nothing. How do you do that?"

I scanned the panel, and everything aboard the airplane was perfect except for the one thing that mattered most to me.

"It's not a world I want you to live in."

"But Mama does it."

I played with a pen to buy a little time while my brain turned itself inside out. "Yes, but she's not the typical—"

Pogo cut me off. "Anything! She's not the typical anything."

"You've got that right," I said.

She cocked her head and looked so much like the little girl I wish I could've known a decade earlier. She said, "What did they do to her to make her that way?"

I suddenly wanted a thousand more pens to buy a lot more time. "I'm afraid that's a conversation you'll need to have with her if she's ever ready to talk about it with you. The world was a vastly different place back then. The Cold War was going on, and the Russians took a very different approach to training operators like your mother."

"Is that what she is? An operator?"

"She's a lot of things. And I doubt I could list them all, even if I had an eternity to try."

"Why didn't you marry her when the two of you fell in love?"

There weren't enough ink pens on the planet to buy my brain the time I needed to process that one, so I said, "Too many things went wrong back then, but isn't it nice how we're sometimes given second chances?"

"Citation Eight-Alpha-Foxtrot, descend and maintain flight level three-one-zero without delay for traffic twelve o'clock, two-five miles opposite direction, a regional jet between flight level three-three-zero and three-six-zero experiencing mechanical issues."

I'd never been more thankful to hear an air traffic controller's voice in my life. I set the altitude preselect and began the hurried descent. "Eight-Alpha-Fox is out of three-five-oh for three-one-oh with no delay and searching for traffic."

"What does that mean?" Pogonya asked.

I pointed through the windshield. "Look for an airplane coming straight at us about twenty miles away. We're descending to get out of his way. Apparently, they're having some kind of issue holding altitude."

She threw her finger into the air. "I see them!"

I keyed the mic. "Jacksonville Center, Citation-Eight-Alpha-Fox has the regional jet in sight, and we'd like to continue the descent when it's convenient for you."

He said, "Citation-Eight-Alpha-Fox, maintain visual separation from the regional jet and descend at pilot's discretion and maintain flight level one-niner-zero."

"Eight-Alpha-Fox is leaving three-two-zero for one-niner-zero with visual separation."

I programmed the descent, and Anya's Citation obeyed the electronic commands like the magnificent machine she was.

"That was exciting," Pogonya said.

I gave her a wink. "You've had quite a night."

She put on her mother's most sincere face. "Tell me the truth, Father. Were you afraid?"

I laughed. "No. It was just an airplane. We had plenty of room to get out of their way."

"You know what I meant."

"It's not really fear, Pogo. It's the reality of the world I live in. If I trembled in fear every time somebody pointed a gun at me, I would've been dead a long time ago."

"Were you scared the first time it happened?"

I laughed out loud. "Can I let you in on a little secret?"

"Yes!"

"The first person who ever pointed a gun at me when I started this job, or whatever this is, was your mother. I was mortified."

"I can't wait to hear this story, and I'm really glad she didn't shoot you."

"In her defense, I did shoot her first, but only after she'd cut my tongue in half."

"What?"

"We'll make that a story over smores when all of this is over. I've got an airplane to land at the moment."

* * *

Back on the ground in St. Marys, Dr. Mankiller buzzed Pogonya and me into her lab while Shawn, Kodiak, and Mongo escorted our special guest to his new luxury accommodations.

"Why are you still working?" I asked.

Celeste wiped her eyes. "Because some things can't wait."

"Where's your help? I thought Skipper arranged for a tech from the hospital to give you a hand."

"She did, and she was great, but I sent her home half an hour ago. Everything's on autopilot at the moment, and I should have some results for you in a few minutes."

"Anything interesting so far?"

She stood and stretched. "As a matter of fact, yes. So far, none of the samples are showing signs of the same amphetamine or LSD that Garland had in his body."

"Oh, that *is* interesting, and it's right in line with our theory that whatever this is, it's targeted directly at Fitzsimon."

"It looks that way," she said.

I glanced across the room full of equipment I would never be smart enough to understand. "Go home, Celeste. You need some rest, and there's nothing we can do with the information in the next twenty-four hours. I have to be in Israel sometime today, I think."

"I can't go home and leave this running without me, but I can shut everything down within an hour or so. I'll get some sleep then."

I stood. "Thank you for everything. You give us capabilities we'd never have without you. That means a great deal to me, and I sincerely appreciate what you do."

She wrapped her arms around me. "I know you do, Chase, and I love that about you. Thank you. I see your appreciation in my bank account every month. You changed my life forever, and I love what I do here. It's cool to feel like I'm part of something, you know?"

"I know exactly what you mean, and I feel the same. Thanks again. I have to run. I've got a very special guest who deserves a little over-the-top attention from me."

"I don't envy that guy, but I'm sure you'll have fun dishing out exactly what he deserves."

Pogonya had been practically invisible during our visit to the lab, but she finally said, "I'm sorry I didn't come help tonight, Dr. Celeste."

260 · CAP DANIELS

"No reason to be sorry. I had plenty of help, but you never need an invitation. The door to the lab is always open for you."

Pogonya put on a beautiful smile that soon became a long-overdue yawn.

* * *

We drove the VW Microbus from the airport back to Bonaventure with my daughter drifting closer to sleep with every passing minute.

I said, "I still have a lot to do tonight, but it looks like you're ready to hit the sack."

She stretched. "I'm really tired, but I'm not sure I want you to leave me alone."

"Let's get you in bed, and I'll put somebody on your door until I come in. How's that?"

"I guess I'll be okay now that I know you've got that scumbag. Tell me what you're going to do to him."

"I'm going to interrogate him and yank everything he knows out of his head, but first, I'm going to let him spend a little time reflecting on what he did to frighten the most important person in my life."

She bit her lip. "I love you, Father."

* * *

With Pogonya sleeping soundly behind her locked bedroom door, I made the walk to the shop where I would encounter Gregory McDonald on my turf and on my terms.

I walked into the cell of a room where Mongo, Shawn, and Kodiak waited with McDonald stripped to his shorts and tied to a steel chair bolted to the concrete floor. I'd done things inside that room that most people couldn't stomach, and I prayed I possessed the self-control to keep that night's guest alive long enough to prove valuable.

I took a knee in front of Gregory McDonald. "Wake him up."

Shawn hit him with a stream of cold water from a massive hose, and McDonald shook off the blast. The shock and disbelief on his face made me want to laugh out loud, but I wouldn't break character. The man he was about to encounter wasn't a man of good humor or tolerance.

He growled. "You have no idea—"

I had no interest in anything that would come out of his mouth, so I shoved a rag between his teeth and wrapped four rounds of duct tape around his head to hold the gag in place. "You weren't told to speak. Tonight, you only listen."

His muffled rage looked like that of a cartoon character on the verge of exploding.

I said, "You thought you knew who I was, but you are wrong. You thought I was the kind of man who would tolerate you threatening my daughter, but you were wrong. You thought I was a man you could shoot in the face, but you were wrong. Clearly, you're very good at being very wrong."

He bucked and growled behind the gag, so I tilted my head and watched him writhe.

When he finally fell limp on the chair, I said, "You're not going to escape, ever. In fact, you'll likely never leave this room."

I sniffed the air and shuffled backward several inches. "What's that smell, Gregory? Did I frighten you that badly already? Oh, I hope not. You're supposed to be some colossal thing—the muscle for the man. Isn't that what you are, Gregory? Muscle for the man?"

He thrashed his head back and forth, trying in vain to expel the gag I'd shoved deep in his mouth.

I leaned in until my face was almost touching his and whispered, "Feel that? That burning in your stomach? That acid in your throat and on the roof of your mouth? The spikes being driven into your ears? Not knowing what I'm about to do to you? Not knowing exactly what I'm capable of and imagining the worst? That's power, Greg. *My* power. You tried this on my daughter, you worthless piece of trash, but I'm a lot better at it than you. Fear isn't a game I play. It's a world I own."

I clenched a fist of iron and cocked it high behind my shoulder. McDonald grimaced against the coming blow, but I didn't let it come thundering down against his jaw. Instead, I drew my knife and sliced the tape holding the gag in his mouth. He spat the rag from between his teeth and bellowed obscenities until I pressed the tip of my blade beneath his chin. "Stop talking, or I'll cut your tongue out, starting just above your left knee."

I turned and growled. "Feed him, water him, and for God's sake, wash that stench off of him."

"What do you want?" McDonald yelled the instant before Shawn shoved a protein bar into his mouth.

I turned back as he gagged on the dense, dry lump sticking to his teeth. "What do I want? Is that really your question, or is your question what do I want in order to let you go?"

He gnawed at the mush Shawn crammed into his face. "What do you want from me?"

"Water him," I ordered, and Kodiak opened the nozzle again.

The wall of water that hit McDonald in the face sent his head flying backward until it could go no further without separating the vertebrae in his neck. High-pressure water rocketed up his nose, gagging him and sending his body into convulsions and maniacal panic.

I waved for Kodiak to stop the onslaught, and he shut off the hose.

In mock frustration, I wiped the water from my shirt. "Okay, I'll tell you what I want from you. I want absolutely nothing. I simply want to make you pay. That's right, Gregory. You're going to pay a price your weak little mind isn't capable of comprehending yet, but I'll teach you. And when that lesson is over, I'm going to destroy everything you think you love because you scared my little girl. And nobody gets away with that."

As if on cue, the heavy steel door to the cell swung open, and the most terrifying woman I'd ever known walked in with an iPad in one hand and a fistful of black hair in the other. Anya held up both for McDonald to see. "Look what I have."

The screen came to life, playing a video of two women scowling at each other and yelling as if each had something the other had once wanted. The first was Gloria McDonald, Gregory's wife, while the younger, raven-haired woman was the one he'd spent six hours with prior to becoming my guest of honor.

Anya hissed. "Worlds collide and crumble beneath people like you when they threaten our family."

Chapter 35

Still Miss?

Anya and I left the shop with Gregory McDonald in our wake. "I think we need to have a conversation with our daughter."

The Russian beside me, who'd spent her life destroying the lives of others without flinching, broke. Well clear of the shop and out of earshot of the rest of the world, she stopped, took my wrist, and locked eyes with me. "I do not want this for her."

Pulling my arm from her grip, I let my hand collect hers. "Neither do I."

She melted into my arms, and we stood, wrapped around each other in silence as the stars peered down on us, just as they'd done since the Creator spoke them into existence.

I said, "She was pretty shaken up on the flight home. I gave her time and space and waited for her to break the ice."

"What did she say?"

"She asked how I could do it—how I could deal with someone sticking a gun in my face and move past it the way I did."

"I am certain you told her something brilliant, yes?"

"I doubt it. I probably told her it was routine and I just didn't think about it, but what I said wasn't important. Her reaction to the whole night was the meaningful outcome. She was terrified."

Anya squeezed my hand. "I do not like her being afraid."

"I misspoke," I said. "Terrified isn't the right word. She was frightened when McDonald threatened her, but when she watched us grab him, it was unthinkable to her that anyone could do that routinely."

"Good," she said. "I am pleased she was not intrigued or maybe fascinated. What we do is not glamorous, and I am glad our daughter got to see the part of it that is frightening."

I nodded. "What do you think about letting her see us question McDonald?"

"She does not need to see the animals inside her parents."

"I agree, but I want her to understand that we'll protect her without end."

"You are best father she could have, and I love how you feel about her."

"She's the most important person in my life, and I'd die for her without a thought."

Anya smiled. "I think this is beautiful thing for you to say, but is better that you are alive for her . . . and for me."

* * *

A shower cleansed the surface, but it would take far more than soap and hot water to erase what lay beneath the skin of the situation we'd created for ourselves. Questions far outweighed answers in those early morning hours, but I felt the balance tipping, and the man with whom I'd sip undrinkable coffee before the Earth could spin another rotation would hopefully lay the weights on my side of those teetering scales.

Although the coffee pot called to me, I ignored its siren song. My body and mind needed the sleep I'd hopefully get on the long flight to Tel Aviv. What I didn't expect was the pair of companions waiting in the kitchen.

"Why aren't you two asleep?"

Pogonya said, "I was asleep, but you said I had to choose between going with you to Israel or visiting my baton upon Gregory McDonald. I made my choice, and Mama is coming with us."

"So, this is how my life works now, huh? The two of you decide—"

Before I could finish the question, she said, "Get used to it. You're stuck with us."

I threw an arm around my daughter. "I don't care much for your mom, but I'm pretty fond of you. You know that?"

"You are a terrible liar, Father. You love both of us, and we love you, too."

* * *

I didn't want to think about the amount of ink on the check we had to write to cover the Gulfstream that Skipper chartered to carry the three of us nonstop from St. Marys, Georgia, to Ben Gurion International on the far side of the world, but I didn't let the expense keep me awake. Knowing Pogo was safe and sleeping a few seats away gave me the assurance I needed to let my heavy eyelids do what came naturally.

Eastbound flights do strange things to the clock inside the human brain. It was barely daylight when we climbed aboard and pitch-dark when we touched down in Tel Aviv. Checking my watch would've been a meaningless waste of time because it didn't matter what time the hands displayed. My body and mind felt like it was mid-morning, regardless of where the sun was hanging out.

Visiting the soon-to-be director of the world's premier intelligence agency had its peculiarities. Not the least of which involved being towed from the tarmac into an enormous hangar instead of walking into an FBO and spending some quality time with a customs agent. Nobody would stamp our passports, and thanks to the blacked-out windows on the SUVs, very few people would see the three Americans who arrived in the middle of the night, on a private jet, with an agenda that would never be mentioned out loud.

Four Mossad officers escorted us into the waiting SUV and delivered us to a private residence high in the hills where Anya and I had been once before. Another officer met us at the door and escorted us into a study that would've made the perfect setting for a scene in a James Bond movie.

"What is this place?" Pogonya asked softly.

I took in the dark paneling, rich leather furnishings, and walls of books in every language imaginable. "It's a place you can never claim to have seen, my dear. In fact, you're going to step out with one of the Mossad officers while we have our discussion."

"Nonsense!" came the booming voice of a man whose head held more secrets than the rest of the intelligence world combined. His dark hair and suit made him the perfect character for the setting, and he reached for Pogonya's hand. "I am Dovrat Rabin, and it is an enormous honor to have you in my home."

She shook his scarred hand and curtsied. "The pleasure is mine, Mr. Rabin. I am Pogonya Fulton."

Rabin glanced at me and then finally at Anya. "You should be enormously proud. She may, of course, stay if you and she wish, but the kitchen staff is working on desserts for a reception. I'm certain they would welcome the palate of a beautiful young taster like Pogonya."

Our daughter accepted the enviable assignment and left Anya and me alone with one of the most powerful men in the world of international intelligence.

He motioned to a sofa. "Please, make yourselves comfortable, and David will be in with tea and coffee shortly. It is a joy to have both of you in my home again."

I suddenly wanted to buy a dozen sofas just like the one beneath me. "Thank you for seeing us on such short notice, especially considering the nature of our request."

David, who was clearly more soldier than servant, placed a silver tray on the table in front of us and offered to pour. Mr. Rabin waved him off and spoke in Hebrew. "Thank you, David. See that we are not disturbed."

The smell of the coffee left my nose begging my mouth to say no thank you, but refusing anything from Dovrat Rabin was tantamount to a slap in the face.

He poured two cups of the steaming brew and glanced at Anya. "Tea or coffee?"

The mother of my child answered in Hebrew. "*Kfa, bebaksha.*"

Rabin smiled and poured the coffee.

We sipped, and I forced the kerosene down my throat.

Mr. Rabin crossed his legs. "I can ask you how your flight was and how you have been, but we are warriors, not diplomats. I owe the two of you a favor, and tonight, I pay my debt."

I placed my cup on a doily on the side table. "You owe us nothing, Mr. Rabin, but I deeply appreciate your willingness to grant us an audience."

He rolled his open hand in the air as if to say, *Spit it out, boy.*

I didn't waste any more of his time. "Sir, there was a boat—a yacht, really—off the coast of Key West, Florida, with four men aboard. Two were Americans, one was Russian, and the fourth, we understand, was Israeli."

Rabin leaned back in his chair. "Next, you are going to tell me a minister, a priest, and a rabbi walked into a bar."

The knot in my stomach tightened. "I wish I could tell you this was a joke, sir, but I cannot."

He took a sip. "Indeed. Please continue."

"A third American arrived, caused a disturbance, and may have killed at least one of the Americans on board. The dead American was a former . . ."

Rabin planted his cup on the table without a doily. "The dead American is a National Security Agency contractor. Yes, of course I know. And you want to know who the Israeli is, yes?"

"I want to know who everyone was, and nobody knows more about who the players are than you."

"Flattery, my boy, is wasted on me, but you are, of course, correct. I know a great many things no one should know. It is the nature of *our* business." With the emphasis on the word *our*, he stared back and forth between Anya and me. "First, tell me why you would travel all the way across the world to drink coffee you can't stomach and to ask me questions about such an obscure event that no more than a dozen people know ever happened."

Lying to him would not only destroy the relationship, but it would also get us thrown out of his house, so I said, "Somebody set up a small-time American criminal for the murder of the NSA contractor, and they're feeding him a chemical diet cooked up in a kitchen run by the Central Intelligence Agency. I want to know why."

Mr. Rabin poured a second round of coffee, but he meticulously placed a sugar cube in the bottom of my cup before pouring mine. "For your soft American stomach."

I thanked him with a silent nod, and he let his focus drift to the ceiling of the ornate chamber.

Finally, he said, "First, tell me your theory."

"I'm not going to play games with you," I said. "I don't know, but my guess is an Iranian–Russian deal—probably arms or oil."

"Your instincts are good, Mr. Fulton, if a bit naïve. Who benefits from war?"

"The victor."

Rabin laughed. "Oh, my boy, no. Nothing could be further from the truth. Those who benefit from war are never the ones who stand and fight. They are always those who crawl beneath tables at the sound of a backfiring auto. Tell him, Ms. Burinkova. You are still miss and not yet missus, I presume."

Anya said, "For now."

Mr. Rabin glanced in the direction of the kitchen. "Ah, I see. So, Ms. Burinkova—for now—it was *your* former countryman on that yacht. So, what is *your* theory?"

I would never be the operator Anya was, but greater than that, I would never remotely approach the level of spy she was.

She said, "This depends on how your officer represented himself and how good his Farsi is . . . or was."

Rabin smiled at me. "You are a lucky man, Dr. Fulton. Only an enormous fool would let this one escape again."

Anya closed her eyes and groaned. "My God. It was a nuclear weapons deal."

The Israeli spymaster laced his fingers together. "It *would* have been a nuclear weapons deal, but the imprisoned American with only one ear was sent to disrupt an operation that Mossad worked eighteen months to create."

"It was *your* operation?" I asked in utter disbelief.

"We would have closed the snare and captured Ms. Burinkova's countryman, thus tearing the heart out of the Russian-Iranian transactional pipeline, but *your* government threw an untrained buffoon into the middle of a brilliant Mossad operation and left the doors swinging wide open for a nuclear Iran . . . Israel's greatest threat."

"Why would we do that?"

"Again I ask, who benefits from war?"

Rabin's ominous tone seemed to echo through the room and inside my soul. I felt as if I'd been kicked in the chest, and no words would come.

After an eternity drowning in my own terror, Rabin offered me a lifeline. "Have you ever heard of Solovetsky Monastery?"

I slowly shook my head, but Anya said, "Of course."

Mr. Rabin uncrossed his legs and leaned forward. "Spies are everywhere, inside every crevice, and often wear the mask—or even the collar—of a man of peace."

I suddenly wanted to swallow every drop of coffee inside the silver pot. "Can you please explain what you're—"

Mr. Rabin stood. "No, I cannot, but Ms. Burinkova can. I'll have Miss Pogonya escorted to the foyer. And Dr. Fulton, I have not yet repaid what I owe you, but if this plays out the way I expect, and you survive it, I, and the nation I love, will both be further in your debt."

Chapter 36
Solovetsky Monastery

Back aboard the charter, Pogonya thumbed through a small, leather-bound book, and I was intrigued. "What's that?"

When she looked up, I saw the same expression that had watched me two decades before—when I was little more than a boy in the hands of one of Russia's deadliest weapons—and I fell in love with her all over again.

She closed the book, tucked it beneath her arm, and smiled. "If you can have secrets, so can I."

"You and your mother will be the death of me."

Pogo grinned. "Can you think of a better way to go?"

"Stop it," I said. "You're way too good at this already, and you're still a child."

She seemed to consider my admonition. "I wish I could've been a child with you as my Poppa when I learned . . . everything."

"I wish that too," I said, "but we're making up for it now, aren't we?"

She unbuckled, stepped across the aisle, and kissed my cheek. "We are, and I love it. Thank you for bringing me with you. Did you and Mama get the answers you needed?"

I shot a glance at Anya. "I'm not sure yet, but something tells me your mother will let me know."

Pogonya trained her attention on Anya. "Well, Mama?"

The beautiful woman who'd haunted me, and even kept me alive when I should've died a dozen times, said, "Tell to your father story of Solovetsky Monastery."

"Mama, your English, please."

Anya laced her hand inside my elbow. "When your father says to me that he does not find my accent to be sexy anymore, I will then speak proper English."

Pogonya rolled her eyes. "Get a room, you two. What do you want to know about the monastery?"

I shrugged. "I don't know what I want to know. Just start talking, and I'll tell you when to stop."

Pogonya said, "Okay, here we go. Solovetsky Monastery is a citadel on the Solovetsky Islands in the White Sea. You do know where the White Sea is, right?"

"I do, but it's not a place I plan to vacation any time soon."

"No, I would think not. Anyway, after the Bolshevik Revolution and Civil War, the monastery became Solovki Prison Camp. And here's an interesting side note. That prison became the blueprint for the Soviet Gulag system."

I leaned in. "This is all fascinating and news to me, but I don't know what it has to do with why we came all this way to Israel to see Mr. Rabin."

Pogonya turned to her mother, and Anya said, "Tell to him story of monks escaping."

"That may not even be true, Mama."

"Tell to him! Is important."

Pogonya sighed. "Which one? The boat or the hike?"

"Both. But first, boat."

Pogonya shook her head as if still disgusted by her mother's accent. "Fine. The prisoners at Solovetsky, mostly monks, were forced to cut timber in a massive logging operation as part of their punishment, apparently just for being Christians. There are rumors of a small group of monks secretly building a raft with a sail and rudder out of some of the trees they cut down. The rumor says they sailed away to the north in the middle of the night in July or August of nineteen thirty."

"That sounds pretty specific for a rumor," I said.

Pogonya continued. "Specific or not, it's still just a rumor. They allegedly sailed to a tiny village called Lesozavodsky. In case you failed Northern Russian geography, that's an extremely rural village in the Kandalakshsky District of Murmansk Oblast, and more importantly, it's *north* of the Arctic Circle."

"Sounds delightful," I said.

She groaned. "That's part of why I don't believe the rumor. Even in July or August, the sea would likely have been frozen that far north, making it impossible to sail all the way to Lesozavodsky, especially on a poorly constructed raft. The monks would've been wet and suffered hypothermia that they couldn't survive."

Anya leaned around me. "I hope you never have to know what a person will endure to escape such a place. When your father rescued me from Black Dolphin, I would have given my life to get out of that Hell. There is no price too high to escape from a place like that."

Our daughter looked away as the thought washed over her.

I took her hand. "That's why we do this, Pogo. We fight so others don't have to."

"But why does it have to be you?"

"It's what we are, and why we exist."

"No, Father. The two of you are my parents, and *we*—all three of us—exist to be a family."

I've been hit by bullets the size of my thumb and men the size of Mongo, but nothing has ever struck me like the words of a teenage girl that day, high above the Atlantic with Israel astern and home somewhere ahead. In that moment, I wanted to walk away from everything my world demanded of me except for my daughter and her mother.

I've always believed that Anya was capable of turning off emotions like a machine when the moment required it of her, and that point in time seemed to be such a moment. She said, "It does not matter if you believe rumor, Pogonya. Tell rest of story to your father, or you will have to listen to me tell him in his favorite accent."

Pogonya groaned. "Oh, Mama . . . fine. So, supposedly, the monks made it to Lesozavodsky, where someone fed them and gave them supplies before they walked a hundred fifty kilometers—that's almost one hundred miles—to the border of Finland."

"Wait a minute," I said. "Are you sure they were all monks?"

Pogonya frowned. "What difference does it make? It's probably not even true."

"It matters because Rabin didn't say anything about monks. He was talking about priests."

Pogonya cocked her head. "There were tons of Eastern Orthodox priests imprisoned at Solovetsky, too, but the story of the escape has always been about monks, as far as I know."

"What about the other escape your mother mentioned? The hike?"

"Now, that one actually has some merit. It took place in nineteen twenty-five, in midwinter, while the White Sea was frozen solid. A few prisoners, including priests, hiked three hundred kilometers across the ice to Finland for over five weeks. That would have been a tremendous feat, but it's more believable than the raft story, and there was even one prisoner who wrote a book about it. His name was something like Malsagoff, and I think the book was called *An Island Hell*."

I leaned back and tried to imagine the conditions those desperate men faced on such a journey. The wonder led me to snatch my satphone from a pocket and search for the book. It took a couple of minutes to download it, and ninety minutes to read the horrifying story of conditions inside the early Gulag and the miraculous escape to the west across the frozen, unforgiving wilderness of Northern Russia. In the final electronic pages of the book, I scanned through the short list of survivors who made their way across the Finnish border. Third from the bottom was a man named Wm. Lamb, who was described only as an Irishman and follower of Christ, but neither the title of *fr* nor *br* followed his name as it did for the priests and monks who made the unthinkable trek for their lives.

I pressed a thumb against the name on the small screen and held it in front of Anya. She was one of the best in the world at hiding her reactions to almost anything, but seeing the name Wm. Lamb sent her hand covering her mouth and a gasp exploding from her lips.

Pogonya said, "What? What is it?"

Anya said, "This is not proper question. We know what it is, but we do not know what it means."

Pogonya raised both eyebrows. "Tell me."

"It's the priest," I said. "Isaiah Lamb. Unless it's an incalculable coincidence, it would appear that a person who could be his grandfather, a guy named William Lamb, was one of the men who escaped Solovetsky."

Pogonya's face bloomed. "Oh, my God. That is amazing. I can't wait to get home so I can talk with him about that."

I said, "No! We're not going to mention it yet. There's far more going on here than we're ready to deal with, so this stays inside the team until *I'm* ready to air it out."

Pogonya flushed. "You don't think . . ."

"I don't know what to think yet, but *this* is what we do, Pogo. We answer questions nobody has the courage to ask."

Chapter 37

A-Caroling We Will Go

When we landed at Bonaventure, my body and mind had no idea what time or even what day it was. The hands on my watch did nothing to soothe my jetlagged senses. What did make sense, though, was Gator and Kodiak singing Christmas carols to our temporary houseguest, Gregory McDonald.

Pogonya stood on the tarmac, staring across the airport at the spectacle. "It's not Christmas, and neither of them can sing. That's just cruel."

I put her in a playful headlock. "Yes, baby girl, it is, and that's why they're doing it. He thought it would be okay to scare you, so I think it's okay to be as cruel as we want to him."

"What will you do with him when all of this is over?"

"That's up to him. A wise man would switch alliances and join the good guys, but so far, there's no evidence that he qualifies as wise. Only time will tell."

She said, "Well, time and his tolerance for their singing . . . or whatever that is."

Anya and Pogonya took the Microbus back to the house while I jogged across the airfield to join the Christmas cheer.

When I arrived on the scene of the vocal atrocity, Kodiak finished a chorus of "Grandma Got Run Over by a Reindeer" and threw up a hand. "Welcome home, boss. Our boy wanted to sleep, but we figured you wouldn't approve, so we kept him up by serenading him for you."

"You guys are the best." I gave McDonald a tender pat on the cheek. "Aren't they the best, Greggy boy?"

He shook his head and let out an exasperated huff, so I said, "You sound thirsty." I turned to Gator. "Doesn't he sound thirsty?"

Our young teammate lit up. "Oh, yeah, baby. It's tactical baptism time."

"Easy," I said. "We're not waterboarding him yet. He hasn't earned that honor, but I'm sure we'll get there. He's tough."

Gator snapped his fingers. "Darn it. That's my favorite part."

I trotted inside the hangar behind the revelry and pulled out one of the Desert Patrol Vehicles and a nice piece of rope. "How's your endurance these days, Gregory? Feel like a fun-run down to the water for a refreshing drink?"

My lassoing skills hadn't improved, so Kodiak played Buffalo Bill while I tied the other end of the rope to the back of the DPV.

As McDonald struggled against Kodiak's restraint, the three of us mounted the DPV and headed for the black water of the North River at a reasonable pace. When the rope went taut, I'm sure McDonald suddenly wished he was still listening to my men sing him awake. The first two times he fell, I slowed enough to let him scramble back to his bare feet, but after the third tumble, Gator said, "I'll get out and set the pace for him."

I tapped the brakes, and our all-American free safety went to work. He pulled the man to his feet, slapped him on the bottom, and said, "You look like you need a running partner, so I'll be your huckleberry."

I pulled away, and Gator turned backward in a run, facing McDonald. I missed the days when I could run an eight-minute mile backward, and in boots.

As our guest stumbled, I tapped the brakes again, and Gator shot an uppercut that would've blinded most men, but McDonald took the blow like a man and stayed on his feet.

Gator said, "Go ahead. Try to fall down again. I've got plenty left in the tank for you."

We made it to the river without any more falls or pugilism, and Mc-Donald collapsed to his knees on the grass, panting like a dog.

I hopped from the DPV and took a seat beside him. "I'll bet you're wishing you'd left my daughter out of this, aren't you?"

The profanity that came out of his mouth earned him some more love from Gator, but this dose wasn't as gentle as the uppercut. The young operator untied his prey and dragged his unconscious form to the river's edge. McDonald returned to the land of the living after three dunks in the brackish water, and Gator threw him onto his back on the bank. "Watch your mouth. We don't talk that way around here. Got me?"

He shook the water from his face and hair, and I watched his eyeballs wobble around in his head. When I believed he was coherent enough to understand the situation he was about to endure, I said, "Put him on his face on the dock. The tide is coming up, and he looks like he could use a good core workout."

Kodiak and Gator hoisted the man to his feet and practically dragged him onto the dock. They laid him down with his upper body hanging over the end and his hips and legs firmly pinned to the structure beneath the weight of both operators.

I hefted four sandbags from the riverbank, and we stacked them on McDonald's legs and butt.

"That should do it," I said. "That'll keep your feet down while you try to hold your head out of the water. Don't worry, though. High tide isn't for another ninety minutes, so you should be fine."

We strolled away and took seats inside the gazebo to watch the show.

"How long are you going to leave him out there?" Kodiak asked.

I shrugged. "I don't know. Wanna take bets on how long he can keep his head up?"

"There's no way he lasts fifteen minutes," Gator said.

Kodiak said, "Oh, I think he's got twenty in him."

I checked my watch, but I still didn't believe it was almost five a.m. "I say we go to bed and see if he's still there when the sun comes up."

Gator hopped to his feet. "Please let me tell him."

"Go for it."

He sprinted for the dock. "Did you hear that, Potty Mouth? The boss said to kiss you good night. If you're still alive in the morning, maybe we'll bring you some breakfast."

McDonald bucked and roared. "What do you want? Just tell me what you want!"

"That's easy," Gator said. "We want you to fully understand how much it costs to frighten the boss's daughter. How close are you to getting the message?"

"Okay! Okay! I got it! I regret that approach. I shouldn't have done it. I was wrong."

"Excellent," Gator said. "It sounds like you're about three, maybe four percent of the way to understanding. See you in the morning."

"Wait! Just get me up. Please. I'll give you whatever you want."

Gator yelled from the dock. "He says he'll give you whatever you want. Please tell me you want him to drown."

He jerked and writhed beneath the weight of the sandbags. "No! Please get me up."

I said to Kodiak, "It sounds like I should get involved before the Boy Wonder sends him to the bottom."

Kodiak nodded. "The kid scares me a little."

I grinned. "Yeah, me too. And I like it."

After jogging to the dock, my boot landed between McDonald's legs. "Oopsie! Sorry about that. I slipped. Does your tummy feel okay?"

He moaned as if I'd broken his legs, and his yelling became pleading. "You don't have to do this. Please, just tell me what you want."

I grabbed a handful of hair and pulled him back onto the dock. "I want you to forget everything else in your miserable life and remember this moment for the rest of your life."

"What are you talking about?"

I tied the rope around the four sandbags and then wrapped the free end around his torso six times. Terror filled his eyes, and his hyperventilation sounded like a freight train.

"Ever heard of walking the plank?" I asked. "Imagine what would happen if you messed with a pirate captain's daughter. And in case you've not figured it out yet, I'm the captain of this ship, and there's never been a pirate as vengeful as me or who loved his daughter as much as I do."

He broke and cried like a child. It took all three of us to get him to his feet, but we accomplished the task while he expended what little energy he had left in a useless attempt to force himself back to the ground.

"Please. You don't have to do this."

"You didn't have to scare Pogonya, but you did," I said as I forced him two feet closer to the end of the dock. "Put him in the river."

My men didn't hesitate an instant. We'd done it. His will was broken, and he was ready to trade everything he knew for his life. The problem for Gregory McDonald was that I wasn't ready to negotiate yet.

The sandbags broke the obsidian surface an instant before the rope went taut and McDonald followed them to the bottom.

My men turned for the house, and Kodiak said, "G'night, boss. We'll see you in the morning."

I liked his commitment and said, "I think I'll take a dip before bed."

"Want us to stay?" Gator asked.

"Nah, I'm pretty sure I can handle it from here. You guys have done enough."

Finding McDonald at the bottom of the river took almost no effort, even in the absolute darkness. He was the thrashing mass working hard to wake up every alligator in Georgia.

The blade of my Benchmade parted the rope like butter, and I hooked the potential drowning victim beneath an arm. After dragging him up the ramp, I planted a boot in the middle of his chest. "When was the last time you were this miserable? Did they do anything this ugly to you in Force Recon School, or did you even go to that school?"

He gagged and spat. "I told you I surrender. What do you want?"

"It's simple, Greg. I want to punish you, and if you have the strength to tell me that you surrender, my work isn't done. I'm going to give you a few hours of peace and quiet so you can think about what I'd really like to hear you say. If it comes to you, and you give it up next time we meet, you'll stay warm and dry. If not, you can expect to get real familiar with that river bottom."

It took fifteen minutes to drag him into the workshop, bind, and gag him, but I did give him the courtesy of stripping him of the wet clothes and tossing an old wool blanket beside him on the concrete floor. He could decide if it would be his mattress or his blanket.

I was incapable of remembering how long I'd been awake, but my waking hours were far from over. With one more stop to make before my head found a pillow, I both dreaded and longed for the final visit of the night.

Chapter 38

Cyrillic and Old Black Men

The twelve-block walk from Bonaventure to Oak Grove Cemetery and Penny's grave took half an hour, but in so many ways, it took over forty years.

In the eighteen months following her death, I'd spent every day sitting in front of her headstone, crying, and drinking Jack Daniel's Gentleman Jack. In the lifetime since then, I'd stopped all three, and I felt a heart-crushing guilt for stopping two of them. My still-broken heart made me believe my body should've been on that piece of hallowed ground every day, my eyes still flooding with tears from losing the woman I loved and who loved me beyond measure. For the living, though, life must go on. And for the dead, the living must be left astern.

Her grave was as clean as though someone had cared for it even better than I had in the days when I rarely allowed a leaf to remain on it for more than a few hours. That left me wondering if God Himself was blowing the leaves away from Penny's grave while most of the other plots in the cemetery were covered in an ever-thickening layer of brown foliage.

The cleanliness wasn't the only oddity I discovered in those early morning hours as the eastern sky showed its first hint of the coming day. A tiny square of grass had been removed and carefully replaced beside the marble headstone, so I picked at the square and lifted it from the moist soil beneath. The earth was soft under my fingertips as I probed and scratched until I touched something cold and hard. Another half minute of excavation revealed a small glass jar with a tightly secured metal lid and a coiled leaf of paper inside.

The lid gave way easily, and I lifted the paper from inside as the curiosity and twinge of anger grew inside me. I unrolled and unfolded the paper carefully, but nothing could've prepared me for what I found. Written in the most beautiful Cyrillic script I'd ever seen was a note only three people in the town of St. Marys, Georgia, could read. One of those people had been awake for at least three days and struggled with Cyrillic on his best day. Regardless, I studied every word, wrestling to translate it into the only language I understood well enough to grasp that morning.

Penny,

It feels strange and somehow wrong to call you just Penny. You were married to my father, so that seems to make you something of a mother to me, although I met you only once and never knew the beauty of who and what you were until now.

I see and feel you in Father's eyes and in his touch. He is a man of enormous power, but his memory of you reduces him to a lonesome child. He speaks of your love every time he smiles at me. The way he loved – and continues to love – you gives me hope that someday, such a man might offer a love for me as truly and as deeply as Father loved you. If, beyond this grave, you have doubts about how he adored you, please allow this letter to erase and banish those false beliefs for all eternity, for he treasured every moment you gave him, and he whispers to God in his prayers that it should have been him, instead of you, who was taken from this world.

Although differently, I love him as truly and as purely as you did. He proves daily to be the man every daughter should have as a father. Thank you for teaching him to love, for it could only have been you who gave him such strength to give so much of himself to and for me. I live in your debt and in your shadow, and I fear that I'll never live up to the grand expectations your husband, my father, has for me. I hope, strive, and pray to one day be half the woman you were and to love with the same passion, heart, and life that you did. You are, in death, as I'm certain you were in life, a beacon of what a wife and woman should yearn to be, and I shed a tear every time I realize that you were never given the opportunity to be the mother of my father's child. I know you would have been the greatest mother any child could hope to know.

I want you to rest in the knowledge that your husband is still loved without end by me, and even though I can't replace you, I vow to be a living reminder of how you treasured him. Most of all, I want you to know that no one, absolutely no one, could ever replace you in his heart, no matter who she is.

Love,
A child on the doorstep of becoming a woman who could've been your daughter in another world and another lifetime.

Pogonya Fulton

I prayed that my weary mind translated the Slavic script as it was intended, and I cried a deluge of tears, sobbing and aching with every breath. How could a child write such a beautiful tribute to a woman she barely knew? How could anyone capture Penny's heart with words, and why would God give me such a beautiful soul as my daughter? I'll never know the answers to those questions, but I'll never stop giving thanks for the love of the wonderful woman I had known and the love of a precious daughter for the rest of my life.

"You all right there, sir?"

The words sliced through the silence like the voice of God, and I tucked Pogonya's note away as if holding it were a sin.

I wiped my eyes and looked up to see a tall, thin man whose back was bent by age and countless decades of work. He leaned against a rake that looked almost as old as him, and I said, "Yes, sir. I'm okay. I was just . . ."

"I know what you was just doin'. I do the same thing myself 'bout every day of my life, 'cept I do it on the other side of that stone wall there. That's where I laid my Myrtle to rest and commended her into God's hands over sixty years ago. Still now, there ain't a day go by that I don't think I hear her voice calling me."

I stared up at the old man, uncertain if he was really there. Between the hours I'd been awake and the letter I'd just read, my mind was capable of creating hallucinations no logical man could comprehend, but just in case I hadn't created the old man from somewhere deep within my insanity, I stood.

"You don't have to stand up on my account, sir. You just sit right back down there and have your fellowship with Ms. Penny."

"How do you know her name?"

He pointed with the blunt end of his rake. "It's scribed right there on that stone, but that ain't the only reason I know it. You don't know who I am, do you, sir?"

"No, sir, I'm afraid I don't. And you'll have to forgive me, but I'm not completely sure that I'm not dreaming all of this."

A broad grin came over his face, and he took a step forward, placing his calloused hand in mine. "It ain't no dream. We're both real men, left behind by women we loved, but that ain't all you and me's got in common."

I furrowed my brow. "I'm sorry, but what does that mean?"

He pointed with his rake again. "Why don't we sit over there? An old man like me gets tired."

I followed him to the stone bench and took a seat as he slowly lowered himself beside me. We sat in silence for a long moment until he said, "That ol' sun gonna be up any minute, and this whole place gonna come to life. Squirrels and peoples and e'rebody else gonna go 'bout their day doin' what they do without a care in this whole world for the folks buried here 'neath our feets."

I wanted to respond, but nothing I could come up with seemed appropriate.

Finally, he said, "Oh, sorry. I still didn't introduce myself. I'm Ellis Monroe, and I'm a member of Brother Jimmy's congregation. That boy sure can sing, can't he?"

I racked my brain trying to figure out who Brother Jimmy was until it hit me. "Oh, you mean Singer. Yes, he's got a beautiful voice."

"And the heart of God in him," Ellis said.

"Truer words have never been spoken."

He slid his gnarled hand across the smooth wood of the rake handle. "Like I said, Brother Jimmy and our departed wives ain't all we gots in common neither. Your great-grandfather, Lyman Huntsinger, bought my granddaddy in September of eighteen fifty-nine at the slave market in Charleston and hauled him in a wagon all the way down here to Bonaventure Plantation."

If I'd been speechless before, I was dumbfounded in that moment.

Ellis kept talking. "The way the story was handed down to me was that your great-granddaddy, Lyman, made my granddaddy a free man that very night by writ and oath and gave him a share of what the plantation made from that day on."

I gripped the cold stone bench. "I don't know what to say."

Ellis grinned. "Don't say nothin'. Just hear me out. A lot of people who look like you done a lot of people who look like me a great many wrongs down through the years, but ain't never been no man nor woman in your family line back above your momma, as far back as my granddaddy, that ever treated none of us like anything other than honorable mens, womens, and little childrens."

I swallowed hard and stared into the face of age.

"You come from fine stock, Mr. Chase. That's all they is to it, and blessing be to God in Heaven that now you've got yourself somebody to leave all this to in that girl of yours."

I sat in silence, shaking my head in disbelief and wonder.

Ellis said, "You know something? Your great-uncle, Judge Bernard Henry Huntsinger, and me was borned on the same day. I looks after his grave, too, just like I do Ms. Penny's. Your family's plots here is just as 'portant to me as mine's is. The way I see it, if it wasn't for them fine people you come from, there wouldn't be no Ellis Monroe in this world today, and I've been on this here Earth for nigh-'bout a hundred and three years."

I stammered. "Why haven't we met before today?"

"Wasn't no need," he said. "I still live on the four acres of ground your family gave to mine after the war. That land won't never be in no hands that ain't Monroes, just like I hope Bonaventure won't never be nobody's 'cept the straight-line descendants of Lyman Huntsinger, like you."

I watched the sun deliver her first golden rays through the mighty oaks and pines of the Georgia lowlands. "It'll be Pogonya's when I go, and I pray she has somebody to leave it to someday."

He patted me on the back. "You just keep on livin' right, the way God intends, and lovin' that little girl . . . Begonia, is it? 'Cause she sure loves her daddy. And I'll keep them dead leaves raked off Ms. Penny's plot, just the same as I do for my Myrtle and the Judge, long as I'm able."

"Her name's Pogonya, but you can call her Begonia if you want. I'm certain she'd take it as a compliment coming from you."

"That's a pretty name, but I ain't never heard it 'fore."

"It means *chase* in Russian. Her mother is—"

He patted again. "I know who her mother is, and I want you to know that neither God nor Miss Penny there would hold it again' you if you made her your wife and had a right proper family of it 'fore that little girl o' yours gets all grown and gones."

Chapter 39

My Spicy Russian

When I finally found my bed sometime after the sun came up, I lay awake as Ellis Monroe's story, philosophy, and advice played through my weary head. His were the last words I heard before exhaustion overtook me and I surrendered to sleep's relentless call.

"Father! Father! You must come now!"

Pogonya's beckoning yanked me from the world of dreams and back into the reality of my life. "What is it?"

"It's Mama. She's going to kill him."

I'd never admit it to Pogonya, but part of me wanted to roll over and let the drama play out without me, but I couldn't do that to her.

"Hand me my leg," I said as I threw back the cover, only to discover I hadn't removed it before falling asleep. In fact, I hadn't removed anything, including my boots, so I stood, gathered my senses, and followed my terrified daughter down the stairs.

We sprinted across the back lawn and into the shop, where an atrocity of epic proportions was on the verge of becoming Gregory McDonald's end.

"Anya! Stop!" I yelled, and shoved Pogonya back through the door behind me.

Anya didn't flinch, continuing her excavation into the psyche of her imprisoned prey.

I'll never know if she was speaking Russian because of some connection to her primal core, or if it was a tactic meant to frighten Mc-

Donald even more, but the slow, methodical monotone of the Slavic dialect sent chills traversing my spine. I could only imagine what the defenseless victim of her rage was experiencing inside the pool that remained of his sanity.

He stood naked, toes barely touching the concrete floor, with his hands tied high above his head, stretching every muscle and tendon of his body to its human limit. Silent tears of terror dripped down his face as Anya traced the lines of his body with the tips of her twin blades.

I'd known that pair of knives as if they were extensions of her body. She wielded them with the precision of a surgeon, but with the mindless disregard of a lifelong butcher. The blood had yet to begin flowing, but the unimaginable horror she delivered rose like a cascading tide driven by the winds of rage.

"Please . . ."

Pleading fell from the man's soul on waves of repentance for his mortal sin. "I'll give you *whoever* you want."

Anya lowered her blades, took a step back, and turned to me. Still in Russian, she said, "This is word you wanted to hear from him, yes?"

That was precisely the word I'd been trying to pull from McDonald's lips with every threat I made in the previous days, and Anya extracted it from him without breaking the skin.

"Very good, Gregory. You finally figured it out, and all it took was a pair of fighting knives and the mother of the girl you threatened. It's not *what* I want. It's *who* I want."

He seemed to lack the will or perhaps the strength to open his eyes. "I'll do anything you want. Just—"

Anya's blade landed against his bottom lip, and she traded her native tongue for the only language McDonald was capable of understanding in that moment.

"*Just* nothing," she growled. "You will make no demands. You will give to us everything and everyone we want, and you will do this *nemedlenno*."

I whispered, "That means immediately, in case your Russian is a little rusty. I'll ask the questions, and you will give the answers *nemedlenno*. Understood?"

His body trembled in some terrible combination of fear and depletion. All that remained within him were the twisted edges of his immortal soul and barely enough breath to sustain his life.

Anya withdrew her knife, and I said, "Tell me who was on the yacht. If you say anything other than four names, I'll leave this room, and we both know you do *not* want me to leave you alone with *her*."

He drew in what breath his strained position would allow and exhaled the words. "Victor Komarov, David Kline, Jacob Miller"—he paused to force another breath into his chest—"and Arash Mousavi."

"Who was the primary target?" I asked.

"All of them, but they demanded Komarov."

I turned for the door, and panic overtook his voice. "Wait. Where are you going?"

I ignored him but whispered to Anya as I passed. "*Ne ubivayte yego.*"

The order *not* to kill him would be obeyed for the moment, but only God knew if I possessed the power to hold Pogonya's mother at bay and keep McDonald alive in the coming hours.

Stepping through the door, I nearly collided with my daughter. "Did she kill him?"

"Not yet, but she scared him enough to get exactly what we needed from him."

"Please don't let her kill him."

I pulled her against me. "Your mother isn't the kind of person who can be controlled, but as long as he keeps talking, she'll let him keep breathing. I'll need your help after that."

"What do you mean, my help? What can I do?"

"You can talk to your mother and implore her to let him live. She'll listen to you."

Pogonya stood until the weight of the moment bore down on her and she was forced to take a seat.

I called Skipper and gave her the names of the four men on the yacht. "Run those as fast as you can. I'm on open-channel comms, so I can hear everything you say. I need you to record what you hear from my end."

"Got it," she said. "And I've already got a hit on David Kline. He was the NSA contractor who washed up with Fitzsimon's ear in his stomach."

"How about the other three?"

"I'm on it, but I've got some roadblocks. I'll need a little time."

"I'll go back in and keep pulling information out of McDonald. Make sure you're recording everything."

"Yeah, yeah. I always record everything. Just do it. Is Pogonya down there with you?"

"Yes, she is."

Skipper said, "Well, send her up here, and tell her I need her. She doesn't need to be anywhere near what you're doing."

Without hesitation, I turned to Pogo. "Skipper needs you in the op center."

She darted from the workshop as if she'd been begging the universe for any excuse to run.

"She's on her way. Find something meaningful for her to do. She's too smart to swallow busywork as anything important."

"Don't worry. I've got plenty for her to do. Are you okay with her hearing the audio from your end?"

I paused to consider the question. "Can you keep it in your ear only?"

She said, "Sure. That's probably best. Who knows what that lunatic is going to spit out. Is Anya going to kill him?"

"Probably, but that's a later problem. Right now, I need the team down here."

"I'll have everybody there ASAP. And Chase . . ."

"Yeah?"

"Nice work."

"Thanks, but it wasn't me. It was Anya."

I slipped the sat-phone into my pocket with the connection still running strong and stepped back inside the locked room that likely contained everything I needed.

The scene I walked into was the last thing I could've expected to see when the door closed behind me. Anya's blade had been far from dormant in my absence. McDonald lay against the wall with his legs curled beneath him and his hands dangling limp at his belly.

"What did you do?" I demanded.

"I only cut him down. He is not dead, but he would have been if I kept him hanging from arms any longer. He needs water or maybe IV."

The room we affectionately called "the workshop" was well equipped with medical supplies to keep our guests alive during those moments when our inquisitions got spicy, and with the possible exception of Gator, no one could add spice quite like my favorite Russian.

I stuck McDonald with a large-bore IV and positioned a bag of normal saline above his head. "We're going to need Singer."

Anya frowned. "Why? To pray for him?"

"No," I said. "He's the best medic we've got, and I'd like to keep your pincushion alive long enough to get what we need out of him."

She smiled for an instant. "He will never frighten our daughter again."

"No, he certainly won't, but I still don't want him dead."

She waggled a hand between us. "Maybe a little bit, I do. I would like to give to Pogonya his head on silver tray."

"She doesn't want his head. She wants her parents, and she doesn't want any part of the world we live in."

Anya said, "She will learn is necessary sometimes to do unpleasant things to keep ugly world from becoming even worse."

"Maybe, but I'd still like to protect her from that cruel reality as long as we can."

McDonald stirred, and I planted a hand on his chest. "Relax. We're getting you some clothes, and we're going to make you a little more comfortable as long as you continue to cooperate."

He squeezed his eyes closed several times in rapid succession and stared down at the needle in his arm. "What are you giving me?"

"Just fluids, nothing more. The ugliness, as she calls it, is over for now, but it's up to you if and when it starts again."

He nodded and closed his eyes again, but that didn't quench my thirst for information. "Was it a CIA operation?"

He mouthed, "Not officially."

"But they were involved, right?"

He nodded. "Look, there are some powerful players involved in all of this. You don't want—"

Anya slapped a blade against his tongue, and I tasted the steel she'd used to split my tongue all over again.

She hissed. "You do not tell to us what we do and do not want. You tell only to us answers to questions, or I will remove tongue one centimeter at a time. Blink to say to me that you understand."

His eyelids fluttered as if he were trying to blow out a fire with them, and Anya withdrew her knife.

I spoke as calmly as I could. "See? I told you that it was up to you if and when the ugliness continued. Is it starting to make sense?"

He nodded, and Kodiak's voice echoed in my ear. "Sierra One, Sierra Team is on-site and standing by."

I said, "Send in Sierra Six."

Singer came through the door and took a knee beside me. "Brief me."

"He's willing to play ball, but he doesn't feel very good. I've got fluid running, but nothing else. Check him out while I set up the room next door."

He hip-checked me, knocking me out of his way, and went to work. Anya stayed by Singer's side as he assessed McDonald, and I stepped through the door.

The whole team looked like retrievers waiting for me to shoot down a duck so they could fight over who got to bring it back.

"Relax, guys. It's just a Q and A at this point. I just wanted a show of force and a few extra sets of ears to catch anything I miss. Let's get the other room ready for a friendly little conversation."

The second compartment inside the workshop looked more like a hospital room than a torture chamber, but with the right combination of drugs and tools, it could be just as terrifying. That wasn't my plan for the day, but we'd have to see how our detainee chose for it to play out.

Fifteen minutes later, McDonald was sitting on a well-padded chair with a much better IV than the one I'd jabbed into his arm. His eyes were open, and his color was returning. Two bags of fluid hung from an arm above the chair, and Singer squirted something from a bottle into the man's mouth.

"It's just simple syrup. Your blood sugar is all screwed up. Are you diabetic?"

McDonald slapped his lips several times and swallowed the sugar water. "No."

"Your body's been through the wringer over the past few days, so it's probably a little confused. You'll be all right. Just do what we say, and tell us what you know. We'll take care of everything else."

Singer's life was a dichotomy of extremes. It's likely that few snipers throughout history could match his lethality, but I was willing to bet that none of them could come close to meeting his level of compassion for his fellow man when the situation called for it. He, somewhat jokingly, called himself a serial killer and a child of God, but everyone around him knew that a more devout soul didn't exist, and none of us wanted him pointing a muzzle at us from any distance.

I pulled a stool in front of Gregory McDonald and took a seat. "Okay, here we go. How do you feel?"

"How do you think?" he quipped, and the team moved in.

I held up a hand. "Easy. Keep it civil, Greg, or it's all over for you."

"It's over for me anyway. They'll kill me the second you release me —if there's any chance of you doing that."

"Maybe," I said, "but they'll do it quickly. If we do it, you're not going to like it so much. Now, take me through it. Let's start with the Russian."

Skipper's voice appeared. "Chase, I got a hit on Arash Mousavi. He's Mossad."

My brain turned into a three-ring circus, but I fought to keep it under control and focus on the questioning. "Let's start with Mousavi."

McDonald nodded. "The Iranian."

"Tell me about him."

"He was the buyer."

"The buyer of what?" I asked.

McDonald suddenly looked amused. "You really don't know, do you?"

I didn't like being caught on my heels. "What I know is immaterial. What you tell me is what matters, and every word better be the truth. What was the Iranian buying? I need to hear you say it."

"Plutonium two-thirty-nine from the Russian, Komarov. And the priest wanted his facilitator's cut."

Chapter 40
My Honey Pot

Interrogators are an interesting breed. There was a time when I was a good one, but I was never great. The best ones go about it with calm resolve and a demeanor of unconcern, as if they don't care if the subject ever divulges the information they want. Just like my days behind the plate in catcher's gear, I was always anxious to gun down the runner who thought he could have second base—which belonged to me. I'd throw almost as hard as my pitcher an instant after the runner bolted from first, and my mask would fly from my face as a result of the force. The dislodged gear never distracted me. I kept my focus on the shortstop's glove as my bullet struck leather and the tag was applied. That's exactly how I conducted interrogations. I threw as hard as I could and waited with the anticipation of arrogance for the shot to land and one more notch to be carved into my mask for gunning down another runner caught stealing. I believed that approach would always work against a detainee with information I needed, but baseball isn't espionage, and arrogance isn't the right approach when a broken man lay in front of me with missing teeth and a headful of knowledge I wanted.

I stepped back to leave the room and discuss what I'd learned with Skipper, but the hand of a much wiser and more accomplished interrogator than me landed in the center of my back, halting me in place, and she asked, "Which priest?"

Gregory McDonald cocked his head. "The nuncio, Father Leonardo Vincetti. Who else?"

I was instantly back in my crouch behind home plate with my mask on my face, and the runner safe at second.

"Keep talking," I said.

McDonald shook his head. "Oh, no. I'll answer your questions, but I ain't walking you through the whole parade."

It was time for Anya's mask to fly off. She lunged forward, planted a knee between the man's legs, and delivered a crushing open-handed strike to his throat. "You will talk, or I will take away your ability to do so. Do not doubt what I am capable of and willing to do to you."

"Get her out of here," I ordered.

For the first time I could remember, my team hesitated a beat. It lasted only an instant, but it happened, and in that instant, I let the team talk me into questioning my decision.

But it was too late to withdraw the command, so I grabbed Anya by the shoulder and pulled her from McDonald's face. In the darkest Russian I could muster, I growled, "Play along."

She did as I said and fought against me as if trying to get back into our prisoner's space and tear out his spine, but Shawn and Mongo stepped in.

They pulled her from the room, leaving me standing in front of the only real source we had. "Well, that was pleasant. Don't you think?"

"She's out of control," he said.

I grinned. "Oh, you have no idea just how *in* control that woman is. She couldn't care less about Fitzsimon, the nuncio, or your vice president. She just wants to turn you inside out for threatening our daughter. And just so there's zero confusion about this situation, I will let her do it if you give me one more hint of a reason. Are we clear?"

The look in Gregory McDonald's eyes said he'd lost all ambition to steal third.

Before I could kickstart his narrative again, Skipper said, "Chase, I've got intel on Jacob Miller. He was, or maybe still is, CIA SOG."

I held up one finger behind my back, and Gator got the message.

So I didn't have to, he said, "Stand by."

I positioned myself back on the rolling stool with my new piece of intel and slid close enough to McDonald to remind him I was still in charge. "Since when does a priest dictate American foreign policy, especially when it comes to the covert actions of the CIA's Special Operations Group?"

He may have had a background in hardcore military operations and high-level politics, but his eyes betrayed him, and he looked away.

Gripping his face in my hands, I refocused his attention on me. "Remember when you were a little boy and your daddy threatened to pull his belt off if you didn't behave? Well, you can consider me your daddy, and that Russian out there, my belt. Look away again, refuse to talk one more time, do anything I don't like, and the belt comes off, little boy."

He swallowed hard.

"Now, tell me exactly how the Vatican's ambassador started this whole ordeal."

McDonald cleared his throat. "It didn't exactly start with him. The operation had been going on for months. The Iranian, Mousavi, was buying plutonium from the Russian, Komarov. The nuncio, Vincetti, had been the ambassador to Moscow for three years before getting posted to D.C. Look it up. It ain't classified."

"Watch the tone," I said. "We're playing nice, remember?"

"Whatever. You and me, we ain't smart enough or rich enough to be on the inside. We're the same, you and me, and next month, it might be you in this chair."

"I doubt it. If you survive this, I don't think you'll ever want to see me again."

I don't ever remember a detainee laughing during an interrogation, but he did and said, "You're a fool if you think any of us is going to survive this thing. The people I work for are the same people you work for, and they'll end every single one of us because we're expendable. There's a line of young, ambitious, patriotic idiots—just like you and me were—a mile long waiting to become us."

"You're good at this, but building rapport with me doesn't work. Nothing about us is the same. You've got one more chance. Tell me the whole story, or I walk away."

"Fine. What difference does it make now? Vincetti got all buddy-buddy with Putin while he was posted to Moscow. It's obvious you know how convincing those Russians can be, don't you?"

I rolled closer and grinned. "Oh, yeah. I got sucked right in, didn't I? I'm the one who defected to Russia and went to work for the SVR because a pretty girl smiled at me. Pay attention, you pitiful piece of trash. I don't get stuck in honey traps. I eat the honey and bring the pot home with me."

He sighed, and I prayed that Anya hadn't heard me call her a pot that I brought home with me.

"So, how did you convince Garland Fitzsimon, a nobody from nowhere, to try and kill two American intelligence officers, a Russian, and a Mossad agent?"

He furrowed his brow. "Mossad? Who said anything about a Mossad agent? Arash Mousavi was Iranian . . ." At that instant, his face turned pale as realization overtook him. "My God. The whole thing was an Israeli op, wasn't it?"

"You tell me," I said. "You're the insider with big, powerful friends."

He sat, silently shaking his head. "Those damned Jews . . ."

I waved a finger in front of his face. "No, sir. That's not how we do this. You're not going to redirect my attention. This is the part where you tell me how *you* got Fitzsimon to go after the men on that boat."

"It wasn't me," he said, and I raised an eyebrow.

"Okay, it wasn't *entirely* me," he said. "I pulled him out of Walton Correctional Institute or whatever, but I don't know what they did to him."

"They who?" I asked.

"The Agency. Who else?"

"Are you telling me that you pulled Fitzsimon out of prison and dropped him off at the CIA?"

"Yeah, that's exactly how it happened. I drove right up to the front door at Langley, just like a New York City cabbie."

I drove a finger at his face. "Do that again, and—"

"Yeah, yeah, I know. You'll unleash your little—"

As if out of nowhere, Gator landed a left cross that rattled McDonald's grey matter. My young operator said, "Sorry, boss, but he was about to say something ugly about Anya, and I really want to hear the rest of the story before you let her kill him."

When our guest reclaimed his senses, he spat blood from his mouth and said, "You guys really are a bunch of cowboys, aren't you?"

I smiled back at him. "Yippee-ki-yay. Now, keep talking, or we'll throw a branding iron in the fire."

He wiped his lip with a shoulder. "Who taught that kid to throw a punch, huh?"

"It's just natural talent," I said. "Now, talk."

He blinked several times as the residuals of Gator's blow lingered. "I handed him off to a couple of guys. That's all I know. Whoever they were, they did a number on him. When he came back, he was like some kind of robot."

I rolled a few inches away to give him a little space. "Ever heard of MKUltra?" He glanced down, and I stuck a finger beneath his chin. "You see, Gregory, I know a lot more than you think, and when you conveniently leave out details, that makes me think you're finished talking. Are you finished?"

His chest rose and fell in renewed submission. "I guess you know about the drugs, huh?"

"Yeah, we know about the drugs, and we know you were the delivery boy to the supermax."

"So, what else do you want to know? It sounds like you've got it all figured out."

"I want to know why Garland Fitzsimon is still alive." His expression changed, so I asked, "Did I strike a nerve, Greg? Something didn't go as you and your all-powerful masters expected, did it?"

"He got a note to his mother somehow."

I said, "You let him go see his mother before you sent him to kill the guys on the boat. Why would it surprise you that he left her a note?"

"The fact that he left her the note ain't what hung us up. It was what was in the note that screwed everything up."

"Don't keep me hanging here."

He let out another of those sighs I'd come to hate. "I can't quote it exactly, but that Fitzsimon kid was brighter than we thought. Somehow, during his time in Maryland, he apparently slipped a few packages out, telling some of his buddies to make sure the contents got to the TV stations if something happened to him."

"TV stations? What year does he think this is?"

McDonald said, "He'd been in the joint most of his adult life. He didn't know nothin' about social media. To him, we were still living in the nineties or whatever."

"So, what was in the packages?"

"We didn't figure it out until the whole thing was over and Fitzsimon got busted in the Keys for starting a fight in some bar. To be honest, we knew he wouldn't make it through the thing on the boat. He was just supposed to disrupt it and kill as many of those guys as he could. Obviously, that fell apart, and he survived."

"Obviously," I said. "So, the package?"

"Yeah, that's when we got to him. We told him to take the plea deal and that his grandma or whatever would go into WITSEC. If he didn't shut his mouth and take the deal, we'd make him watch when we took care of his granny."

I leaned in. "You keep using the word *we*. Who are you talking about?"

"You know, like the royal we. I was the point man on the thing . . . the muscle."

"Yeah, I know. You're a scary guy. Just look at you."

"Whatever," he said. "The kid was smart enough to take the deal, but one of the packages surfaced anyway. It was all about what they were doing to him in Maryland and what they were telling him he would have to do. You know, on the boat."

"Maryland? I thought you said the CIA was running the program."

"Yeah, what do you think? That the CIA only exists at Langley? Grow up. They're everywhere. You've probably got one of their guys in your little posse and you don't even know it. It ain't the kid with the left cross and the uppercut, though. I'll tell you that much. Ain't no CIA puke who can throw that kind of punch. Know what I'm saying?"

I stood, rolled my stool into the corner of the room, and settled onto a real chair. "Okay, I'll buy most of that story, but you work for the VP, and you left out the part about *his* involvement in all of this. Nice job trying to protect the big guy, but I'm not gonna let it fly. You either tell it all, or, well, you know."

He said, "So, what do you think you're gonna do, huh, tough guy? You gonna take down the vice president of the United States of freakin' America?"

I crossed my legs and inspected my fingernails. "No, tough guy, I'm not. You are. And I'm finished making threats. You talk, or I walk in three . . . two . . ."

"All right already. The boss is a Catholic, like me, and he's got the backing of the church from his days in Florida. You know, with my cousin, the archbishop. We got the same name, me and him. It's a family name from way back. It's a whole big thing, him and the nuncio Vincetti. They're all old pals. What do I know? I'm just a guy, like you."

"You might be just a guy, Greg, but you'll never be like me. If the VP was in bed with the nuncio, why did they try to shut down the deal by killing the guys on the boat? I thought the nuncio wanted the deal to happen so he could get his cut from Putin."

McDonald said, "You don't know nothin' about nothin'. When somebody like the VP gets cold feet, he'll do anything to shut something down and sweep it under the rug, and until you showed up, all of this dirt was nice and gone under that rug. You're the one who flipped it over and stirred everything up, and you got no idea what kind of storm you're bringing down on your head because of it."

Chapter 41

Laws and In-Laws

With my head bursting with new information, I stood. "Make him comfortable, but he's not free to leave."

Gator nodded, and I reconsidered my instructions. "On second thought, let him go if he wants. He's right—he won't survive twenty-four hours out there."

McDonald said, "Hey, wait a minute. What are you gonna do?"

I gripped the doorknob. "We've got your confession on tape, so we're going to the U.S. Attorney . . . and probably the president. I've got him on speed dial. Wanna see?"

He said, "Look, man. You really don't know what you're in for on this thing. You should really let me—"

"Let you what?" I asked. "Help me bury your boss? I don't need or want your help. As you've probably figured out, we're pretty good at what we do. I will make you an offer, though—if you're interested."

"What kind of offer?"

I turned back to face him. "The kind that keeps you alive and maybe out of prison."

He huffed. "You've got an overblown opinion of yourself, Cowboy. What makes you think you can do either of those things?"

I gave him one of Clark's crooked grins. "I got you, didn't I?"

He turned to stone, so I said, "Oh, that reminds me. We let your wife and mistress know that you're alive and well, but you can probably expect some legal ramifications arising from those two getting to know each other. I'd offer you a phone to give them a call, but I doubt they want to talk to you right now." Turning back for the door, I made one more dramatic spin. "I almost forgot. We've got Pat Fitzsimon, too. She's tucked away somewhere nice and cozy. I told you we were good at this."

His sigh made its return. "You know none of this is admissible in court."

I laughed. "I don't need it to be admissible. It's more than enough to initiate an investigation and rock your boss's world, no matter how it shakes out. The U.S. Attorney is standing by, but just in case your people get to them and shut this down, I'll release the audio to those same TV stations Garland Fitzsimon mentioned, but we'll make sure it finds its way onto every social media platform in the world, too. Nobody's going to bury this one, Greg. You can go down with the ship or stick around. Something tells me that your interview with the U.S. Attorney will be admissible."

Gator followed me through the door. "Do you really want us to let him go?"

"He's not going anywhere," I said. "Feed him, let him bathe, and get him some clothes that fit. I've got a lawyer to call."

* * *

When I walked through the door to the op center, Skipper smiled as if she'd just won the lottery. "Chase, that was a master class. Well done! I've got the U.S Attorneys in Atlanta and Tallahassee queued up. Who do you want me to call?"

"Dylan Duncan," I said.

"The attorney in St. Augustine?"

"Absolutely. She's about to earn her retainer and then some."

"What about the U.S. Attorney?"

"We'll get to that, but we've got to protect Fitzsimon before we light that funeral pyre."

* * *

"Ms. Duncan, Chase Fulton here. How are you?"

"Good evening, Mr. Fulton. I'm fine. Just wrapping things up for the day. What can I do for you?"

"You can get on a Citation jet at St. Augustine Airport and come to St. Marys. I've got someone for you to meet."

"I don't have a jet," she said.

"You will after this case, but for now, you can use ours. It'll be on the ground in thirty minutes. Triple your hourly rate, and start the clock now. I'll see you in an hour."

Without giving her an opportunity to protest, I ended the call and dispatched Gator and Anya to fetch the lawyer.

She arrived just over an hour later, and the team escorted her into the op center.

The lawyer's eyes wouldn't blink as she took in her surroundings. "What is this place?"

I motioned toward a chair. "Have a seat, and consider this the nerve center of our little operation."

"Operation? You told me you're a writer."

"Yeah, well, I also write—just not very well. We've got something for you to hear."

She timidly accepted the offered seat and pulled out a legal pad.

I said, "I have to warn you before we begin. You're going to hear some things that aren't as palatable as you might prefer, but listen for content, not setting."

She said, "Mr. Fulton, I can't be party to anything illegal."

"Relax. I may have pushed the boundaries of a scumbag's civil rights a little, but I assure you he's not going to press charges. Garland Fitzsimon and I need you to hear what the man had to say."

Skipper started the audio, and Dylan listened carefully, scribbling furiously on her pad.

I expected her to demand that we stop, but the longer the audio played, the more engrossed she seemed to become.

When it was over, she said, "Play it again, right now."

Skipper eyed me, and I gave her a nod.

The attorney made more notes on the second pass than she had on the first. When it ended for the second time, she dropped her pen. "You know you can't take any of this to the U.S. Attorney, right?"

I said, "Of course. That's why you're here. Let's clarify a few things in the interest of full disclosure. I'm not writing a book. I'm throwing one at the vice president of the United States and maybe the Vatican if this thing's tentacles actually reach that far."

She scowled. "What are you, Mr. Fulton?"

"You're still my attorney, right? And privilege still applies."

She nodded, and I said, "I'm the leader of a team of paramilitary operators. We aren't exactly contractors, but we work in the interest of the American people. We're not cops, but we enforce a law that isn't exactly codified."

"I see. Okay, well, in that case, I need to know who you work for."

I glanced around the room at the stone-faced team of operators hanging on to what was about to come out of my mouth. "We work for Garland Fitzsimon, Ms. Duncan, and so do you."

I learned Gregory McDonald wasn't the only person in my life who was capable of producing a definitive sigh.

Dylan Duncan let out one of her own. "Give me a minute and let me think."

We sat in silence as the electronic cooling fans for Skipper's equipment and the HVAC system produced their soothing background whispers.

I envied the attorney's ability to stop the action and think before reacting. I'd never enjoyed that privilege on the battlefield. My decisions were made instantly, and their consequences often came in the form of blood and scars. Something told me the consequences of the lawyer's coming decision would be far more painful . . . for someone.

"Okay, I've got an idea," she finally said. "My ex-husband's father is a senior legal advisor to the governor. I was in the process of joining his law firm when I found out his son—my husband at the time—was doing a little legal probing of his own with a couple of cute little clerks at the courthouse."

She paused, and I said, "Sorry to hear that, but how does that have anything to do with this?"

She said, "Michael may have been his father's son, but that doesn't mean that senior approved of junior's lack of prudence in his jurisprudence, so to speak. Believe it or not, he represented me in the divorce against his own son and offered me a junior partnership in his firm."

"Why didn't you take him up on it?"

She tapped her pen against the yellow legal pad. "I wanted a clean break, and I wanted to prove I could do it on my own—that I didn't need Michael Duncan, senior *or* junior, to succeed in the law in Florida. I may not have a flashy twelfth-story office with three dozen associates and half a billion dollars' worth of clients, yet, but I'm paying the bills, and based on what I see around me, it looks like I just landed one whale of a client."

I drummed my fingertips against the table. "You should be proud of what you've accomplished, but I'm afraid you still didn't answer my question. How does that affect this?"

She glanced at Skipper. "Can I have a copy of that audio?"

As if in practiced unison, Skipper and I said, "No!"

Skipper continued. "It exists here, on a secure server in Silver Spring, Maryland, on one of our off-site secure servers, and nowhere else."

I took the reins. "What do you want to do with the audio?"

Dylan said, "I want Michael to hear it, and then I want the governor to commute Garland Fitzsimon's sentence, or maybe even pardon him."

"Is that even possible?"

She leaned toward me. "Mr. Fulton, not only is it possible, but I can practically guarantee one of those two things will happen within the next seventy-two hours. Where is this McDonald guy now?"

I checked Skipper, and she brought up the video of room number two in our workshop. I pointed to the monitor where McDonald sat, clean-shaven, comfortably dressed, and reading a copy of *Don Quixote*.

Dylan said, "You bugged his hotel room?"

I chuckled. "Not hardly. The room is ours, and he's our guest."

"You mean your prisoner."

"Look around. The people you see in this room make up the entirety of my team, with the exception of a flight crew in Oklahoma and our technical services officer in the lab. We don't have a guard on McDonald, and the door isn't locked."

"Can I talk to him?" she asked.

"Why?"

"You told him you were calling the U.S. Attorney. I'm an attorney, I'm definitely from the U.S., and I suspect you've got a set of credentials lying around that will pass as official from across the room."

Anya slid her U.S. Department of Justice cred-pack across the table. "I like her. She is going to fit in nicely on island of misfit toys."

Dylan opened Anya's credentials and smiled. "This isn't counterfeit."

The Russian said, "No, of course not. I am real deal, baby."

"You're a fed?"

Anya shrugged. "Not anymore, but I did very good work for them, so they let me keep souvenir. I will need to have it back when you are finished, though."

The attorney pocketed the cred-pack. "There's no way any of this is legal, but it's going to be a lot of fun. Is that guy dangerous?"

Shawn, Mongo, and Gator stood in unison, and the SEAL said, "No, ma'am, not as long as we're with you."

The four of them headed for the workshop, and Skipper said, "There's no chance of this working, is there?"

I laughed. "I have no idea, but like she said, it's going to be a lot of fun."

We locked eyes on the monitor as Dylan and her security detail stepped into McDonald's temporary home. He laid down the massive book and stared up at them.

Dylan flipped open the cred-pack. "Remember that U.S. Attorney Mr. Fulton told you about? Well, here I am. Would you care to have a chat?"

Skipper snapped her fingers. "She just impersonated a U.S. Attorney and did it with style."

"No, she didn't," I said. "She asked McDonald if he remembered me mentioning a U.S. Attorney. She never said she was one."

Anya said, "I like her even more. We can keep her, yes?"

I chuckled. "I'm not sure that's how it works. She's not a puppy, but if she pulls this off, we'll definitely write her a check every month to keep her on our side. Having a gutsy, no-nonsense legal eagle like her in the nest can't be a bad thing."

McDonald said, "I'm not talking without my lawyer."

My gut tied itself into a knot, but Dylan didn't blink.

She said, "That's fine. Would you prefer to surrender to me, or shall I call the Marshals Service to take custody of you?"

"Wait. What are you talking about? You're arresting *me*?"

"Oh, no, Mr. McDonald. You're not under arrest yet, but you're a material witness in a federal investigation. Protective custody is absolutely essential and non-negotiable."

"But I haven't agreed to—"

She cut him off. "Oh, you mean the immunity agreement. After what I just heard, you can call that one a done deal. It's just a matter of paperwork. So, which will it be? Me or the Marshals?"

McDonald's face morphed into a melting ball of wax, and Dylan said, "Of course, if you have concerns about your safety within the federal system, considering the potential defendants' positions, I could probably arrange for authorization for you to remain here under the protection of Mr. Fulton's force."

Anya almost squealed. "Yes, we are for certain keeping her. I will feed her and clean up behind her if she makes mess on floor."

"You mean I can stay here?" McDonald asked.

Dylan contorted her face. "Only if you're comfortable and feel that you're in no danger here. I *will* need you to make an official statement to that effect, though."

"Okay, yeah, sure. I can do that. Do I need to sign something or what?"

Dylan sat on the sofa across from McDonald and wrote a paragraph on her legal pad, then she asked Shawn, "Where's the camera?"

He pointed to the corner of the room, and she asked, "Audio, too?"

The SEAL nodded, and she handed the paper to McDonald. "Raise your right hand, and read this for the record."

He took the paper, read over it, and tugged at his collar. "Are you sure I gotta say all of this?"

"No, of course not." She pulled a phone from her purse. "I'll have the Marshals here in half an hour."

McDonald said, "Okay, okay. I'll do it."

Dylan took a step back, positioning herself beneath the camera and out of the frame.

McDonald stuck his right hand in the air and said, "I, Gregory Mc-Donald, swear under penalty of perjury that I will remain at this location in St. Marys, Georgia, under the protection of the individuals under the direction of Dr. Chase Fulton, who I have selected, believing that they represent the highest degree of safety, protection, and preservation for me while I await written confirmation of an immunity agreement with the U.S. Attorney in the investigation of events surrounding and involving Mr. Garland Fitzsimon, a current prisoner in the state of Florida. So help me God."

Chapter 42

Yourself, but Better

I've spent a lot of time in my beloved gazebo, with so many people I love, but there was no one I enjoyed in those old Adirondacks around the cannon more than Pogonya.

"Do you want to hear something strange?" she asked as I pondered the situation the team and I had created for ourselves.

I said, "My whole world is strange, but let's hear your version."

She tapped a bare foot against the ancient cannon's cradle. "Sometimes, I come out here by myself and pretend that gun can talk. I know you said it might be French, but it sounds British when it talks to me."

I said, "If anyone on the planet needs proof that you're *my* daughter, there it is. We may not be insane, you and me, but we're certifiably not normal."

"Who wants to be normal anyway? That's boring. Are you still going to let Mama kill that man?"

I shook like a wet dog. "What? Where did that come from? Weren't we just having a conversation about a talking cannon?"

"You said it, Father. We're not normal. I don't want him to die."

I stared across the old gun and at the beautiful young woman so full of wonder and hope for everything. "We're not going to kill him. That's not what we do."

"Mama was going to."

"She gets a little excited sometimes."

"Can I tell you something else about her?"

I tilted my head. "Sure. This should be good."

"She's better with you. Sometimes, before she brought me here, she would sit for hours and stare at nothing. I always wondered what she was thinking about, and now, I know."

"Oh, really? What was she thinking about?"

"Come on, Father. Surely, you know. She was thinking of this place . . . and of you."

"How do you know?"

"Because if I had to leave, that's exactly what I would think about all the time. I love this place. And you, too, of course."

"This place has been in our family since the seventeen hundreds, and now, it's yours."

"Mine?" she asked. "What do you mean?"

"It means that I'll end up in the cemetery across town at some point, and Bonaventure will still be in our family. You're the only descendant I'll ever have, so it belongs to you just as much as you belong to it."

She stared out over the cannon at the winding, lazy river making its way to the ocean, and I watched my daughter become part of everything in my world, while inside my heart, she was becoming my whole world.

The chirping phone on the arm of my chair pulled me from a moment I'd love to relive a thousand times. "Hello, this is Chase."

"He wants to meet with you, privately."

"Who?" I asked.

Dylan Duncan said, "The governor. He wants to hear the audio."

"When? Where?"

"He's coming to St. Marys."

I thought about the logistics of hosting the governor at Bonaventure and asked, "Should I plan a dinner or something?"

"No. Just try not to do or say anything crazy."

I palmed my chest. "I'm offended."

Dylan huffed. "Yeah, right. Just don't blow anything up or do anything, I don't know, covert while he's there."

"Covert?"

"You know what I mean."

"You sound nervous. Why don't you come, too? After all, you are my lawyer."

"It's not that kind of meeting. Just be yourself, but better."

"I'll do my best. What time will he be here?"

She said, "I don't know, but you should expect a call from Michael Duncan. That's my former father-in-law."

"I remember. I'll keep my phone handy."

"Okay. Call me the second it's over."

I said, "I still think you should be here, even if you're not in the meeting."

"Can you send the plane?"

"I can do better than that. Pack an overnight bag, throw on some jeans and a T-shirt, and meet me at the airport in forty-five minutes."

"Why jeans and a T-shirt?" she asked.

"You'll see. And if you get motion sickness, take a Dramamine before I get there."

* * *

It wasn't the best landing of my life, but I kept all three tires on the pavement and taxied the P-51 Mustang to the ramp in front of the FBO. When I hopped down from the wing, my attorney stepped through the double glass doors. "You've got to be kidding me. Are you for real?"

"Come on, counselor. I'll take you for the ride of your life."

She shouldered her bag. "I think you're already doing that, but what the heck? Let's do this."

I strapped her into the front seat and fired up the massive Merlin engine that made the most beautiful sound in the world and helped win the Second World War. Memories of my first time in the Mustang played through my head, and I vowed to repeat the performance Dr. Robert "Rocket" Richter gave me all those years before.

When the wheels seated themselves in the wells on climb-out, I retracted the flaps and lowered the nose to build the airspeed we'd need for what was to come. When the needle passed two-fifty, I pulled the stick into my gut and let *Penny's Secret* dart into the heavens.

Dylan alternated between giggling and screaming until we passed thirty-five hundred feet and I rolled the old warbird on her back.

"Oh, my God! We're upside-down! This is crazy!"

"Welcome to my world, Ms. Duncan."

"I love it!"

We rolled upright, and I said, "Take the controls. Pull back to go up, push forward to go down, left to go left, and I think you get the picture. I'll manage the rudders. Just have some fun and keep the coastline on our left."

She flew the airplane poorly, but the Mustang and I let her get away with it until she said, "Okay, that's enough. You do it now."

"I have the controls."

Penny's Secret seemed to relax in my hands and settle in for the short flight to Bonaventure.

"Did Michael call?"

I said, "He did, and we're meeting around three this afternoon."

Although I couldn't see her around the seat, I was confident she was checking her watch.

"Are you nervous?" she asked.

"About meeting the governor?"

"Yeah."

"No, I'm not nervous. I'll pass you my phone, and you can call the president if you'd like. He's in the contacts as L-O-T-F-W."

She said, "Leader of the free world, huh? Cute, but I don't believe you."

I leaned forward and dropped the phone over her shoulder. "Go ahead. It's connected to the airplane's intercom. He'll answer. He always does."

"You're serious, aren't you?"

"When you do what I do for a living, Ms. Duncan, you don't get nervous around dignitaries. I've never had a head of state point an AK at me. I can't say the same for the rest of the world."

"You're an interesting guy. You know that, Dr. Fulton?"

"No, ma'am. I'm just a dude with some pretty cool contacts in my phone and an even cooler airplane. Look to your left. That's Bonaventure. We'll be on the ground in three minutes."

I chopped the power and started our descent, but I missed the three-minute mark. We rolled to a stop in front of the hangar, and Don Maynard, our airport manager, helped Dylan from her restraints.

"Did he roll you upside down?"

"Yes, and it was awesome."

Don held her hand as she stepped from the cockpit and onto the wing. "He does that. Did you hold onto your lunch?"

"So far," she said. "But it would be worth losing it to do that again."

* * *

Dylan and I were having a conversation in the library a few minutes before three o'clock when Skipper called and said, "Chase, someone's pulling up to the dock in a really nice boat. Should I send the guys?"

"No, I'll check it out. It's probably nothing." I stood and said, "Why don't you run up to the op center with Skipper just in case this is more than just somebody at the wrong dock? I'll be right back."

Dylan said, "Unless it's somebody pointing an AK at you."

"If it is, I'll be right back after killing somebody with an AK on my dock."

As I trotted down the gallery stairs onto the back lawn, I couldn't believe my eyes. I raised an arm and waved. "Ahoy!"

Dominic Fontana, Clark's father and my first handler in this business, tied the Hinkley to a pair of cleats, and a second man stepped from the boat behind him. "Ahoy, yourself. Hope you don't mind us showing up this way. Confidentiality and all . . . You understand."

I continued across the lawn until reaching the dock, where Dominic said, "Dr. Chase Fulton, meet Governor Glenn Morrow from the great state of Florida."

I extended my hand, and the governor shook it. "Great to meet you, Chase. May I call you Chase?"

"Sure, Governor. You can call me whatever you'd like. Welcome to Bonaventure."

I shot a look at Dominic and mouthed, "What are you doing here?"

Instead of retreating to the boat or otherwise disappearing, Dominic said, "Glenn and I go way back. I thought the trip up here would be a nice chance to catch up. He's got a place on Amelia Island, so the governor taking a boat ride from his own dock shouldn't raise any eyebrows."

"Well, thanks for coming, I guess."

"Quite a place you've got here, Chase," the governor said.

"Thank you, sir. It's been in my family since before the country was a country."

He said, "But not before Florida was Florida."

"No, sir. Not quite that long."

"There's no need to call me sir, Chase. I'm just Glenn today, and I hear you've got a little audiotape you'd like to play for me."

"It's not exactly a tape," I said, "but if you want to hear it, follow me."

We took the elevator to the third floor, and I thumbed us into the op center, where Skipper, Anya, and Dylan were having what appeared to be girl time. They leapt to their feet, and I said, "Sit down. It's just Dominic and the governor of Florida."

Governor Morrow spent a moment with each of the women, starting with Skipper and ending with Dylan. "Ms. Duncan. You're Michael's daughter-in-law, right?"

"Former daughter-in-law, sir. I was married to Michael Jr."

The governor grimaced. "Sorry about that."

Dylan said, "Thanks. Me, too. But it worked out. I'm in practice in St. Augustine now."

The governor said, "And also here in Georgia, it would appear."

"Well, yes, but only recently. I can leave you alone to do . . . this, and if you need me for any reason—I don't know why you would—but I'll be downstairs."

"Nonsense," the governor said. "Have a seat. You're part of the reason I'm here. Besides, I may need your legal counsel before all of this is over."

With the formalities astern, I said, "Play the audio."

Skipper hit the button.

Governor Morrow took no notes, never changed expression, and simply listened. When it was over, he said, "Ms. Duncan, what would you do if you were in my seat?"

Dylan straightened her lawyer hat and said, "In light of what this audio obviously brings to the forefront of—"

"Stop. Stop being a lawyer for a minute, and tell me what you'd do if you were governor."

Dylan said, "I'd pardon him, of course."

"Of course," Morrow said. "It's always so easy for someone who doesn't live in the governor's mansion to say they'd pardon him."

Dylan didn't back down. "I can't imagine that kind of power and responsibility, Governor, but can you imagine spending the rest of your life inside the North Central Florida supermax for a crime you didn't know you committed because you were drugged and brainwashed by the government you thought was supposed to protect and guarantee your rights as an American citizen?"

I was both impressed and frightened at the same time, but the governor seemed to have a different reaction.

He leaned back in his chair, crossed his legs, and said, "Michael was right about you, Ms. Duncan. You are a firecracker."

Dylan wasn't finished. "No, sir. I'm not a firecracker. I'm an ardent defender of the rights of my clients and a firm believer in the system of government that was created by some of the greatest minds the world has ever known, even though that system let my client down and likely cost him his freedom for the rest of his life."

Morrow said, "By *your* client, I assume you're talking about Garland Fitzsimon and not Dr. Fulton. Am I right?"

"Obviously," Dylan said before quickly catching herself. "I mean, yes, sir."

The most powerful man in the state of Florida cracked a smile. "Relax, Ms. Duncan. You're not arguing a case here, and I'm not a judge. What I am is a man with the power to turn *your* client loose, but if I were to do so, I would become a politician responsible for the actions of a lifelong criminal."

"With all due respect, Governor—"

Morrow laughed. "I always love it when people start sentences with that phrase—with all due respect. It usually means something delightfully belligerent is on the horizon. Please, do continue, Ms. Duncan."

"With all due respect, Governor, my client served his sentence for the crimes for which he was convicted. He's now in prison for a crime that was perpetuated by operatives of the federal government, and we have a witness prepared to cooperate and testify against the very people who did this to Mr. Fitzsimon."

"Cooperate, you say? Based on what I just heard, this McDonald fellow was—shall we say, coerced—into admitting what he knew. For all I know, he could've made the whole thing up to keep Ms. Burinkova here from . . . how is it you like to put it? Gutting him like pig?"

As much as I wanted to watch Dylan and Morrow duke it out, I jumped into the ring. "Governor, it's obvious that you, or someone in your office, has done your homework. You know who and what we are. No doubt, your friendship with Dominic played a role in that knowledge. If I may, I'd like to show you one short video clip that might put both your personal and political mind at ease concerning Mr. McDonald's willingness to play nice." I motioned to Skipper. "Go ahead. Play the statement."

She clicked her mouse, and the large monitor above her head came alive with a full-color version of Gregory McDonald's sworn statement that he felt safe, protected, and prepared to cooperate with the U.S. Attorney pending an immunity agreement.

The governor removed his glasses. "This does indeed change things, but I must ask. Was this statement coerced in any way?"

Dylan stared at her shoes, but Anya didn't flinch. She slid her credentials across the table and said, "Is permitted in all fifty states for investigators to mislead or even lie to suspects, witnesses, and potential witnesses in course of investigation. You should know this. You have law degree, no?"

The governor cracked open the cred-pack and peeked inside before sliding it back to the Russian. "I'm not going to pardon him."

Dylan clenched her fists. "Governor, please. If you'll only hear me out."

Morrow raised his hand. "I'm not going to pardon him, but I'll commute his sentence. The conviction remains in place. Write the commutation order, and I'll sign it. The state of Florida will not, however, assume responsibility for your client's safety, welfare, or upkeep. He's yours, Ms. Duncan. If he breaks the law in Florida again—I mean, so much as jaywalking at Disney World—you're a co-conspirator in that crime."

Dylan froze for a moment, and the governor continued. "Welcome to the big leagues, counselor. The ball is in the air. It's up to you whether or not you swing. Just remember, Florida is a three-strikes-and-you're-out state. You and your client are looking at an oh-and-two count, so if you swing, you'd better swing for the fence."

Chapter 43
Lincolns for Franklins

With my—and Garland Fitzsimon's—attorney sitting in stunned silence, I said, "Why don't we give Ms. Duncan the room and go for a little walk. I'd love to show you around, Governor."

Dylan Duncan mouthed, "Thank you," as Dominic, Governor Morrow, and the rest of the team rose from around the table.

I caught Shawn's elbow as we left the op center. "Where's Singer?"

"We put the priest back on the island, so he's doing a little babysitting, just like you asked."

"And Pat, the grandmother?"

"She's in the mother-in-law suite at Skipper and Gator's place because you haven't told us to take her back to Arizona yet."

"Good," I said. "I like those arrangements. And McDonald?"

Shawn chuckled. "He's not going anywhere. That book you gave him weighs about twenty pounds, and nobody's shooting at him. That's a better deal than he'll get anywhere else."

"If this works, we'll need to work on a plan to get Garland and his grandmother somewhere safe. As soon as he hits the streets, he'll be a target, and it'll only get worse when this thing breaks."

"We're on it," the SEAL said. "Are you planning to set them up somewhere?"

I said, "I'm not sure yet. I don't plan to write them a big check, if that's what you mean, but I might find a place on the payroll for them if we can come up with something meaningful for them to do."

"I'll float that balloon, too," Shawn said. "Surely we can come up with something to keep the guy out of trouble and off the streets."

An arm wound its way across my shoulders, and I turned to see Dominic snuggling up with me. "If you wouldn't mind, Glenn would like to see your shoot house."

I smiled and stepped beside our distinguished guest. "I understand you'd like to get a glimpse of what we do here."

The governor said, "I'd like that very much if it isn't too much trouble."

There are moments in my life when I do things purely for my own amusement, and such a moment had just blossomed in front of me.

"I'd love to give you the behind-the-scenes tour, but I'll need you to sign a non-disclosure agreement. Do you have a clearance?"

Governor Morrow froze. "Are you serious? You do know I'm the governor, right?"

"Yeah, but not of Georgia."

A politician at a loss for words is a rare and amusing sight, but I couldn't play it out any longer and broke into laughter. "I'm sorry, Governor, but I couldn't resist. Come on. Let's go pull some triggers."

We began our tour in the armory, where the governor picked out a rifle and pistol that seemed to meet his approval, and when we made it to the shoot house, he proceeded to school me up on how his A-Team cleared rooms when he wore the Green Beret.

It took a lot of work to hide my surprise and ignorance about his background, but I made no effort to hide my approval. "I'm impressed, Governor."

He pulled off his shooting glasses. "Call me Governor one more time, and we'll find out how much hand-to-hand I remember. We're just two old soldiers turning gunpowder into noise, Chase. Please, just call me Glenn."

"I'll try."

He cleared his rifle and let it fall against his chest on the sling. "How long have you known Ms. Duncan?"

"Not long," I said. "But I put her on retainer the day we met."

"I think you made a good move there, but I believe I got under her skin a little with the firecracker comment. What are the odds she'll take me up on my offer of commutation for her client?"

Although we were sealed inside the darkened shoot house, I glanced in the direction of the op center. "The truth stings sometimes, and if I were you, *Glenn*, I'd make sure I had my pen handy when we go back inside."

He reached into a pocket and withdrew a Montblanc. "I never leave home without it. Say, have you ever played Lincolns for Franklins?"

"I'm afraid I don't know that one, Gov . . . Glenn."

He stowed his pen and dug into his pants pocket. "Do you have any change?"

I pulled out a handful of coins just as he did the same.

He plucked eight pennies from my palm and six from his. "Perfect. These will do nicely." He led me to the end of the long central hallway running the length of the shoot house and placed the fourteen pennies along the top of a target frame. "We'll start at five paces and alternate shots. If we both hit a penny, we'll back up five paces and start again, counting hits along the way. The first to miss owes the other the sum of the Abraham Lincolns we hit in Ben Franklins."

I stepped off five paces and raised my rifle, but Glenn pressed a hand against the top of my upper receiver. "Oh, no. Anybody can do it with a rifle. We're using pistols, and we're doing it left-handed."

My confidence soared. I'd fired at least as many rounds with my left hand as I had with my right, and my lifetime round count was well into the millions. Former Green Beret or not, the governor was going down.

By the time one of us finally missed, our fourteen pennies were riddled with holes, and I owed the honorable governor of the great state of Florida almost four thousand dollars.

I paid my debt, although he made great effort to refuse, and we climbed the stairs back to the op center, where Dylan Duncan sat with her legs crossed and a two-page document resting on the table in front of her. Glenn sat down across from her, slid the lawyer's Cross pen aside, and uncapped his own. With little more than a cursory glance across both pages, Governor Glenn Morrow signed, Dominic witnessed, Skipper notarized, and Garland Fitzsimon was a freeman.

* * *

It turns out that you can't simply show up at the supermax with a two-page document—even one signed by the governor's own three-hundred-dollar pen—and pluck an inmate from his cell. It took almost twenty-four hours for every box to be checked inside the State Attorney General's office and the Florida Department of Corrections, but just after five o'clock the following day, Garland slid onto the back seat of my Suburban and held his grandmother's hand for the first time in what had to feel like an eternity.

I installed Garland in Gregory McDonald's former room in our workshop and called The Ranch. Dr. Fred Kennedy, the board-certified psychiatrist who'd crawled around inside the heads of warriors for decades, became Fitzsimon's personal physician throughout his recovery from the litany of drugs the prison system had pumped into his body at the behest of the Central Intelligence Agency.

McDonald got an upgrade and moved into Dominic Fontana's guest house in The Bahamas on an island that probably has a name, but nobody seems to know what it is. The U.S. Attorney for the Eastern District of Virginia proffered the expected immunity agreement, and McDonald accepted, setting in motion one of the largest investigations into the Office of the Vice President and the diplomatic branch of the Holy See in history.

Security at Bonaventure tripled when we contracted thirty-six gun-toting knuckle-draggers to keep everybody alive and everything intact.

Word of Fitzsimon's commutation made it to D.C., and Gregory McDonald's absence from the vice president's staff was noticed. Panic ensued, and federal judges' phones started ringing, but it was too late to stop the steamrollers that had been unleashed by McDonald's sworn statement.

With Fitzsimon's full knowledge and consent, Dr. Mankiller finally tested his blood. In spite of Dylan Duncan's efforts, the precise formulas for the drugs manufactured by the laboratories of the CIA and various contractors since the 1950s couldn't be released, but Garland's blood and brain would forever bear their scars.

Heads rolled. The vice president and the director of Central Intelligence resigned, while the president built a massive wall separating himself from the actions of his number two and the highest-ranking intelligence officer in the country. Claiming victory in a second election wasn't in his future, but his legacy would likely survive without too much of a stain.

* * *

It was one of those rare late September nights in coastal Georgia when the north wind chilled the air just enough to make long sleeves feel good. My team—my family—filled the gazebo with a few additions, making the time together even more interesting. Pat and Garland Fitzsimon sat side by side, and the demons that had called the young man's mind their home for so long were absent from his eyes. Under Dr. Kennedy's care, his calm, almost shy demeanor gave Garland the look of a humble, hardworking man—not that of the criminal he'd chosen to become as a teen.

I asked, "How are you feeling, Garland?"

He looked up and tried to smile. "Thanks to you, I almost feel like a human again. I don't know how to thank you for everything you did for me and Mamaw, but what I really don't understand is *how* you did it."

I said, "The how isn't really all that important. The main thing is that it's done. Now, let's talk about what happens next."

He straightened in his chair as if he didn't want to miss a single word, and I said, "Second chances are rare and precious things in this world, and you've been given the biggest one I've ever seen."

He pressed his lips into a thin line. "Yeah, I get that, and like I said, I don't know how to thank you."

I watched his expression and weighed the sincerity in his eyes. "I'll tell you what we're going to do, Garland. You can thank us by taking full advantage of the life you've gotten back—a life you wouldn't have had without the men and women sitting around you tonight."

He stared at me, and I continued. "Take care of the woman beside you, just like she took care of you when you were a boy. She deserves the love and attention she gave you, and you're the only one who can give it back to her."

He turned to his grandmother and squeezed her hand.

I said, "Dr. Kennedy says you've still got a long road ahead to get and stay clean, but that *has* to happen, Garland. There are no other options. After what your body and mind have been through, you can't put poison inside yourself ever again. We'll make sure you have the support you need to make that a reality, but it requires an absolute commitment on your part."

He nodded. "I'm an addict, and I will be forever, but I'm determined to stay clean, no matter how hard it is."

I said, "I'll say one more thing, and then the lecture is over. We've got a lot of work to do around here. None of it is easy, but we pay well, and we've got enough eyes to make sure your feet stay on the straight and narrow. If you want a job, you've got one, but it comes with conditions. You'll stay clean, work hard, take care of Pat, and you'll go to church with us."

"Church?" He pointed at Father Isaiah Lamb, dressed in his black shirt and white collar, and sitting between Kodiak and Singer. "Like, *that* kind of church?"

In that instant, the priest reached beneath his jacket and drew the 9mm Glock we'd given him to protect himself. He raised the muzzle to bear directly on Garland Fitzsimon, and then he pressed the trigger twice. The report of the pistol echoed through the air. A pair of brass casings flew from the weapon and bounced off the iron cannon between the priest and his target.

Garland didn't go down, and my team didn't move. The priest jerked the trigger seven more times, sending roaring reports through the night and brass flying from the smoking weapon's ejection port, but nothing left the muzzle, and nothing struck Fitzsimon.

As realization came over the Jesuit, he lowered the pistol, still half full of blank rounds, and slumped in his seat. "How did you know?"

I took Pogonya's hand in mine. "She figured it out. Your grandfather escaped from the prison that had been Solovetsky Monastery. Your hatred for the Russians, despite your faith, has been blatantly obvious since the first time you heard Anya speak a word. You tried to hide it behind a feigned look of amusement, but your contempt was obvious. Garland was supposed to kill Victor Komarov on the yacht that night, but he failed, and the soldier in you had to make him pay for that failure."

Singer lifted the pistol from the priest's hand and said, "You may be a Jesuit, but you're no soldier for the God I serve. You hid behind the collar and the vows to avenge your grandfather for what the Russians did to him on that island in the White Sea almost ninety years ago, and you tried to use our family as a tool in that ungodly pursuit."

Our sniper glared down at the man who never deserved to wear the collar, and I said, "I told you when all of this began that we'd find the truth, and we did. We know about your alliance with the nuncio and the archbishop, who you claimed was out to get you. It was a clever ruse on your part, but the truth has a way of coming to light. And sometimes, that light burns awfully hot when it hits you in the face, doesn't it?"

He couldn't look at me, but I didn't expect an answer.

"The authorities are waiting out front to take you into custody. It's over, Isaiah. We'll pray for you, but you have to pay for the role you played in all of this. I just hope the faith you claimed to have wasn't all a lie, because you're going to need it where you're going."

Epilogue

Shawn, our SEAL, waved a sealed envelope in the air after dinner. "You guys thought I forgot, didn't you?"

I laughed. "I'm the one who forgot, but I'm glad you didn't. Rip that thing open, and fork over my cash."

Gator said, "Not so fast. We still have to read your prediction, which I'm sure is cryptic like Nostradamus, but you'll claim it's right anyway."

Shawn tore open the envelope and slipped the pair of hundred-dollar bills from inside. He unfolded the slip of paper and read what I'd written when Gator bet me that I hadn't figured out the case early in the investigation.

The SEAL cleared his throat and slipped on an imaginary pair of glasses. "Hear ye, hear ye, hear ye. Our fearless leader did predict thusly . . ." With a flourish, he shook the paper and read, "Father Lamb is a liar, and given the chance, he'll pull the trigger on Garland Fitzsimon, himself."

Gator slapped the table. "How? How could you have possibly known that so early in all of this?"

I slid him a piece of pie. "Stick around, kid. You're doing great, but you've still got a lot to learn."

* * *

After the dishes were done and everyone was gone, Anya said, "I have confession to make for you."

"What kind confession?"

She said, "I was doing for you laundry—"

"Wait a minute," I said. "You do my laundry?"

She recoiled. "Yes, of course. Someone must do it because you do not know how, and I am this person."

"Well, thank you, I guess. I didn't realize you did laundry."

She looked up at me with those smokey blue eyes that could drown any man alive. "There are many things you do not realize, but this is conversation for only confession."

"I doubt you really have anything serious to confess, but I'm all ears."

She looked away. "This is not true. I must make to you sincere apology. I found inside pocket of pants note written in Cyrillic."

My heart sank, and I wanted to punch myself in the face for not burying Pogonya's note back in the earth beside Penny's headstone.

Anya said, "I should have put note back inside pocket and left pants on bed, but I could not. I thought terrible thing. I thought, who is writing note to my Chasechka in Cyrillic? This is why I read it, and I cried tears for emotion I do not have English word for. It was not note for you. It was note for Penny from Pogonya."

I swallowed hard and looked back at her, wishing I could say something, anything, but the words wouldn't come.

She said, "Even my own daughter knows that I can never be person to replace Penny for you."

I took her hands. "That's not what she was saying."

She pulled away. "I am not finished. This is all of confession. I read note, and I should not have. For this, I am sorry. But you have to know, Chasechka, that I would never try to replace Penny. No, this is wrong word, *replace*. I want for you to have beautiful life, but I know Pogonya is correct. I cannot be for you what Penny was. I can be only for you what you let me be. And I want to be person who gives to you happiness when all of rest of world is terrible for you. This is thing I want most of all."

* * *

Dolphins broke the surface just ahead of the starboard bow of *Aegis*, my beloved catamaran. The shoreline and beach lying a hundred feet away could've been a thousand island paradises in tropical waters anywhere on the globe, but that evening, the secluded stretch of sand dotted with volcanic rock was ours alone, and the dolphins seemed happy to offer it to us as their gift for a job that I considered to be well done.

The two women, twenty-five years apart, could've been the same person without the relentless passage of time. Both were tall, lean, and beautiful. One, however, wore the scars of a lifetime spent giving herself for the protection of others, while the younger wore only the innocence of her youth. I loved them both, and I also feared each of them for the power they possessed to crush my heart. Losing either of them would destroy what remained of me. I'd said goodbye to Penny and much of my past. The future ahead of me rested, at least partially, in the hands of Anya and Pogonya, who lay laughing, captivated by the dolphins.

Pogonya rolled onto her back. "Come join us, Father. The porpoises want to see you."

I lay down between them and gazed through the trampoline as the sleek, grey backs of the ocean mammals slid beneath the surface. I couldn't remember the last time I'd felt such peace and tranquility—and so much like the man I was meant to be.

Pogo said, "I wish it could always be like this."

I ruffled her hair. "The fact that it's not always like this is what makes these moments so precious. If this were our everyday reality, we'd take it for granted, and that would be a sin."

She tugged at the grey hair streaking my beard. "You're pretty smart, you know that? I guess it comes from being an old man, huh?"

"I'll show you what an old man can do." I scooped Pogonya from the mesh of the trampoline, and she landed in the water only inches from where the last dolphin had surfaced. She giggled even as she sank beneath the surface.

I lay back down beside the woman who'd given me the most precious gift I could've ever dreamed possible, and I took her in my arms. "Do you remember what you said to me while you were sitting on my lap aboard the first *Aegis*... after I'd shot off your toe?"

She ran her fingers through my hair and whispered, "Of course I remember. I said to you, 'We should kiss.'"

Author's Note

We've done this together thirty-four times now, and I still can't believe it's real. It means the world to me that you'd sacrifice a few hours of your life to read a story that fell out of my crazy head. As Anya would say, I do not have, in English, words to say how I feel. I can only say thank you, but that doesn't feel adequate. I'm truly in love with the enormous gift you've given me in making my dream of writing professionally come true. I've said it before, but I'll never stop reminding you that I will never take your gift for granted. I will always pour my heart into every story I create because that's what you deserve. And that's what you'll get from me. Now, let's talk about some of the craziness that happened in this outrageous story.

Let's start with the Vatican. Although a few Catholics turned out to be some of the bad guys in this story, I do not hold any animus toward my Catholic friends. I pick on everybody, so please don't take it personally. Every religion has its share of bad apples, and sometimes, those apples float to the top. I love writing Russian bad guys, but just like the Catholics, I have absolutely nothing against the Russian people. It's the bad guys I detest, regardless of their affiliation with any religion, nation, or organization.

I wrote a lot about pharmaceuticals in this story, and I probably got most of it wrong, even though I forced myself to do hours of research on drugs like mescaline, LSD, quetiapine, and clozapine. The drugs I mentioned exist and are in common use; however, I used them criminally and cruelly in this tale. If you happen to be a physician, pharmacist, or just somebody who knows and understands drugs, I apologize if I butchered the details.

It's time to talk about one of the ugly truths I discovered while researching material for this book. Everything I wrote about the Solovetsky Monastery, which became a prison, is true based on the available information. It was, by all indications, a horrifically inhumane hell after the Bolshevik Revolution and Civil War. I encourage you to pick up the book I referenced — *An Island Hell: A Soviet Prison in the Far North* by S. A. Malsagoff. You will be horrified by what you learn on the pages of the almost unbelievable story. I must tell you that I added a bit of fiction to Malsagoff's book to support my story. The list of men who escaped does not appear in his book, and there is no record of anyone named Wm. Lamb ever having been held at Solovetsky.

Now we've come to the North Central Florida supermax prison in Greenville, Florida. I'll keep it short, sweet, and simple. It doesn't exist. I made it up, I made it all up, I'm a miserable liar. Sorry, I got carried away. Although there are several prisons in North Florida, the supermax is not one of them. The moral of the story is this: Don't go to Florida and do stupid stuff. They'll lock you up for a really long time in a place that's over a hundred degrees in the shade in December. Okay, I made that part up, too.

Lacunar amnesia is a real thing, and it isn't as uncommon as one might think. It is generally a gap in a person's memory involving a specific event, just as I described it for Garland Fitzsimon. If you're curious, there is an abundance of information available about the condition online. It's not really that interesting, so I'd recommend grabbing another one of my books, which may not be true, but it'll be a lot more entertaining than reading information about amnesia . . . that you'll probably forget.

And here's the big one — MKUltra. It is also real, as terrifying as that may be. Although I'll always believe the United States is the greatest country in the history of the world, we have done some horrible things, and some of those things are still going on. I won't go into the details of the MKUltra program here because it would make this book weigh twenty pounds, much like *Don Quixote*, but I hope you'll do a little reading on it. A quick Google search on the subject will keep you awake at night. You've probably heard the term "manchurian candidate." At the heart of the MKUltra program was a doctor named George Estabrooks, who practiced mind control through hypnosis and massive doses of mind-altering drugs for the purpose of creating manchurian candidates. There is some evidence that he was successful on a limited scale. Just like the overall program itself, I won't go into detail on Dr. Estabrooks because I'd like to be able to sleep without waking up drenched in sweat and screaming like a howler monkey . . . again. If you're brave and curious, feel free to fire up the Google machine, but prepare to be petrified.

I'm not an attorney, and I've never played one on TV, so I probably got most of the legal maneuvering wrong in this story. I did, however, do a lot of research, and the most important element of the legal craziness in the story is both plausible and possible. Although rare, the governor of Florida can reduce a sentence through a process called executive clemency, specifically through a commutation, which lessens the penalty but not the conviction. That's what Governor Morrow did for Garland. For the attorneys in the audience who cringed every time they read a legal scene in this story, I apologize, but I tried.

I'm getting close to wrapping this up, I promise, but I want to cover a couple more things before saying goodbye until next time.

The First African Baptist Church on Cumberland Island is real, and its history is absolutely fascinating. You can still visit the site and the church, and I highly recommend it. If Singer were real, I believe he would spend quite a bit of time there.

Finally, Jay-Dub. I've wanted to write this character for years, but I'll never possess the imagination to create such a fascinating personality. Only God could pull that one off, and He did. Jay-Dub is absolutely, thoroughly, completely, and in every other way, one hundred percent real. I didn't exaggerate a single element of his personality. He is a dear friend who I consider a brother, and he's impossible not to love. He is, without a doubt, one of the best people I know. He'll wrestle a bear for fun and give you the shirt off his back if you need it all on the same day. The town of Ponce de Leon, Florida, where Jay-Dub and the fictional Fitzsimons lived in this story, is also real and just as I described it. The barbecue joint has moved to DeFuniak Springs, but it's well worth stopping in if you happen to be in the neighborhood, and the Tom Thumb gas station sits exactly where I put it in the story.

If you'll indulge me just a bit longer, I'd like to wrap this up with a true story about my friend, Jay-Dub, that will sum him up beautifully. In another lifetime, I taught folks how to breathe underwater, and I did much of that teaching at Morrison Springs, just south of Ponce de Leon, FL. One evening, after a long day in the cold water of the springs, I was driving home and saw Jay-Dub's truck sitting at a horrible angle in the ditch on the side of the road, less than a mile from his house, and my friend was sitting on the tailgate having a drink as if nothing had gone wrong.

I, of course, stopped and asked, "Is everything all right, Dub?" (Here in the South, we often shorten people's real names for simplicity.)

He said, "Oh, yeah. Everything's fine. I just stopped here to have a drink 'cause I didn't want to go home yet." He then slapped the tailgate beside him and said, "Come join me."

And *that* is just one of the billions of reasons I love Jay-Dub.

About the Author

Cap Daniels

Cap Daniels is a former sailing charter captain, scuba and sailing instructor, pilot, Air Force combat veteran, and civil servant of the U.S. Department of Defense. Raised far from the ocean in rural East Tennessee, his early infatuation with salt water was sparked by the fascinating, and sometimes true, sea stories told by his father, a retired Navy Chief Petty Officer. Those stories of adventure on the high seas sent Cap in search of adventure of his own, which eventually landed him on Florida's Gulf Coast, where he spends as much time as possible on, in, and under the waters of the Emerald Coast.

With a headful of larger-than-life characters and their thrilling exploits, Cap pours his love of adventure and passion for the ocean onto the pages of the Chase Fulton Novels and the Avenging Angel — Seven Deadly Sins Series.

Visit www.CapDaniels.com to join the mailing list to receive newsletter and release updates.

Connect with Cap Daniels:

Facebook: www.Facebook.com/WriterCapDaniels
Instagram: https://www.instagram.com/authorcapdaniels/
BookBub: https://www.bookbub.com/profile/cap-daniels

Also by Cap Daniels

The Chase Fulton Novels Series
Book One: *The Opening Chase*
Book Two: *The Broken Chase*
Book Three: *The Stronger Chase*
Book Four: *The Unending Chase*
Book Five: *The Distant Chase*
Book Six: *The Entangled Chase*
Book Seven: *The Devil's Chase*
Book Eight: *The Angel's Chase*
Book Nine: *The Forgotten Chase*
Book Ten: *The Emerald Chase*
Book Eleven: *The Polar Chase*
Book Twelve: *The Burning Chase*
Book Thirteen: *The Poison Chase*
Book Fourteen: *The Bitter Chase*
Book Fifteen: *The Blind Chase*
Book Sixteen: *The Smuggler's Chase*
Book Seventeen: *The Hollow Chase*
Book Eighteen: *The Sunken Chase*
Book Nineteen: *The Darker Chase*
Book Twenty: *The Abandoned Chase*
Book Twenty-One: *The Gambler's Chase*
Book Twenty-Two: *The Arctic Chase*
Book Twenty-Three: *The Diamond Chase*
Book Twenty-Four: *The Phantom Chase*
Book Twenty-Five: *The Crimson Chase*
Book Twenty-Six: *The Silent Chase*
Book Twenty-Seven: *The Shepherd's Chase*
Book Twenty-Eight: *The Scorpion's Chase*
Book Twenty-Nine: *The Creole Chase*
Book Thirty: *The Calling Chase*
Book Thirty-One: *The Capitol Chase*
Book Thirty-Two: *The Stolen Chase*
Book Thirty-Three: *The Widow's Chase*
Book Thirty-Four: *The Sacred Chase*
Book Thirty-Five: *The Assassin's Chase*

The Avenging Angel – Seven Deadly Sins Series
Book One: *The Russian's Pride*
Book Two: *The Russian's Greed*
Book Three: *The Russian's Gluttony*
Book Four: *The Russian's Lust*
Book Five: *The Russian's Sloth*
Book Six: *The Russian's Envy*
Book Seven: *The Russian's Wrath*

Stand-Alone Novels
We Were Brave
Singer – Memoir of a Christian Sniper

Novellas
The Chase is On
I Am Gypsy